Furniture

by Kevin M Sheetz

for the gods,

wherever they are

As to what should be done in a day, when the eating and drinking has been arranged, let one sit straight with his mouth shut, and not allow a single thought to arise in his mind. Let him forget everything, and keep his spirit with settled purpose. Let his lips be glued together, and his teeth be firmly pressed against one another. Let him not look at anything with his eyes, nor listen to a single sound with his ears. Let him with all his mind watch over his inward feelings. Let him draw long breaths, and gradually emit them, without a break, now seeming to breathe, and now not. In this way any excitement of the mind will naturally disappear, the water from the kidneys will rise up, the saliva will be produced in the mouth, and the real efficaciousness becomes attached to the body. It is thus that one acquires the way of prolonging life.

- from the Zah Yung King, *translated by* James Legge

Concealed deep in the center of the moon is a spherical egg. It was laid many years ago. Inside of the egg is a small airplane. There is snow around the ankles of the passengers, the snow breathes like slender blades of green grass, the snow has been to the sea.

Hello.

How are you? Where are you?

What is occurring around you?

It was summer when I met this woman named Gasoline. She was nineteen years old at the time and nineteen feet tall. Instead of breasts she had two turtles on her chest, one was the sun and the other was the moon. Their heads were her nipples, retreating and emerging like eyes. She owned two dogs who were rectangular prisms; they shone brightest by the light of the moose. They would communicate by ringing the bells which were their noses. They did not communicate often and nothing was misunderstood, it was very easy for them. In the center of each of their eyes were small gardens which no one tended.

Growing there were fig trees, diamonds, paper airplanes, voices, onion-peelings, goose-down, carrots the color of sky.

Whenever I was with Gasoline I would crouch down near her ankles, holding my breath, holding my mind. It was very similar to the interior of a pyramid, the shadows looked like hieroglyphics which swayed and breathed and mingled like jingle bells. Her cough sounded like tinfoil, the albatrosses are preening. With my good arm I would hold on to things for long periods of time without getting tired, I would extend them over my head. Time would visit us in the park, at the cinema, on the street; it was always dressed very nicely, beautiful headdresses and fluorescent robes and lavish shoes. One of Gasoline's toes was a mirror wherein I would observe time and myself holding hands, pressing our ears together.

What is it like outside?

How is the weather in the interior?

Is there something you'd like to accomplish today? Could it be put off until tomorrow?

The bridge is being worked on by lurid salads inside of wooden bowels. It'll be another week or so until it is fully operational again, another route must be taken. The fountain at the center of town has also fallen into disrepair; someone has been commissioned to create a new one. The old fountain is a statue of a lion, a symbol of older times; lions no longer symbolize anything. Once a day, the two optometrists of the town can be seen conversing secretively near the fountain. What they are discussing is anyone's guess. The question of the optometrists has plagued me of late.

I stood with Gasoline near the fountain and I was vomiting. I vomited up a rocking-chair horse, a dolphin, several old newspapers, an infant child, the flesh of oranges, a straw hat, an exaggerated kaleidoscope. The sun did not rise. Pure skin, stretching on for miles and miles. It grew cold, and something vast and dark gathered up my vomit and went away with all of it. I was sad to see it go. The question of the optometrists has plagued me of late. I could've been a shoemaker or a sculptor. Gasoline's breath was in the shape of tiny airplanes; there were lights on in all the airplanes and they drifted away like trees out of the atmosphere toward the center of the system. It is unknown whether they will make it to their destination or not.

The new statue in the fountain will be a wooden peacock, ten feet tall, with a lighthouse in place of its neck and head. It was not my idea, it wasn't up to me. I am not sure whether the peacock lighthouse will be functional or not. Ask yourself these questions.

I grew up inside of a blade of grass. At all times I could hear soft breathing; where it originated from I had no idea. Something was alive. This much I knew. It was around here somewhere but I didn't know where exactly. I grew up to be a marvelous washing-machine; there were none like me in the immediate vicinity, everyone would bat their eyes at me, it sounded like tiny bells chiming against the dark of night and quiet of snow. There were many stars planted in the sky, they looked like amoebas, mosquitos. When I was alone I could hear them coughing. My eyes are just painted on my face in black ink, you could remove them. I had my esophagus removed because it was getting to be too large. I gave it to Gasoline as a gift. She would put it on top of her tongue, underneath her fingernails, along her spine. Her spine was a vertical series of metal birdcages and when she was underwater you could see through her skin. In one of the birdcages a thimble was arguing with a train. Several were empty, the doors swinging on their hinges like voices. The stone inclemency is shouting into evaporating air like quicksand, inclement patterns pattering. Trifling handprint invasion precious addition. In another birdcage was a stone. Tambourine enema tangerine enamel.

What do your thoughts look like? Can you see them? What is their shape and size?

Do your thoughts look like writing? Written in colored ink? Invisible?

Are you talking to yourself? Are your thoughts a conversation or a monologue?

The dimpled rendezvous of the fraudulent corporation corresponds to the skeletons of water. As you read this, my mind is speaking with the voice of your thought. Is that true, or not? A thought is best expressed as a thought, when they escape the mind they become filtered, impure, diminished. A thought is best expressed as a vacuum-cleaner. Action is thoughtless, action is indifferent. What is the difference between mind and thought? Thought is the surface of the mind, thought is the mind's excrement. Sometimes we find our mind's waste products to be very important, we want to promote our thoughts, share them with other people, hold them in cupped hands. Sometimes our thoughts make us smile or cry.

If you are reading this, then a line of communication has opened up, though I receive nothing from you. But I am here, in the back of my mind, listening. I am waiting for response, waiting to see if there is an echo. Everything is a bouquet of echoes; it looks like this, it sounds like this.

Are you there?

What are you doing?

Is anything troubling you?

The giraffe had a mind of its own. It was different than the other giraffes but it was not hostile toward them. It knew its limitations. It lived alone on the moon, it would eat the craters. The giraffe enjoyed moving imperceptibly slow. Nothing would cross its mind. One of its hooves was a funeral procession and another was a man and woman having sex, they sounded like parrots. The giraffe could regenerate its tongue, which would detach itself and fly down to Earth. I was in a building in the city with Gasoline when one of the giraffe's tongues landed in her inner drink. The next day was spring. The giraffe's tongue and my esophagus jumped out of the window and into the branches of a nearby tree, which whinnied out of disgust. It sounded like roses, like rosemary.

The giraffe and I share the habit of collecting picture-frames. The question of the optometrists has plagued me of late.

Did you do anything enjoyable yesterday?

Will you do it again?

What do you do the most often?

The top of a lighthouse is in my mouth, there are flowers growing out of the roof of my mouth. A bird made out of eyelashes lives in my mouth, it flies around the lighthouse, it eats the darling flies that frequent the flowers. Sometimes all this becomes too much for me and the light from the lighthouse erupts out of my nose. Should you and I ever meet in the flesh, I will give my nine nostrils to you. Smooth white flesh, stretching on for miles and miles inside my mind, outside my mind. Are you inside my mind? Am I inside yours? Are we inside the same mind? Or are we outside? The inside of the mind is the same as the outside, a thought occurring on the inside is occurring on the outside, inside and outside are not two. We must make sure that the bed at the back of our mind is tied up with yarn and string, bound tightly, smooth wire. Make a soothing noise.

All I'm asking is for you to help me build some sort of magic machine that can reproduce thoughts outside the mind with no alteration. I think we're getting close. Perfect thought production sans body, sans mind. All I'm asking is for you to help me build a robot that is exactly identical with a human body, down to the veins and blood, the bones and breathing, the mind and thoughts. I think we're getting close. We should work to produce a will independent of a body, a mind, an intention, a cause. A will without desire. Is there anything that is without a cause? Is there one source or many? There is no will but thought. The will is like emotion, the will is not like an appendage or viscera. Feet, tongue, will, breath, organize, compilation, excitement, crying out, taking a bath, taking a void, taking a bath in the void, producing a void out of void, pulling a nose out of the void. The will is our sole responsibility. The vast monster has been activated, it breathes through our senses. Horses are our sole responsibility. Activity and maintenance. I think we're getting close.

The function of the living organism is reproduction. We should work toward covering the Earth with human beings, until there is nothing else but ourselves, room for nothing except more human bodies, covering everything. The Earth will wear its human skin like a crown of crows and show it off to the other planets. The other planets will not be envious. They are alive in their own particular way. The planets behave as we do, as fire does, the planets behave in the same way as wind-chimes do, as thought does, the planets behave exactly as you do, over and over again, stretching on endlessly. Space is alive, vacancy is alive, things that are alive are not alive. You and I are not alive, are infinitely alive in every direction. Is it the living organism that is alive, or is it the atoms themselves that are alive? What do the atoms think? All the atoms are joined together, there is only one atom. There are no atoms. The mind is the pit of the fruit that is the universe. We are the exterior, we are the interior. I am interior, you are exterior. You are interior, I am exterior. Superior, inferior. Congealed, misappropriated. The beautiful success, the most wonderful failure. My languid tears are smiling as they drift through the universe toward distant vacancies. Suddenly: a hand bursts through the black of empty space like the tongue coming out of a mouth, it clutches at my tears but they are sand in its fingers. The hand lopes along through space, trailing my tears. It approaches a planet which it engulfs like a white handkerchief covering a green ball, like a black handkerchief, a black rhinoceros, a golden dodo. From the right-hand corner of the universe comes sauntering a long white tongue that you've helped me create.

Hello?

What time is it?

We have forgotten that the sun is the visible, tangible God; it is over there, we can't look at it, we can't touch it. Everything is a monument to the sun. The laughter of children is rain, the sorrowful lovers are rain. You and I are sunlight in the rain, or are we? We have forgotten that Nature is the mother of All. But there is something outside Nature. Or is there? We must do away with the old symbols, they've become meaningless. Get caught in the net, do not get caught in the net. The glittering trap out in the open, closed control.

Are you tired? Are you full of energy?

Are you in your house?

Do you think I am being honest with you?

Do we feel the same?

I keep three mummies in my mouth; each one weighs about 20,000 tons. They sleep rolled up in my tongue like anchovies or sardines. The tallest mummy says: "Feed yourself to animals." The smallest mummy says: "Do not feed yourself to animals."

There are so many processes at work, it's difficult to be aware of them all at once, it's more gradual, sequential. One process replaces another, perpetually. I keep my awareness in a box in my mouth, the box looks like a tooth slightly decayed. Or is it just one process that includes everything? This process, these processes. Awareness is substance. Awareness is the great prison, there is nothing outside awareness, there is nothing inside awareness. Existence is a nesting doll in the shape of the universe; opening outward, opening inward, indefinitely. These things are very near at hand, you can touch them sometimes. They quiver like images in a mirror, like a horse in a trap, teeth in a mouth. Once you've gotten the horse, you can forget the trap. Everything is a multiplicity, there is no singularity. You are like teeth in a mouth, I am a horse in a trap. There is no object, there is no process, it is a process of carefully balancing objects. Why should you and I be excluded?

What are your parents like?

Do you dream of them?

Do you resemble them in any way?

There is a small violence in the corner of the room. The seahorse who resembles an anchor, the awareness of an anchor, is struggling to fall asleep. Its bed is a clock that resembles a washing-machine. The seahorse mimics the harsh rasping noise it produces every eight seconds. Suddenly, without warning, the sun does not rise. The absent sun spoke: "God is appearance, God is awareness, God is the image of the universe." God is difficulty breathing, God is static, God is very long and drawn out. The seahorse falls asleep and dreams of visiting the North and South Poles. Tomorrow it would be winter, fingers, palpable.

Have you taken a lover? Do you have children?

Is there much difference between your awareness, your lover's, your child's, your parents' awareness?

Do you and I share the same awareness?

The sound of silk tumbling up the stairs. I am at the foot of the stairs, Gasoline is at the top. Between us, in its room, the seahorse is dreaming of white whistles. The fumigated serpent rose cordially to greet the suitcase; everyone knows that snakes are stairs, and this serpent was a spiral staircase made of tree bark, leading from the roof of the mouth to a cool pool of eddying water some distance away. Stay inside, do not go outside. Stay outside, do not go inside, however you may feel at the time. It gets better with age, like chimpanzees or escalators. Wooden escalator at the corner of your mind, with your mother and a tree whose leaves are small bright moons, so many mouths to feed.

How good is your memory?

Can you remember what it was like before your parents were born?

How often do you feel the same way?

These things are being revealed to us, almost casually. Things making themselves apparent, being made apparent by some outside agency. Someone told Dogen that "there is nothing in the world that is hidden." These changes are very real, cloud of illusions like a bouquet of oysters. I can almost taste it, I smack my lips, my mind has the same shape as my lips and they inhabit the same place on my face.

Have you experienced any pain lately?

What is the difference between physical and emotional pain?

What do you find funny? What makes you sad?

There is only awareness, everything is awareness, manifold awareness no awareness. There is not awareness. When I was born it was so cold that everyone's eyelids froze open, they had to find something at which to look. Some people would look at animals or other people; some people would look at smoke, nonagons, material, electricity, the orbits of nearby planets, calamities, exotic plants with living fruit. The doves had frozen in midair and hung suspended like thoughts. The quality of the soil was sounding alarms. I was born inside of a man who wore test tubes on each of his fingers. He loved to touch things in this way, to caress and fondle. He would touch trees, infant children, arrows, octopuses, whispers, the wings of living insects, insects like animate molecules, errant angles. It was his greatest pleasure. I was born out of the top of his head, his hair was passed on to me, covering my whole body. The passers-by submerged me in water and the hair fell away like laughter. A gathering of dust, a gathering of perfume. The mind is very thin. The top of my lungs is also the bottom of my lungs. The mind is fat and ugly. I was born out of the top of my head. The kitchen lagoon pervious to misfire. The ass of my lungs spewing spiderwebs in all seven directions. Mistaken caterpillar dining in the sepulchral condensation.

There is no disappearing, no revealing, no masks to be taken off; there are only masks, some easily and quickly removed, others gradually and with difficulty. I prefer the endless putting on of masks. Everything wears the disguise of itself, everything the counterfeiter of itself, nobody is suspicious, nobody the wiser. The fools are all juggling themselves forever like a soft rain. Rain is associated with smiling, angels, angles, phalanxes, optometrists, trysts, ovulation, spears stuck in the mud, spears stuck in the mind, spears stuck in bodies endlessly endless falling like rain. The gradual colossus is wearing thin. I wish I could save your life, in an instance of courage without deliberation, then you would know the love I have for you, for everything, my immense reconciliation. The relationship of the mind to itself, which resembles the world so perfectly it would fool even itself. The living orgasm. I would call the tombstones liars and paint them white so that they disappear in the snow that falls graciously over all the eyeballs, closed open. The place where light and darkness do not enter in, where there is no noise. The immense reconciliation. Fruits that resemble lungs, tongues, teeth, hair, faces, lined up in a row like grave-markers. A cordial brainstem makes for an exclusive panorama of the floundering disembowelment in its charming hydrant of gooey metal nettles.

The light of a bluebird illuminates a small room, where in the shadow of a tree crouches a chest of drawers. When it rains in the bottommost drawer, a sun in the shape of a smile is revealed on the dresser's hind-legs, springing to life at every quarter-hour. This usually causes the glass of water to fall out of the hand. When the crowd of policewomen comes to investigate, the chest of drawers goes outside to observe the dolphins in the fountain. The dolphins are always very sick, vomiting flowers, vases, armchairs, cherished brocades, lilting airplanes. A passenger in one of the airplanes, speaking into a large armchair, arouses the lionesses nesting beside the fountain. The lionesses enter the bookstores, cigar shops, cafes, museums, portraits. At the very least, the nude woman in the museum is enticed by the sudden eruption of lionesses and writes a very long letter. The nude woman is Gasoline, at the time about thirty-four feet long. I haven't seen her since. She wrote:

      The sundown, apprehensive, appreciates the gradual taxidermist under the eaves.

      A bright blue sundown, a closing sundown.

      The closure of a bird taking a nap under the eaves.

      The fish

            like a revolver

    into a giant's hands giantess

            the blind streets

    knitting sweaters, scarves, dolphins,

            mussels, muscles, hair,

                    bread

    a growth of colorful flowers

            around the giant's feet

    like hands

like the moon in two hands

      breaking apart

in a flourish of ants

the window bats its eye

      you turn to look

      only to catch a glimpse

of something indistinguishable

      a clock, marble

         a cough, violets

you place the clock on the stairs

      it waits

that is the best place for it

      not underneath the arm

      not in a tree

not in the rocks and sand

      along the beach

at the back of your eye

      along narrow teeth

each with one eye

wide open

like fish gaping into memory

distant unremembered carnival

blue orange green

    While I was rereading her letter I was interrupted by the arrival of three men huddled very close together like the flame of a candle thirty-four feet long. It seems to me that life has no leitmotif, that it is unclear whether there is any thread or through-line. Existence is without a spine, we are all vertebrae in the great spinal column. Some dinosaurs had huge backs, stretching on into the distance, entering the eye like a train entering a tunnel carved into the side of a mountain. If all the chairs were destroyed, there would be no more chairs.

    I've seen a black ant in a black room slowly going nowhere, unsure, struggling laboriously under some huge weight. I've seen a black armadillo shaped like a star ascending a lamppost like teardrops. It's all just a feeling. I am your mother, you are my father, the seashells are my brothers and my sister is coughing weightlessly. Everything is just a feeling that we have, that we share. These words are a feeling, you reading them is a feeling, clowns are a feeling, shadows are a feeling. There is no sharing. The feeling is uncertain. Life is nobody's feeling.

    Do you prefer night or day?

    Do you have many acquaintances? How many would you consider friends?

What is the self, that we are always yet never alone?

Is our burden imaginary?

Giraffes are imaginary. The self is green and shaped like a bell, a hollow, a well. A well so deep that it requires a ladder for entry/exit. Pull the ladder up, leave yourself stuck at the bottom (of your self). Put the bottom on top so you can fall into the well ceaselessly. You are my shoulders, my fingernails, I am your left ear, your anus, the hair on your feet. Assuming, of course, that you have feet. Find yourself in blue underwear, bright underwater.

How often do you feel guilty?

Have you travelled to many different places?

What is your favorite sound? Do you hear it often?

Rising up out of a remote location in the Specific Ocean is a beautiful golden temple, with twisting spires and exultant domes and huge windows with glass like a god's eyes and staircases like arabesques carved into the air. Two men stand guard at the foot of the temple, where it meets the ocean. They let their feet flit about like birds just below the surface of the water. There is a horse on a ledge near the top of the temple who eats the air, which is never exhausted. On the northeast side of the temple is a single statue protruding from the wall; it changes position twice every four days. It is tied to the horse by a single string of jade that gives off a musical hum. The sound is akin to the center of a tree.

Inside the temple is a vast jungle resembling the interior of a human body. No matter which route you travel, it always takes two weeks to reach the temple at the center of the jungle. This interior temple is an exact replica of the exterior temple. The horse near the top of the interior temple eats the moist jungle air, which is never exhausted. The two men who guard the interior temple are blind and have enormous heads.

A limit implies that there is something beyond it, that it is part of a larger context or framework. I would say limitlessness is more restrictive. You can't escape from something that is unlimited, there's nothing outside it. Limits offer possibility. There is something beyond limit and limitlessness. Shadow characters like things taking place in the mind. Above the interior temple in midair a pelican is turning inside-out endlessly. The meeting place of object and space, the limit of the object, distance, extent. Limitlessness is its own limit. There is no extension or depth, only surface, near and far disgorge the sparkling trunk. The slipping surfaces. There is no 'other side', there is no digging through, no getting past. Things have to take their turn, there's no jumping around. It has to be this way, things are the way they're supposed to be. There is no mistake, no error. How could it be otherwise? There is no alternative. Things follow each other, it's perfectly put together. Seamless, no crack to enter in and disrupt. The changes are unchanging, change is unchanging, change is changing. It appears to be moving, appears to be still. It is all self-contained; nothing inside nothing outside. The surface of nothing. No more is required, it's finished, not in want, not in excess. It is a perfect emerald statue, flowing like ripples across the water across the mind. We are the surface of nothing, of everything. Both quantum orthodontists parlor trick trinket twinkling. Forever is wet and sticky like one hundred cows in a trap like teeth like soldiers. Into the soldier's shoulder. Likewise the cumbersome swordfish on fire, within the sardonic sarcophagus.

Use a shovel to dig a hole in your back yard. It is recommended to then masturbate into the hole and put the seed of a tree of your choice in your emissions and fill the hole with your old newspapers. Take a train to the second furthest destination from where you are now. Place hats on the heads of strangers. Make animal noises when you are alone. Cough without needing to. Fly a kite while swimming in the ocean. Spend your entire day waiting around inside government buildings. Be naked whenever you are indoors. Paint things different colors as often as you can. Act sexual with unfamiliar furniture. Blink rapidly. Breath very slowly. Force your breath into little piles. Run whenever you have nothing to do. Refer to people by their eye color. Drink only hot water. Stack things on top of each other whenever you are in someone else's house. Keep your money wet with coffee or tea. Carry a ball around with you wherever you go. Leave something in every location. Lick policemen and the elderly. Never close your eyes while having sex. Crawl backwards on your hands and knees whenever you notice the time. Create meaningless rituals. Create meaningful rituals. Don't masturbate. The longan is trembling credulously.

Often I can feel my limit. It's easier this way. What would you do if you were unlimited? How would you interact with something that is limitless? Are there some things with limit and some things without? Is everything limited, or unlimited? Limit is identity, it gives definition. There is no identity that is limitless. We are all in this together, we are not all together. There will be a great awakening from the dream of life, there will not be a great awakening. Things cannot be divided, there is no division, there is a ceaseless division. Perpetual unfolding of things without end, or perhaps with a definite end. There is no unfolding, no expansion no contraction. It is not working toward something different, something other than this. It is a corpse that does not decay, it is a child that does not grow. Halted time like a frozen waterfall. Energy and mass cannot be created or destroyed. Is this false? Is nothing false, nothing true? There is nothing that 'goes away', yet there is no return. Memory is a hallucination, the dictionary is empty, the body is a fragile ecosystem sodden luggage.

How are you feeling?

Has life turned out like you imagined?

Do you wish for it to get better?

Do you have hope?

The Ritual of Movement and Sound takes place in two phases inside the interior temple. The first phase is performed when all the windows of the interior and exterior temples are in alignment with the full blazing sun. The second phase is performed when all the windows of the interior and exterior temples are in alignment with the full blazing moon. The Ritual takes place whenever possible. The participants wait unmoving until they are called to action, which could be days or months. They receive nourishment from little silver bubbles that float out from the jungle and burst upon their foreheads, knees, shoulders.

Prelude to the Ritual of Movement and Sound

Testing the depths

the naked strangers

calling out across time

to perchance hear an echo or response

seeking something softly that is not myself

the mind that thinks on its own

coming out of the recesses

the avenues between grass and rock

that delicate balance

fragile as glass

cupping gently the waves

those footsteps down the long hallway

there is a light above each door

a colorless light

not white

like a sigh from the next room

the fanfare of trumpets

The king is old, his cape hangs about his decrepit shoulders and runs through every room of the castle, envious of the rugs, a bat's wing is a crow's wing's table, crawling napkins and forks, spinning plates and glasses; a moon razor bottle filled with soap and a washing-machine left out in the sand. Towards dawn, we see a young man, who cowers up against the veiled face of a woman twenty times his size and mass, reaching her lips toward the sky, he finds that, within her teeth of ivory and rosemary, a lion is cavorting as if he were an umbrella, from whose mane protrudes blasphemous tree branches. These itch her almost to the point of ecstasy, as he steps one foot blind and hobbled, cobble-stone scarecrow as a stairway, the other leg a dangerous yet alluring invitation to a charitable swan gathering, proud and benevolent. He swings his ass to the sky and from above encircles the crown of her head, coming to rest upon her shoulder, sagging and leering, a full breast, caught in the bramble of springtime sunlight; minimum pack of dogs, pack of cigarettes, in an old telephone booth between four and nine o'clock, these are an old horse's two eyes, set against a harsh light, hold the phone to the snow and wind, oiled markers holy oily. A thick spiderweb she would cast about his teary eyes, alight with sea-and-chrome flames that leap amber tresses, stirring marble, a frozen banquet that the hair on her face seems to admire, cascading a billowing green, the frozen char-horse, breasts, when suddenly tightfisted his eyes, as a lock of frozen marble, howl into the night, the daylight, a succession of countess the crows.

Taking the nails of her fingers in handfuls and the nails of the door in barnyards, the gelatinous smoke which coughs and snores a delight too, fish the last from a ditch, flies, alight, a sinister eyebrow of flies and bees and foxes, into the sky, take a wing, to the wing, with the woman's fist, she is swooning, he bats her eyes and with each procession of admiring sighs the swarm becomes transparent, reaching with an arm that rivals the arm of Achilles, in silken and somnolent tresses, momentary and eluding, a wink that surprises the stars. Let the obscene char-house, burrowed and fur beneath the other farmhouses and fountains, the tip of each outcome of water, of jasmine, of toothless angels that crowd the sewers and the summer sky, at the peak, as that of a mountain, we find the woman sweeping and careening between the fainted stars, dissonant and reflexive to the extent that each comment as she rebounds from one to the next becomes in itself a miniature parabola, a work that encompasses a passage of northern crows, horned vestibules that take the sky alighted, destined, and fit the entirety of it into a coughing and laughing and sneezing fit of hysteria, candle lit at the top of a match the mouth, clockwork top lit, a seamless birdbath that eclipses the elliptical crows, scoffing into their rabbit-fur napkins and hand-brushes, towels to the sun and with which the number seventeen, as uncountable the countess, the remains, the countess, a sudden star bright, the young man takes her navel into the wind!

It is viewed that as he takes along her hair a golden rope-ladder that glides and sings, each rung a noose and the knot that can be seen from one eye, to the other eye, pull the eyebrow down, tightly the eyelashes full of spring the chance of the fingers while it curls, a bright bird cough, he resumes his travels, each knot of her spine a delighted pigeon or a lewd damsel under duress, the trance at last, coiling around her ankles and her brow, the swan noose, her dress alas slid upward like Maldoror from the mass grave. Toothless and gnarled, her buttocks upon the horizon beat as breath and wings descending from the stockpile of tortured fish and veal, two monsters looming, each buttcheek a single eye from both barbarous creatures, a cretin to the end and of the end a journey from the night through the day, a day, at last, TODAY, eyes held out as toothbrushes and clothespins, a field great enough to feed the sun, plough the soil, the man, eyes wide and without temper, her heel, now bound to each hand, he ploughs the field, to release a great spider that unfolds as a bat's wing. She catches his missteps with each gale of laughter, a sacred cat and more so a formidable gray heron, laying its eggs, cracked open sprout its own feet misplaced and birthed from its loins alcoves of sea shepherds, to the south, at last a summit which secretes a soluble shriek heard throughout and through in, the eagle catches its eye in a tear of hot laughter that sounds through a forest almost as though it were a desert, with her elbow he sips wine from the glacier of two continents open and divine, divide, he buckles around her knees, slinking, four or five women, all in dresses of copper or amorous fiend-calls, a dish or soluble lizard, creeping away from the circus, her knees alight, her knees a tortoise-shell aflame!

Brick-backed whale, spine of bricks, together with the young man, a light to fire the silence, the storm that weathers the fevers of children, drinking from pools of grain and silk-water, alas both as one, whale and young man, a city consoles them between the two walls barricading the street, a full moon a crocodile, shops expand and contract as a retina, host of the whale, a full bones crate, silver, windows that are each of your own hands, a wave, tap on the shoulder, the excuses, a range failing the mountains, clothing that writhes throughout the cracks which lay upon the street-side, hair mussed and beautiful into a full face, a marvelous lips and breasts, the eye and the nose, hand strikes with a cobra's fangs, burnt sun, burnt lightbulb, a twist in the road, turn your side, the street, alas: the tide is in, waves of gracious water and foam, from the lips of a cougar, surrendering your ankles to expand into complete skeletons, stride and cast away, a lonely bat, a shadow that is hidden amidst the company of others. The woman is lying down, a flurry of parchment draped across her body as a suit of arms, young man smiling along the curve of her nose, feet trembling and sliding a soft shout, the crook of her back, whale and man approach a bridge which seems to consist entirely of many flags and ribbons, duct tape and talcum powder, the coat of arms of mice of street bends, behold, the whale is peering at the young man from the other side, a courageous wind makes his arm a part of the glowing picture, a heart upon a glove, tulips that serenade the skylight, winter and spring, summer, the autumn, the glass chandelier. There, a boy with a golden arm outstretched, finger extended, pointing illustrating, there in her eyelashes, swept up amongst the curls, a leopard-skin swings and cavorts promiscuously, that makes the moon blush scarlet and rosemary, sending toward Earth a procession of roses which by the time they finally reach her eye have become small grass chandeliers, squashed against bathroom tiles, the boy of the newspapers, who transcends this day and the following day but never the previous one, an old book or a forest, wings spread flight of six nights a daredevil with fingers for lips, the young man's eye, upon which the woman's eyes set, as the sun, crying sweet moonbeams, kerosene, he runs his hands, bound by string and a wooden noose, through her pubic hair as the wind along the trees, nook of her elbow becomes a harbor for eyes, wrists and for cellar-doors.

Candlestick, a five-arm march, at the peak of this mountain a hand flickers and jumps more like a shadow than itself, across the woman's face an ocean swells and breaks against her nose, her lips full of sand, wind of the summer dawn blowing from her ear, the raise of her handkerchief to catch a lovely cough coincides with the passage overhead of an immense cloud, turning her face almost into caviar, almost full of snow and a forest which breathes uniformed policemen into the air, emerald sitting-rooms into the sun, the young man witnesses all of this as a group of women kicking their feet underwater, he and the whale sitting cross-legged in a trolley-car, each bump brings a new twist into the city, streets growing and becoming illumined by that flickering hand, jumping and crossfire, cussing, a sun within a bicycle wheel, the trolley-car travels down these freshly birthed streets mirroring the caress of the woman's knuckles along the back of each of their heads, city torn and rustling to match the king's cape, palm of a hand in the night sky, there is a whore, merely a single eye and set of lips, looming as the treetops outside the trolley-car, screaming that 'a horse and carriage will become an ocean when a lightning of birds is cast upon it,' alas, the young man is walking along the top of her left eyelid, which opens and shuts to a horse's little ninny whinny. Her breasts gazed upon him through a chest of drawers, were to him a gleaming sword, nine-sided, one side a bright lizard, while two of the other sides consisted of newspaper articles and battering rams, dust caught up in the sunlight, her bosom was the ruins of an ancient city, the young man, accompanied by the whale, for whom the most insignificant detail of the immediate surroundings transposed itself upon his being, the whale took on the shape of her breasts, of fallen castles and crumbling abodes of times past, the shape of an open gate, an amusing drawbridge that would speak and tickle if it were permitted, alternating one before the other they progressed through her bosoms, at the peak of the rightmost breast the young man laid his eye across a swollen bee, wings creaking as cellar doors, tossing about the nipple, the bee bursts open and reveals twenty thousand more bees, emerging simultaneously, a nine-bladed sword, the young man and the whale were engulfed in an ocean, swept across a herd of straw-horses and rocking-chair horses along a field, filled to the brim with elegant birds the shape of an elderly drawbridge, the whale wore this as a hat before it is knocked off by a gust of wind, a gust of her breast, gangplanking like two swords. Masculine linearity, average succession cessation. Is and is not play together like diamonds, perfume of choicest boundaries. Life is like granulated sugar. Life is like this.

What is your motivation?

Do you have any pets? How do you treat them?

What are the differences between animals and human beings?

Ritual of Movement and Sound, Phase One

He knocked on the door with the barrel of his gun, a small gun, no larger than a bird, the sound of his knocking woke her up with a start and she fell out of the bed. The sun shone deeply through the window and curtain, the sun of an early morning, and clouds filled the sky, billowing clouds like white smoke, like white breasts, and he knocked harder against the door, for he did not know whether she had woken up or not. He assumed that she had, for he was knocking awfully loud. She stood in the center of the room putting on her clothes, she didn't sleep with her clothes on. The clouds cast shadows on him. He hit the door with the gun and it went off in his hand with a frightening noise and the clouds split apart like dying birds. The sun fell softly to earth, the sun filled the man. She unlocked the door and pushed it open and knocked the man over and the sun spilled out of him and blinded her. The gun lay on the ground covered in dirt. All she could see were patterns green like emeralds and birds that held the earth with the claws of their feet and the sun growing and shrinking in the morning. The man reached forward and got his hand caught in her hair, she yelled, the door swung on its hinges and closed, a bird come out of the sun. A second man approached and picked the gun up off the ground and held it loosely and watched the two figures sprawled on the sun. The clouds came down like rain and no one could see, not the woman, not the two men, not anyone. In the sky the moon hung distantly and the woman's shouts evaporated into the air. The man with the gun retreated into the room out of which the woman had come. The remaining man was covered in dirt and the woman's hair and the woman collapsed against him and the birds all surrendered to the sunlight and moonbeams and the morning swirling and expanding and breathing as if it were a living organism, the sun was an organism, the spaceship was an organism, the woman collapsed against the man and the moon faint in the morning sky rested on the man's head and for all he knew the moon was a flight of birds. He wanted to shake the moon off his head, but the woman was leaning on his chest and the sun clouded his sight and covered his back and legs with light thick and wild and tangled like the woman's hair. A spaceship emerged from the horizon, from out of the morning, and enveloped the sun and was filled by the escaping birds. The woman escaped in a flight of birds. The sun burst through the door and the man with the gun was seen lying on the bed curled beneath the sheets and a nude African woman stood over him whispering in a tongue indecipherable. Then the man with the gun was gone, the space grew amongst the clouds and morning light and the remaining man entered the room out of which the woman had come and into which the man with the gun had vanished. He walked slowly toward the nude African woman, slowly as if he were sunlight or a bouquet of feathers fallen from the moon, distant in the sky, eclipsed by the spaceship. The spaceship was filled with light and the woman slept within. Her dark form and the shape of birds.

Quietly the nude African woman led the man through a long hall and into another room much darker than the first, through many rooms wherein the light grew progressively dimmer and a strong smelled overwhelmed him, a wild and unknown stench that spoke to something deep inside the man and caused a stir in him. The final room was very small in width but very tall in height and a bed hung suspended by umbilical cords ten feet off the floor. When he entered the room, his feet were bare and covered in dust and dirt and the nude African woman was sitting on the bed, her large curving feet dangling like stars and the man reached out and held one with both hands as if it were a bird. The woman opened her mouth and a bird flew slowly out, a dazzling white bird like a star, and the woman sat watching the man, her nipples were dark and her eyes were dark and her skin was color of the very first humans' skin and the room was damp as if it had recently rained. The floor was wet and a small light was emanating from an unknown source. The man gasped and sunlight spread throughout the room and vanished and the moon lay beyond the nude African woman's head in a torrent of clouds and birds and faint distant light. All was still, the nude African woman breathing softly, the man breathing softly, as the man with the gun entered the room and slumped against the dark wall aiming the weapon at the moon. The man whom the nude woman had led into the room ascended and hid beneath the sheets, the other man stood underneath the bed and let the gun fall to the floor, where it was lost, and the Lost Pharaoh emerged grinning from where the gun had landed. He stood as tall as the room and his headdress was beautiful and golden and he winked and disappeared. The man who was not in the bed searched in vain for the gun, he was on his hands and knees and he was crying, crying. The man who lay in the suspended bed held out his hand and the nude African woman placed the gun on his outstretched palm and the gun fell to the floor with the sound of a bird. She was on her knees with her hands clasped as if in prayer and her billowing hair black eclipsed the moon until it descended onto the bed. The man took the moon in his left hand and the nude African woman brought her shimmering body to his body and they made love while he held the moon.

The Lost Pharaoh slept within the sun and out of the sun the spaceship was birthed into the morning and the sky. The spaceship hung in the air motionless, as still as the sun's rays, the moonbeams, the woman exited the spaceship and returned to earth on a cloud. A desert and a vast woods had surrounded the building containing the two men and the nude African woman and the Lost Pharaoh, who often was many places at once. A cloud of birds. The woman stepped into the forest and was lost and the leaves were of sunlight and bird feathers and of the birds themselves.

In one hand the man held the moon and in the other hand he held the spaceship. Underneath the bed, in a pool of sweat which appeared a faint green in the dim light, in the swallowing dark, the other man stood with the sun pressed against the small of his back, his spine grew and writhed and broke through the bed and into the nude

African woman's vagina. Her eyes poured out onto the moon in a soft glimmering haze of old colorful patterns long forgotten, and she spoke in an ancient tongue undecipherable. Her skin was a vague memory and the man made love to her as if she were a pyramid, a pyramid of shifting stones and sand and birds and the dead men and the dead women. The pyramid was a labyrinthine forest, full of sunlight. The other woman leaned against a tree to rest, she was out of breath, the tree was the man's spinal cord, within the nude African woman's vagina. Everything was an inescapable ecstasy.

The Lost Pharaoh says:

"The sound of a piano

is like rain

escaping this heart the flight of a bird

toward the sun

birdcage heart where no one goes

the stillness of clouds

and the morning sunlight

unbroken

it takes delicate fingers

chandelier fingers

to play the piano

like rain

and in between the black keys and white

birdsong

these eyes

looking out into the distance

at the silhouette of trees

there are wolves in the city at night

you can hear their howls

surfacing through the sound of cars

rising far between like monoliths

only to return

to no-source."

A man opens the door and closes it, stepping into a white room. At the center of the room is a statue of a nude woman made of stone. The man approaches to investigate. Her lips are not smiling but nor is she frowning and her eyes reveal nothing, for they are of blank stone. The room is vacant, and slowly the door fades away. The man was not going to leave but he had no intention of staying for very long. He had arrived by train, followed by a walk, it seems. The statue had flowing billowing hair, which he supposed would be blonde or red. Her bosom was ample, like a cloud or plume of smoke, her thighs smooth and bare and attractive. The room an echo of itself, disrupted by the man, now circling the statue, inspecting. He looked down at his left hand, the veins distinguishable under skin, and the hair on his arms, and the bones of his hand. His flesh arm became her stone arm, and he realized that he was looking at the statue. He shook his head and noticed a small wooden table in the corner of the room. It had four legs which converged to a single stem which held the flat circular surface. On top was a clear glass of water and some feathers beside it. They were light blue and the pattern subtle and beautiful, authorless work of the Great Artist of its own design. He approached the table and let out a sigh. The air in the room was clean, pure, gradually transformed by the man's breathing, imperceptibly. Air birthed incessantly from the statue of the nude woman. The vacancy of the room, its limited void, seemed bound and produced by her, her form, silent breath, in and out without distinction. The curve of her stone ass, not in view of the man, who put his hands on the table. What to do? he thought. He spoke it. "What to do?" it sounded. And slowly the room usurped his body as the home of his mind. The white walls, floor, ceiling, and the statue, the table, all writhed with constancy, motionless. There was light, but from no source. Is there a certain way a man must act? He must not give himself away, but of course there is nothing to give away.

He took a drink from the glass, and the water felt cool going down his throat and disappearing in his body. Someone began to speak, but when the man turned there was nobody. And still the statue stood, her feet just barely touching the ground. He saw the nude woman as a well, and he came to the well and gazed upon it, into it. The descending wall was at first brick, then soil, plunging. A heart lay at the bottom, so far away the man could not see, the light was lost to it. If he were to throw anything into the darkness, it would not reach the ground, the heart, unknown fruit. And it was the statue again, and he took another drink of water. The feathers toppled softly to the floor, his breathing was heavy. The man walked across the white room and sat leaning against the wall. And the ceiling was an eye, the whole room a fruit, and the man became the eye. Its lashes swept through the fruit, the statue wearing a dress, and the man was seeing, seeing a boy and a girl, young but not children, and the eye was no more.

The blessed ones

holy

stand upright in infinite coffins

daybreak crooked broken

temples in ruin

whilst birdsong echoes in ocean

swollen to the fallen buildings

like rain

comfort

In the horse's mouth

a white dove escaping

against bright sunlight

seen peering out from the

dining-car of a passing locomotive

a young boy with hair like wheat

with countless eyes

frozen tongue

grey-haired mule

slumped like an old woman

in the snow

brays at the grey moon

weightless grey burden

like an echo

the kites and skates

flitting in a little pool

further down the cave

could not be heard

over the sound of voices

at the cave's mouth

wooden ball

thrown into the night

a shout broke open

like a diamond

drowning in the snow

diving in the sow

equestrian

the winged psychiatrist

emboldened

raises the first ray of celadon

and settles the second

along the curling tail

of a one-eyed dog

graciously

Ritual of Movement and Sound, Phase Two

The village closely resembled a descending hand, through
water, through air, through eyelashes, suspended in motion by the edge
of a vast desert, along a twisting river quiet gentle as a wink, and the
people lived in huts made of grass and sticks and mud and sand. To the

north and east was the great desert, to the south flowed the river to the sea, and to the west were the grasslands and plains and further the forests. No one of this village had ever ventured far in those forests, where it is said trick-playing spirits live and strange beasts. Owls yell out in the night, voices echoing against the huts before being swallowed into the empty horizon of endless sand. Travelers seldom came to the southern shores, but such occasions were times of great excitement and joy amongst the villagers, for travelers are often inclined to share fantastic stories and bring foreign objects and materials. The people of this village were generally happy and were in no shortage of food or water or wine.

Sometime during the course of the country's history, among the sprawling generations, two men lived in that village by the desert. They were Abua, which means Restless Sleep, and Chandelier, which means The Stiff Grass In The Fields. Both were of strong families with good reputation. Abua was well-educated and could recite many sacred hymns, whereas Chandelier was big and open-hearted, suited for work. The two were friends and lived in nearby huts, close to the river. The river was of great interest to them and they were often to be found there, cavorting about or quietly conversing. The river played a large role in the lives of the villagers, and there were many rituals and ceremonies dedicated to it. Abua and Chandelier were intelligent young men and filled with curiosity, and each liked to participate in ceremonies.

One day when the air was warm and the grasses were brutally green and shimmering with the sun's tears, one day when the sand in wild abandon begins to invent shadows of impossible things and the birds hang from the tree branches upside-down like lamps, like furnaces, Abua and Chandelier took a wooden canoe to the river and drifted downstream, leaning sensually over the sides in glorious fatigue, identifying the creatures and plants they happened to glance while lost in dreamy contemplation. The canoe went far with the water, past the last of the huts, past the pastures, toward where the river becomes the sea. They got into the water and pulled the canoe ashore and thanked the river god for a safe voyage. Abua and Chandelier dragged the canoe through the sand to the path, and hoisted it into the air, each carrying one end in both hands. Water was in the canoe and it sang with silent ecstasy, causing the hearts of invisible fish to become visible. Abua swallowed a fish's heart, aflame, without noticing. Walking along, they became aware of a great figure standing beside a tree, engaged in some activity. It was a god, and to Abua it was in the shape of a fox who had in addition to its four fox legs one human arm, with a slender and masculine hand, and several eyes, placed in different locations; to Chandelier it was in the shape of a large human head, but so distorted as to blur any human qualities: strange geometries were explored in the curves of the skull, teeth introduced in peculiar positions and of varying length. The god was dividing a sphere, which hung in midair like the ring of a bell, in half, and then into fourths, and then into eighths, and so on, in a continuous process of division. It was operating at such minute levels that the two young men could not clearly see, nor fathom, its actions. They stopped and looked on, transfixed, mouths agape, when another man came down the path from the other direction and upon seeing the god flung himself before it in reverence. This beautiful act disrupted the spheres and sent them off flying in all directions, some maintaining their height while others fell to the ground or ascended to the sky. And the god became upset and tumultuous. It demanded of the man that he bring to it a tiger's fur, lest its anger be stirred into wrath. The man clamored and wailed before the god, who climbed the tree and reclined in its branches. Abua and Chandelier approached the man, who implored them to help him, for he is a weak and lowly man and surely could not kill a tiger singlehanded. Abua and Chandelier agreed and the three men continued on to the village.

Tigers were known to frequent the edge of the western forest, so they gathered spears and started out, making haste. Across the plains like tumbleweeds, silent before the midday sunlight, wind moving about them with the ebb and flow of a distant voice, careful for snakes and vermin under bare feet. No sight of any tiger as they approach the first trees. The man introduced himself as K'oahno, meaning Gentle And Bothersome Fly. He seemed as frail as a pair of insect wings, and the two friends took pity on him. Whilst K'oahno lay in the shade, his spear at his side, Abua and Chandelier looked out over the plains and into the forest for signs of a tiger. Chandelier climbed high into a tree and called out to the birds, imploring, but they offered no response. The hours grew ripe like ancient fruit but still there appeared no tiger; it was decided to construct a shelter for the night and the three gathered sticks and branches and settled amongst the grass a little ways into the forest, though not far enough to be out of view of the plains.

Much as the men willed and feared for a tiger to wander upon them, no such animal was to be found. Three nights came and went, and with it many dreams and patient waiting. K'oahno was slowly becoming cold and his skin pallid, as result of the god's temporary preoccupation with his being; he would be of no help when it was time to conquer the beast. Abua looked to his dreams for solace and guidance, but the swell of mischievous energy seething from the depths of the trees obscured any comprehensible meaning. Foul visions often befell the three men when gazing into the darkness and awful, curious noises evaporated and assembled as if divorced from any source. On the morning of the fourth day, as the sun began to weave its way through the fog of dawn, Chandelier took up his spear and gathered his courage and moved swiftly toward the heart of the forest, his ears keen for any noise, eyes discerning sharply uninhibited, searching. The trees grew closer together as if frightened and the light of morning halted outside the dense branches, night continuing within hidden and inexhaustible. He couldn't prevent his feet from rustling and crumpling the leaves and twigs in his search, the sound breaking the silence of the fog. But soon he heard another pair of feet, moving as swiftly as his own, a short distance behind him. Chandelier paused and turned to look, and seeing a spear emerging and a man bearing it, he kept on.

The two made their way through the wood, quiet and no more than an arm's length away, Chandelier maintaining the lead, and in this manner they came upon a clearing. Sleeping in a pool of sunlight amidst the pale darkness and fog, before a dying tree, a mother tiger. Her fur was a complex and jagged red, stained gracefully by black and dark blue streaks, and thick. Her chest rose and sank like a leaf on the surface of a lake. A sight to behold, beneath the dying tree as if it were a shrine. Undone arabesque of muscle and fur and beauty. An eagle flew along the clouds. The sight touched Chandelier's heart. He began to hear a noise, footsteps, many men. They will surely wake the animal! He turns to the figure beside him, and discovers it to be himself, as if a reflection on water. The figure does not take notice of him but watches the tiger slowly. More men have entered the clearing, and all are himself. The sound of their (his) arrival has awoken the slumbering animal, who rises quickly and begins circling the tree. The tiger roars like organic gunshot and the men are frightened and run away. Chandelier remains standing still, looking at several of himself running in all directions, and the tiger gives chase. He follows closely behind, bewildered. The figures would run and vanish behind trees and reappear elsewhere, and the forest was a confusion of bodies and trees and growing sunshine. When Chandelier raised his spear, suddenly all of them turned and charged the tiger; as the spear left his hand in flight they were upon it, and his spear stuck in its ribs. Like a swarm of ants, the men and the tiger writhed in a passionate drama, like the play of two gloves in midair above a table. He dived into the formless motion of men and tiger and was lost to it, before another spear came through and struck the final blow to the beast. Chandelier looked up to see Abua standing some distance away. All of the figures had disappeared. He looked around the forest but there was no sign of himself, and the tiger's corpse a ruined temple of vast color. They wait leaning against some trees while K'oahno skins the vanquished animal. The sight of the naked dead tiger caused a stir in the depths of Abua's heart, and a shadow fell across his brow.

It was nearly evening by the time they returned to the god, who was dozing in the branches and leaves of the tree. It appeared to them all in the form of a luxurious woman, with starlight breasts and a bouquet of boundless dark hair, brown as the heart of a tree, wooden, nearly. They laid the tiger's fur on the ground as it descended softly. It spoke with the ambiguous and complex voice of a god:

"Chastely the clam climbed

to the top of a tree and

its pearl dropped down down

down down

down down immaculately it fell down until it landed on a camel
passing by and became a fountain

When the camel reached the city

the waters of the fountain

turned violet

and the clam could find

no rest

neither the camel nor the tree

knew which wind was stirring the gossamer wind

the windmill wind

the tunnel wind

the dried wind

the wind's wind

with all horses

and bells at its dismay

the playing-cards belched forth

out of the fountain

and the seagull wind laughed

and laughed

if only were tomorrow Sunday!

then the lepers would

find a sparrow in each of

their skin's new pockets

eight-balls hiding in the patches

of lepers' skin

closed tight like a virgin window

full of chimes

and the windmills turned upside-down like chandeliers in an alligator's

mouth

too porcelain to make

any difference any difference at all

would be acceptable and the camel sat down

for its lunch in the bath

the fountain was picked up by a little girl

and scattered in the sky

to make new stars

each one braying like a damsel in disdain

the bath well lit

like a reindeer's rainbow antlers

too much like a carriage

a miscarriage of daffodils

and what was it I just remembered? was it I or someone else?

I in the dark courthouse

you hearing the tremendous falling

of leaves in the damp courthouse that could hardly be put back
together to resemble a crown, a crow

a laugh

a stagecoach

drawing nearer and nearer

to the blue infirmary

dotted with rose lashes

so sinister to be seen

and I

and the velvet raincoat underneath a white handkerchief

a white smile

croaking a daybreak song altogether whose lips

I often remember

being twenty yards long

or the White House

in the smile of fire

in the ankles of water

It is quiet in the eaves and

it is quiet under the sties

It is very noisy in the teeth circling overhead like a catapult branches
pulled out

from the blue laundry

at all hours of the day

there is a tiny city in the dust beside the cases

that in the daytime is called Darkness

and Rut at twilight

the pretty blue cases

the pretty blue cases

trapped under the eaves closing the stars

the crooked bedframes tumbling through the city

quiet as a pinto bean

hatred of the snarling umbrella grown milk dust

the poultry is too effervescent

to be startled by the

rutabagas in their underclothes

the poultry is too effervescent

to be intimidated by the

rutabagas in their underclothes

the poultry is too effervescent

to be circumnavigated by the

rutabagas in their underclothes."

Sun fish rivers danced like snow, night's white bicycle, white angels of night roll along the surface of the water temple hidden in the corner of the eye, light light light, dark of forest cloak run white bones feather white of the nightingale carrying snow in its beak, winter bell in the talons of the moon dripping long tulip petals across the water fountain fire of soft running coat-heels, stone fish with eyeballs running the hourglass into sand dust rain particle of water loosening its tie to join the sun in its cavern of light blue light light, wingtips, wing rose at the petals and drenched with rain white black skeletons froze thunder and lightning with hair trailing at the heels of the canoe sliding down the throat of wind and sand, blow hounds of night blow the dandelions into the forest below, below the paper cranes diamond run red icicles run the forest at the teeth of the heels, thousand white seagulls danced sun red danced danced down blue petals forest night at the winter bells hidden in the vines and briar of the woman's intestines, the white intestines of diamond birds scattered paper pelicans at the forest of the young man windswept at the heels bedlam boat across the palm of the woman's hand inside-out; as if her legs were white sun snow horn blow, across the fountain slowly out the mouth of the nightingale birdcage teeth drawn trapdoor shut and fire drawn over the bed simply simply, quiet quiet the rain.

What is your favorite activity?

Do you feel good when you help other people?

Do you enjoy being alone?

The libraries lap at the rug like tongues at the ocean's shore, too swift to smell the exhaust produced by the precocious bird whose ribbon is choking it, caught in its throat, caught in the throes of that argument which has swept the stairways of so many physicists, the inexhaustible torn rug that is host to a diamond for every facet of truth the woman's great face conceals, the squeak of a robot is forever heard by the cough of the young man, when it has ceased to be heard and retreats fearful into its vacuum, its birdcage filled with cigar-smoke that screams sweet star eyes, hoof-prints left by the corridor of the whale, in a fit of twirling hands, some with rings and chains on them, cavorts into the moon night. Through the ceiling, by the staircase and storefront mannequin that quivers at the bow-and-arrow stretching across some nude woman's body, holding open a glass door, veiling the raccoon slinking around like an old dress worn to the bone only by the young boys and girls who feel like the fin of a dolphin rubbing up against the thigh of the sun, a burnt-out lightbulb that the raccoon kisses, raccoon who is simultaneously crushed by the weight of the moonbeams and rides above them as a carpet of pubic-hair back in the rain and fog, clover hidden blue-eye moon, raccoon is a basket of leaves when leaning against the glass door, under the grass is the moon peering out as if from a ghost's lampshade, viewing in its immediacy a collection of bones from some creature, almost forming a complete skeleton; the head is made from fish bones, the body is of old table legs and the workings of old machines that startle the eye and fill the heart with melancholy, the tail and legs are salamander tears sewn together to make a coat or candlestick, green shit, that under the living wing of the woman is a stray hat made of the lore of sailors and countrymen when they make love against the coiling snake, teeth bared and the skirt pulled over the knees, revealing the incomplete skeleton found in the swamps and alleyways and fish-scales, that etching of a young man who resembles a whale, a diamond-shaped whale that completes the young man's eyes when he is at an expensive restaurant combing the lips of the beauty of the afternoon with a bathtub or soda grin, marvelous flowers are curved around the bottle, when glanced at it through the crack in the door, silverware impaled through a globe half-frozen grin suggesting the coming of a gunner to remember in the salamander's soup-dish.

At this table, legs of men and horses and goblins are limp to the early tides, smoking forerunner fortnight four runners too late past the evening meal of table-legs chilled to perfection, upset of woman's bloated hair turns the waves of the plates and waiters, causing them to tumble to the floor and once broken and in pieces they travel to the ceiling to mock the cooks who eliminate the horse's teeth with a brew of manure to the cold runner, locked at the chair front, the backs and seats of the chair match the image in the candlelight of an old fisherman cutting the horse free of its table-legs, but when the wine is finished the waiters collect themselves into a dustpan and fish the dishpan from the fire of the night, fish ghost leaps from the green sun into the eyes of the young man, blinding him in one eye, momentarily, and he misses an entire revolution carried out by the tablecloth, napkins and silverware against the plates and the meals upon them, coloring the seagulls gray with delight at the premise, the old woman and the sea select from the bread basket a couple who are fighting over who will pay for the nose and eyelashes of the chef and the socks and shoes of the waiter left by the table, like a boat left in the sand on a foggy morning, whales erupt from the stern of the boat and collapse on the sand as if enlightened, while the bow of the boat makes its way off with the silver spoon and the tulip fork, cowering in the frothing tide, undisturbed by the toss of a lock of amber hair used to fill books with water, so that the beauty of the afternoon can frolic in front of the immense wonderful woman, whose body is wrapped around the hermit's sunken house, stretched out four limbs by the mule submerged in the daylight and fine fire that grows with the destruction of each glass cup full of herbs.

A mummy is quite similar to a tree, shake a leg and sit crooning like an emperor or mad phantom coaxed by the impossible hump of the flute, a mummy is several cats' tails emerging from a pot of soil and a tree is fourteen lily-pads rising to the surface of the clouds, woman shining moon dazzling and leaping, places against the tree a voluptuous hand with all the lips of a rose, quite silver; when placed in a diamond, the mummy turned on its head is the spitting and hissing image of the tree, where the old men and women perform tangos and waltzes and beehives and rocking-chair seahorses out of the branches reaching like grinning stars across the water where dummy legs are branches covered with leaves at the bottom of the lake, only the mummy's head can perform the necessary functions of the tree's roots, hoof tooth and nail and old meat left out in the starfish, the old men and women fall out of the tree onto the dirt and form a circle around the trunk, a Grecian statue with mummy lips and hands. That a tiny red spider climbs on a string of smoke and produces gales of horse lightning, spreads through the veins of a rock's pupil the spectacular dance of peasants set on fire and goblin roses for every thorn and throne of the bush, touching toes with a bridegroom's veil, tumultuous in the dust cloud eye, well through the nursery-rhyme a dog bark pierces the bones in the hand of the window, the peak of a mountain, causing stairways to tumble down the chest of the woman and up the thigh of the young man, while along the wall the whale full of breath is covered in soot and fragments of passing ghosts, sundial in the forest embellishes the traveler weary of the weight of that solitary stone, large and engraved with invisible etchings of the tempests, squirming underwater the spider emerges in a time of war and a time of robins' crowns, thrown on the chairs of kings and queens littered on the porch and lawn, laundress of the light and falling smoke that breathes with the passing of each season as if it were its brother or cousin, reaching with the sea branches of the colossal footprint that disrupts the teal party until the sky clears its nose.

Quiet sound of church bell

distant and heavy with sadness

echoes across the countryside three men nearly collapsed

move like shadows lengthening in failing daylight soldiers all

guns swollen with bullets

and muddy boots

broken voices and extinguished eyes

through the wind and sunlight

to the lonesome church-house

unobscured

rising out of the horizon

like the pale moon

or a cloud

as the hours grow

the distance evaporates

tall white church-house vacant and beautiful

the bell like an eye

gazed into the men beneath the soldiers

and cried tears the wind brought

inside, the full sound

of the tolling bell like

swelling breasts or waves whispering to shore

surrounded the soldiers like a distant lover's embrace

as they climbed

standing beside the now-still bell

the entire horizon offered to them

a silhouette behind the church

caused the men to raise their guns

but it was only a scarecrow motionless and silent

amidst a forgotten garden

the sound of a bell

is born of its emptiness

such it is with a man's heart

such it is with everything

tiger lying in wait

like curled sundown

lone shadow thrown across desert plain

behind skin and hair

birds sit in tree of bone

beneath skull always frowning

brain

so many lashes to unseen eye

within fruit-flesh... what?

can a line be traced all the way to empty space?

what does space occupy?

something holds all boundless space

like a diamond

fleeting as a glance

between lovers

downstream

motion is violence

the softest violence

if any ear listens

to the sun always relentless

it speaks of loss and what is lost

pushing to give last fight fish gaping with open mouth

the battle is already won and lost

why this scramble

why the ruined flowers like abandoned eyes

why broken coat-hangers

in fields below blue skies

the battle never waged

is this bruised place

why the thrownaway words and useless talk

it's already lost

lowdown light and spaceless dark

dropping like loosed fingers descending or violins

without all these things everyone

everyone

everyone

everyone

everyone

heart without all these things heart

heart

heart

everyone

heart

quiet nebula unfolding without commencement

without all these things

fragile as dragonfly wings

in without entrance

gone without departure

it's all center, and nothing is without

it is the same it is not the same

      I wish I had been there for the first dawn, I imagine it was pretty spectacular. Unrivaled perhaps except for the first dusk. Assuming of course that things had a beginning. The beginning of a beginning, prior to a beginning, after the beginning. Things are beginning. Will you begin with me to see again the world forever new? A false topography. Standing beside a tree in the snow, beside the trunk, peering around it to see the other side. And finding nothing there. Do you remember? It wasn't so long ago. Do you remember being at the top of the stairs, holding in both hands a transparent green vase filled to the neck with ice delicacies? It was autumn. There was brown hair draped down along the middle of the stairs. You closed one eye and held your lips. It was exactly like this. My lips are becoming transparent, my mind is becoming transparent. My parents are transparent.

      Did you have a formal education? What was it like? How do you learn?

      What is the difference between you and your learning?

I think we've got to come to some sort of understanding. Or misunderstanding. We should be able to agree on our misunderstanding. Consolidate the illusions, delusions. Suppressed occlusion. We must distinguish things together like falling snow. Would you please point something out for me? There is something between us, there isn't something between us. There is a piano between us, a vacuum-cleaner, there is a dancing bull between us, kicking its legs, nonthreatening, rejoicing. **The dinosaur rose and stood before it in a vast clearing enclosed by a great forest.** The merry anus that eats kilometers and lion-cubs with appalling zeal, zesty trickle. Mercury cubical, mercurial cube slouched menace infatuated fatiguing.

Soon overhead a thunderclap is observed, commencing the lineage of the lamp of life to triple twice-fold, fold the tablecloth so that the breadcrumbs which dance and lose their way are suspended in midair by an invisible plate of necklaces or a broken guitar, caught in the oven as a small mouse is forgotten as a fish and is served as antipasti until the wind boils over and the night is young, when the sun is old and the sun is young and the moon is crying over split milk, though it dislikes the absolute flavor of cranberry juice, it finds delight in the taste of the pepper-shaker and onion-bulb one thousand feet long and fifty feet tall, a crowded neighborhood, by sundown, that whale's oven is as open as a lightbulb in winter, smothered in overdressed clowns who take it upon themselves to cause disdain for the lion and its meal, soiled to the point of ecstasy, the point of the knife, in the mirror a bent spoon, a kiss so soon spent, the point of the corner of the drawer, way in the back, where the dust is unfettered as the crease of the moon's ray-gun is smoothed, wind carries it's basket several yards toward the east, last night or this morning, which ever brought about the bread of change or Mendelev's coin-purse bathed in the innocent golden locks of a young boy in the shape of a rocket-ship, a clock chimes under the surface of the water one hundred leagues. Seventeen means she'll hold the rocket-ship nape of your neck in the cupboard, twelve means the she'll cover the steaming scalp of you at a young age in a terrapin tarp made from clothespins, sixteen means that winter will turn the rust earlier than the steamboat will turn into a cup of water that only the sun can grasp, while the shark tails its sweetheart around the bend, corner of the eye-socket filled with metal filings or fish-teeth, next time or other, ere the cold harness of sweet perfume licks my cheek when the sun is up, king of the marshes, slow descent of red marsh waters, emphasis on the coattails, twenty-nine means that the young man has to coil his robe around the handsome arm of the next airplane to happen across the shivering skyline, tomorrow's sun danced the late blues and greens away from the corner of the ballroom, toothed and crooked, wicked moonbeam snap under the buckle, a triangle loose from all of the obscenities cast to the shoreline, the foam of the ocean cleanses the wounds of the cosmos.

The whale is under the hermit's old shell, a spiral mimicking the laughter of countless crows' wings, flashing lights startle and prey upon the footholds of a suspecting snake, abracadabra, the snowfall wakens a melancholy cadaver, covered in words spoken in ancient times, multitudinous in the histories they relate and the poetry they weave, a wave of amber nails and fingernails cascades from the woman's tears, seeping through her bellybutton, a red or silver button that spills the live tide whenever a millionaire is present the sun goes out, until their money is spent on the old torn shoe three feet by the lowside, autumn will arrive and with it azure tides, a crumpled table shattered like a leaf of paper holding the next glimmering of the stars' brassieres. Hooting owl, cast your skeletons and new papers over to the windowsill, where the cadavers sleep in the newspapers that come into print several days in the future, but which are still curling with the flames of time, a breast of time that heaves and quivers under the triangle and square as they emerge from the soil as a cube or cylinder or pyramid, the greatest of all tapes, where the Universe was born and where the great turtle sits balanced, the woman is hovering alongside the world atop the tortoise's shell, a light eyeful of courtesies and oven-mitts, a small blanket or suit of animal fur retrieved from the animal which has no name without its knowing and inevitably has changed the course of its life and death in that they no longer exist to it; should that animal be human or has the era of awakening yet to befall our mountain of picture-frames and pillows and newsreels unspun?

A wedding-carriage is only as thick as the tuba turned inside-out, as the old saying goes past the window and darts into the tool-shed, playing with the whale's sense of direction and courtesy, the young man hangs a painting from the fishhook nose of the whale, continuing on toward summer, winter dress is dragging in the sand at the moment, the woman hurls the iron ball of modesty toward the window in the starlight, the moon is nigh when the coat is removed from the sewing-machine, machine to start the news, end at the roundabout tree in the center of the driveway, three-hundred yards from the center of the Earth, wearing a beautiful golden maroon dress, the fringes are two ivory snowmen, coiled in the smoke of the late summer afternoon, blue mouth over that part of town, where only the old men go to sleep and where the women dressed in coattails and donkey ears are shown the door, a glimpse of the sound of dolphins weeping tables and chairs of forlorn days past when lovers traverse the corridors of the woman's bones, a sprawling array of bones on the carpet which only promotes the guests of that certain party where cold beverages are never served but where the crown of engagement is placed on one of the men with closed eyes, the crown is one hundred feet long and can accommodate every being in existence, though it is only the humans who wear the crown of the skull backwards, facing the golden gloom of the sun and moon, bluet, the bones on the rug drift off into the sand of tomorrow's sunset.

The young man, in the rain one day late in the evening on the woman's shoulder-blade, carries a lioness in the corner of his foot, with a tail subdued orange bat wings, twirling chandelier that costs too much to look at directly in the eye, lioness covered in thirty foot long hairs and crestfallen leaves, a rowboat leaning against its heaving side from all this sprinting into the dingy yesterday's rain, when overhead an enormous sapphire suffers the air with it's incredulous remarks about the nether weather, upsetting the lioness who in midair takes the shape of a clump of leaves resting in the crook of the woman's elbow, up along the forearm, up along the rowboat that this winter is blind and taking every precaution against the wind in this rain, the wind is dressed in a ridiculous suit of rain and lightning, obscure but not at all appropriate for this occasion, lightning-bug a smile and a tear, look in the box. Cobwebs are alight in the winter sky, as the cuckold runs the good year around the forest walls so well, black as a coat, night sky a deer inside-out with two tears trailing dark antennas, a cobweb could pluck a single cherry from the horseshoe of the woman curved in the lamp's light, four legs by the bluebird tree, the forest trees play the illusion of a hammock for the bluebird to see, caught up in the cuckold's reverie, as it sails from shore to shore under the trees in the soil, caught so well; the cuckold is confronted by a minister who has bestowed upon his boot-heels the color of a rope hanging from the largest black or white spot on the cow, taken for a walk to the sundown tree, over by the water that runs so well you could swear it was a piano-stool in a paper bag, all dressed and prepared for the morning-glory to fall, fallen handshake by the old winter tree and blood is exchanged through their veins as a gift, a summer night that is too rundown to be broken by the cry that the bluebird makes when it is under the soil, dressed in soil for the crown of the woman's head, bluebirds' bones, the eight-ball can pocket nothing but the phones, the minister and the cuckold sing as a single bard from days of yore, distinguished as a toaster or lampshade from the future, and their song is blood, hurrying home from the office, where the coattails are spun about the spiders' webs alight in the daylight, by the end of the night.

Giraffes are imaginary. The self is purple and shaped like a bell, a hollow, a wheel. A well so deep that it requires a ladder for exit/entry. Pull the ladder up, leave yourself stuck at the bottom (of your mouth). Put the cinders on top so you can fall into the well endlessly. You are my eardrum, my anterior, I am your left icicle, your ants, the hair of your feet. Assuming, of course, that you have a creation, some invention. Creation invention, life invention, life creation, feet.

How often do you feel guilty?

Have you travelled to many different spaces?

What is your favorite antelope? Do you hear it often?

Spouting up out of a specific location in the Pacific Ocean is a beautiful golden pear, with twisting bears and exultant domes and huge widows with glass like a god's umbilical cord and staircases like arabesques carved into the bakery. Two men are standing guard at the foot of the temple, where it meets the proscenium. They let their feet flit about like birds just above the surface of the breasts. There is a horse on a ledger near the top of the cabbage who eats the poison, which is exhaustive. Toward the rear-end of the temple is a single statue protruding from the orifice; it changes position twice every four artifices. It is tied to the morsel by a single umbrella of jade that gives off a musical honk. The sound is akin to the center of a dancing bull.

Through the Japanese dishtowel, through the curtain, protrudes a daft sort of blue, covered in the rings that it drew too well, well, well, by the night's alight nightlight the hammer saw the swing and it wasn't too well, oh well, by the rope's knot and the clothes on the floor know only too well, finger-licking well in the know, down swept the broom in hopes and fires of casting off the shackles of it's furtiveness, dressed in the dishtowel, only it didn't go too well, and the dinosaur though it knew only too well what the sight of the dandelion was like, when the dandelioness curtsied and caught the wind by the snout, blowing and coughing hard into it, and soon an immense tunnel was birthed by the shoreline and hillside and by the very fringes of that dress which the wind wore did the coast of this new ocean toss up into the air only too well, the stone monk sits alone and full of company, by the hairs of the sunlight's beard did the horse fall. That space-ape full of goldfish and oils, brings rocks and carved stones from his country, with a golden eagle climbing do his feet breathe softly like mice teeth on the leaves and snow, space-ape your fur is an island and the jail-cell where you were born has crumbled and there is now a toy store in it's place, a ballroom gown that you wear, space-ape, looking at the whale because he is full of water and pearls, you see the young man in the whale's esophagus, trimming the hedges of the whale's phlegm to suit your senses, oh glorious space-ape how you have grown from the thorns and from the ivory, whilst the songbirds explode and blood is thrown across your dinner-plate; the woman looks over at the ape of space, the crow from the cosmos, and exhales miniature rocking-chair seahorses, to the wind's undercoat, blue shells descend from the sky as the spiral on the space-ape's eye, looking forward to the long winter and the salad dressing up in colorful ideas and thoughts that only the autumn can imagine, curled up by the bottomless stairway space-ape is full of balloons and feathers and silver coins brought over by the people of his galactic county.

Across the woman's immense and beautiful form did the young man and the whale venture as if they were straw dogs, encountering various secret embassies of coral reefs and cigarette ashes painted to resemble a diabolic little girl caught in the furies of playtime with her dolls. She had three dolls: the first doll was a bear, red and silver, that reflected her mood in the gold of summertime when the dandelions shone no more, shown hazy sun-smiles, a coiled blue cobra can withdraw its venom from the tongue of this little girl, the second doll was a mule with detachable limbs who spoke ivory tulip blossoms very slowly; the third doll was a deer, whose front left hoof contains the Four Horsemen of the Apocalypse, whose positions have differed to better suit the arms of the Cosmos: the rider of the white horse is a fallen leaf, the swordsman has become two clouds of opaque smoke that grin at the mention of unkempt gardens, the other Horsemen have since their formation been heard of only in the whispers of this little girl, no different from any other girl, except that when her hair reaches a certain length the old tool-shed in the backyard crumbles to reveal a dress suspended in the air, with a forest of severed hands, feet, teeth, fox legs, ghost eyes, dolphin screams and other phantasmic apparitions that protrude from the headless collar like a bouquet of flowers ripe for the picking in the middle of winter, when the cold hitches up its jeans and turns its hat inside out.

The whole robot makes the short trip to Heaven. All around are soft material images, large overflowing wells, wooden fences, voices in and out of the ear, non-material inventions. The whole robot allows itself to become a river, snaking its way slowly through Heaven. Everything floats in the river and light is emitted by every object, there is no sun in Heaven. Pyramid or in a snowstorm, the belly of the beast.

One is desirable, one is not desirable. Heaven is missing its toothbrush, its armored-car, its anvil. Guerrilla spring sprang sprung singed spigot. The plastic environment is shrewd and disparaging asparagus. The paralyzer, addicted like so many before it to the effulgent circumference of pilots, barrels regularly into swarming swarthy tiles. The missing mixers maximum miser. Miserable crisps, fraternizing elegantly. If you'd please direct your attention to the grunting knuckles, you might notify the arsenal; quickly now, before they wrench the dependent policy, before they drench the repellent horst. Glinting flanges along the Ganges. The visitation of the burnt apple upholding sympathetic delinquents. Perseverance like so many windowless peaks.

How are things going?

Do you think you'll continue to read this book?

Do you care about what other people think?

Do you enjoy your own appearance? What is the difference between you and your appearance?

A storm-cloud gathered at the tip of a bird's wing, a nightingale's wing, where the glass of fresh water is overturned by the waves that adorn the woman in her dress, the storm whose eye is the sun and whose feet are the feet of a crow or a pallet swimming in the song of the golden palace known as a hospital or fever-head, sliding out from underneath the wormhole the clock with all its gears curled around the lips of a tulip, a rose by the tip of the wing, all along the closed window the vehement whale danced by the hospital; slowly, a skeleton as if it were a garden emerged from the pearl, hung closely by the cork of woman, naked and full of grace, a pendulum swings at the heels of the clock intoxicated with all of its feelers, the curtains are drawn closed because they resemble swinging heels, the skeleton wears a pearl at its neck as if it were a garden, danced all night, the forest was in full bloom, the forest emerged from the flower and revealed itself to be the night, marble columns and the cost of meat at the deli relay races, the flowerpot hands the torch of night over to the forest who spills it at the heels of the clock wound around the waist of the woman whose pearl is acting as if it were either a skeleton or a garden, vampire-bat wing closed at the morning sun glow, a womb brushes the storm-cloud into its eyes and wishes the curtains away.

Toothless comes the thundercloud bursting at the seams, cut open a torrent of water is expelled and the woman will have to find a new rat, or at least a handful of tree bark, carved from the finest yellow suggestions made by those men and women who frequent grocery-stores in order to accumulate mass quantities of tombstones, whenever the listing books spill open they can house Attila the Hun or Avicenna with their coffins, whenever the books lose their words, wrap a red scarf around a purple tree or else the flowered ground will overturn and the corpse of Aristotle will hover over the moon as if he were an eye, but when Gandhi is preparing the worms and soil, brandish your spades and jacks and hearts and the seven of clubs and pour the entire grave into a glass of water, a hurricane will swirl the liquid and light will emerge from the dirt, close your eyes, you shall be free again. When the whale tires, it returns to Africa so it may rest in the shade, its tail flails over Sudan and one flipper stirs the soil of Ethiopia and an eye looks over Madagascar, but if there is a great horse looming over Ghana, shield the clovers and unravel each mummy, the thunder sounds deep overhead and under head the beetles crawl like silk, any open mouth can be a hoof or thoughts slinking across the tiles of the kitchen, rattle the pans and a fog winds its teeth around the trees, fish-scales scour the seas, 'assume the heavenly flowers as your gown, madam,' read the thoughts of the young man as he addresses the street outside one of those little plots, a glorious temple made from triangles and circles, from the Heavens and Earth, columns and the ruins of a town; before the march, before the sun swings, a great leap into the northern doghouse with seventeen the ghost years, sixteen ghosts a year, a hot year and cold dog hero the moon hero thirteen and a sinking lampshade which casts a hand into the ear, strong steel a frozen iron barstool and a fist with clenched tinctures outstretched wings flurry jumping snow full blown through unknown winter; throw a hand into the snow and the blood moves outward like a loud echo into a dark cave, the steep hill pulls up its boots and makes its way towards the East, leaving in its wake a rusty railroad track and the only train that comes along is a lion whose mane is a tumultuous rainfall of broken tulips and steel pipes, screaming dark silver into the moonshine sun.

In the cat's bag, four seashells have wings, collared-greens and a limousine full of the voice that calls through the corridors of the Arctic, the tundra removes its dress at the sight of the sun, but whenever the wind and moon shake their fists, the eyes bulge through the ice and a copper-wire fence tangles the rodents at the call of the wild, the blue yonder window bright like a copper penny, a grain-eyed moon full of ideas and the cornea is a shimmering baseball-bat, the pupil is an achilles-tendon with a broken wrist the arm can fold a tablecloth before dinner, someday the forest will call the lion home and great lemon-peels form disembodied hands in the sky, a cloud of birds for the morning's song, a rocket-ship that bursts through the trees, a torn belt-buckle and the lion's eyes are in the beehive, the queen is in the kitchen cupboard, the king is next to the bedside table, the prince and princess are both underneath the peradam with a shovel and a hot iron. A silver seagull without its eyes is a diamond, and a diamond without a skeleton is a bridesmaid attending the four simultaneous funerals of four brothers, each a rabbit with a tree in its whiskers in his own way, a balloon rolling down the lead pipe of the night, scorpion arching its eyes like the spine of a book, the woman is kneeling and a well emerges from one of the knots in her spine, a celebration, a burly burglar's sack covered in hair and filled with wreaths made from teeth, frog hair forest hair, ghostly sunken ship runs up the creek lifting its skirt, a dress worn as a crown, worn as a crow, the kingdom of the stars thrown across the back of a chair and a lamp tips over, spilling hornets into the daylight, turning the stone into a bundle of roses, mimicking the shape of a bush or hedge or lamppost or hyena, only when a cat yawns and closes one eye does the rain fall from the coattails of the Heavens, clouds each grin to pass the tide, lowside of the belly where Buddha sits like an overturned stone, a tower yawns and bends over, rousing the tide of passions to come bursting out of the tiger's mouth, the abandonment of desire leads to the soul's unfettering, the fish reads a book and loses the goose in a snowstorm, loosens the noose in a glowworm, a golden puppet is the bluebird's swelling bosom fresh water.

A calamity of apes grasped by the wooden hand twice out of the mud, carved block at the wayside of the toothless hold-'em-high, at the length of rope, the space-ape swept the members of the orchestra into the windmill and closed the eyes at the foot of the site bent over the bed stage overlooking the growth of hair from the tulip's eye, a book with no cover and a foot for each length of bread that wrens at the nightingale bluebird sing, highland the low and far across the eyeball, the pupil stretches like a monastery at the heels of the tooth and fork, crouched along the corner of the bed apes collected and sewn together to complete the fabric which is known as 'Egyptian hand-races', blowing flower bulbs and loose leaves from the trees in time for the young man to sneeze and cover his mouth with the curling fingers around the bedpost, at long last the stowaway crumbles his paper neck and tie, loosens the heels of his shoes, bids the hermit farewell, grasps a crab in the palm of his hand, eagle eye, and locomotive long gone past the chimney stowaway and port to starboard all along the eye's watch toothless and bygone at the lowdown and swindling the feet right from the crow, a wink or a foghorn at the shark roosting on the edge of the cliff over looking the ocean, a green eye with fog eyelids and sailboat eyelashes, city of marigolds and golden lions and dandelions further than the elbow of the sailboat caught in the trench-coat of the evening. Underneath the skin and bones of the human is a seashell or garden pearl, coattails of the old crow, sweep like waves, water falls over the sand, a desert in the garden of the sky, the eye of the moon coils a snake of rope around the lips of the sun, black rope of smoke and snake eggs curling, coattails of the winter wind, breathless along the five o'clock, shoestring, covers the eye of the woman and Arabian night falls all over her, trembling day retreats into the curves of her spine, the young man turns leaves over and leaves the eyelashes under a seashell, spiral staircase to the cosmos; a lightning-bug casts lightning to the seashore of the trees and their leaves and snakes, the leaves the rope-bridge, drawbridge to the sandcastles of the ant colonies, centipedes over the hand-rail, frail bones of the green skeleton ant colony, frail at the fingertips and lips the ant bones hoist the smokestack at the heels, too many bones, bend at the rocking-chair horse called 'seashell' by the ants and leaves; the coral reef dress of the skeleton drags along the ground, catching in the grins and hollers of the ants still lost in the seashell at the foot of the seabed, a banquet hall of skeletons and tulip-bulb horses where the woman addresses the clouds about to rain and leaves with bulging paper wire veins and hand-me-down locomotives, the clouds and the whale's eye shrinks like a hermit-crab into a seashell spiraling toward the beautiful azure grass field, the corridor gets longer the further down the ball is left in the sand, driftwood, the stomach of seashore dogs is a jungle.

A handkerchief of the night cuts like a knife the diamond white: the sun cloud beat down as wings upon the raindrops heavy and fluttering ghostly above the houses and courtyards of the men with feathers for hats and shoelaces around their feet, the ocean wall rises up to the sundown and by the corner window a salamander of light shrieks by holding in its cupped hands a poison dart or toothbrush or lampshade, golden coat around the damp shoulders of wet light drip the tails into the sea of dirt swirling around the nightingales feet flickering like candles in the blink of an eye, stolen eyelashes and a bruised orange around the stomach in an ivory knapsack bound with the gold teeth and whale bones of yesterday's stones and leaves and hair winter takes down the mustache of the frigid air and breaths a sigh of relief as the ghost of a gold summer reenters the room slowly as a foxhole and with too many feet stuck by the teeth-marks in the wet fingers by the doorknob embraced and collapsed the city of green flowering waves and sandcastle walls and fallen horses' knees thrown around the side of the barn door swinging open and handling the air like a mother handles the wet teeth of the cookie-jar spilt over the tabletop loose and cloth rings smoke around the long nose twofold; sweet rain bells ringing dewdrops and cartwheels by the windmill cause the waves of violet air to melt tulips at the fringes, sautéed in the breast-milk and sweet meat of the passing doctor and his ghost who wears a top-hat like a frown, winter clothes and the old foes always know how the winter goes around the snow-filled ditch at the sea-bend in the crack of dawn, dust and brooms by the handles were swept into the eyes of the passing ocean, covered in eyelashes and fallen trees the woman wades into the eyes of the moon with the sun in its mouth, the cotton clothes that bear the mark of the sweet ghost trembling as the garden pearls melt the tulips and the lilacs and lilies rose like golden fawns in the winter's breath cowering at the shoulder-blades and drawn from the hilt of the sword blood meets the blue sky as if it were a blue bird covered in a green fabric too thick to be called a womb.

As the elegant lightbulb births light in the shape of a table that in the sun transforms into a badger and in the moon is a small tree which the woman sits against, storm-clouding the vehicles of her mind across the tapestry of past days and the beauty of the afternoon, gliding on stair-legs the golden horn of violet plumes arisen from the ghost of ashes passed on the way down the road toward violet umbrella loose towards the light, producing animals for the shadows to make love within, a hand tangled up in the bramble curses the flight of bookcases and books from their shelves following summer sunset of the courageous fingerling twilight book night, under the arm harden by the winter's eye and the thought of old maidens wandering above the ocean, a fish jumps through their dresses collecting the dust and leaves and snowballs from the surface of the water, billowing blow horn horse jump across the apocalyptic hoof dangling from the clouds, a shower which leads invariably to the enclosed area where night and day refuse to tread even for a moment, the ground there is too quick on the draw and the roof of the mouth is a garden with little bushes and trees, flowers for every throat to catch in its snores, whistling as the thistle coils a ball of yarn in its mouth while under the cat sprays the closeted mammoths for any soothsayers along the furlong.

Where the end of the water petal meets the moon saying words illuminating and joyous, graceful goes the woman to a bridge of ice and eyelashes and cloth napkins over a rambunctious eggplant reminiscent of the Tigris or Euphrates, but without the tail-wagging that comes with the Nile, the Amazon is an old grin that leaps from the face of the whale to the woman to the young man and so on and so forth trudges the weary rice climber across troubled bridges over brass and ivory fountains containing by their lips the secret essences known of only by the woman, but alas they are known by all, under the dirt in the Way of Nature, looking by the glass fountain the woman sits and ponders these things, which makes her soft, hoof-print under her eyelid, and the grace and beauty of the Cosmos is seen when observing several rocks tumbling down a hill, Truth is a tiger's tongue, throbs like autumn and spring leaves through the veins of every heart. The soldier with long teeth is by the deep pool out along the balcony of the cyclops where the fisherman with stone feet uses the hair's razor to comb the breath out of the fog, twofold diamond wing to light up the swing-set under the rug, along the woman's tooth, swallowed by the deep pool, seen through a different eye is a garden where the hedges grow twenty feet tall to caress the glum gum or the one eye with feelers and toes that touch and burn every bird singing old songs because they are lovely, organ raises the moon from the gravestone hedges to eclipse the sun, releasing the hornets and creepy-crawlers to gaze at the blanket set on fire, horse-prints fill the meadow at the sight of the year-long loose-fitted gown worm cowering by the foot of stone, the tin passage of purple penguins.

Grass and trees grow along the brainstem causing thoughts of the circular nature of things to harbor wishing-wells under their arms, full of thunder and bird beaks, haystack thrown away at the storming sky grinning with bicycles in the teeth, in the brain, roughneck squalor polar eyes feeling foot-long, neighbor lays eggs the size of trees with the ghost's spine of winter under the knife whose blade is switched with the cat's meow, handclap the bug life winter crow, leaning against the mane of a lion up against the corner of a tree or a nail or a cloud hovering above the breast of the woman, the man is riding the cloud as if it were an automobile and the whale is acting as a robotic dog, slow to the touch but along the wayside is a cobra at its haunches hunching over the caught napkin escaped from the dinner table erect like a butterfly around the five legs of the table loose wind dancing and serenading holy spokes of the train run loose, over the garden and field at the dog's lark, run up against the house under water where the hermit smiles at something known only to him. A snail raises a green flag at the train whistle in order to vanquish the alarming procession of candlesticks, catching the dogs and mountains on fire, only the fire is a ruby or emerald that grows legs like a laser-beam and swallows it whole, only the hairiest fires can grow eyes and cover them with lids like pyramids, drenched in snow at the beckoning call.

"Honey," she called out softly from the bedroom. The word evaporated against the dark apartment like a lasso of smoke.

He was sitting on the couch in the middle of the living room as it hummed silently with cobweb shadows. The television was off and reflected his outline hesitantly. He rose and the darkness did not scatter.

Standing beside the bed, "What is it?"

"Could you run to the store and get me a few things?"

Her swollen belly writhed inertly with hidden cultivation. Appearance was held at bay, under the surface of the skinny light, under her skin the child growing. They could not make out each other's faces.

"Sure, anything you'd like."

Her hand arced toward him, contorted as if holding an apple. Her hand arced toward him, shaped like a pear.

"I'll have a rhinoceros, thirteen bluejay eggs, a pink garden hose, a broken aquarium, an orange, two or three buttons, some sparks, a drunken daffodil, some hot soap, tree ark, a handful of feathers stained with kaleidoscope semen, several wooden cuffs, and some danger danger danger. Oh, also: a brick, a canary, a brick canary and two waffles, please."

Thank you, deer.

What are the things you cannot touch?

What are the things you are not allowed to see?

The man clamored and wailed before the god, who climbed the tree and reclined in its branches. Abua and Chandelier approached the man, who implored them to help him, for he is a weak and lowly man and surely could not kill a tiger singlehanded. Abua and Chandelier agreed and the three men continued on to the village. Tigers were known to frequent the edge of the western forest, so they gathered spears and started out, making haste. Across the plains like tumbleweeds, silent before the midday sunlight, wind moving about them with the ebb and flow of a distant voice, careful for snakes and vermin under bare feet. No sight of any tiger as they approach the first trees. The man introduced himself as K'oahno, meaning The Horse's Long Eyelashes. They stood in a row like pillars for several hours. Night crept up from behind them and nestled on their shoulders; they shook their heads simultaneously, producing falling snow. You came up to them, carrying the candlestick. Abua extends his hand to you and lets fall the candle made of ice, it sticks in the ground like laughter. K'oahno begins to vomit and the antelopes come to devour it, they are always at the ready. A bird makes the sound of a freight-train. The candlestick begins to vomit, it is very beautiful. You overturn the glass of water, the pitcher of night, the vial of canaries. Bay of twigs, the vulgarity of the oatmeal is annunciated poorly, the clear running linguistics purple exposition. If only humankind could walk with invisible feet from Venus to Neptune to Saturn to Earth and from there until the finale, when the cougars of silence descend against the stage-curtain, tearing into it a single hole, circular, and thus life is refurbished, tugging on the night with all its force that Mercury becomes Jupiter and when the Earth's moon enters Saturn's ring fail not to locate all the lost minds and the whisking corpse of Jesus, their eyes are surely two golden orbs or cubes that dislocate the light cast onto them and reflect the amber tresses of a maiden voyage across the turning waves that greet the cosmic traveler when two oceans collide and form a mountain fit for the footfalls of Venus, snow falling from the beards of Chinamen and the curtain is a sausage eaten by the lost mouth of Babylonia, bygone sight and beams of sand that interrupt the scanning eyes of the driftwood and here is the dog corpse, all things are in the likeness of a sphere, when the sailboat plunges skyward, recoil the rope or else the poison will swing from the left to the right or wrong, deaf cobra with one fang to hang all things, set against the crown of the great woman squinting.

When the woman blushes, nightingales fall from the sky, leading the young man and the whale to a diminished castle nestled away on a hill where the river is grinning with bones in its teeth and purple ruby roses in the gums, where they crouch hidden by a dancing raspberry-bush, unattended to, and observe the goings-on of the family who lives in this castle of sand and jewels and stone and ancient bell tolls across the Universe, the mother who feeds the roosters and the boy who wanders down the lonesome road, giving it company, and the father who is exploring underneath the bridge to find that crystal in the lips of a troll or goblin which makes itself visible only to those with many chores to accomplish, so while the father is off trekking through the murky waters and feathering the ears of young djinns with a clump of soil, the mother comes upon the troll who speaks in fragmented slabs of marble that rejoin the structure of the castle, increasing its marvel, only to be taken down when the father returns, upset and swollen with icicles fallen from the tree, like a bat's wing or the head of an ant, and the line drawn by the pen of the ant leads to the jewel tucked away under the corner of her eye. With such a crown, with such a snow-flurry; the jewel of the night blossomed into a dancer hidden amongst the shoes of the trees and bushes, where the stones overturned themselves only to be rejected by the women that they find favor in, their loa is but a diamond nose, chilled to the bone of the morning, each sunset mourning for these women, abandoned to the ocean's devices, where trembling the iron manta-ray is consumed by the pestilence of this world, only further developing the vampire-bats to sound off their whistles and cat-calls and stone jeers that turn only the horniest winter golden, with a brush upward of that incredible nose indelible, nostrils envelope the horizon and the linear passage of dog-walkers into the gaping orifice of a train tunnel, where the man with closed eyes is by himself and comes upon himself alone and quivering like the arrows of a valiant knight under the blanket of the dreaming sea.

The Birth of the Will

When the dinosaur awoke, it was still there. It always has been and always will be. The dinosaur rose and stood before it in a vast clearing enclosed by a great forest. The world was a primordial labyrinth of giant twisting trees coiled against the sky like smoke, savage creatures unclouded by thought, flowers and plants of deepest color and exquisite pattern; the world is the manifestation of existence, and it is beautiful. Life is being, it is the ten thousand forms and it is the essence both.

The dinosaur gazed unmoving upon it, which began in the ground as a stalk no thicker than an inch around and grew into a wide hollow opening three feet across, seven feet high. Along the edge of the rim were carved ancient, cosmic hieroglyphs indiscernible by any eye or mind. The object was of smooth earthy stone and filled to the brim with water so clear and pure its reflection was perfect. Within the circular surface were the clouds and the winged creatures overhead and the sky, the trees and the dinosaur as it watched itself in complete fascination, the large humming insects.

It has grown in the clearing since the dawn of time, and as of yet nothing has issued out from the stillness of the water. The dinosaur visited it and contemplated its own reflection for many years.

On a day similar to all others, the dinosaur watched and listened as the earth trembled and groaned. The sky was stained various shades of purple and green, brilliant and shining and violent, and from the waters of the object crawled the naked shapes of four dark-skinned human beings, three men and one woman. They fell to the soil and dust rose into the sky, which was fading back to its natural hue. Water beaded on their muscles and they lay in the dirt writhing and howling. Becoming silent they stood slowly and began to move in a circle around the dinosaur. Their pace increased and the woman started to chant, primitive half-formed noises of an unused tongue. Soon the men opened their mouths and allowed the sound out, and they were leaping and running in an echo of the blood coursing through their veins. The dinosaur fell back and tumbled to the earth screaming. The naked dark-skinned humans were dancing and chanting and hollering. They cast their blind eyes to the heavens and knew the sun to be the face of God.

thus coming, thus going

take care

as you walk these valleys

and streams:

there are so many beautiful things

to trip on!

the view is blocked, the view is not blocked

slow and steady bloats the pinwheel graciously

the water is stilled, the dust is settled

with no effort

it is likened to a sphere

balanced carefully on the tip

of a pyramid

in the depths of boundless

nothing

Alas! to die, tumbling down

the crags and cliffs and

jutting rocks

of a mountain as high

as the heavens

the few birds

in the dead pines

will not weep for me

the tears no one will cry

glitter like jewels

in the dazzling sunshine

under the cloudy sky

full of stars and bright moon

ghosts slink amidst the trees

like the notes of a zither

slowly

ah, night

which the day so cleverly

hides away!

if there is a call,

respond;

if there is no call,

no response

through the pines atop the mountain:

the sun about to rise

(cold morning)

it takes continuous practice

practice that is toward no end

practice

practice

practice

repetition

repetition

repetition

pool

pool

pool

reverberate

reverberate

reverberate

solvent

invertebrate

moderation

immoderation

though he stumbles over it in his search

it is not found

the old songs have new meaning

grasping, not grasping: useless!

it cannot be forced
it is free of intention

there is no proof
there is no evidence
prized possession
relieving itself
of the choleric
valor

first bell: clouds breaking up
second bell: clouds drifting away
third bell: clouds disappeared
fourth bell: sky drifts apart
fifth bell:

O, the stillness

of the trees and the motion

of the river:

their activity is not the same,

or is it?

the motion of the trees

is not like that of mind,

the stillness of the river

is not like that of mind,

or is it?

existence or nonexistence or in-between:

there is not a trace

it is not one, not two, not zero

letting go of self and other

the mountain embraces sky

Chuang-Tzu says: 'assimilate to the Great Pervasion'

no source, no root, no branches, no extension

no source of sound: what is hearing and what heard?

no source of appearances: what is seeing and what seen?

no form, no substance, no emptiness, no fullness

no place to put a finger, no finger to place

dark dark the night

the night who

does not move

the night who

is not still

dark dark the night

who does not come

who does not go

it is like the blade of a dagger

hidden in the drawer

now open now closed

breathing in breathing out

the eyes open

the eyes close

and the dark dark night

the bright bright day

if there is no ground below no sky above

what is it?

if there is ground below and sky above

what is it?

nothing exists independently of its occurrence

nothing exists independently of anything else

how could it?

considering everything

no one part is more prominent than any other

sitting, standing, walking, reclining:

breathing in, breathing out

it is not in preparation for anything, not working toward some goal

ceaseless activity:

it is covered in snow, it is not covered in snow

the sunlight on the floor

does not lie

heavily

remains undisturbed

by the gentle wind

this morning

the birds sing with the

voice of the sun

shining through the green green

leaves

covered in snow

the river in

the background

knows not of the

whiteness of the landscape

nor this human body

trying to quiet mind

in reflection of

the world

melting dripping snow

a bright song

world no world

this world, that world

word no word

this word, that word

things need tending to, things do not need tending to

there is nothing contrary

nothing unusual

suffering is only suffering

talking and thinking are only talking and thinking

there is something

that is not talking not thinking

not suffering

the world and the mind

perfectly integrated

"This is not mine, this is not myself."

Drinking margaritas with Li Po on the roof of a hotel in Brussels

chopping leafy greens with the sunrise while Ptolemy takes a tour of the Vatican naked

the crow is naked, the sheik is naked,

the dogs and potatoes are naked,

Thomas Aquinas is naked, the president

is naked swinging on the naked vines

a thousand sunsets

a thousand rocks

a thousand fists

a thousand Lenins

twenty thousand scorpions inside

naked pomegranates

Ptolemy takes a tour of the pyramids

Ptolemy takes a tour of the sunsets

Ptolemy takes a tour of Memphis, Tennessee

the naked Indian Ocean with genitals like shoelaces

left untied by the old tire-swing

a thousand moonbeams ago

ingrained speciality

why does it seem so easy to be mindless

and so difficult to be mindful?

mindless mind mindful mind handful of minutes

where should our energy be directed?

why is it so easy

to fall into the habit

of not being

present?

      Sometimes the coroners are alight with jingle bells; the
marionettes have been in the stable all day, unable to receive the bright

milk offered them so carefully by a silver dove, an amber dove, a colloquial dove. The optometrists met twice daily in the umbilical cord at the southern edge of town; there are two optometrists, and often they are accompanied by a third man, whose profession is unknown to me. I am beginning to suspect that he is the shoemaker. I myself am in the habit of spending my time near the fountain at the center of town. When is it necessary to change shoes? Is it enough to repair and mend them again and again, so much that eventually a wholly new pair of shoes emerges? It is its own evolution, adapting to the grey current of time, blind and restless like an umbilical cord. I considered perhaps two or three lions, but that seems to be a bit too much. A bouquet of lions perhaps, two hundred or more, but that lies outside my ability and resources. An older woman with her two children ambles by me, huddled close together so that they seem to be a single entity. Their image won't do either, charming as it is. They are close brothers, wind and water, their children are the birds and fish. A bird with a fish in its grasp could work, but is perhaps too morbid, as is a fish with a bird in its mouth. A flock of birds together with a school of fish, as indistinguishable as the children and their mother. I abandon my curiosity like strawberries. Plump buffoon of obstacles, stumbling application apparent. The mineral holds on to its gloves with the force of a transparent horse transplant. Fissure is chicken, a startling diameter in bad taste, barometer of sign. The scream-emulators are marvelously sufficient, salmon nonsense. Horses and cacti are our dual responsibility. There is liability, there is no liability. There is well-meaning.

We see it

the day withdrawing into night

night giving rise to day

the body lies down to sleep

only to awaken and stand once again

on two feet

trailing footprints in the sand

casually effaced by the wind and

tide

what of this death which lies just

behind everything

coming to the fore and receding

like a breath

the skin falls away

leaving the grinning skull

and fallen bones

is death just a sunset

or a gentle dreamless sleep?

it is what we cannot know

it is ourself

it is of no concern

the debts will be paid

either way

death the omniscient God

death the forgiving God

death the vengeful spiteful God

death the indifferent God

looking at the choices

and choosing neither

the extension of clouds across the

sky like a

spinal cord

planted into that vast brain

which holds the sun revolving

humans twitching nerve-endings

feels along with its vast hand

feels along the atoms and molecules

alas, it is a horse

it is a house

it is an ocean

the atoms perform regardless

no applause necessary

no audience

the atoms in a coffin

casual acquaintance

overlooked

hegemony

disparate antlers seek reproach

removal of external esophaguses

the blatant espionage of a bouquet

of antennae

the atoms in a pair of sea-legs

overlooked

the crowd slowly diminishes

like the flame of a candle

until night finds no companion

besides the sea and land

the atoms in a crowd of people

the Pure Land is right here

in death's melody

in life's chorus

death's handprint life's extension

the atoms are dirty only with themselves

death is time

death is a womb

death is lost at sea

death is a leaflet

death is an earhole

death is an earlobe

death is turning around but finding

no one there

death is with child

death is horizontal

death is an unmarked crate made of wood and

leather

death tourniquet

death squalor

death peach

death forward

death depth

death is never absent

life is never absent

life and death

are absentee parents

it is lost in the crowd

it is never going home

the tallest mountain does not reach the sky

can I even look sideways

and know the

phosphorescent call

of some unknown duty

to be laudable

to seek unknown climes

to carry on

the vast weight of the

inexplicable

the impossible climate

the look of discomfort

vanishing swiftly before

undying eyes

swelling

rainfall

darkness that slowly passes away

a dawn brought on by

no sun

daughter

laughter play

crucible

Sanscrit

bellowing trunk of

foremost

consciousnesses

these are just

playthings

the loud banging of the closed window

the sound of God coughing

coughing up smoke

like a pedestrian daffodil

the laziness of a daisy

turned over

in the bathhouse

unaccustomed to such misgivings

the succulent low-hanging fruit

bathed in the song of all

the species of insects

calling out to shadow

along the river bank

a man walks slowly past

the flight of a seagull overhead

whose shadow trails behind it

like a child trying to catch up with its mother

as she moves through the street

heavy with thought and age

Dreams of the Interior

in an instant I am slowly awake

gradually the light of day

and of consciousness

filters through the blinds of

an open window

and for a moment I have no regret

no sadness, despair

longing or otherwise

my ego alights on me soft as

an insect

unnoticed until discovered

I don't worry

don't play

just awaken

slowly

the insect does not burrow

or bite but

becomes larger and larger

slowly

until it is the weight

of myself

and in that instance of awakening

I wish that I were not awake

not assailed by the confusion of

thought and feeling

heavy as a piano with broken strings

not pushed ever onward

by the force of my

decisions

but there are

obligations to fulfill

and with heavy heart I rouse myself

from bed to greet the day

curl up to sleep

in the harsh soft sand

the waves

monotonous

ever different

push upon the

shore

with a sound like

the caress of

slowly blinking eyelids

over eyes

looking out

on the beach

with its endless horizons

with its beautiful primordial

tedium

always the same and

always different

I wish you were there

then you would know

all the things I've lost

wilting tree made of sand

stifling a laugh, a cough, tears,

anger, a fart, memories

the things I've lost

in memory I'll run to them

and wake upon the threshold

of knowing what they were

who they were

what I once was

before the skin of time

drew taut over my soul

and with vanquished foes I

ushered in a time

of unsteady peace

seething with tumult

seething like bones beneath

hide

breakneck breathtaking

ostracized lobotomy

twofold

ask me again some other time

my throat is too choked with

unreleased sobs

and bitter tedium

Descartes found himself alone

and I pity him

almost as much as I pity myself

who writes these words

that perhaps no one will read

I who am so quick to take responsibility

for my actions

as if my willingness to be held accountable

would somehow alleviate me of them

I bow down and

pray to distant heaven

if you're up for it

one can imagine a thousand Christs

stained on crucifixes

scattered in the slowly rising

dawn of a new day

a million Buddhas waking up

beneath

billboards and stop signs

anguished cries

dirty laundry

foiled hope

languished dreams

subsidies

afoot

the cleaning-women of time

going through all the drawers

looking underneath

the rug

that sweet interior of fruit

with its subtle organic colors of life

the interiors of those vast machines

of metal so unknowable

full of the unrevealed workings

the somber interiors of buildings

which are so decorated as to not

resemble the exterior

the wet and dark interiors of bodies

bulging with contents and writhing

shaking trembling

so unwilling to show to the light of

sun the swelling blood like the rivers and

oceans

the organs like sculptures

the bones like white gasps, whispers, thin trees

transparent vegetables empty fruit

     Moonbeams filled the glass tipped over onto the lilacs and centipedes, cemetery in the bosom of the night across the mountainside gathering together as if it were a garden. Tombstone blue tombstone tombstone the thunderhead at the foot of the bed, at her heels raindrops squeak like wings across the sunbeams bearing morning sand, sand covering the pearl until in its place is a piano or handkerchief which she uses to pat her brow, her shoulder-blades,

blades of grass, a rhinoceros, tombstone tombstone. Seashell across the garden of sand, the oceans are the tulips and dandelions that burst from the seashell at the corner of the mouth and the squiggly lines run out of steam. The other people are thinking, too.

Do you have many habits? What is your favorite habit?

Have you ever met someone with no habits?

sometimes it is like being in

an all-pervasive ocean

floating and bobbing in the water

but the ocean is only

yourself

the invisible skin

the sweet loving caresses

absent caress careening

sometimes the self

is a screen

a veil

so delicate

as to appear to be

absent

the two soldiers

bent at the knees

look out past the horizon

and wait

for their shadows

to fade

build

the illuminated world

adorned with images

sick with images

gritted teeth of deceit

a lapse

the roll of the waves

plummet

plumage

the strength of the valuable object

the object generous with its appearance

the tiny invisible objects

the stench of spaces

water is the most like time

gentle turbulent undulations

across expanse of void

invisible tempest

howling

the strength of tears

the loving object the love of objects

the invisible spaces

the green green hooves

covered with snow

tears like snowflakes

vacant daffodils

trees like flames

licking at nothingness

trees like flames

licking at nothing

there is no isolation

though things seem to be

only of themselves

there is no preservation

why do humans wish to hold fast to their failing flesh

and vigor of youth?

their thoughts and passions and

motion carved into space and vanished like smoke?

they cling to imagined separation and call it soul

clutch at bone skin blood desire as if it were not bone skin blood desire

there is no self in isolation

brain is bound by skull

but if allowed

the mind is unbound

seeds sown by reigned mind yield no harvest

only unrest and calamity

only forced and mutilated thought

torment

why wish for ceaseless birth and death in perpetual distinction?

pursued happiness is never caught

only glimpsed from behind

run from suffering

and you will know it as your shadow

never leaving your heels

see the world forever new

as when you were a child

the rain

the moon

the trees

the clouds

who has seen these and desires more?

who has seen these

and still believes there is

life and death?

before and after?

this and that?

here and there?

you and I?

as the wind moves the clouds skeleton bride with dress

slinking down her bones like

raindrops

some voice is

hollering nonsense

but I can't keep the sun

from getting in my eyes

sending off sparks that reach the sun

though you can hardly tell

and I took it with a grain of sand

when you broke all the china

please remember there is a seat at my table

when you lose all the feathers of your wings

and all the waiters make origami shapes with the napkins

a delight

an outstretched fist

seething

if we see the individual nature of things to be their essence

the world is an unbound bouquet of essences

infinite, without birth, ever changing

if we see past individual things to the nature of all things

there is but one essence

neither coming nor going

as if it was never there

the world is likened to a man

always wearing different masks

never revealing his face

the world is likened to a dream

appearances always shifting

without core

concealing nothing

it is like a colorful ball

that if burst

displays only vanished air

when we consider the world as a front put up by nothing

we may know ourselves truly

for nothing is beneath appearance and we see

form as essence as emptiness as form

nowadays pretty girls always wear little shoes

and make quiet steps

soft as descending sunlight

as a descending flower falling in silent arabesque

soft as a descending ear

lovely girls with small shoes

your being is wasted here

be gone

come hither

decisions that bear no fruit

the hieroglyphs hidden in your motion are wasted here

savage men

turn your eyes away

and listen

what do you hear?

what do you hear?

the search for nothing

is unending

because there's always something

a paralyzed fly

carried into

the bowels of an anthill

clouds

clouds like a dragon

shifting

leaving its entrails in the

blue vacant sky

the shade of a tree

and every movement

so much is unnoticed

but felt by the wind

there is nothing

without consequence

there is nothing

there is everything

so much

so much

so little

from the looks of it

a left-over puddle

by the side of the road

is depthless

depthless

like all things

the search for nothing

leads you

to all things

so little

there is no heart

the heart of all things

heart heart everyone

heart

        everyone

racing from desire to desire thought to thought

action to action

no tree of sleep can relieve the

tiredness this brings

gnarled roots in frozen eruption

pouring into and out of earth

falling leaves

gnarled roots that are eyes swelled with tears

swelling with leaves

tears born of no sadness and no happiness

smile

reptiles and amphibians

fathers and sons

vision obscured by flowers

released petals like tears

some think that a man is more than his

reflection

have they not seen

a garden corrupted by weeds a broken windshield

an animal smile?

have these women hunted

for food

or gathered the storm-clouds?

one's reflection cannot be seen

in the decaying sunlight

in the startled insects

birthing flight

tumbling amongst stones like laughter

a child is neglected

whose passion

is checked

adulthood

adulthood bears no fruit

one's head aches

but is lost to foreign lands never visited

the difference between shadow and reflection

is a fly rubbing its back-legs together in soundless observation

against a bathroom lightbulb illuminating

some human who remains awake

despite the pregnant night

and in darkness

the reflection is lost

reflected is only

absence

there is no birth

there is no human body

there is no apprehensive mind

there is but

soundless plummet into gaping nothing

into gaping everything

the mind is an hour-glass always filling up

always becoming obscured

until turned over

and the sand

slowly falls away

leaving empty clarity and

full understanding

the wise man

does not allow it

to build up

even a little

without desire

the mind turns of its own

all things fall away

thoughts and senses fall away

location and forms

fall away

self

being

mind

all falls away

what then is there?

what remains?

after all this

golden eye gazing in looking out

finds nothing

the world

just one sitting

exulted is the mind empty of all experience

uncarved

a stream dappled by sunlight

each tumult pure

the wise man

knows the whole world

like the palm of his hand

because he is neither

coming nor going

and every eye

is an emerald tear

the mind full of all experience

room to move

the reality of illusion

      dinosaur migraine transit

thoughts are sticky material pull your hands away

pull your hands away

either way

there is no human

made up of words there is no human

being

it's always springtime

in your understanding

me too

only you

     Changes

The mind is where the two Heavens meet in sublimity,

with a quiet caress as soft as the embrace of existence.

But in the selfish mind there is no heaven,

the selfish and destructive mind is alone in itself, with no one to talk to but itself,

yet it only seems to listen.

Clinging from thought to thought

like a man falling down bottomless stairs, hitting each step,

unable to stop. This is sorrow unending.

The unselfish mind wanders aimlessly, absorbed in the ecstasy of everything, the body too wanders, full of light.

This mind is a smile as boundless as the cosmos!

her dress was like the city at night

a dream

women with baskets

balanced on their heads

snow

so easily

rainfall

and she wouldn't even

give me the time of

day

everything nowadays is impenetrable

even as I gaze into

the winter furnace brimming with turquoise latticework

the winter sun furnace

Open

the stillness in the flight of a bird heavy as snow

silent as rain through the fallen leaves

the eyes that behold it the act of seeing

trees living speechless

on the mountain for many years

a man from beginning to end

in the morning

when bird cries out echoes in the cold mist

rising from the lake

echoes in the empty mind

thoughts like trees grow

unknown

it is always raining in Paris and men are so easily lost

in the wet and melancholy streets

women lifting their skirts

the Seine drifts along every corridor slow and dirty

tall buildings unknown leaves like reptiles

blinking slowly

to the girl lifting her white hand to stifle

a cough

to the men alone

turning the corner and gone out of sight

Paris offers a love letter

stained by a muddy footprint

I remember Paris in this way

and it will never change

memories are all the same

especially if you look upon today as having already past

it is always raining in Paris and these lost men

have no destination

no conclusion can be drawn

from a man's life

depthless emotion and loftiest thought

spent energy

he is a vanished eternity

and the tears he weeps are naught but rain

sordid symphony

when it rains

the sound of footsteps

disappear like a smile

crying eyes

so often hidden

dissipate slowly like clouds through the boundless sky

a ceaseless chase

stone building crumbling in ruin

do the dead pile so high

as to usurp the heavens?

generation after generation

like a forgotten friendship

and still I'd like to hold your hand

that is enough

let us reorganize matter perfectly

empty boat

bumping around aimlessly

slowly

in the breeze

slow descent to

red marsh waters

indiscriminate

there is no remainder

a finger lingering

to touch the night

to touch the stone

that is not there

      The young man has recoiled into the small of her back; he has lost the flame that enveloped his eye and whose tendrils extended further back into his brain; only charred coals remain which at any moment might become frozen for eternity or burst into a pristine violet wildfire that gropes the world he perceives and moves about it so that the world may kiss him on the cheek or lips, the tongue of a lizard protrudes and withdraws at the sight of a match being lit and the head of sparrow emerges from his lips, eager to penetrate the golden sea, the diamond fields of flowing grass; he is sad, causing a bruise to spread around her shoulder blades, he has crawled unknowingly into the dark of his heart which may smother him, the woman shed a single and luminous purple tear; to the young man it looks like a piano or small elephant falling into an infinite void, he leaps halfway around her body to catch the elusive tear that has crystallized and has taken a somber green hue, the color of his eyes and his hands, clutching at her kneecaps, observing the descending star erupt into a bray of laughter and a swell of seashells against the city past the woman's body, city which he knows not to be called 'Charlotte.' A slaughter-house, erected by the left hand of a bird of prey and the left hand of a small collection of arrowheads, sunshine that curves through its windows like the touch of the virgin against his first and only prying lemur, proceeds into the late spring bearing on its shoulder a scarlet sack, swelling, the young man who bites his lip in an effort to reveal his wit and audacity, leaps into the air and lands upon the eyelid of the slaughterhouse, still moving quickly through the seasons, now resembling a grassy field ripe with eyelashes and kaleidoscopic flowers that shake one's hand with each breath of their erotic and grateful scent, a wolf that squirms and slowly evolves into a stream of water; the young man, momentarily leaving the woman, catches his foot on the streams and cascades into it the way a sailor might descend a great fish, carrying him on its back; the Great Fish of which only the woman knows and man has barely seen out of the corner of his eye, leaps from the sun into the ocean and from there swims into the depths of whichever mind casts its lines, its linens, now the young man at the creek bed, falling asleep.

As the woman crushes the sweet winter into a fine powder, a forest opens itself up to the young man, standing with a single line through his skull extending all the way to the center of the sun, the string shreds and expands to the rhythm of a heartbeat, the woman's, a fish's, a dining-room table's, when the young man steps with heavy boots that are shrouded in feathers and jasmine, who uses her two hands to grow the young man's beard, a startling sunbeam, into the forest he swims like a bird through the tall grass of a childhood backyard in the abandoned farmhouse and silo, birthing constantly small undecipherable creatures that convulse, fornicate and expire until the sun gives a howl to the moon who receives the shout and turns it into a fine powder, shortly after the woman stands up again and take a step back; the trees in the forest are as beautiful and loving as the Earth of which they are part, tirelessly he moves among the foliage to come upon a stunning violet and emerald green daffodil, that will teach him to see through the leaves, before they are swept away by the wind and soil broom the sky wields as a catamaran or sailboat. As slowly as the woman contemplates this phenomena, the young man approaches the western coast of a solid diamond lake, complete with the faeries playing sail-boat across the surface, a smooth field of grass and haze, until the water, boiling, returns to the source, is swept out to the shore, open and flowing as a bloody wound, a sight for no eyes, sore eyes to fly the haze of this early afternoon, before the releasing of the trench-coat belts, revealing, as the young man steps up: a hermit who is carrying his house upon his back, towering above the clouds and obscuring the sun, which stretches its tendrils until it is holding hands with the moon, confusing the hermit, who kneels; as this occurs the young man can make out that the house upon the hermit's shoulders is three stories tall, with eight windows and a small garden, the kitchen is untidy as well as the living-room, the dirty beggar is cloaked in armchairs and sitting-room desks, table-lamps and a multiplying array of mounted deer heads, each frozen death is more grotesque than the last, when finally the beggar glances at a majestic buck, winding antlers mimicking a set of dollhouse bedrooms, is displayed falling into the open mouth of an elephant, ready to mash the poor buck into a more suitable meal, perhaps for himself, perhaps for the beautiful woman, perhaps for those guests who are silently waiting in the hallway about to enter the living-room, which is thrashing to and fro, upsetting the kitchen and the downstairs bathroom; unbeknownst to the upstairs bedroom and office, the living-room, grumpy from too many feet beating upon its great head, will climb the great stairs.

At the flicker of the candle, the donkey's bray, as sweeping as the woman's eyelashes, the young man kneels and cocks his head to the side, his eye is cast, a horse's whinny, to the woman's shadow draped along the gigantic rocks to the northwest; her shadow is alas a jungle or seabed, if she is a lioness then her shadow is a spider's web, all Ten Thousand Forms are ensnared in the sinewy ropes, at the toss of her lustrous lungs, and a man equal to the woman in size emerges from the illustrious shadows emanating from her body; just as quickly as he emerged, he is extinguished by her breath as a flame or cloud of sheep's wool, a quake of her thunderous knees; the young man has one eye closed, has the moon rising quietly behind his brow, until the ocean is folded over the breast of the woman and the crown sun simultaneously; at the toss of her stomach, from the tumultuous snow-capped mountain tumbles a rainfall, which at closer inspection is a flock of tremendous crows, throwing shadows across the rocky terrain of the woman's neck and shoulders, shadows that mimic the shape of multiple young bears, perhaps ten or eleven years old, a tip of the hat from the sun's point of view, crosshairs of seven blades of grass on the front porch of the old house now filled with water, heavenly water, the hermit is now a boulder, some driftwood and a sea urchin, all Ten Thousand Forms are the spines projected by the hermit/sea-urchin; now, the coil of the resting snake, blessed by the moonlight of the woman's gaze, upon the young man's knee.

A slow wing, disembodied hand climbing the sunset, until tomorrow, guess who showed up under the lovely eye of the woman, when all over the night a forest was growing in every mouth and each tear that fell was a replica of the longest hairbrush ever made, to scale, at the arrival of which a long cat appeared, cloaked in a suit of arms, each limb writhing and crying out for a body to latch itself upon, slowly, a knight in shining clamor, coat of armor that caresses your lip and brow as a cloud, that a tiny cadaver, no larger than a teardrop of the sun, could fit into the gaping hole where no shoulder hangs, of the night's severed arm, a closet full of arms, that he might find if his eye, flat and draped over his shoulder, could tear the arm from a suit of arms, that a lightbulb would burst and the woman would not cry, galloping across the ewe of tomorrow, the knight can see his damsel, see her legs crossed around the moon, her breast high up in the branches of a tree, the roots tugging at the hem of her dress, so as to unravel her smile into a mouthful of lightbulbs, full of arms that seem to love her with the grace of the young man, casting a sad smile over the soil, could see her eyes throughout the sun, her teeth that may hang from a suit of fingers so lovely, so thoughtful, when the woman's tears brought an avalanche, burying the knight in a suit of lightbulbs or mirrors. Dripping heavily over the arm of the young man, while each coil of the yarn is the departure of a ripe bluebird, orange in this light or that, throw the wind some other way, while her hand is turned toward her mouth, to capture any tiger that may escape, and through her fingers the tiger's stripes extend, swimming around in the hair of the trees once more, while the cornerstone of the graveyard reaches and brushes the comb from the tooth of the gentleman in the path of the young man, sauntering through the wooded road of the woman's toes, hoping she does not put a boot on, a boot that will send the air into a fit of laughter, of uncontrolled animals and clothespins, overcoming the zoo and the cages in which they were bred; long blonde-white hair that curls at the whistle of a hot stone, smoke rising from the painted mouth, as if it were a clown that ventured too far into the belly of the ruckus and was from then on never permitted to throw stones over the fence, as when he was little, to the cold horse's yell, in anger and in love, large teeth that grit through a broken tambourine until closing time at the yard-sale where only various rocks and stones are presented for inspection by the arrival of a flood of raspberry birds, cloaked by the sound of their own voices, in a suit of arms and hands, joyously spilling onto the carpet.

During the night Abraham had a dream. He was wandering through a dark woods. Though the sun was not visible, the sky was not completely dark. He leans against a tree to rest. A noise from around the other side of the tree startles him. He walks toward the source of the sound. Gradually, through the hindered light, Abraham can make out his son Isaac. He is crucified against another tree a few feet away, his head hangs limp and dead, huge rusty nails protrude from his wrists and ankles. Abraham falls to his hands and knees and begins to weep before his son.

"Here you are, God! Here is your sacrifice! You have requested the only thing I could not give, and yet I have given it. Your will be done. Here is my son, my son Isaac for you!"

And God sayeth naught.

"Are you gone? I hath sinned for thee! My God, my God, why have you forsaken me? Are you gone?"

There was no response. Birds can be heard chirping, animals tittering, and Abraham runs off through the woods, weeping and shouting. Then he awoke, shivering in the dawn.

"You were having a terrible dream," says Isaac, who was sitting beside his father, looking at him with concern.

Uncoiled came the sun from the silvery trenches of the woman's finger blades, soiled nails loosen the wood that unites each building to the warehouse of the new tongue, that slaps and itches the ear and eye of the young man, so it would appear to the trained eyeglass crushed and dazed, ablaze cold moon yelling, that his dreams in the Chinese palace lapped as waves over to the shores of these words as a train hollering and tool blue to the zoo spool, yarn told yesterday on a closed eye, mouth of the marshes, snow mouth, blind eyes and no eyes no mouth, which would rend the spiraling sun in the shape of a piano's shadow in the hot earth's quick glance, thrown to the lowside, under the sun, underneath the distant run of the rainmaids who clutch hair-brushes to their lips, snow lips of the no-eyed king, too cold to taste the breath of their wrists, curving round his knees and elbows, swift canoe into the winter's deep eye, dark as the light twice-fold over itself, one night, this book that gave paper-cuts to each cat that meowed in the early evening during the unveiling of the woman, while the young man wrapped himself around her left heel and ankle; rainmaids, song of the graveyard fence betwixt their tongues, song growing out of their gaping snow-mouths as the branches and leaves of a small tree, until each sun is rotated in the fashion of the woman's choosing, 18th-century farmhands that destroy the hot breath of their cattle in the rain, come in out of the rain, come in out of the rain, come in out of the rain, come in out of the rain come in out of the rain, with a glass tongue and cold shoe to the side of the door, broken and off its hinges, come out into the rain; rainmaids weaving a tapestry of disembodies hands and feet, that the sun may look down and see a golden chariot, through the no-eyes of the moon, return, return, return!

On Saturn you hold these pages with skeleton fingers, the woman's breasts smell of sulfur and then of ivory, ivory that chills the rain to the noise of the ocean's yawn, lo and behold the presence of the whale constructed out of her eyelashes, circles alongside the young man, to his surprise, the whirlwind that the whale creates is fashioned in the likeness of an old city in ruins, beautiful on the Earth, three stars fallen to the holler of the whale cold nose, toe of the nose, to be understood upon the forest where disembodied torsos hang suspended in the air, a wispy devil's sandwich-bread, smoke curling with its teeth and eyes and toes; tail of the old whale spiraling infinitesimally, the young man clutches it in his right hand and traverses the smoky plains of the woman's scalp, a thunderhead, snowfall in the Amazon, goddess, who climbs the stairway of the mind as a boat raining along edges of a river that runs for years and years to the sweet sigh of Japan's golden climes, sunny window, day for a stool to unwind in the shape of a pinecone coming out to graze in the patch of hair covering the woman's vagina, a snow-mouth moving quietly overhead, seabird-like, to the songbird's handclap, crumbling skeleton's ribcage, coiled bird laughing, that looks down the slope of the hill as the road to its life and its own twisting spine is the road to its demise; vestibule of spring's wrinkled sooty wings, overlapping like two hands converging, diligence is but a bone-brown key on the skeleton's piano, a gold coin wing, plummeting to the Earth from a hidden trapdoor in the roof of the woman's mouth, wide in the throes of a rickety sigh, similar to the guardrail along a winding staircase, a set of self-contained iron bars return to the shape of a wing, the woman shakes her head in azure, one eye wide, one eye gone and one or two more limbs tumble loosely, the young man shakes his head and thirteen hundred wings remove the crown of the long grass fields surrounding the pond, a winged being in flannel asparagus chirps the laughter of blades of fruition and is a crumbling armchair's four wings. The azure cadaver spills as a liquid onto the furthest corner of this drawing table, throwing it into asymmetrical gales of laughter, a chortle of blue rain that cries out in the dawn of seven fingers, balanced only by the light of a candle dwindling, the wick is a hand and the wax is a fallen star constructed out of bird beaks, down by the clever edge, colored eyes and flowers with grinning mouths sip the loose fraying street corners into a gale of icebergs, with the young man acting as a small boat and the whale in the shape of a crown of moonbeams splendid in the early dawn air that clenches and unclenches the teeth of fifteen airplanes hurling upward to the roof of the Earth, roof of the hoof and mouth, with the diamond candy wrappers and soiled eight-tails of the climbing scent, tortoise whose shell holds the sad smile of the woman, the curved Earth with tremendous breasts and pelvic bones filled with the cherry tree down the hill, the hill of tombstones that breaks water across the sunrise and sunset and blue-eyed stars across the moon whistling, vacant buffalo of the streams, blanket of spurs.

Hanging partially in moonbeam stairway a street cat flails and clicks a blue lagoon, and as happenstance would have it, another high-top top-hat removed its shoulders from the thunderhead of the woman, across the hall behind the stairs, cooking up an after-midnight meal that clanged and brushed and parted the air with its hand sonorously in the great bird and the ants are going for the soda-pop cans, your antlers swaying in the purple glaze and thunderbolts, laughing very quickly, nightingale; the young man naps between the woman's eyebrows while the whale colors her high rosy cheeks with skeletons loose as a noose around the blind man's one good eye, Saturn with a quivering hand removes its rings and alters its path to the sun's kitchen, Venus swims out of the disembodied planetary rings and tells marvelous songs of her house, invisible, with walls made from leaves and tree branches hanging suspended in the air, the main hall is a giraffe's neck and the ceiling-light is a sand-dollar, all the faucets are penises and the refrigerator has ants in its butthole, from out the ocean swells her bedroom and dining-room, until the great woman upon which everything in existence is based snaps her fingers, twenty collarbones and drapes are thrown forth onto the fraying carpet of Jupiter, brushing its feet on the teeth of one of its rings, no longer hanging around the planet like a crystal candle, the phantasmal pharaoh, whose shadow tosses pearls into the oven, in the sunlight. The shoes of Order and Chaos hovering over the ocean during those summer days, shoelaces embedded in the soil of that hard afternoon, tolling are the bells that sing in the flowers' faces, caught in the hailstorm and fire of their trouser pockets, each to loosen and squeeze these lemons, these avocados, the citrus fruit that is divine Unity to the carved stone of the swinging emperor, Chinese mountains drop jewelry into the hands swarming like bees to the tobacco shop on the corner of the dawn, as oil dripping into the fusillade of handclaps, the woman puts on her three shoes and runs down the street to the corner where the man with the beard and the disembodied mustache greet and take the names of the passersby, laundromat by the oven, each wave in the seabird's tongue is a ripple, the kitchen of the stars and planets, on the palette of humankind's tongue dances integrity, a dustpan to the glue eyes of the subconscious.

He pissed and washed his hands and with the water still running looked at himself in the mirror. There in the reflection were his eyes and his mouth and his nose and everything else. All that he was, looking back out at him. He spoke softly, and then asked himself who it was that he was talking to. He turned the water off and left the bathroom. She had taken off her shirt and her bra and unbuttoned her pants. Her breasts were small but the shadows they cast were beautiful. She said something to him and he took off his shirt and knelt on the bed. They made love once and fell asleep in each other's arms. The night fell away to a subtle dawn and a sky filled with clouds.

When he awoke she was gone. He sat up in bed and looked about the room. The door was shut and she had taken all of her clothes. His clothes were folded on the chair near the television. The sunlight fell through the shades onto the bed. He lay back down and closed his eyes and opened them again. He felt very alone. Slowly he got out from under the sheets and put on his clothes and went to the bathroom and urinated, leaving the door open.

As he was driving away, not heading to any place in particular, he turned down a road and the sun shone down on him unobscured and he shielded his eyes and began to cry. The brilliant light and his tears made it difficult to continue driving safely, so he pulled into the next available parking lot, which belonged to a church. He got out of the car and walked up the steps and entered the building. A young couple was talking to one of the priests and an old woman was reading an inscription on the wall. He continued on past the front hall, wiping his eyes with the back of his right hand. A statue of Christ on the cross stood prominently, overlooking the vast room. There was a black man sitting three rows from the front, praying. Several other people scattered about, some praying, some not. The tears would not cease and he stumbled forward and sat down five rows behind the black man. He put his hand together and got on his knees and prayed to God. When he was finished he was not crying any more. The black man was still bent in prayer. He looked around the church, at the statues and paintings and stained-glass windows, at the other people praying, at the architecture and wooden benches and the priests and nuns preparing for mass.

Everyone is striving. For happiness, for the companionship of others, for a spot in heaven, for a reason to live through the joy and hurt. For a lucky break, for a smile from a stranger, for a sign from God, for something. Everyone is striving and praying that life is worth the pain and the happiness and everything else. No one knows what we are doing here and we all end up dead in the end and sometimes it is enough just to hold someone in your arms, and sometimes not. We all want to be forgiven. We all want something, because we don't really know what we have. We want heaven to be worth our life on earth. We want God to be worth something. For our lives to be worth something, for thought to be worth something. Everyone is striving and praying. Or they have stopped.

The man left the church and stepped into the lion, which was acting as an elevator. There were three buttons on the wall next to the doors: one with the symbol of a man, one with an arrow pointing left, and the last with a dark circle. He pressed the button with the arrow and the lion-elevator began to move down into the alligator's mouth, its eyes were polar bears, a flock of cranes could be heard outside the lion-elevator from all directions, a murder of canoes. The man put his wristwatch in his mouth. Elevators are the best form of travel. There is something to this. A flock of flowers in the sky, releasing insect excrement on the rooftops. The souls' excrement. A pelican with one hundred mouths inside each other. The laundry has been left unattended, like a garden, like an apple.

Born from the Heart

Outside the night was thick and hazy, like a dream. The lights of the city kept guard against the unknown darkness. Henry sat at the bar and ordered another drink. A shot of whiskey and a lite beer. They say that idleness breeds discontent. Soon, three men entered the bar, they were young, and they meant trouble. You could see it in their eyes. They approached the counter, staggering and laughing to themselves. They were looking around. The man two stools away was holding himself together. Henry looked at the boys; they were dangerous. The man two stools away ordered a drink and one of the three said something unkind and the others guffawed.

"If you have something to say, then look me in the eye and say it," said the man two stools away.

The boy repeated what he had said, only louder so the man could hear more clearly. The words were unkind, and the other two boys stifled laughter.

"When I was your age, I was making something of myself," the man said, "I wasn't going around being a worthless shit."

The boy stood and took a step forward, "What of it, old man?"

"Just leave me be," he said.

The boy struck him across the face with his fist and the man fell off the stool.

Says the bartender, "Let him alone."

"Fuck off."

"Get out of here if you are going to stink up the place."

The three boys drag the man outside. Henry followed like a shadow, unseen, unheard. They took him around back and the boy who had been talking hit him again in the face. He was bleeding and on the ground with the filth and garbage. The others took turns kicking him.

The man tried to fight back but to no avail. They were really taking him apart. There was blood everywhere. The boy who started it all pulled the man to his feet and spit on him. Henry observed silently. In one fluid motion the boy took hold of the man's left ear and tore it off. The man cried out. The other two pushed him to the ground and the man was out. The boy walked over to the nearest garbage-bin and threw the ear away and closed the lid. Laughing the three went off into the night, which swallowed them without hesitation or discrimination.

The man lay on the ground in a pool of blood and filth. Henry moved slowly into the alley and raised the man to his feet and walked him into the bar and set him in a booth. This took some effort. Then he went back outside to the garbage-bin and collected the man's ear and went back inside. He set the ear on the table near the man's head and paid the bartender what he owed him and left the bar. The night was gracious.

Henry stumbled along the sidewalk in the dim light of the street-lamps. His hands were stained with blood. The night was heavy and hung menacingly in the air. He was a little scared and looked behind him frequently as he walked. The darkness of man is seemingly impenetrable.

Four or five blocks from his apartment, Henry came upon a man wearing a suit. The man approached, whistling softly to himself.

"Hey, man, do you know what time it is?"

Henry did not own a watch. "I'm afraid I do not. Sorry."

The man laughed. Henry began to walk away but the man said something further.

"Of course you don't. No one knows what time it truly is. That's because there is no time," the man said.

Henry said nothing.

"Hey, man, follow me. I know what you ought to see," says the man, taking Henry by the hand. His grip was unusually strong, and not exactly being a tough guy, Henry followed him.

The man led him into an alleyway seven blocks away. The journey there had been silent. Henry was unfamiliar with this part of the city.

"Help me push this away," said the man.

They leaned their bodies against a large metal contraption similar to a garbage-receptacle in size and pushed. Slowly it gave way and they moved it about ten feet further into the alley. The sound was nearly unbearable and sure to wake up anyone sleeping in close proximity. On the ground where the metal contraption had been is a stone no larger than a watermelon.

"Here it is, man," says the man, and vanishes quickly out of the alley.

Henry stares at the stone and after a long moment runs off, into the night, into the vast unknowable oblivion, into God, into nothing, into the heart of the city.

You can't touch what's not there. Let us make countless duplications, an exact forgery of everything. Let's you and me go to the tops of trees and shed our tears. Shred our clothes. Let's tumble playfully up the stairs, backwards. The stage is set. The rings are in place. Opening all the bottles. Let us wear ghosts like necklaces. Let us shoulder the night with fur coats, feather coats, leather coats. Boiling. Boiling over softly. Under gentle caress. Everything is elsewhere. Let us exhaust possibility. Exhausted impossibility. The place where everything else is.

Do you have a lot of money?

Have you built anything lately?

Do you know anyone who is genuinely insane?

What if the stars, planets, sun, moon were not really what they tell us they are? What if they're lying to us: we have no way of knowing. Walk into a police station and demand to see the truth. Stars are actually distant escalators, the moon is a closed eye, the sun is conversing with itself, the faraway planets are actually a group of people huddled very close together, exchanging clothes. The police station smells like vomit, smells like unicorns. "It stinks like unicorns in here!" someone said. The escalators smell like dandelions. It has been confirmed, the pattern is unmistakable, like handprints in the sand. Sand is often associated with hair and feelings. Shadowy form on the horizon, the painted kisses. It is retreating. You can decide it for yourself. Distribute advertisements for imaginary products. The ribald habitats are the cucumber's cuckold, the globs are serenely garrulous. The argument lasts forever; long live the short-lived! The mind is the enemy, the mind is not the enemy. The rote camel must consist of the strictest caffeine. Dissociative configured flatulence obese tourniquet.

What do you think?

How do you think?

When do you think?

Is there a difference between thought and object of thought?
Subject of thought?

The brain is subject to thought, object. Brainy lumberjack
inside purple passage massage. The brain is important the brain is not
important. Caught between the greasy folds grassy knoll merry marry.
An eye climbs the tree twisting and whirling an umbrella down the
flight of stairs leading to the sun's memory, a loose-fisted elephant
hoots and heckles the wind at night by the sundown and clothespin
army men strap their helmets to their knees at the braying of the wolf
down flightless stairs at the birdbath golden emerging from the soil, a
beautiful spine reaching toward the stars, undulating as a crow lactates
and the milk from the udder is only a shovel when compared with the
thunderstorm of lonely birds beyond the veil of wind dirt trees and in a
vacuum, windstorm nightingale and the lost fragments of a statue one-
eyed sphinx a thousand pieces that to the untrained eye seem to be
wavering in the sunlight at dawn, an umbilical cord threatens the piano
as it walks awkwardly down a flight of birds, hands in its pockets and
two spinning wheels at the lightning-bug forever against the dawn
wind heel, trying with all the forever green, a shovel in someone's
pant-leg, hovering over the windmill a silver hoe. By the bedside,
hedges grow like dandelions, concubine of the forest swinging long
strides and squirming bees feather the horn blow that seeks a nest in
the bosom of the crow, last but not least a chair and a bat with dove's
wings twofold; the chest of drawers blew out telephone cords like

swine, like smoke rings by the evening fire, pale danced lightly mahogany twilight earthbound, bound to the Earth almost in the silhouette of a camel or tortoise, past the ceiling fan with one leg loose, so that the wires coursing with electricity are caught at the horse's hoof and undressed the umbrella slightly tomorrow forgone bystander to the curious left hook of the corset, chandelier, to the curious bookshelf with velvet pattern coat of arms danced slowly at the floorboards foot step tulip by the rose tomorrow, of tomorrow with the coiled skeleton fingers neatly by the row, streetlamp top-shelf almost cornered the fingers. Unscrupulous moral cowboy exclusive trepidation, bedbug syncopation.

The hanging of the stranger was a delight to all the strangers. They gathered around with as much fish as they could carry, in their shoes and hands and pockets. There was a locomotive in their arms; it could whistle a strange tune. The hanging of the soldier was a cascade for all the bulletin boards. Hanging is very singular. It is different from the gun shot. It is more real. Hanging is very real. Dolphins are very real. Discs are not real. A handclap, a thunderclap. The sun is applauding the behavior of empty spaces. A bookshelf is a monument to lions, lions are a monument to lions, monuments are monuments to monuments. It seems very familiar. Familial. The industrious facsimile. The quiet ineptitude. The virgin microscope is ululating gorgeously. The weather in between is rocky. It is advised to be both indoors and outdoors. Pick a side, there are five sides, six. Which would you prefer to believe? The collapsing door is out of breath, let's give it our hat, the hat that you and I share. Snowflakes are actually the body-segments of an enormous centipede, everywhere scattered. This happened a very long time ago. It was the crime of the turtles. People don't know turtles very well.

What do you know very well?

What do you know the most about?

What is your favorite thing that you know?

What do you not like knowing?

Before this, there were three men climbing the bookshelf. They
wore turtles instead of hats, they had clocks in their shoes. One man
was very near to the top, he looked down at the other two men but they
were gone. On the floor was a dead pelican, it looked very beautiful.
You were standing behind the bookshelf, breathing harshly the harsh
winter sunlight. There was snow on the bookshelf. The man sneezed
and toppled to the ceiling, which admitted him like a mouth, like an
elevator, like a vestibule. The vestibules are wearing thin. You took
the shards of glass and laid them on the bookshelf. The bookshelf was
aroused by this and grew warm. Its tears were light, were white. Your
armpits were gaping fish-mouths. The sun closed its green eyes
sequentially. The hanged man inside me was restless, the hangman
inside me was inside-out. An exact soundtrack. The soundtrack of life
played over the image of something else. The antiquarians have been
generated sloppily. Chloroform tigers draping newspaper eagles along
the banister, chlorophyl diamond white open, relieving the antennal
cooperation adjunct.

Instructions for first undressing a lightbulb

Second is emerge from this season you behind the hand-mirror mounted upon the back wall as perhaps a rose or a tulip grows ever more across green landscape which draped along the walls high as a curtain swept back by fast eyelashes This is where we will dress the eye bulb in two by two before grappling with the air hands spread unseen cloud carpet Fingertip to finger sword electricity and torn wind as skin flow beneath shutter fold eyelids

The third will follow the fifth appear glass spied alphabetically now crops with long stalks slipping through the night between the second and eight, fourth and thirteen, the sixth, any which is hair underwater tree branches casting bluejay and moth shadows in the dirt

Man in the shadows you are the envelope withdrawn hidden array of sunlight fourth step follow through this man will only be with shadows late see you see see against tossed side of a building pairs of hands which have flown their last cloud pierced through hot moonlight hot man with feet as forty-five seconds a walk brisk match the gold light caught window flurry like bat wings shards of glass raining down as the window they once were once hole in his cheek blood a red hand which crowds the soft wire high rope billowing eyeball glazed cracked rolls flies through his teeth choke down his feet gone tied with his hair around your back A sudden shade of high-hat straight line chance happenstance across forest trees through down their limbs as blankets in sleep in between more or less and less more so will as along the seashore and the ground caught idle a stickle

The fifth is all the steps in order and none of the steps It is not a step as it is every step

Step aside bright fingers flashing as door knobs silver quick lightning wait one minute two minutes a trance departing train night passenger regard a follow through turn around cleverly alluring this

fast paced fake sale into curling a sandcastle transfixed water winds
feet running through this five hundred foot tall amber palace as one
might run fingers through a train's hair curling wrapping itself around
evade through disguise several lamps light turns to and forth not
dissimilar to breathing

Involving this revolving drunken peasant as yourself into this
boat writhing a naked Sumer as one's hands breeze moves behind fresh
as antlers a set of lips on the shore sand in her eye lips are her tongue
alas this woman is sure sign your mind has wandered off from your
resolution shared with it the light bulbous Taken a trip where you build
as is wont old dusty shelves raked with mud aligned across the walls
they are curtain as the count exclaims breaking and breathing this
manor in this manner grammar

are flown to the ground

the whore who speaks too softly

her lips an entire marching band

beat against the sky fluttering

in the same way these birds

in the sky form combs and pant-buckles

encircling

they use the whore's spine to plough the

sun

which a deep red acts as her fingernails

when she plays the piano along the

cellar doors of distant playhouses, courtyards,

murder trials, drawing-room carpets

whore who's eyes cut grass

leaving only the marble

across the diamond, the switchblade of the

night

of the goose's flight

each of her toes peel an orange

the skins rise up against the night sky

pairing up with disembodied hands, fingers

as long as apple-guard watchmen

together they migrate

and greet the next day

as it

arises from beneath the rivers

and stones

the skeletons are on parade

playground of the stars and planets

the cardinal girl

counting trees with a razor blade

tea kettle boiling

tea kettle kettle boiling

bird beaks open

     to receive the male

as long as there are

     cries in the sky

the night sky

kettle tea boiling

     over bird beaks

   and spinach wrists

     the hornet's transformation

     Three times upon a time, a sudden eagle engulfed the land, before the present knew it was present and when yesterday became the future; the future of the town with no hat on with hot dogs barking, hot coals with showers in each hand. Each eagle was a sharp horn blast, big fan going on and off over a period of six or seven times; fifth cat expands and can no longer find its way through the doorway, head in the past, body in the present, rear-end in the future; this remains a constant.

Land of ungulate honey where the

burglars jump like pearls

hot and cold cider

a warm arm winter's breath

length

three rain forest

      The morning sunlight came down and shook him by the shoulders; his eyes swung open like an old garden fence. Coughing grey and green flowers he rose and shed the blankets which he wore like a marvelous cape; he had worn them throughout his stay at the palace of dreams. He crept into the bathroom and as he emerged he thought he saw a girl standing before the end of his bed, but his mind was deceiving him.

      air sun red violin lattice clock slunk rain billow twenty Aramaic candle loose the cow over silver flirting quantum blue sleeve an third twice count horde sink deep well toward fallen alligator name broke soak done onion a quitter quintet soft solve dove divorce cut food big mile hot home home driver water winter host dryer sing sorbet sober quiet tumbling roast coy smog plight dwell seat cucumber aspirin smite ghost ahead bird cute faint painting part progress inside and than of dove glutton barrier barracuda saxophone which crab toot sweep errand eighty luxurious validate combination sworn post pacify rub

Fresh complications arise when the spool is turned over on its side; if it is upside down, how can the birds be considered? The room was so full of breath that it could hardly stand. In the bed, a fresh application of wherewithal was acclimated by a forest of tongues, of glass and seashells, of violet rope burning with invisible fire, of the bouquet of hands turning each marble over and over. And to think it was summer! Summer spread over with autumn like dust on a worn cold shadow, hissing with fatigue, until a farmhand lost his name in the supplement, for the fourth fortnight. Quite a hold on things in blue ascension. Toward the curved edge of the summer, now shaped like a bowl, an end of the feathers was seen just below the horizon hundreds of kilometers in the distance. A horse sat down abruptly on the wooden curtains

kite bark squirm eat fast too soap spit benign subterranean trail rope shadow quote right fought stop stoop pots still weaver thirteen aim crow torch turn run straight court curtain dip sub wrinkle stone broke throne coat host horst hoist stern starboard hull grass scene white worst camera action single unitary twenty-six wolf curb urban twin frost again soon upon blue ravine ribbon canyon swarm birds soot twilight bath burden breathe sought pinky raspberry old gone still forged coat cope underhand

Pale pale the good sun hidden in a garden, where a little girl happens upon a fountain in the midst. Pretty fountain with golden eyes, in one fist a clump of dirt coming apart like marble. The little girls goes to behold her disrupted reflection as the departing good sun, squawking like a titmouse, caused a lion of ants to emerge from the fountain's water. Her hair, dangling like fingers, in the blink of golden eye, playing music in the water, tossing and turning, a statue on its side asleep in the wind. The little girl takes her rest in the lion of ants, assimilated like the atoms of a beehive, full of water, sleeping as the fountain hikes up its skirt and hurries away toward the furthermost reaches of the garden, calmly expressing its feelings through a series of renovated garages, each filled with the various artifacts of trees, oysters, antlers, the sort of kind known to frequent the taverns at the highest elevation in town. The town, alternately called Furlough and Somnambulist, was of such varying elevation that its residents are required to carry small amounts of ice when in the mouths of the streets. The fountain passed by the little girl's father-mother, whose eyes were closed as (s)he skated somberly forward to the gaping purple hole left by the receding fountain, now wearing a crown of highest achievement, and leaping and curling. The great hypotenuse was extinguished courteously, transexual traditionally, metronome ticking nowhere endlessly soundless. Dr Faustroll brandishes the lady legs. The water growing bitter.

manipulate the

pollution

clockwise

counter

there is only one ocean

and it is yourself

it is

myself

who

who

who?

knock knock splat splat

who's there?

the painted whispers

the surface of painted mountain

resembles painted sea

collapsed woman sunflower

the colosseum is full of noise

      a whisper can't be heard

the wind through the tall grass

all this

has only the weight of memory

but who's remembering?

what are these things?

even statues crumble

if they aren't toppled

by hands or wind

is it the flesh?

is it the undone motion?

there is no preservation

the self is wind

and topples flesh

there is nowhere else

and this place

is no place

everywhere

   is

vanished flame

       slow hand

vast and unholy consumption

      manifest in

      countless bodies

writhing in pretend ecstasy

scampering flesh

      like unpersued thought

the growth of

      fathomless depth

growth of hurried

      unseen flesh

      like broken smiles

collapse of piano down

a flight

      of stairs

like rain

      old man birds

I wonder what he sees

when the wind moves

along the trees

that obscure the horizon

when he feels the grass

beneath his feet

does he long for home?

he's coughing

looking out past the door

repulsion

the bedsheets are in ruin

like windswept hair

but she isn't there

to make them up

she isn't there

her neck

and her hair

her lips

her eyes

are somewhere else

looking upon things elsewhere

no longer upon this wretched body

whose reflection

is in no eyes

except his own

exhaustion

the child

offers a small cupped hand

as if to receive candles

or coins

delicate hand

like the small birds

which come after rain

the world was made for children

but men have forgotten this

alas, they have forgotten themselves

who cannot smile at a child

whose clothes are dirty from play?

and nowadays the playgrounds

are no more

like burned-out stars

there are so many good things

and still much is unacceptable

no discrimination between the

acceptable and the unallowable

some ceaseless river bears them both

into the nowhere of tomorrow

that we will never know

and the nowhere of today

that we pretend to know

and the nowhere of yesterday

that we have forgotten

some day there will be no laughing child

and the men are unable to cry

looking out at you

from the back of a train

waving at me

too far away to see my eyes

days passing like someone

playing the piano

unruined puddles

like your voice

too far away to

reach my ears

the rise and fall of each day

I'll go

I'll go

I'll go

I'll build a home in your heart

with forgotten wood

it felt just like the old days

tapestry of rain

full of forgotten colors

so far away

reach out to touch

only mirage

only a loosed mirage

and tangled heart

there are some things

that can't be gotten used to

there are some things

that can

drips and pulls

lathering lazy

you know

you've got the prettiest eyes

I've ever seen

but sleep won't come

rain dresses the sky

     in a smile

     in a smile

that few will see

and fewer still are those

who return

that wide-mouth grin

did you break the law?

or was it already broken

by the time you dried your skin

wet from the fallen rain

was the world ever young?

and those things undone

I'm crying into a white handkerchief

who's to say

it's not a dove

with folded wings?

all those men

like fallen rain

get up and take the A-train

but only eyes are closed

lashes upon lashes

a forest

no-water

the sleeping cat

awakens

startled by its own dream

      on the death of someone else's child

sitting alone

by the river

I watch my shadow grow

until it is gone

in the newborn night

I rise and depart

ceaseless flowing water

getting further and further

from my ears

not a trace remains

soon I am falling asleep

though it seems

that I am just now waking

inside and out

not a trace remains

of what?

this emptiness is a fullness

of what?

the scarecrow in the field

casts the shadow

of a man

what is the sound of wind

before sound of wind?

what is the sight of chair

before sight of chair?

what is the touch of lover

before touch of lover?

before and after

trade places

and forget their order

self-awareness does not belong to anything

empty of something and nothing

empty consciousness

empty consciousnesses

in a row

what makes you so special?

the mosquitos don't discriminate

falling rain reflects from all sides

before hitting the ground

broken rock reveals

rock

he is scrambling

the ground crumbles

the rocks and stones fall away

does he keep going? or does

he stop?

in the distance a bird calls out

no response except for the trees and sunlight

parting the branches

the clearing becomes clear

empty with sunlight

fullness of moonlight

so heavy as to never be lifted!

one mind

thinking

there is one sight

and it is seeing

there is one sound

and it is hearing

there is one surface

and it is touch

don't mind

no birth, no death

uncreated

not coming, not going

faith in mind

vigor

cessation

no limit to what is true

no limit to what is false

"how can it be likened to anything?"

all things present themselves as they are

all things do not present themselves as they are

rivers flow just as it flows

flowers bloom just as it blooms

things happen when you aren't looking

There are certain birds which resemble soapstone chairs and are called Lightbulbs. They hang like fruit from the vines crawling up castle walls, crawling up the castle walls so far as to reach the moon, only to be buried in its reflection. During the Lightbulbs' mating season, occurring between the afternoon and evening of every sixteenth or seventeenth day, and every other winter solstice, those birds which are closest to the ground leave the embrace of the vines and venture as far as the cliff, where they descend slowly in unwavering vertical lines until the voluptuous lips, hiding amidst the crags and ledges and vegetation, open wide in scowling smiles and plummeting frowns to allow them access. The male Lightbulbs enter the smiling mouths; the females turn upside-down and fly into the frowns. The lips then close in fleshy arabesque and the sound of a car engine starting is issued forth every so often for the twenty minutes ensuing. The mouths open: when sunlight pierces the interior, water rushes out, bearing the birds and their newborn offspring. The adult Lightbulbs then return to the vines and the young are carried down by the water to lie in pools at the bottom of the cliff until they can understand what to do.

The birds that recline on the vines closer to the moon burst into shadow like a shout. To hold a Lightbulb in the palms of both hands is enough to make any human cry.

Crying being.

Do you believe in God?

Does your belief or disbelief in God affect your behavior?

density is mass over volume

43567 + 6367 - 888888 = 3757.5433211

23526.343434 - 54351090 = pleasant stay

2 + oligarchy = 2020.0202

A clementine for every last word

    she spoke

Fingers windmill spiderweb toward

    the knight who tilts and rainstorms

    through and through the knoll

    Big Stuff

    Situated as if it were a machine such as an automobile, the dog-star-ghost stretched its tendrils and gripped tightly its cloud. Being a ghost, it travelled in this way for a long time, going many miles. The avaricious dangles threaten disaster. Too little too pale the frail rain pail. The woman closed her hoof daintily. Let us pray that time skips. The lettuce drinks the Shedeh. Urgent chamomile penguin spurting French caterpillars, the thermometer behaves like a daffodil to sort the tonsils, nests, utensil. Shedder shedder shudder recently abhorred boring spurt, dirt.

lively, of sorts

the immaculate cadaver

the cadaver casts moonlight on its gravestone

one man to another

the finite trees

lightning eyes darkness

little ants

the three charities fourth

the sun beat down on the shoulders as wings

the king is old, his tattered capes hang about his decrepit

body and run through the rooms of the castle, envious of

the slugs

what breathes the life-breath of existence? is it breathing in, or out?

what is it that casts the shadow of the universe?

a shadow has no weight

the world is also like this

breath, water, food, sleep

why ask for more?

four shining jewels

three crows wing

she has seashells covering her eyes

five hands drawn

old torn shoes three feet by the lowside

red train to elsewhere

Buddha's sewing machine

Saturn, throw down your marvelous rings, permit Venus to traverse
your azure corridors

a heavy heartbeat

cuisine well worth the trip to Mars

this deep moon, only as firm and blue as the moon twice-told

the misfortunes of tomorrow's sunsets

the sun shines on the saxophone players of Neptune

room for two

the dentist

by the beside, hedges

grow like dandelions, concubine

last but not least a chair

and a bat with dove's wings

the dancers are stationed at the woman's toes

the umbilical cord mimics a glass of wine

toppling up the flight of stairs

the corpse was wearing a real pearl as if it were a garden

the skeleton emerges from the pearl as if it were a garden

pearl = garden

corpse = pearl

does the candle seek its flame out?

what is reflected

in the mirror of everything?

what is revealed

in the mirror of your self?

in the mirror of the mind

nothing is absent

nothing is present

perception is understanding

one is oneself

leaving things alone

China sunfish

this is understanding

       sandcastle sans castle

       sans sand

The soldier says:

              spiderwebs spiderwebs, old

               crow's feet are mirrors,

               sunbeams, as short as I

               am concerned, as far as

              the grass grows by the side

              of the bed, sailboat bed,

            grass sailboat of sun feathers,

              soft as a butterfly passing

              over the bare eyeball,

the exposed fancy,

tulip bulb wings

around the eyeball dancing,

a rainforest of wind, sailboat

that I can feel against

the corner of my eye, the

butterfly carving designs

into my window, the sun,

tombstone, tombstone,

open window of flower beds

running the rain into the eye

of a single tulip,

gorgeous, gleaming, hair

is coming out of the center

of the tulip, hair and leaves

are emerging from the sandcastle's

petals, the drawbridge is made

of feathers and eyes,

an old crow with ruby wings

by the window, I can hear

the rain dancing through the

sandcastle's corridors, overturning

the flower-pots and taking

the books from their shelves.

Ballroom water caught

in a glass shoe sunbeam,

china sunfish blooming in

the ruby garden the ruby

golden meadows

under the woman's lips,

woman by the fountain,

I'll give a rose to a lion for

its two eyes and the flowers

of its tail,

in the eye-socket of the whale,

under ballroom water,

the woman puts on an

armful of mirrors by the wayside,

long tail road

curling dust at the edges of the

broom, the broom that the woman yields

is a road, the flower's throat.

A tarantula is only as hairy as the pitchfork in its eye, a
carpenter ant is a knife only when the window is closed, creaking attic
door barnyard along the closed eye, with a fistful of bat wings and
golden embers pale in the moonbeam but smiling at the coiled dinner-
table; a colony of miniature wine glasses at the foot of the bed, moving
with remarkable efficiency for their stature, a statue of ice and dirt
topples off of the toilet-seat and crumples the glasses until they mimic
the light reflected off the toilet-bowl, open air too loose to swim, forest
dwindles at the back-porch of a great fire which is actually the
woman's wrists, a child's swing cuts through the paper seahorses like
so many hurricanes, and against the dawn's window the maker of toy
soldiers croons for the hermit; unbeknownst to the toy soldiers, the
whale has the hermit in a sack, twelve thousand legs like a fish bone.
Crescent shape swings into the low night, making an outline out of
which crawls a various assortment of forms: triangles, circles,
rectangular prisms, the tooth of the forest wrapped in the waist of the
woman, swing gently as a spider's web brings the sinking moon out of
the shadow of that eye which hangs in the air menacing and inviting,
the sun or perhaps the antlers of a deer whose hoof is a snarl from a
coyote caught in the toes of the whale, flung against the bow of a
sailboat painted red and diamond and garland; swamps fall over one
another in the footfalls of a giant cone, at once a bucket full of leaves
and at twice a snowflake with fingers emerging from the wondrous

and labyrinthine corridors that tell of all the ways of the ancient people who crawled about as lizards and drank from the purse of the sun, always covered in the overhanging bramble and moon's legs that hang down like spiderwebs.

Many clouds return to Earth and lay their eggs and seashells along the bags under the woman's eye, the young man covered in horse-hair is available to sweep up the ashes, hovering sweet the moon is engulfed by a reindeer, and from this form the shadows of crows and lions merge to create a drum, played with a cigarette as angels overflow from the handkerchief, quite a display of showmanship as the winter passes for a duck whenever it is riding in an airplane or the cold laugh materializes and withdraws its hand from the deck, thrown all over the table grinning like a bat or fountain, the way fountains smile is a rainforest, the way fountains frown is a cause for investigation, covered in mulberry-leaves and fern trees with eyes too old to be seen from afar, hand caught fire through a window thus broken all over the buttocks of the woman, in the shade of a crow and the fence of the young man, cold is the whale whose shoes are elephants' ears or jugs of lye. Toothless comes the thundercloud bursting at the seams, cut open a torrent of water is expelled and the woman will have to find a new hat, or at least a handful of tree bark, carved from the finest yellow suggestions made by those men and women who frequent grocery stores in order to accumulate mass quantities of tombstones, whenever the chemistry books spill open they can house Attila the Hun or Abraham Lincoln with their coffins, whenever the books lose their words, wrap a frail scarf around a lurching tree or else the flowered ground will overturn and the corpse of Aristotle will hover over the moon as if he were an eye. The Way of the Silver Goose is established carelessly, clay moose bound and gagged in the estuary tepid concussion, splitting headache blessed illusory famished. The aching acres of ochre arcs actresses dietary assassin, golden asinine.

Flying dish with perfumed skull full of urine wherein the tiny moons elicit their buoyancy. The hollering of gibbons from within the offspring.

Standing before a forest which spilled gently into the orbit of Newgrange, I could distinguish faintly the form of a woman, leaning against the trunk of a tree; with difficulty I could see that she was wearing a white nightgown. She had it hiked up around her waist and was inserting some object into her vagina, I could not make out what it was. The size and shape reminded me of a pineapple or kangaroo. Looking at the area around her, I noticed the figure of a man hiding a short distance away, watching her. The man is holding an object, is dressed in dark clothes. Once she has gotten the object inside her, the man approaches and the woman reacts as if she had been waiting for him. She takes the object from him and pushes it slowly yet swiftly inside her. I watch intently, unsure of what I am witnessing. The man then removes all of his clothes, which he lets fall to the ground. Once he is completely naked, the man slowly makes his way into the woman's vagina, arms and head first, then wiggling his lower body and legs into her, slowly. The woman assists as she can. My mouth hangs open. Once the man had vanished inside the woman, a second man approaches and the figures are seen conversing, but the words are too quiet for me to hear from my vantage point. The second man removes his clothes, which he lets fall to the ground, and opens his mouth wide, so wide that it would be impossible, the pain excruciating. The man makes no sound and the woman bashfully climbs into his mouth and struggles down into his throat and is gone. The naked man remains standing, now alone. I rub my eyes in disbelief, I have half a mind to make some noise as to alert the man to my presence, but I refrain. The man's skin appears to be changing colors rapidly, and he crumples as if fainting. Before he hits the ground he vanishes in a cloud of feathers, a clout of warts, and a mechanical beeping sound is issued. Only his anus remains, lingering faithfully. I listen to the beeping as it fades into the sounds of night. A large disembodied human head watches me from a distance, suspended above the tops of the trees. In the sky the clouds form an immense vagina, weeping tears that are penises and seahorses, gently into the night, directly into the night night night.

cut open a swordfish by the sunset and a lion will emerge from the intestines

the night's testicles knight

lovers grow in tulip petals

you can find a lion inside of a lightbulb or by the seashore or behind the spiral staircase

break open an emerald and one thousand bees will come out

amiable distraction amulet

only noses grow along the moon

only lions grow along the moon

only tulips grow by the moon

ball of night

she is sure something

you put animals in my wounds

       green sand in the mind

if all the truth were in this stone

all the rain were in this feather

by glass castles in the forest green

forest walls nightingale

cries the sun with night in its eyes

shows like a forest sandcastle

to the Heavens and Earth

in the sandcastle

chandeliers

lights

blue

as forests grew

into dove's wings

beautiful towns in the wind

the sea has come to the shore of the mind

fragrances hid by miles

bouquets of the souls

in the skin bind All Is One

the fruits of the seasons are ripe

on the frontier of the One

each eye is freed from its gardens

sits on perfumed clouds

a beautiful green purple temple

through the forests of time

on the eye but a bird from beak to wing

from each sun a bird to cry

freed on the boat a foreign

lullaby

on the vast frontiers of the

mind corridors of forest blue

green in the eye

sand from the boat sits

uncounted gold for the

seashells

a bird sits green soft as a cloud

in the eye sand finds the harps

and bounding leaping pearls

sandcastle in the water a

forest labyrinthine pearl

the sound of the sea is on every wing

nightingale

blue forest hiding in the eye

of the sandcastle

songs are cities burning down

in the soft green cries of the moon

as green eye around the sun

the seashell with golden wings

in each eye come out like

night

sandcastle sunshine

blue in the coiled moon

around each sailor's eye lies a cobra

with night and love at the rose tips

blue night eyes

sank into green

forests of sunshine and sun

coiled at the foot of the nightingale

sleeps

the sandcastle

into silent blue

of the cobra's eyes

of the tiger's eyes

seashell in the sands of time

blue forests of the moon in the

nightingale's feathered locks did fall the

winter bell

and her silence was the great

feast of snow and cold and ice

the sun on the sandcastle lakes

leap in green sometime

around the heel coiled the

sand crowns of blue ocean

nightingale kings in forests that

drift from scene to tongue to eye

for the oceans of kings are

green nightingales along the corridors

of the sandcastle forest

at the heel of faraway shores

curves in the woman's shape sleep

silent and green forest upon

forest

a tongue is

white as the lotus flower

the petals are a woman's hands each in snow

the curves of seashells sit in soft

green waters swimming at the

cobra's heel

summer in the eyes

ocean eyes

winter bell in the sandcastle

forest blooms

castles in the tulip's eye

a snowy mountain of green forest gold

a pale black mountain

caught in the spiderweb dove's wing

each shaft of light

in pale moon islands

sitting sandcastles

by the

lake

eyes of forest green as my tongue

castles on my forest tongue

bleached white skeletons

in the pale moon snow

in pale sun grows

the seashell howls

of some forest nightingale

in the street

the lotus flowers

coil the sun

in their eye

each moon smile brings cold oceans

black as sandy mountaintops

up in snow

down in sun petals roll

in sandcastle labyrinths white as

snow the woman's eye

sun fingers

are sure to go

white castles in green forest

seashells where the woman reveals

her pearl to the ocean

sandcastle

ruins

seeped in green

forest silk, nestled in the heart

of the nightingale swimming

sinking in the sands

a white boat over time

the beautiful sun of rivers

cries the green night into our

dreaming sandcastle canals white and green

snow and lizard pendulum swung in the lizard green

in the snow or rain the sandcastles

are forests and the same the same

windmill giants hiding in the sun

silk passages sit white birds

at my brow

the winds play at the sea

coast, my eyes, the feasts

of rain and nights, doves

and woman bathed

black in gloves

the snow silk

rain sun flower

rivers through her skin

green sandcastles at the forest

snow drifts on each

beam of light

a lizard's tongue

in dark crystal

sun-eyed in the dew

wore time

at the heels

sandcastle eyes

in the forest sink

snowy heavens around each finger

a pyre of foreign lullabies

syrup of words

running

down the

sandcastle

of her eyes

all is all and is to is

the heavens cry

the forests shrink

Should you be doing something other than reading?

What is important to you? What is unimportant to you?

the sensitive syrup

the duplication of necessities

the duplication of ponies

false advertising

the sensible armoire creates its own ambush

inchoate

the flesh bursts

the flesh expands

the flesh extricates the exultant occultist

your eight urinates

the bowels are corrupting the languid tendrils

my life glows in the dark

every time

immediate fascination

immediate vaccination

the gorillas are exempt

put your broken teeth in my mouth, I'll suck them like eggs

the winning smile

winding trees

the flea is screaming from within your ear

though you hardly seem to notice

it sounds like ice cracking

shifting

the resemblance is remarkable

the elephant emerges vertically from the lake

like a saucer of milk

a flying saucer

the fingernails growing out of skin

coils of flesh

bees of white flesh

stretching on

for miles and miles

the discreet anatomies

are perishable perishable

we've got a good thing going here

little ducklings across the treetops

hollow acorn stuffing

concrete duckling figurines into its lavish

bellybutton

chrome ancestor barking liquid

it's all happening at the same time

no time

sumptuous time

with no tail

the mahogany ghosts like sandcastles, tears

      sword of the high afternoon

Assaulted by the gangrenous stare of a robed king whose height may be measured in oak trees or silver birdbaths, the woman hangs her womb to be washed by the sunlight. Her name, her true name given by her mother while her father gathered stones and feathers for the preservation of their house, is of a mild significance, so we shall bestow around her head an ivory crown with ivy strewn about it and the name Gasoline shall be spoken in reference to her from now until the end of the season for the eyes of a bird. She moves as a silken curtain in the moonglow, leaving the king devastated to the extent that he shall order the army to slay the royal jester and the wizard, but to leave alive the majestic gardeners who allow his palace to mirror the face that the king wore in his youth, at the time when Gasoline was conceived. The mother and father hurriedly take their daughter off to another town quite far away, where the people no longer wear glass skirts but instead pronounce words such as 'chair' or 'hilltop' the way one might speak 'Egypt' through a blade of grass. Gasoline was left in the care of the innkeeper and is given a room behind the staircase in exchange for her functioning as the inn's sole receptionist. Her duties are as follows: take reservations, place customers in any available room, handle the affairs of the customers, cook blithe lunches that remain in the eye of the eaters until the next meal, light and extinguish the candles and solitary chandelier, lock the door at night and allow the nightingale to frequent the halls as is wont of any small town hotel or inn. Slim the innkeeper is rarely in her field of vision but the sun is a frequent guest which allows her smile to wander. In the kingdom of her birth, the king is decorating the mountainside with disembodied torsos as a result of her absence and the devil of the mountain uses these as its sandwich bread; the king creates men from locks of his hair and has them executed, his son the prince is weeping and the image of Gasoline has made a great depression upon his heart, the king stands before the window, caressing each bird and fish with the wind drawn from his cape which hangs about his decrepit shoulders and runs through every room of the palace, envious of the rugs. He makes short use of his weathered shoulder-blades capable of slicing an orange diamond into three table-legs. From afar, the king does not love Gasoline but is entranced by her, obsessed with her, almost to the point of loathing.

Goddess, with all of her glittering jewels nestled underneath her eyelids, so that whenever she may speak or laugh, one's eyes are drawn to and fro about her face, unsure, and the tongue is forced from the cascade of teeth; Goddess, with the sun's knee to rest her breasts upon, bears down in the soil moist and crumbling that rocking-chair horse forged by her mother while she was birthing her, the husband was in the rain upon the reaching seashore where the wood and stone is collected. Into the sky a howl is unearthed and becomes eventually a typical garden rake, used to sow the apple-seeds in the garden of Yellow Emperor; the coil of the snake in this garden is not dissimilar to the flip of a coin, light is reflected off this coin in midair and the goddesses are seen making away with the Nile River between their teeth. The other gods raise a silver heel as wings stretch from their shoulder-blades, sharp as the sneezing of the wind when it has a cold.

Diminished clouds, half-seen smiles that arouse the windfall, diminished smiles, where must one find the call given by the fruit of the sun? All the gods in their play give the idea to those still living on Earth that the summer breeze is death and the absence of wind is the door to the heavens swinging as gently as the waves lapping against the eyeball, the bulb of an amusing flower. Can you distinguish between each child if they have yet to become entwined in their parents' lips?

Golden blonde curls and locks flowing as a a smiling bath, with tight and wrung lips, tongue like a lizard peering out from the rocks of their teeth, this young boy is flying through the air, hair dancing vaudeville upon their shoulders, slender like a sculpture or sepulcher, blue eyes that look to you as the moon and sun, body like a hen or bluebird, this young girl is always bathed in sunlight. Their joy comes rolling fat down the dirt brown tongue road. Paint this picture for me and from the ocean of my mind swells the image of death. Just birthed into life they are closest to death; birth and death sing with the same voice, throats tangled as tree branches. This young boy and girl swim in the clouds; they have created the world, to them I am grateful.

Heart pumps and beats faster, sending through the veins not blood but leaves, from the heart moves as a breeze to the tips of the fingers to the curling lashes to the toes and the knees; cut in half right down the middle discover that the skin harbors a tree with branches reaching and crying out to heaven, growing and growing out from within the cave of bones so tall and sturdy; the heart and its veins the tree and its branches. Travel down the road in a car made of ashes for so long your mind gropes from within your skull something outside to trigger your brain's jism a dream; your eyes meet with another's, gangplanking like two swords. A hitchhiker with his fist clenched and thumb skyward, out of his fist a flower grows beautiful before turning into an arm and hand with fingers gnarled like old tree roots. This third extremity leaps off to join the sun as your heart pushes leaves through your veins; I emerge beside the hitchhiker and begin your dream. My lashes gain one hundred feet in length and tangle up with the road, your car bumps and spills forward the hitchhiker with head all over the dirt blood looking like a tree branch winding its way through the soil. Teeth ablaze before you can stop me I devour him entirely; I take his heart still beating in my fingers as if I am keeping something from the moon, I put his heart on my left breast. Veins rise through my skin and bones enough to make a graveyard fence and this new heart thumps and breathes and writhes above my chest, I feel blood rushing to and fro on top of my skin. Sing the song of the trees and leaves pour from my eyes and mouth; blood be my constant and infinite companion, not dissimilar to the skin or the sky of a dead man. You know it through the trees.

9:45 am = 5:23 am

4:41 am = flotsam

January = 11:12 pm

Further exploration of artificial orifices; creation of orifices, creation of artifices. The voice of the mind is not your own. The mind is a deception, the mind is not a deception; nothing is a deception, everything is a deception. The false deception. There are two minds. You should always read a book backwards, that is how they are designed. Privet to take care, privy unmatched unattached. Crucial designation, prying the whiskers that are sold, that are cold. Someone with no rabbits.

Do you have a lot of possessions?

Are your favorite things tangible or intangible? What is intangible?

What is your favorite sense?

like a man perpetually swatting at a relentless insect

like a man falling down endless stairs

what a terrible feeling!

what authority should one follow?

are we all experiencing the same thing, or not?

what are the things that should be discussed, that are worth discussing?

self and not-self:

what is it?

let us decide between all the false statements and true!

we can do it!

I can almost taste it,

it tastes like

silver

slivers of pitch

I'll see you when I see you

The young man looks inside of himself with five hands, one of the hands compared to the others resembles a blind lumberjack, a frozen azalea bush that moves and grows and hisses as the woman's eyebrow, the young man's eyelashes, shattered lightbulb flower steaming smoking bulb in a blue, in a blue, out a blue yonder, heavenly wood words, carved from the Earth's smile, a coarse tangled brush that weaves old sweaters for nickels, sandlot built along the cold coast, mirroring a gold ghost that flourishes in the weeds and bramble, a slice slick red dog's bark, sounding as a girl speaking softly, of things the young man wishes to comprehend, cracked knuckles and a tidal wave, thunder wave, for a blue bright farther the lighthouse is sent onward at the bray of a severed torso, cascading down in golden tresses, a little boy of four a little golf-club of stone and weasel-wood, from a cold sheep's wool, red lamp cushion, several of the young man's arms raised heavenward; behold, the heart of the blemish is the soul of the worn hangers!

It is morning: the birds and insects beat their wings upon the woman, who brings her hands together to form a beautiful flower, a falling wineglass, to which there is not given a name and the fluttering of the sunshine is like the rainfall of rose petals against her breast, now swelling to the size of the moon, two moons, a horseshoe long river winding; lazing along the edge of the water is the young man, a small stick trailing behind him as a tail or moonbeam, he is thinking of her; as she coughs, she is under his eyelids, in between his eyelashes cavorting as a lioness amongst the group of zebra and buffalo who marvel at her ferocity and electricity, the greatness of her paw is matched only by the latitude of her roar, three swans rising, three women on a raft center of the river blue, a steel shadow they cast with both hands furling, the young man may just have wings under his skin, a heartbeat which emits dirt and leaves like a satellite, stone wall erected toward the heavens, heaven-sent behind the thick trunk of a sandcastle, hidden in the bowel of the florescent woman's brow, bosom towards the moon and howling. These mock-women on the river's bow-and-arrow are but disillusions, cast off as the true woman's eyelashes, rosebud petal fawning in the green sunlight, shine the gold tomorrow, bearing a trench coiled dirt robe, hoof-marks all over the soil, a ghastly eyeball fallen from the horse socket swims alongside the women as they disappear into the haze downriver; the young man finds refuge in the shadow cast by the early morning sun, two ravens' claws, thick bolt lightning a thunderhead handclap, saddened and dampened by aspirations to reveal his soul to those women; the woman who stands taller than him by several thousand feet watches as her breasts resume their regular stance, nipples that smile like the tops of palm trees, good hand given to him, his foot, writhing, catches the sand and he is tucked into the riverbed. The young man must learn to reap the bounty that is within himself and within the woman, that which is without any woman is a finger gnarled and beckoning, invitation to become lost in the cracks of the sidewalk, carved from the stones of men past and future, a deep forest in snow, the young man views from beneath the carpet of water, a splendid home for the Wendigo who makes his abode in the hearts of men and in the heavy smiles of ice, cold wind blowing south the song of the creature who is not only itself but those three women, as well as many more men and women alike who cast their eyes into the dirt and with them their souls, reaching with cupped hands, one around the soup bowl and the other around the breast and the testicle. Waves that wrestle about the water, searing a golden nest for the ear of several days, toss your pianos out of the door, stair bound water the heaven door same way, harpsichord playing rosehips on the ceiling of a ballroom, filled to the cup a large knee cap that is the woman's, people and trains swinging the sweet starlight, bite me south the other drunk, skip to your loose toes undone and flying sky airplane toward the center of the room which mimics the suns in that they are the same when viewed by the left and right eye separately, woman whistles for a moment, the young man leaps to the garland, picks up the treasure for her, lost in sultry glances over the shoulder against the steaming wall lifting tight cloud-banks: a three-bladed scissors of dark diamond and oak tree branches; soon, high above, a flame that casts shadow instead of light, a lamp that casts rocks instead of light, a blue eagle with a two-hundred foot long beak.

A Terrible Device

This object is singularly designed to disorient its user. In order to construct it, you must first find some way of producing two hollow tubes, each about 1' long with a 1" diameter. The cardboard inside of a roll of paper towels or toilet paper works just as well. Next, you somehow secure the two tubes to each other, so that they are a single unit, resembling binoculars; they should be as far apart as your eyes. Now you have the object, which does not have a name. Let us call it object L.

While I do not recommend it, the use of object L is as follows: first, find two different images (such as from photographs, paintings, television or computer screens, etc) and place them side by side on some surface that is about the same height as yourself, so that they can be seen together. Object L functions in the same way as binoculars, except it does not magnify. Stand five feet (or whatever is necessary) from the images and look at them through object L so that you see only one of the images per eyehole. The goal is for your eyes to receive separate signals, as opposed to receiving the same signal as is natural. You can probably imagine that this gives the brain quite a nasty shock. Just thinking about it gives me the heebie-jeebies; just thinking about it makes my eyeballs throb.

Oops!

When he opened his mouth he looked like a flight of stairs, when he opened his mouth he looked like a flight of birds, when he opened his mouth. He yawned and reached his hands toward the ceiling, arching his back. The painter stood before a canvas stretched across an easel, in an almost bare room with a single window which revealed the sea less than a mile away. There were no boats on the water, as far as he could see, and the sand was dazzling in the near-blinding sunlight. The waves progressed unbroken. A young white woman is lying on the beach. To the painter, she appeared to be sleeping.

The door shook on its hinges as someone banged upon it from outside the room. The painter nearly jumped out of his dark skin. He walked slowly to the window and opened it wide. A gentle wind flooded the room and a profusion of odors permeated the silence that followed the outburst of noise, saltwater and sand and stiff grass. He looked out of the window, then back at the door. No one entered. He heard the shout of bird from somewhere within the apartment building. The room in which he painted was on the second floor, and the room directly below his was occupied by an old woman who sat in a rocking-chair all day long. He could hear the creaking of her chair while he tried to sleep at night. Her room was empty except for a smooth stone no larger than a watermelon. She sat in her rocking-chair near the window, and the stone sat near the center of the room. Everyday it was like this. The painter didn't know about the other occupants in the building, but he heard other people occasionally, especially deep in the early morning, before dawn, before light. During the day, he would paint. Each movement of his hand as he brought the brush across the canvas was a symphony.

The painter turned his head and looked through the window. He saw the sea and the woman lying asleep beside it, the woman asleep in a flower of sand. He looked around the room. The woman a flower of sunlight. He distinguished the picture of a mountain range hanging in the upper right corner of the wall opposite him, and against the wall to his left, beside the door, was a small table with a single drawer and a thin vase atop it containing a bluish-green flower, with a long stem and very small leaves culminating in a flourish of radiant petals. He saw the sleeping woman in the petals. She moved through the petals as if they were trees in a forest, as if they were flames. The painter reached out to touch the woman, but a change in the movement of the wind knocked the vase onto the floor, spilling the water and the flower and the woman, who vanished. He bent down to clean it up, when the door swings open and a small white man wearing a suit enters. The man closes the door behind him, leaving it opened a crack. The hallway beyond it was lit by a small lamp hung on the wall. The man loosened his tie and took a step further into the room. He looked around and settled his gaze upon the painter, who was turned in his chair to face the door. The half-finished painting lay on the easel, the sea rose and sank in the open window.

"When it rains, it rains, doesn't it?" says the man in the suit.

"It does," says the painter, "it does when it should."

The man took another step forward. Sunbeams fell through the window and lay heavily on the floor at the painter's feet, the light filtering into the rest of the room like a haze of butterflies or octopi.

"I don't mean to be barging in unexpected like this."

"Then why are you? If you don't mean to do something then why do it?"

"You don't understand," says the man, "there are larger forces at work here. There are bigger things than you or I."

There was a hollow silence. The painter looked upon his painting and traced his dark fingers along the surface of the canvas.

"What a lovely painting. Really, very interesting."

"It isn't finished."

"Then what a lovely painting it will be!"

Silence.

"What are you doing here?" asks the painter.

"Well," says the man, easing forward slightly and fiddling with his pockets, "I've been sent to request your presence at the police station."

"What for? I have no reason to be there"

"You have been implicated in a burglary. You are a suspect."

"Are you pulling my leg?"

"No."

"This is absurd. I have been here in this room painting for several days now. I haven't left this room except to go to the bathroom. I haven't eaten!"

"The police have reason to believe you were involved in the theft of a tree."

"What reason do they have?"

"Please just come with me, sir," says the man, closer.

The painter stands. "Theft of a tree? How can someone steal a tree? They don't belong to anyone."

"Somebody stole the tree from the lion exhibit at the zoo," the man says. "You say you have been here for the past few days, painting?"

"That is exactly right."

"And do you refuse to come along to the police station?"

"Absolutely."

"Then I guess there is nothing I can do. If your name isn't cleared by tomorrow I will come back with a warrant."

"I don't have anything to do with any crime."

"Then you should have nothing to worry about."

The man in the suit turns to leave and notices the floor. There are three holes in the ground near the small table, one in the shape of a flower, one in the shape of a vase, one in the shape of a puddle. They extend all the way through the floor into the ceiling of the room below.

"What happened at the zoo?" asks the painter.

"I told you," the man says, opening the door, "someone stole the tree from the lions' den. Their behavior has been greatly altered by its disappearance. Something about the absence of the tree disrupts the flow of the lions."

The man in the suit closes the door behind him as he exits the room. Silence settled like a roosting bird. The painter looks out the window. The sun is setting, the woman is gone. The tide has become rough and the waves more defined. He raises his hand and presses the dry paintbrush against the canvas and is still.

The sight of movement catches his eye and he turns to face the window. It is now early dawn and the reflection of the moon rides the waves all the way to shore. He had seen from the corner of his eye an old man walking slowly away from the building along a path which lead to the beach. The old man moved slowly yet swiftly. The painter stood and crossed to the window, leaning out of it to get a better view of the old man walking quietly in the mist of the fading dawn. The waist-high wild grass that grew on both sides of the sandy path rustled and swished in the breeze. When the old man arrived at the beach he vanished from sight. The painter heard the sound of a bird from somewhere within the apartment building. On the beach, the old man reappeared, accompanied by the woman from the day before. She was completely naked except for an enormous headdress. They were carrying a rowboat to the edge of the water. The woman moved back out of sight and then returned bearing two oars, which she gave to the old man. She stood facing the sea as he got into the boat and pushed away from the shore. Slow, labored strokes that just barely broke the gentle surface of the water.

The painter did not see land out on the horizon. The old man was rowing toward the open sea. He sat straight with his head up as he rowed, looking in the direction of the painter hanging out of the window like a piano full of water. The sun rose behind the old man as if to envelope him in an eternal abyss of light.

On another day, but at the same beach, a man was reclining on a towel in the sand, in the shade of a large umbrella made for such occasions. He slowly looks down the beach to his right, and then turns his head and slowly looks down the beach to his left. There are only a few people out today, mostly couples with young children. The man closes his eyes. The weather is mild, the blue sky and shining sun concealed by thick white clouds that came together and parted and came together again. The man looks out at the ocean, at the horizon of water. He then turns over onto his side and closes his eyes and falls asleep.

He awakens a short while later. It is early afternoon. The sun is showing a bit more clearly through the cloud-banks, like someone peering into the window of an abandoned house. The man sits up, rubbing his eyes. There are a more people out than before, but still not many. No one is near him.

He stands and stumbles slowly forward to the waves dashing gently on the shore. There is little wind. The water is cold and bracing as it sweeps over his feet and brushes his ankles. The man submerges himself, surfacing shortly thereafter, keeping afloat leisurely. It is still cold but much more comfortable now. He looks through the beads of water on his eyelashes at his surroundings. There is something floating a short distance away, a dark heavy mass that appears to be glowing faintly. He can't make out what it is. The man dives under the surface again, suspending himself in the water. He opens his eyes wide and closes them and propels his head above the waves. He breathes heavily and begins to wade back to shore. He stands and shakes himself off at the water's wavering edge before continuing on to his towel. He can now see that there is a seagull diligently going through his bag.

"Hey! Get out of here!" the man cries, waving his hands above his head and advancing sternly. The seagull squawks at him and ruffles it feathers. He is almost upon it when it honks disappointedly at him and flies away. The man inspects his belongings, and nothing seems to be missing. He looks into the sky at the retreating bird, who lands a stone's throw away, eyeing another person's icebox.

As the man dries himself off with his towel, he looks out at the ocean. There is a small sailboat midway between the shore and the horizon, with a single mast and sail, which was white with two yellow stripes. Two men wearing dark suits are standing in the sailboat; the upper half of their bodies was visible to him. He could not make out their faces, but they appeared to be conversing. The man finished drying himself and hung his towel on the umbrella.

When he looks back at the sailboat, it seems to be empty, the men are nowhere to be seen. He furrows his brow and sits down. He gets himself a beverage from his bag and turns back to the ocean. Now there are three men in dark suits standing in the sailboat. The new arrival is significantly larger than the other two.

"Hey! Get out of here!"

He turns to his right to see a middle-aged man flailing his arms as a seagull departs leering from his belongings. He resumes his vigil. There is now only one man in the boat. It strikes him that the boat had not moved the entire time he had been watching it, it remained as if anchored, though it did not appear to be, no line or rope was noticeable. The man remained standing in the boat. Slowly, a dense cloud withheld the sun, seeping everything in a dim, somewhat squalid light. He rubbed his eyes and the man was gone; the sailboat was now empty, moving faintly in the current of the waves, but rooted in place.

Time passed and eventually the man packed up his things and left the beach. The sailboat remained, empty still. Later that day, though no one was there to witness it, the sailboat lined up perfectly with the sun as it submerged into the horizon, bathing the world in night.

Silhouette   silhouette   silhouette   silhouette   Silhouette

the lovely

unscarred mind

Of what does the Earth speak when it trembles and bats its eyes? Surely there are etchings bigger than you or I. Surely the moon, with its tired noose and cold feet, must sweep a broad and dusty hand to her mouth, the woman looks down upon the whole of it, the whole into which all pieces fit, the hole which the sun and moon drape over their shoulder, hiding the woman's vagina, awakening the young man asleep by the riverside under a sword of fallen leaves, delicate as the tiger's tongue racing through each room of the palace, covered in snow and grease and blood, the only hand straight from the ground, the only hand straight from the gourd, as soon as the wind cries into the woman's mouth, "set your cloak into the night so I might be able to ride my automobile along the crumbling roads, ruinous and beautiful, that traverse, as the fingers of a tree, the entire body," but especially her brain, which the young man sinks his boots into in an effort to hold steady the wind against the battered sail of the slow boat to China; with a seventy foot long paddle and a loose hanging smile never dampened by the sudden yawn of the sun or the bright yell of the mouse, as winter changes, every one of his dreams, soon as the water rises and the water must be the way; which tongue fits better your mouth, that of the lark or that of the locomotive? The wind cries into the mouth of the cadaver only what he knows; must each arm's length of tightly-knit twine unravel and meet the sun, three bluebirds into the sun, while the young woman crawls forward twenty feet, each of her limbs gnarling and twitching as a mechanical witch's smile, pushing and pulling her forward toward a destination that the young man does not know but wishes to supersede, to unclothe the desirous face of this woman who is thousands of miles greater in mass than himself, who may be a giant or a dwarf depending on which wind blows; the summer knows, each length of grass is a woman covering her eyes as her escort disrobes himself and the gardener, thrown as two mice into the center of the Earth, a twirling huge knotted smile, a broken river on which no one sets their eyes if the storm of humankind shields their helium.

How often do you think about death?

Have you ever had serious injury or sickness?

When is your birthday?

When are your parents' birthdays?

The days do not come back, there is no renewal. Every day is new, every day is the same. They are not stacked up in a pile. They are in a briefcase, inside a flower. It is laughing. The past days are laughing, triumphant. The future is distraught. There is no today. Today is a rectangular prism in midair. It bursts! Today scattered everywhere. Today gathered up like cobwebs. Today casts the shadows of yesterday and tomorrow, yesterday casts the shadow of today. There is only tomorrow. Yesterday is a mummy. Tomorrow is eating a sandwich of fingers. Today and tomorrow make love and produce yesterday, yesterday makes love with today. The loud singing everywhere heard. The ear-canal is a single screw. Hearing is very upsetting, I don't want to hear it. I am wont to hear it. It is everywhere, crawling like insects made of sand. You know the ones I mean. Everything is making love, we should look away. Cast our eyes away, our eyes like sails. Our owls like sailboats, over and over. I believe it to be true. The fetters are silly. The tongue is silly. Skin is very serious and fragile, like a sick little girl. The ass is fickle. Distribute false dignitaries abroad. There are four trains. The mechanical mule train is unfettered. The blades of grass notwithstanding, let us counterfeit sand-dollars and give them out to the banks. The blind mechanical dawn lurching forward like a drunk, the vision of planets, sight, sighing. Sight makes its exit. Like a glass fountain, a fountain like a menagerie. A man like a menagerie. The collapse of planets infinitely far away is like a gentle breeze. The spaces heavy with fatigue. Emerald lion passing through a seashell: the ocean hid sand in the forest, the garden hid its pearl in a woman. If all the silverware were destroyed, then there would be no more silverware. The platypus of geometry brazenly unfolds its genitals, revelation revealing. Discolored carbuncle scabrous decibel.

Underneath our skin is a birdbath, we just assume we have organs and bones. We don't often peek beneath our surface. You and I share the same surface. The surfaces are shivering in the cold. Surface doesn't have a surface. Your surface is showing; mine is too! I always display my surface. I am the surface of my extension. I always display my height. I forfeit the surfaces. I have several surfaces in my mouth, they are combined to look like a peacock, a padlock. I counterfeit surfaces, I counterfeit peacocks. An unfinished peacock, a functioning peacock. The functioning of the peacock is severely exaggerated. You could read it in a book. You are reading a book, you are not reading a book. The extent of my hands is severely misappropriated. The fickle lobotomist. The lobotomist receives a lobotomy, the lobotomist receives a lobotomist. The optometrists receive a canary. The surface of the canary is identical to the surface of the bee. I've seen it on television. You've seen it on top of the television. A very small man lives inside the television, he is sleeping most of the time. Nobody has ever seen him. He doesn't have a name but we wouldn't know it. His name is Gasoline. He is in the habit of collecting picture-frames, he breaks them down to their atoms which he keeps inside the TV with him. He sleeps on the atoms of picture-frames. He abhors sneezing in all its forms. We shall all have our share of the pleasures. Should we share pleasures? Exchange pleasures? Advocate repeated tonsillectomies? I am a big promoter of shoeshiners. I do it all the time. You should never watch television with the sound on. I hope the act of shoe-shining doesn't disappear, committed a last and final time and never again. What a sad state of affairs. What a happy state of affairs. The state of the porcupines is waning. The armadillos are restless. The coral reefs have begun to perform their own lobotomies. The smells of fish. The birds build picture-frames instead of nests, they're so silly. Insects are very serious, they are frightening, they are very small compared to us. Compared to the buildings we make we are very small. Insects are not like buildings. The lives of insects are short, it's unfortunate. Perhaps to them their short lives seem like a lifetime. Time is very long like a sausage, like a penis. It has performed countless lobotomies. Time is performing these things, we think it's us. We are like living puppets. The grandiose verbatim, the wilting dead. The quarters are quarreling, we should intervene. What does it mean not to intervene? What is important? It happens very slowly, it happens very quickly. Imperceptibly slow, imperceptibly quick. The penis of time comes ineffectually. History is naked, history is clothed, let us make love to history. History is open, history is closed. History is an orifice, let us reproduce with history, let us make children continuously. Maps make great lingerie, to be worn in the advent of partial transmissions. The exhausted quantities cannot be obtained without further restriction, advice hairy lice device devise. The calk is very cute when administered feloniously astern.

How do you feel?

Let us share hands

purple circles rising from the horizon

inclusive, exclusive

explosion

Tolerance

empty noose

swinging in the stillness

of some forgotten afternoon

perfect in shadow

not dusty or frayed

blood-worn teardrops

like petals

spreading

what do men see

when they look at one another?

how many are still proud?

What are you proud of?

What's going on? What's happening?

How does it feel?

nothing everything

a fire stuck on repeat

a scream stuck in the air

buried on the surface of the egg

is a rectangular moon

it was dual

many moons ago

Furniture

time is the great mover

preparing space for the next

inhabitants

always in want

never satisfied

the furniture is never arranged

to its liking

what a mess

blind mechanical time

moving animal furniture

it is all motion and noise

and I the sole witness

but I am furniture

I witness the snow furniture

the tree furniture the street

the people furniture

arranging my thought furniture

reusing replacing

time shifting the furniture

to fit the space better

make it look more presentable

the furniture of sound

that falls on deaf ears

the furniture of appearance

that falls on blind eyes

touching furniture touching myself

touching nothing

yesterday's furniture is today's

the atom furniture

arranged to suit nobody

there is no further witness

there is no getting rid of furniture

there is no room for more

it is the same furniture as yesterday

and

tomorrow's furniture will not be different

from today's

just shifted around moved appropriated

we stumble dumbly over

the furniture and cry out

the furniture does not listen

there is no removing it from space

our furniture motivation

to seek out where there is

no furniture

where there is no furniture there is

no self

we are furniture requiring furniture to

sustain ourselves

furniture that hurts and abuses other furniture

that cares for and helps other furniture

we move ourselves day to day like

furniture

there is no getting rid of the furniture

in our mind

which is itself furniture

there is no motion no noise

just useless furniture

furniture is time

not static not flowing

there is no change left over

it is all balanced out

both sides are even

with our furniture eyes

our furniture sight

we witness nothing

taking place

nowhere

all the time

the atom furniture forming molecule furniture forming

cellular furniture forming material

furniture

forming earth furniture forming universe furniture

forming forming on and on and on

there is no limit to furniture

infinitely outward infinitely inward

no interior no exterior

it is just furniture

not one not many

not big not small

these words are it

and you reading is it also

space furniture order chaos

the furniture of absence

there is always vacancy

there is no vacancy

no absence no presence

furniture no-furniture

perfectly fitted

no space to admit anything more

anything less

there is no possessing

the furniture is thinking but we

pretend it is ourselves

the furniture is this thing

that thinks and does not think

that moves and does not move

that is presence and absence both

that is singular and plural

that is self and other

that is writing these words and

reading them

that is before and after

possession and change

fear and love

that is good and bad

the make-believe furniture of

our furniture imagination

near and far

we are somebody else's furniture

and our furniture minds

look sound smell taste feel

like the furniture that is

the world

that is life and death

time is furniture

and there is no host no guest

no resident no sojourner

no entrance no exit

no guards no prisoners

just somebody

else's furniture

what a beautiful ugly mess

there is an infinity in the finite

an eternity

stretching on endlessly

right before our eyes

unseen activity

quite spectacular

nothing unseen

enormous quivering mass

finite infinite

emptiness is behind everything
at the fore

a man swimming in the ocean

nothing is intrinsic
a swan at the window
everything is intrinsic
foul-weather porcupine relations
limitless domain
ceremony proposal
tribal penetration

time is motion
movement
stillness
time is like the giraffe
perpetually eating itself

over and over

undercover

wearing the disguise

of the world

of you and me and

the disingenuous steps from the ether

my piston is frequent

the stems are frequented

the stems are attached the stems are unattached

let us make children

out of bread

a fog of fingertips, eyelashes, birdbaths, bird brains

cigarette in water

smile = cough

DNA = jewelry

The distance between the stove and the court-martial is calculated by weaving several flowers in your engine. If the engine is lacerated, remove all the flowers and replace each one with a toad. If the engine is calculating, take a bite out of the third flower; whether or not you choose to swallow is up to you. Should you swallow a swallow, do not panic: merely accept the bright milk and translate your engine into Hebrew. Reward yourself with several lacerations. Remove all internal lacerations and put them in the bright milk. Can you hear me shouting? I am crouching low behind the trembling birdbath decorated with lizard-skins and harmonicas. You could mistake me for a brightly colored marble. The diameter of the marble is unfortunate. Insert the marble into the bright milk. If you can hear the swallows chirping, then it is too late. If the pigs are howling bright blue dolman, it is not early enough. Clearly not enough, not nearly enough. Your wrists are transparent and very loving. I keep my love rolled up like a rug on the roof of my mouth. The silk curtains are gangrenous. The Chinese doorman is undulating harshly in the soft pool. I have never had to choose between the birth of rocks and a frequent footstool. The clever toadstools are rocking reverently. The clever batch of cookies. The distance between the stove and the fishhook is calculated by screaming obscenities in the courthouse. Do this often. The languages are all false, the bacteria notwithstanding. Language is a mockery, silence is the true language. Love is having contrary or conflicting opinions in your mind at the same time. The sole functioning is responsible. The talking mind stops on its own. Parakeet explanation.

The ambitious bacteria is at the height of my uncle. It can see for miles and miles in no direction. Be careful not to listen to what it says. My uncle is a mute. The bacteria is shaped like my uncle. It says: "Put pressure on the building materials." Also: "Alleviate the gradual taxidermist under the eaves." There are no eaves, of course. Alleviate the mucus. There are several dolphins along the curves of the bacteria, barking with laughter and rain. Do not close your eyes tightly. Tightness is to be avoided, looseness is to be avoided. The avid avalanche blanches at the marble bacteria. Its curses are dolphins. Penguins are obscenities. The loose-fitting clothes are mistaken for a calendar, everyone is trying to mark the date in coughing ink. Is it more closely related to the tangible or intangible? Perhaps it has nothing to do with either. The goal is to touch everything at least twice. The goal is to reveal the stone sitting in your mind. The ball-bearings have been shed diligently. The pale grease is coughing out bright blue geese into the doldrum humidity, dolorous humility. Tabletop skeletons in a circle around the night bulb, copulating like chipmunks. Either/or is a delusion, both/all is not a delusion, no seclusion.

What do you prefer?

What is your favorite amount?

When is your favorite time of day?

How do you see things?

An exact bestiary is mimicking the courtship precisely. It's not unsettling. The walruses are unsettling, they're settling down to a meal of ivory anchors. The fountain takes its meal in the fountain. The fountain is eating the staircases, the sacrifices. The staircase alights on the fountain in green shadow. This is a common occurrence. The sedentary occultist is masturbating calmly, be careful not to frighten it. The maidservants are sent to the mill for repair. Overhead there are blue letters in the sky, they do not spell out anything. The sky is a map, a marketplace, a grindstone. It is very heavy under the blankets. So many blankets! So much fighting! An army is like the curled tail of a sleeping cat beside the fountain like a fireplace, an apple. The guns are shaped like pinwheels aperture.

The Arabian nights are in a bottle overturned on the stairs, in the fountain, glittering like teeth in the eye. The castrated illusion is gathering steam. Weeping willow overturned on my heart, steaming. Walk around my heart hundreds of times. A noose is revealed on the goose, gently. Turn over my heart, heated on both sides. Place both stems on my heart and count the dice, one two three four red clean willow open soldier sixteen eight calibration. Truncated operations casually defecating. Defecating triumphantly on the spores. The spores are sore with rain and weeping willows. The numbers are incompatible. Bthftyvv sdgi uhik bjsrgio ivdbfbv vgidrgih wwpef pofwu efhj sdffjfjfsiie hwef wgv hfsiefsief hffjfjfjfjfjf f. Truncated defecation on the pores of ice. You should clean the spores, they're getting awfully flagrant. The ruinous fragrance. The ruined bedclothes. The ruins like bedclothes overturned on my heartbeat, hunted fragrance haunted. Truncated gestation heating up nicely. The gesticulating defecation.

I love when you wear the green garland of red umbrellas. The vast penumbra. I love when the night is dressed in inside-out nightingales. The shards of the penumbra are defecating lackadaisically over the hillocks and hiccups. Can you retrace your steps? The wicked wrinkled ankles are standing in a line. Each one is hiccuping masochistically. It is difficult to look at them. More difficult than the underwater clowns, less difficult than the blood of seagulls. The blood of clothespins is very difficult. My teeth are blood. My blood is octagonal. The nonagons are loose-fitting, hand-drawn, diffidently animated. The difficult animals collapsed on the septuagenarian, coiled. The antiques are frantic, but only when you're not looking. It's okay. I only breathe out, it is advised never to breathe in. Always stand on one leg. Twice on Saturday. And again under the sun. When you are on the son, it is advised to only breathe in. Do not breathe out. Be always submerged in water or oil or lenses. The vast tentacles are my favorite. Twice on Tuesday. Shouting lugubriously abroad. A broad toad on the board, precariously shimmering. Shouting lugubriously abroad. The barnacles must be shot. The youth should be confined to gardens with iron fences like batting eyelashes. Try to guess my age, you could count it on one hand. Assuming, of course, that you have hands. The stalwart gynecologist embroidered on the vast newsreel like a figurine with thirteen tentacles. Clench the mourning dew in your shouting fist. The wall is a bridge. Hear the indefinable noises. The instant point of departure is a magnolia blossom on your left. I can hear children all the time. The swift elevation, halted elevator, the swift elation. The acorn fetishist was greatly renewed, mouths agape aghast.

   The elaborate eucharist, trains like rainfall. Taxation with or without condensation, vexation textile. Tactile: a stone's throw-pillow one thousand times. Where is time? It has made its exit lugubriously. The granulated tax-payers are shimmering on their hinges.

fish = fist

flight = height

a volume of volume = ragged flower of volume

I realized to my astonishment that these words are already past, when you read them they are not current. You reading them only sheds light on them. You are present, I am not present. They are not new even as I write them. They are not current. They are only current in my mind, and become immediately frozen when written. They are fleeting, and if not writ down they would vanish like tears or footprints in the sand. Writing is an attempt to translate the mind, the world. Writing is etching in stone, it is object. In my mind it is subject. Object is still, subject is moving. Perhaps they are both still and the mind is object. Or both subject, flowing. Writing does not change. It is still. Thought is changing clothes perpetually. The boundaries are inflated. The infant is inflated like a grasshopper. The moon's tears are grasshoppers. It is very beautiful. Ants are beautiful, they all work together. It's lovely to watch. Watching ants is like watching owls. You have these thoughts, too. The words 'two owl' look like a palindrome. A ghost among pajamas, the fullest season. Nothing is current, nothing present. It is the absence of a present. Opening up the presents, all at once. This is my present to you. My present to your present. You thinking these words, these images, these symbols gives them life, reality. True and false are made of the same material, they are from the same source, they inhabit the same space. The transparent lobotomists all in a room together like cows. Do not sound the alarm. Sound one hundred alarms, sequentially. I love when people applaud in the streets, on the rooftops, in the trees. I think we should clap our hands whenever we're outside. Or rather, inside. We should be absolutely silent when outside. It is an absolute necessity. We should mimic the silence. What is the absence of noise? Is it an object? Is it subject? I'm asking you and me. The courtship of doves caught in the candlelight. An absence of proctologists, a fullness of bananas. Is sound a single thing, or is it manifold? Are there many silences?

Silence is a hose, a nostril. Two boats, a coat. I have silence in the fibers of my shirt. Have you wondered if I was clothed or naked? I am clothed, I assure you. While I write this I am riding on a horse, wading through an undisclosed seashell. It's very cold. Doves the size of clouds make love with the blue powder. A clock-tower is produced three weeks later, covered in kisses and eye-prints. The red powder is in the clouds heavy with snow. Snow is associated with kisses, rhinoceroses. Armadillos and rhinoceroses are siblings. You could read it in the stars. The technology flying saucers, the thought, poignant processes. The saucers are playing like rhinoceroses. We should work toward preserving rhinoceroses and flying saucers. The almanac is frozen in red ice. The nettles are frozen in paint, a streetlamp comes on like ejaculation. Light is very smooth like a piston, like a stamen. Light is very loud. Sound is silent, sound doesn't make any sound. Silence is the sound that sound produces. You told me that the other day. Sound and silence are nothing. We were standing knee-high in water at the supermarket. The lobsters had escaped, they were eating all the food. The custodians were listless. The lobsters had become huge so we dived into the water and resurfaced out of the face of the clock in the aviary. I was coughing listlessly. You threw your hands into the condor. It was smiling and coughing. The canyon was quite pleasant.

I love botanists; we should all become botanists. That would not please the botanists, I'm sure. The botanists are very long and made of suede. There are horses on their tongues, it's partly disgusting. I don't imagine suede botanists are very charming, not like quadrilateral fawns, deer are very charming. Anchors are very charming, confident, dynamic. Your eyes like frozen eruptions, the halted explosion of distant planets. These words are my eyes. Touch my eyes with your fingers. Put your toes in yogurt. It's all too much, the birdcages are upset. Birds are antiques, you should take a closer look. Silence is antique, sound is antique. Things in the future are antiques, everything is an antique. Everything is new, there is no past. It could be both ways. It's not up to me. What is power? What is powder? The antique powder on the powerful seashells. Sound is powder, silence is snow. What is now? Is it then? Not yet? We just assume the universe is very old. Existence is not old, there is no past existence. It is all being produced right now, there is no production, it's already produced. Is it one or many? The horse stomps its hoof in response. The sound is muffled, the sound is fettered, the sound is erect. The wild horses are fettered and the pigeons are fettered. Let me open the door for you.

The ships are sinking off the coast. It looks like a jungle. The huge paper boats are sinking soundlessly. The albatrosses the size of large green ships are sinking into the water. Sinking into water is like the motion of escalators. The primate is sinking into the surface, seeping through the air. Each ship has its own cargo of spiral staircases, cacti, dogs, billiard-balls, icicles, soot, wooden dolls. All the money is steaming. The faucets are sinking, the engines are sinking, the stalks are sinking. Into what? All the giraffes are steaming, all the giraffes are sinking. Your steam-engine imagination, my steaming imagination. The cellular litigation. The stellar star light. Moonlight. Beast light, breast light. The light light. Phenomenal light, nominal light. Loving lighthouse. The lighthouse is a ghost. Don't take it too lightly.

What is the weight of the image of men in suits busy inside the rooms of tall buildings, working with papers, dealing in a wide range of affairs? What is the ideal image? Is photography true? Are we to believe the photographs? Just because it is on television doesn't make it true. I believe everything, I don't believe anything. Must we make a choice? Who's choosing? Get to know your neighbors. No body is isolated like an icicle. Everything is isolated, nothing is isolated. Icicles don't exist. Icicles aren't isolated, isolation is an icicle. The solutions are fallacies. There is no solution, there is no problem. The problem of the icicles has plagued me of late. The optometrists have flown away on brass wings and are dozing in the treetops like clocks. Ducks are very appealing. They like to be in water even when it is cold. Every time ducks go underwater they are trying to drown themselves; they always fail. It doesn't bother them in the least. Ducks are like repentant criminals, former junkies, ex-alcoholics. Their eyes are clothespins. The ducks do not have a language. Stones are a language. Do you think that the world is God's language? Maybe not, maybe so. There is no speculating, it's all very apparent. The ducks are apparent, my parents are apparent. Fiendish homeostasis across the globes. It is not always night, it is always night, there is no day, it is just one day. Two days. Two days over and over: what a bore! What a chore! What a whore! The day is a sore, time is a wound, we are a gradual healing of the great wound. Someday it will be healed, no matter how hard we try. There is no wound, there is no wounding, no healing. The winding wound is apparently fixated. Courageous fixation, vexation. Vulpine volume vulture, euphoric distance. Time is hesitant, whales are hesitant, tomorrow is hesitant and today. Yesterday is not hesitant. The windmill has suddenly ceased to exist, ceased to exit. The exit exists vehemently. What is the universe's intention? Is our will the will of the universe? Who is at the helm? It appears to be nobody, a shadow cast by nothing. The vibrant pustules alight. What color are bats? The color of bats is excruciating, the violent postulate violet.

The optometrist says:

"Who is it

that sees his reflection in the trees and rivers

in the clouds and animals

in the mountains and every person?

He has no face

and no name

he does not move

but goes everywhere

Can you grasp the moon without looking at it

without touching it

without smelling it or tasting

without hearing?

What are you grasping? Who is grasping?

Words drift away like dust like thoughts

like all things."

It is getting further away, it is coming closer together. The sea-anemones are conforming to the artichokes, the unbroken primates like throngs of time. The uniformity of anemones is misleading, the sea-lions like artichokes on the currency of time. The enormous immediacy of storks in the vicinity, the storks unhinge their facets and let fall the gliders. The enormous intimacy. Counter-production. The sartorial equinox is burrowing into the insect, it is furrowing its brow like an insect, the insects have all resigned, they did not give two weeks notice. The caravan is the employer of insects and escapades, the caravan frozen in tan ice. The silver ice of glowworms and eels like mouths across vapid aridity. Space-apes of tomorrow in long suspenders, suspended motion of coarse arguments all over the day like vomit or pistons, the days like urine or formaldehyde. The gradual revealing of the pistons, of the stamens. The statements are obvious, the stalemate is an immense vaccination. Let us hope that the señoritas do not become incinerated. The prismatic basilisk swimming in feelings like shit and piss, flaccid chimera of practical experimentation. Moonless egg dipped in iron water. Depraved saints upside-down and furious, the priest of ointments.

The dysfunctional funnel has become activated, allowing access to the screens; there are screens all around like fields, the screen of fields. The screaming charley-horse, the eloquent char-house, ambrosia all over again. Did you not glimpse the field of particles cross-examining the pulpit? The limited conformity is agile and looping. The antelopes elope with the slopes of pearl and jasmine. It's not too late, it is too late. The evening ascends viscously. The functional funnel is embroidered on the slops, making cuts all over. The cyclops is a disdainful isotope, two three. Is and is not play together like amulets, perfume of choicest borderlines. Life is like granulated antelopes. Life is like this, life is like that. Life is a game, life is like a movie or play; life is not a game, life is not like a movie or play. The past does not change. Or does it? Where is it? It's right here, it's right there. The past is right now. The world is an etching in stone, an etching in nothing. Accelerated declamation. There is no replacement antidote, the corpuscles bristle.

What is your motivation?

Do you have any quantities? How do you treat them?

What are the similarities between animals and human trapdoors?

The Ritual of Movements and Sources takes place in two ovals inside the diaphanous ritual. The first phase is performed when all the windows of the interior and exterior temples are in red ice with the full blazing spider. The second phosphorescence is performed when all the windows of the interior and exterior vegetation are in alignment with the full blazing colloquialism. The Ritual takes place whenever it is raining. The participants wait squirming until they are called into the foam, which could be days or lemurs. They receive sustenance from red and silver octagonal nodules that float out from the jungle and burst upon their pustules. The sources are exchanged politely from a distance. All the places have been taken, all the places have been taken for granted. It has been calculated indefinitely.

I love the hugest mummy gradually clandestine. The mothers are wet silk, damp porticoes, portfolios. The fathers have been duplicated, implicated in the darkest porticoes. The clandestine movements of tabletop mummies in a row. The mummy in the fountain is wearing thin, wearing thick harnesses of upholstered lobotomies. The blue hearts are actualized frequently in cold harnesses, the horses wear the stale harnesses of the sun in green hearts like green sand. The green heart is a blue lobotomy, sequestered casually. The storm-clouds are pooling their resources, are pooling their sources. The sources pulled apart at the seams. The sources pulled apart at the sources. Bite into the storm-cloud like you would an apple, it tastes very affluent. The affluent pustules are misappropriated carefully; indeed, the pustules are very eloquent like falling leaves, the cataracts are very eloquent like balloons.

The moist amulets are foreboding, the moist amulets are foreclosing on the pustules organized like bananas covered in snow. The top of the curve is a bounty, a boundless breast of gold milk and crying primates shedding their fish-scales. The primates are hiding inside of a breast, the light coming from the stems is flippant. The sequestered equestrian is unbound, coiled, ghastly. The pedestrians are afoot, are abreast of the mountain, are a breast of the whale. It is coughing into the envelope. The equestrian languid with stars, laden with white telescopes, antelopes, furnishings. The pine tree in the snow bustling with amulets and dislocated bones, the bones of sheep and grass. The pedestrian catheter is elongated stringently and lies heavy with sweat and grain. War is very colorful and likes to bite the tadpoles. War is naked and embarrassed, hiding behind the lamppost. War is humiliating. Globs of furniture sticking to the flagpoles. It is inherent, communicating like melting candle wax, pyrrhic tenacity. It's hard to ignore.

Change is a prison, let us seek the things that do not change. The thing that does not change. Change is a piston, freedom is inescapable. Let us do away with freedom and bondage, let us do away with the mind. Let us seek the things that are not mind, the thing that is not mind. The mind is a prison, the mind is a prism, the mind is a piston, the mind is a clothespin. The mind is freedom. There is no freedom, no slavery, freedom and slavery are in the mind. Let's change our mind, let's duplicate the mind. Let's mimic the mind carefully. The things that are not alive are alive, everything is alive. Philip K Dick said that "information is alive." There is, of course, no such thing as information. We are information, we are in formation. Information is a machine, a monster. Sublimate infrastructure for total recollection, incompetent subterfuge incomplete subterfuge fantastic. Information and understanding are exclusively in the mind. The world is a deception, the world is not a deception; the word is a deception, the word is not a deception. There is no deception, everything is a deception. The world is not in formation. Where did the idea of deception originate? Antelopes are a deception, the antelope has a thousand clothespins in its uterus. This is the ideal state of things, this is not the ideal star of things. Preference is a deception, the self is a deception. What is the goal of discernment? To count the black fish that suck the pollen from the eucharist. It is ideal to always have large amounts of pollen on your eyeballs. Eyeballs are glowworms. What is the goal of diameter? Soak up the pollen with the vast newsreel. Newspapers should be written in pollen, not ink. Ink is a deception. Cranberries are a deception, they are actually rutabagas in their underclothes. Yesterday is a deception, tomorrow is a deception and today. Today is an antelope. Yesterday has new clothes made of pollen. The antiquated periphery. There is no distraction, no concentration. Rhetoric mouthwash falling teeth drooling spaghetti pasta malfunction nutrition expectation, rheumy potsticker eye gourd fellatio motto.

The submarine on the moon is a drawbridge. It is undulating like a violent saloon. All the mosquitos have little flowers instead of proboscises. Turning the corner and gone out of sight. Inside the submarine is a game of lawn decor and polyamorous thimbles, fish-tails. The lunar piston swaggering softly. The moon inside the submarine is looking under all the rugs, it is the captain. It is looking for the lost smiles. They are not under the rugs, in the cupboards, behind the fences, or on top of the chandelier. Every smile is a bale of hay, as the saying goes. The sayings head west. The western head is coiled like smoke, vapor. The eastern head has its mouth full of grasshoppers, it is always chewing. The same thing occurred long ago, before the blue medallions. Let us put our heads together, it sounds like the flesh of western icicles. The western head belches, it is the submarine on the sun. It is very inspiring. What effects the causes? Is it one or many? Every smile is a blade of red grass. The burned-down barn looks like an aquarium. My own private terrarium, the public terrarium, the public tantrum. The eastern head belches only in its mind. The manifold aquariums. There is only one aquarium and its shoes are untied, are undulating. The promiscuous proboscis has a startling laceration on its eye. The single eye looks like a cyclops, a cyclopean menagerie. The gaunt menagerie. The eye-sockets like electrical outlets, outlet store preposition. The celestial totem, the celestial sockets. An illegible antelope persecutes the legality hitherto snowman angelic circumference deeming. Expedient experience referential. The answers are in the dictionary the naked encyclopedic ribbon. Going down slow. Nincompoop compartment to assuage the prevailing lozenges.

Briefly, a vision of multiple totalities, a bouquet of totalities like a confused mind, like multiple minds. It exudes the scent of jasmine across the spaces. Space is not one, not many. There is no multiplicity, no singularity. Multiple singularities, a single multiplicity. The etchings in stone by an unknown author. The dizzying heights are an extrapolation of fragrances. Become very tall and step on yourself. Trailing mud on the self. The self is a bell that smells of jasmine. The mind is a bell. The mind is a bellows. The straw dogs like bellowing quicksand, aforementioned affidavit. The confusion of spaces, illusion of vacancy. Vacancy is not a deception, vacancy is the only deception. Occupation is desertion. The vast discrepancy. The illiteracy of crepes. Arrows flung in all directions: will they ever reach their mark? What is the consensus? Space is infinitely heavy, infinitely weightless; space weighs as much as sixteen armadillos. Space shares the weight of snow. They are both very colorful and shake hands exuberantly. Sometimes it is polite to watch, sometime it is impolite to wash. Silverware is impolite. The polite policemen wearing wristwatches as heavy as space. They drag their wrists along the ground, stirring up dust and thorns. The antelopes like laughter, the rain like a shout. The immobile policemen like swollen vacancies. The swollen pollen like testicles. The cyclops' testicles are in a race against time to the death, to the depths, to repay the debts. Time flies when you're peeling back the surface of the nuns. The anthropomorphic shout, the amphibious shout, the darling shout. Replace the shark with a cactus. Let us remove all the mouths, they are revolting.

Grimacing apothecary, casual apothecary, moribund. The frozen capillaries are electricity, sunspots. The sun black with white dots, white with black stripes. The sunspots are dysentery, flagpoles. The dysentery is breathing heavily like a maraca. Oil is the main producer of sound and employs the lampshades thoroughly. Insert all necessary perimeters, centimeters, millipedes, dysentery dignitaries. Collapsable flagship complete with retractible flag, gorilla. The gorillas are retracting, are replacing their steps, their hoof-prints like heartbeats around the corner of the room. The moon is a cold colorless room, the moon is a silver moon. The moon has retractible blades like hair, sunspots. The fragrant moon, the vanguard moon, close-quarters. Disassemble your mouth and put it back together in the shape of the green moon. Glass clothing fading from view. The disseminated seminary is trout semen. Elastic coughing wineglass with no module. A big noise big nose. Everlasting dripping water echoing across the spaces. The ocean is a mouth, the arm is a trenchant wrench. Cacophonous sunspots heralding the new fawn. The agile seminary is laughing at standing ankle-deep in water or mucus. All the secrets are mucus. Necessary logistics, hot logic, topical orgy cerebellum. All orchestras are enemies, all enemies are orchestras. Memory is an orchestra and an orca whale. Orchestras and orca whales are illustrations running back and forth like time across the room. The capillaries are frozen orchestras. Same difference, different difference. Causal deference orchestrated. The vast face silently effaced by the dawn. It doesn't make any difference, it makes all the difference in the world. The morbidly obese production of differences and similarities. Vast penetration of surfaces, quiet inebriation of depths, unexplored volume. A wide white handkerchief dazzling spectacle. Vile defiance of surfaces. The vial of golden matchsticks is twice as important, twice as long. The amoebas are psychotic in the white barn. Silken grimace of the aviaries white brine. There are dromedaries in the spherical estuary, in the frowning pulpit. Marriage of spaces. Rocket-car chortling down the highway, spilling a bunch of chickens onto the lumpy road, veil of chickens rudiment. The flaming pulpit boiled alive three times, the paw-prints boiled alive in their stalks.

3 = platypus

19 = sloping

partner = 112

dark hair coming out of the mind

a frightful apparition

like a rancid dove

like black stones coming out of the mind

from the ephemeral depths

glittering like jewels

or snowflakes

The glazed world is singed. The peculiar world is opening wide its mouth and anus to admit the sullen bluebirds covered in snow. Grimacing apothecary swollen with estuaries. Diligent headrests are loading and unloading only. The feeling of cold similarities. The matchsticks bloom in the eye like a lily, like matchsticks. Diligent headdresses loading and unloading only.

What occupies your mind? What does your mind occupy?

The sole inhabitant of my mind is a red church whose skin is made of bells. When I nod it rattles inside my brain like a rattlesnake. When I tilt my head to the right I can hear the long languid screaming of misfortunes. When I balance a pyramid on the tip of my eyelashes a canary emerges unscathed. The tip of my eyes is tipped over on its side, the tip of my birds is upturned on the mummy. The parenthetical wastes are an enormous operation. Never cooperate, always burst at the seams. The dry height of the water. The bells are blowing their noises, the hypodermic discussions notwithstanding. Not without standing! Standing room only capable of explosion. The sole tenant of my mind is an elephant shaped like a waterfall. Soul tenement of the mind. The vast cages sound like bells. The intimate differentiation, vast intimacy, vast infancy, corrugated infantry. Imitate the immediate function. The immediate cornucopia is transparent, the intermediary cornucopia is copulating reverently. Do not upset the burrowing library or the furrowing cornucopia. The billowing librarian is too exquisite. Opulent ornithology. I halfheartedly disagree with tautology. The amateur topography is startling. The bowling-pins are frustrated with ecstasy the bowling-ball is a mute, ball and hand in the hamper, hamster-wheel of time skimming the ledges and ledgers. Skin is sufficient. It is like the elongated elephants standing on azure coffins like shark fins. The sinks are lactating grease, goddess with a thousand teats. What a treat! A crowd of esophaguses like ambulances in shambles. It's very stimulating. The feeling is mutual, death is a small fishing village. Somnambulist in shambles. It is very distraughtening. You are the result of your effort. Do you agree? Do you know what I think? The void is a tempest, the tempest is voided. Let us be self-effacing. The mind is not viscera. H.P. Lovecraft once wrote: "Illusion is the One Reality, and that Substance is the Great Impostor." What is your inclination? The viscera is ephemeral, the viscera of my youth.

   By the bedside, hedges grow like dandelions, concubine of the forest swinging long strides and squirming bees feather the horn-blow that seeks a nest in the bosom of the sow, last but not least a chair and a bat with dove's wings twofold; the chest of drawers blew out telephone cords like swine, like smoke-rings by the evening fire, pale danced lightly mahogany twilight earthbound, bound to the Earth almost in the silhouette of a camel or tortoise, past the ceiling fan with one leg loose, so that the wires coursing with electricity caught at the horse's foot and undressed the umbrella slightly tomorrow forgone bystander to the curious left hook of the corset, candelabra, to the curious bookshelf with velvet pattern coat of arms danced slowly at

the floorboards foot step tulip by the rose tomorrow, of tomorrow with
the coiled skeleton fingers neatly by the row, streetlamp top-shelf
almost cornered the fingers and slipped a goose-leg emerald by the
cauliflower coven-mitt suspended by the loose and shivering leaves
and twigs and grasshoppers and storms eager to make their arrival at
the glass horse wrapped up in corners by the ceiling of several
diamonds and vagabonds coursing through the roots of the piano,
whose player is covered in seahorses and four-leaf clovers, by bye bye
bye by and bye. Single row of iron bird curtains switched their feathers
to diamond glass and the drinking water to the yesterday's
newspapers' flower petals, petal dancer tears fetal, along the taut curve
of unknown material, slightly windblown, lost by the cellar door
opening and closing at the sneezing produced and distributed along the
ceiling kiosks, ever watchful of those deities dressed in a horse
costume, the wooden hose delivered to Troy hangs in the mouth of a
bird swimming at the end of a vine dangling in the air madly,

a skipped stone bears no fruit,

a stairway can be overturned, a flag waving at the eye of the pole suits
the two men beneath it with the thirty-five colors of the two lamps that
are held by the man with a suit and tie emerging from his eye or his
mouth, depending on whether the day is Tuesday or whether the
sunlight can be cast to the tips of the woman's eyelashes as moonlight,
feint, horse clover and the boat by the scenic breeze, ridden past sweet
blue and vomiting garlic gloves like handkerchiefs, peddles the boat
near a house of ill-repute, a house is only as good as its serf, swamp
water by the curling fireside and the coiled tulips by the foot of the
tooth and nail. Roses rolled and the titan raised the roof of his house to
make room for his bellow, scarlet bluebird courses through the wires
of the tree by the bay sweeping and lovely, of sorts, the crooked
window-frame like a picture of a sailboat across the sky, while the

lighthouse lifts its dress to reveal in between its legs the lighthouse-keeper clutching a lightbulb and a miniature bull or steer, the lighthouse-keeper clutching a lightbulb as if it were a woman and clutching a lamp as if it were a flower or the bird of a bird, the wing fashioned to the likeness of a horse, the wing of the horse, a swarm of bees fashions itself in the likeness of a man; the highest honor is to be left for deaf by the king as the fingers of ice grasp the bramble and thorns that climb up into the chimney and the wind instruments need to be cleared, the fire is at the top of the chimney and the curling smoke is a manta-ray at the foot of the bed; holy smokes, forest of the bed, an armchair and a rocking-chair seahorse side by side at the curve of the arm the bend of the ocean the sweep knights riding green across the blackened sky holy smokes a snake and a stingray two wasps exploding in ice; head towards the coat, rising above the treetops where blue and red fish find their gills and treasure is heaped swinging at the heels the hermit's brain scattered like footfalls in the desert; an eye leaps from the sun, roses bowled and bow-tie necktie laced, an eye leaps from the sun into the oceans of earth, a single golden beetle teardrop is caught on a star, a star reflecting the light from the high-heels and necklaces of Jupiter, pools and swans, the star unfurls and reveals itself to be a long salamander gathered at the heels, the swans, feel, long salamander with many arrows stuck in its rear leg, the front left leg egg is a bow and hanging from the tip of its tongue is a chandelier, behind the trees a cold arm skeleton from limb to limb harvests chairs, windows with stained glass, tables elegant and ivory foothill footstools from the ears and ankles of juniper crawling with lizards and piano-stools, the long salamander lays down on a bench and the tear falls from its tail through the gears of an old rock into the hat of the woman, dressed for an imaginary occasion, the tear becomes a feather, when the woman, on whose coattails and tall tales and writhing tails stand the young man, dressed as a chest of drawers, and the whale, frozen in ice with a purple candle burning at the peak of its frozen snout, lawyers and phalluses and gold doubloons crawl out of the frozen blow-hole, blow whole, when the woman arrives at the ballroom, the men are all soldiers and the women are dressed to resemble pearls and are very beautiful; the waiters, members of the orchestra and barmen are all clams, oysters and blazing oil-lamps, hollering through the curtain or dress, hollering through the open window and the moon through a closed window, or flowing gown, is the mother of pearl, gesundheit blue diamonds, at the curious circus umbrella, dancing and wheezing, ballroom water laid by the arm coiled by the line where the ocean and fog and strands make love, tripodal mathematicians aggravated believer restoration.

Straw-colored long-man near the horse's clover of the wolverine twist footed alligator swamp underwater carousel, trampled wind when the rose is a windmill and the antennas are doused in fire water, last drink of water, by the barn door the woman's nose a spiderweb rose like a lilac to greet the ceiling of the sky which is the air in your nostrils drip like fingertips along the mosquito flower pedal to wring out the autumn by the wind's heels, the moon's necktie hung like a drowned man by the corner of the eye, and swim swung loose was the wind around the moon's neck glowing lightning swallow storm fly at the alligator underbelly, that sleepy town crept past the hermit and settled by the mountain where the bees float in the same likeness as wine, windmill tick bloated pointed-head curved fetus tips and swing side to side; underwater kumquat silo silken sliver glistens at the edge of the silver river, silver boat river danced as flames curling the garden the mountain retracts and howls to resemble the crow, mewling and crawling glistening at the metal of the dandelioness whose center is the sun or moon depending on the wingspan of the bird composed of stars and broken sea-glass at the ocean pass lying driftwood dog leaped and hung midair like the frozen leaf of a hand in resignation swatting a fly or spider.

Does life seem long to you, or short?

Would you make a deal with the Devil?

Are you coming or going?

Does the ointment who cries softly at the dinosaur's wing, who has birds to sing, who runs under the red come around dawn a sapphire fox with emerald drawn at her lips, cries into the waterfall a blue hornet a morning dove, who yearns for the forest from each tree hangs a winter bell, the sun scope cock ran darts and circles a sandbox underneath, cries at the coil of bees and ghosts who tie their dawn like shoelaces and furnace where the wind grows, monster crows the dinosaur with windswept heels dances toward the little girl's wing, who cries at the night and sleeps at the gates of day, the moonlight is but sunlight in the corner of her eye, shadows of dairy-cows and run down lowside of the fire gone road loses its necklace of the woman's intestines where she sleeps garden pearls, the doorknob turns and the beggar learns that each sunset is a child's wing, the girl crying sets the beggar aflame with sobs and caught in the hoof of a frightened bee the girl cries and screams into the breast of the woman she does not know, the ghost learns about fire from the sapphire and the emerald runs its fish intestines around in knots whilst the crocodile starts at the sound of any crow or morning glow. Crooked finger of lilac eye bright and peeling at the morning song, bird flight up the deck of stairs spiral and coiled around the nearest tree branch stingray at sunset moon snow, pair of hands pile of saliva-glands swings down into the forest of her intestines at the hour when the sun mimics the coattails of the bullfrog dressed in glow diamond white, the man crosses his eyes and reappears inside of her see-saw spinal fjord, where oceans of gore and blood and crystal insides flit about the ballroom of her ribcage, a bear in a birdcage sings a deluxe too, rope at dawn, sinking into the sand the whale imagines what the birth of the woman was like, how many doctors were horses, how many nurses where invisible or naked, the amount of waves that crash softly on the leech, the girls in irony white, the forest blue in one thousand boys' eyes as clear as a winter bell, the sea shaped the whale's passion into a woman's foam and swung the door off its coat and onto the floor where the baby was swallowed by life, at the foot of the call of the wild blue yonder, the see-saw set against the sun was one thousand bees clapping hands at the performance of the woman's vagina, which was now a lotus flower white as the golden sun.

There is a lake in the woman's heart hanging from the trees, she grows her thoughts in moonbeams, she collects, wanton rumpus ablution, her thought is the sun's ray, drifting like sand-dunes across the green labyrinth, the sun pours its fingers into the cup of rain outstretched before the temple, junk feathers sink from the tree's fingers against black glass sand stones, the winter bell a dark forest falls among the woman's skeleton, reflections glint from the lake's surface rippling expanding labyrinthine where the young man finds a dove in the inside-out water, a dolphin with water glistening on its skin skull skulking like dandelion urinary petals, the lion has found its skeleton key mortar and pestle and the door of night opens onto the lake in the woman's heart caught in the sand of the vast oceans of emerald mystery, the phantoms leap from the water and disappear before any eye may fully apprehend them, tarantula down the legs of the stairs. The futility of words, images, lawnmowers, the futility of skeletons, action, the feudal activity lawnmowers, pile of salvation ikonography turnstiles.

How often do you watch water boil?

Have you ever seen ice form?

The titans of industry have golden balloons, the captains of industry are distended. They are reclining in the meadow like a dream with savage apostrophes. The intricate stalks positioned apropos further development clemency, apropos periphery sustaining. The decals have lost their lobes remotely. Fate takes a short break, is discontinuous. Fate has polio. Polio is a bird in an elevator full of water. The eyes at the treetops are singed, lumpy treetop mummies filing jointly. Disingenuous corpuscles of rapid anatomy. I do not believe the horse's whinny. And neither should you. It is collapsable under the matchbook. Sawdust on the horse's eyelashes. Installation of the incredulous crucible, fastidious organism. The organisms are remote. I don't think I would live in the swamp, the horses there have very long legs, as tall as the trees. It is always snowing insects. Phenomena are cordial, leprous. Gravity takes a short nap, gravity is good friends with the sun. Icicles are the source of gravity. Ask the scientists. Bake a scientist for thirty seconds before scooping soundlessly. Undermine the twitching catapults. It is very itchy. Itching is of utmost importance. We must itch the surfaces. The trees are very itchy in the snow, the leopard is very itchy in the cold iguana. The mind can only itch itself. Itching is the source of pinwheels. Itching depends on the fragrance of locomotives. Rhinoceros sinking into the mind. The sink full of dirty itches. Abusive awareness claustrophobia diarrhea; legitimate circumstance.

The crying animals should be held in your arms. The laughing animals are hidden like tears. If you pinch me I'll rub the red elevator. The sand is like smoke. Pouring smoke out of both eyes, out of both icicles. Airplanes are imaginary, a collective hallucination. The sockets are boiling over again. A collection of hallucinations like playing-cards spilled across the stairs. The weightless teacher is smothered in colonoscopies every red moon. The provinces are alighting, the air is a flame. The air is a wooden bell twenty hands long. I wish existence was one continuous surface with no distinctions. Grey and brown in color. Then life would be worth something. The daffodils are criminals, breadcrumbs on the toilet. Keep your oysters in the toilet. Inflate them only in the evenings. Put your cellphone in the toilet. I have only two oysters, one is a lamp and the other is a chromosome. Vanquished chromosomes in the milk and dust. The chromosomes have been vandalized gently. The wastes of space, space's excrement. Matter is unaffordable. The washing-machine's excrement is flourishing gorgeously. Place your valuables underneath the trashcan. Sever your lawnmowers. The best hiding place is underneath the snow, the place that snow occupies. Snow is the best hiding place. The hiding places are effervescent and comely. Snow is the best hiding mitochondria. Limpid fixtures descending, distending. I believe you when you tell me that I am protein and water. It has red smoke, red wings, flowering teeth.

I am a new tube of toothpaste twice removed. Existence is a clenched fist, a coiled fish, the universe is a clenched anus. I am a sad umbrella recently impeached. What are you? Sometimes you are a cloud of apples, recently exposed, bellowing softly. For optimal capacity use two different types of soap. Never use soap or gnostic gills. For formal capacity exude the bright milk. The evidence is scattered all over the spaces. The spaces are soapy excrement. The pyramid is approximately a soapy funnel under the garland, under the glands. A beautiful life-size feather the shape of amnesia. The putrid puppies rabid with anchovies, the massive anchovies swollen with pride. The massive jeweled lion looks like a peacock's coccyx.

What say you?

How do you like to do things?

How do you impact the world around you?

What is your height?

The library is clothed in jewels and ivory ivy. Fecal matter monies. The aquatic domicile is laboring nicely in the breeze. The reptilian rapture responsible for the production of ivory ivy is under new curtains that are not apparent. The husks are accumulating, acclimating to improper sheathes. The quantities are accumulating bright noises. Something must be done about it. Cessation of opulent noses, tertiary septum. Soiled likenesses. The well-oiled machine is separately exaggerated for the ages. Do not cross the oiled lines, the oiled times. A violent fixture engages the warmth. Do not articulate the counterclockwise crows. I will allow the curtains to fall drastically. What do you allow? Are you allowing the feathered hemoglobin its adamant gesturing? I wouldn't like to be caught inside of a dorsal fin at this hour, it is too rigid. Rigid duplication of aviaries in the salt. The feathered rain. The dorsal fins are raining like feathers inside the vast amplitude, dorsal splitting and rotting. Solipsism is such silliness.

Depersonalization, derealization; realization, personalization. Reverently unscrew the husks from their orifices. The orifices have amnesia and forget their places like limpid furniture. The artifices are accumulating gorgeously like the growth of orange and white plants. The vast milk, the vast honey, the vast dust. The vast husks getting further and further away. Train getting further and further away from the closed window. It is advised to hang ivory icicles from your hunk. Distribute your artifact clockwise. Avoid the blue tar. Increase all expedient avalanches. The ingredients are accumulating languidly across the smiles. You should either sleep 5.45 or 16 hours at a time. In between there is nothing. The vast activity: it is this activity. The mind is a vast insect. We are all following a false lead. There is no activity. You are not external to the world, not internal. Eternal latrine.

the golden arm of

some ghost will comfort me

a stone shaped like a woman

full of tears of light

a bird is filled with blood and a bell

is empty

    Underground Moon

a boy

with light golden hair

he is an emerald

by the riverside sitting

a fish has one of his eyes

while the grass

that is dressed in

a wet sand necklace

his other eye is a pearl

can the boy see

the dinosaur on the

opposite shore?

he doesn't know of any cloud

that isn't hid in the tree branches

like a nightingale

his wings breathe open and closed

the window where

his mother leans

and shouts his

name

the letters

creep along the dirt

lose their way in his hair

swim in the pool

emerald where his eyes once were

a quiet bird leaps

from the water

gentle at his heels

a bird of blue feathers

a bird of eyelashes

and a smile

drifts along the ripples

and catches the boy

a spider that looks like

a skeleton hand

as the boy

who is young

takes off his shoes

a sandwich

is now a sandcastle

for a family of ants

the letters of his name

there is an ant boy

with blond hair

looks out over the water

but to him it is an ocean

and all the evening clouds

are mirrors

the woman by the window

there she is

I see her eyes in petals of water

the dazzling water that washes us all

she keeps away the clouds

that I can't keep away

soft alive morning

"… it doesn't matter where you're from, it doesn't matter who you are…"

everything weighs the same

on the cosmic scale

scaly scale

bless you

the self is time

it belongs to everyone

it belongs to no one

the watching

the waiting

is yourself

the doing

nondoing

undoing

fruitlessly

fruitfully

moaning

a man is the same

as the sun is the same

the tolling of winter bells

feathers of sunshine

at a cool glance

cities reflected in flexing

exerting muscle

windows and windows and windows

straight up along air and sky

a man's eye in blank window

reaching vacant overhead

man's cruel teeth biting sky

streets curve along buildings

streets dry with blood and

sweat and come

and tears and

nameless liquids out of humans ebbing

crowding the coughing roads and

streets

men like staircases all pushed

together

no one behind eyes under hats

to keep gentle freezing wind

from pulling cut eyelids

to show tears

that men are really men

his eyes are in the fogged windows

that descend from heaven

in blood roads and drool

man is alone in the city

just as he is alone in

himself

standing motionless by the lake

he can glimpse the fading

waves

so much like himself

in the chilling wind he can hear

the chorus of his heart

each bird made filthy by the

shit that the city

breathes out into the air through

every machine pore

every bird is a smile

that he did not give to anyone or himself

people are each other's shadows

clouds do not allow the

city too much sunlight

his city is an eyelid

a closed eye against blank

whiteness

when the forgiving sun

seeps the man in its waters

dries his machine bones and wraps him

in skin

fills the buildings with blood and muscle

during winter the city is

a skeleton

and the men dance around

its bones like flies

dirt bones flung like rain

into open white mouths

of humans

empty men empty of tears

sobbing shameless women

during winter

the blood of the city

is cold

he suggests his future in his

immediate movement

observing all the hurrying uncontrolled lost muscles

that fill a city the way

teeth fill a corpse's mouth

wasted ejaculation

dirty man masturbating reverently into the black pores

into the alleys

the buildings

the churches

the schools

the streets

the tourists

the residents

the city

city reaching and grabbing clouds

stealing them back to man's private earth

city like a dying star

drooping its dead occupants back

into dead reality

city screaming and hollering silent as a bell

in the city man's voice

is an echo

mourn not for the cities

not for the men

or the women

mourn for the children

and yourself

the mourning period is eternity

we do not have time to mourn

the silent eternal courtship

of being

and nonbeing

they are in love

writhing like ageless lovers

in the blissful sands

of time

the Adult

He couldn't see, the gray darkness came across as a dim tired light that revealed nothing; a forest of shifting light and shadow peeled over his searching eyes, waiting, he couldn't see anything, but sounds were heard, men arguing and women whispering, children coiled in smoke, muffled play and happiness and sadness; feeling out around him, objects shrank and grew, and suddenly he could see but there wasn't anything to see.

Wet Soil

you set off light at my fingers

a dark touch stolen sideways

a crawling spider

hand of feathers

blown dirt road in wind

cold rain alight in your tooth

and grin

smile at the door to winter closing

a splinter

in my lip

travel one-eyed down the throat

of black alleyway

go toward the fire

in between two tall buildings

silk ran down in rain

I feel the wind and silk fingers

can you swim

very well in this rain

tonight that falls

around our eyes and lips and feet

and our hair like grass

that shimmers in wind gentle

spreading skin drift in soft alleyways

dark of night

in sweet cold air

porcelain trees grow out from

frozen grass

doll's fingers trailing

light down the alleyways

blind

Thunderclap

I have got my eyes on you

but you've got to give them back

so I can see

I've given my heart to you

but with no blood

I'm just a fallen down tree

there are wolves in the graveyard

and some of the tombstones are lightbulbs

I've got twenty thousand bones

in my left foot

and they're all dancing in their skin

since you came through like a

thunderclap

thunderclap thunderclap thunderclap

you make me feel like one hundred miles

of unpaved iguanas

you've got a tornado in your teeth

it's stirring up your mice

there are owls in the windmill

and the wind is a forest

I'm on a tugboat headed south

and my bleating heart sounds like a thunderclap

thunderclap

Fever

the old worn-out sailboat

along the crow's feet

along the sunflower bent

over in eyelashes

dead of night

along the ferris wheel

each seat has a scarecrow

facing backwards

the boat looked

only too much

like an elephant

many men were on the tusks

hollow grey body tired

in the wind

only thoughts blew by

roses of sand

paper sand crane roses

out of the window

into the cool machine air

that smelled

of an elephant

the weight of each foot brought

forests collapsing into sand

mouths filled with

sand in the air

glass cup with morning sand

from straight

out the

sun

      howling out in wind

      howling inside-out wind

the sky is white

white air

I only know the snow as

it passes along

the trees

houses in the distance

the white sky looks like an

angel

the river warmed by the sun

fish leaping into white air

to know cool life

escape

hot death of time

the snow carries white sky

over earth

white hands folding a

twisting smiling eye hot

hot hot hot hot hot

white smooth life cool

death hot hot

hot hot cool cold

hot thought feeling

white snow eye twisting

tears joined life death

thoughts running over

body river thoughts cool skin and snow

white white white

a feeling that is

heaving and breathing

white breath of sky

breathing inside the mind

a feeling of the mind

white thoughts

a gentle river

the sky

air

moon's drawbridge antlers

through the woods pillars dressed in snow

a moose a palace colonnade

slips like the noise of a sparrow

submerged in the waves

by the ocean

a great eye

butterfly along the corner of the sky

moose streaks across the horizon

multicolored birds swimming

in the brown fur

that moose

to the silver eye of a

man lost in the woods

amidst the pillars bathed in snow

virgin birds in the hollow sky

the isolation

amidst all things

the moose is not a man

other men are feather

bouquets

snow erupts from every pore

the eyes leap like birds by the

ocean of the mountain

     dressing gown

dancing down the slope

of the mountain

in whose eyes I see

the flowered dawn

riding the overcoats

of ghosts like lambs

dogs like seashells

stones like icicles

a crimson skeleton

no longer confined to form

a heap of bones

blue and orange

the sun hiding in the waves

the bones when viewed

from the peak of the mountain

were birds building golden cages

around themselves

when viewed from the ballroom

where a slight woman

turns a pearl over on her tongue

the bones were several lengths of paper

the birds were green ink words

if one was to read these ancient papers

by the lake near the mountain

a story is told of a woman a nightingale

who in her dressing gown looks like a palace

of embers

seagull

ouroboric rocking-chair

screaming jaybird

rising with the ruins

of an old town

white eyes where the fires

held out plates of peeled grapefruit

to the mouths

of an old chimney

stones

coiled in dust wings

breathing out the empty walls

houses life-like fishtails

wound under

the lotus of time feathers

bent like an eyelash wet

where the jaybird

rinses its talons in the

well beak faucet

old love in the well

a son of the sun rests out of the well

breathing in tulip clouds

and feet stretched out to the

jaybird who can see past

the white fence

the buildings a crown of teeth

on the skull of the well

where the smoke is dust

the wings are lungs

the lips are lungs

a sunset can reach the days

breathing quietly in the

dust and sawdust and bird ashes

waiting for the doors to open again

a sun by the roses a son by the roses

always will come

always will come

always will come always will go

the common ground

is understanding

agreement

spread assent wherever you go

if you please

encourage stealing

theft

hygiene larceny

the gnomes of disillusion

the gnomes of security

the doves of disaster the gloves

distasteful

ancient

farm

      Earth

a series of diamonds

leads to the performers

disassembled in the shining lightbulb

the diamond fetters the diamond fetters

jump for joy

the magnificent toy jumps on its own

red proposal

war at candle-flame

these long roses are guns

out of the barrel

these tendrils belong to an igloo

the one I know

by the fountain

where under the night of the octopus

trees give out their doves

and bathe in the waters

and drink of the waters

the sun rises from the waiters

the beak of the octopus

breaks open the sun's egg

like a gun or umbrella

gun by the roses grow

an octopus snow

lays its sun on the eggs

while under the tentacle of night

the fountain takes the

umbrella from the gun

and leaves the trees

for the snow

out of the egg

a gun

an octopus

uses the umbrella to keep

the heavens near the sun

egg filled with snow

gun whose lips are a rose

the sun is an octopus

whose forest is

covered with snow

by the fountain the sun roses

skeleton chord rang out

in butterflies

broken carriage down the mountain road

stole the green light of the forest

the day to blacken its wings

hearts on the vanishing treetops

broke the forest smile into a frenzy

of trees and perfume

at the foot of the mountain

a birdbath

calls out to its lover

a nightingale with seashell feathers

and the wheels of a broken carriage

for eyes

raising fruit from pure soil

butterfly rain at the treetops soil

night is the shadow cast by day

as it looks in on itself

the forest swings on the dust of time

pendulum

tree branches like golden soldiers underneath

a great frown

when rain moistens the heavens' brow

keep your umbrella of nightingales

the garden hides the light of day

in ruins

quietly

the salamander pales green light

blown from the forest over

seashell cemetery at the corner of night

quietly

winter roses peel

black felt

sorcerer

weave thine crown of moon white

and stolen willow's tongue

to the fantasies of oceans

the shoreline resting in the

curve of the

woman's waist

sun stole the bird dark from the sky

ants like skeleton leaves

arrange the words to

resemble the teeth

of a funeral

windblown tapestry over the

forest sunbeam peals

flesh pale coils into bleached white

tentacles

wrapped coiling over

the oceans of a woman

taking a nap at the four corners

of a moon

drawn over the sun's sand

wash the bones of earthly tone

into pale black mountain

pale black mountain

like a shout or cough

echoing in my mind

endlessly

into silence

sun stream

ran river against

coal ashes skeleton birds

over the wind boat curls

it is better to hold a bowl of salad in one hand

while urinating

by yourself

      white movement

a sparrow with a cloud of smoke for

a head

has fingernails and centipedes in its feathers

leaves its wings at the funeral parlor

each of its legs is a woman

the left leg used for picking up twigs

and eyelashes and pearls and gardens the

bird full of rain to the eye and a rope

about its beak for the winter

the left leg is a young red-haired woman

with all the attributes of a garden

sunbeams full of nightingales, razor-blades,

diamond intestines, fevers, feather bouquets,

ice, the mouth of a lion

the right leg covered with a light blue vine

which has the words 'come toward the

sand swirling white at the throat' printed

along the central leaf

the right leg is an older woman, pale chandelier

with midnight arms and feet, dragging her

white mist heels at the edge of the bed

a wonder in the winter of night

slowly the chandelier with a chicken or

fox-head drowns in the sand, at the

foot of the sand is a pearl

      sundown

from the tree's great finger outstretched

did fall the leaf upon the stream

the leaf wandered across the stream remote

it sought no direction

nor wished to return home

to the tree's great finger

outstretched

down the stream the leaf did go

never minding where to or fro

across the waters ablaze

the way of the leaf

remained the same

sunburned mast broken hull alive in the grass

a worn-down shack

sits under the sun

almost as if it were a portrait

of a distant sailboat in the clouds

who knows what fish and seashells are

in a sailboat that will never know the touch

of ocean

does the sailboat with ant legs and the

eyelashes of the moon know that it

will never be caressed by the waves

a tulip bulb against the escaping centipede

hurrying away from a smooth stone

in the middle of the road

the ocean is a garden of pearls to the

sailboat forever dry

distant umbrella

returning to the source

      slight

candle-wax spiders spin webs of

grey shifting light

through idle corners

and the halls of dark waiting night

fish bloom in silent pools

candle-flame in the eyes

of a woman

fills out the way into night into daylight

man trips and stumbles

over ghosts in alleyways

lightning wings and a shade of pale

darkness

loose wet lips spiders and flies

raincoat of the windowsill sitting a

black naked bird

bone toes

hair like a cloud in black air

night is the clearest shadow

trailing dark tendrils

through the gardens of day

when you speak sand and water

fill the corridors of lonely

seashells at the tongue

of ceaseless ocean

night that forever meanders

over the heaving gentle waves

your skin is water and your teeth

ghosts are certain shadows also

the blinding night makes me

smile to think

of you

I see in your shadow

the emerald light

of waiting day

days and nights and winters and springs

waves that cover

my body with sand

if only

if only

I could live with you

in a sandcastle in the flight

of a golden bird

forever by the sea

my hand is open

my mouth is open

in my eyes you are an open world

that is filled with the sun's

loving breathing light

as it sets

against the waves

in rain flower

in night screaming black and roses and

icicles clinging

to lips

wet tooth and nail frostbite

day discreetly sends out three white birds

birds of light

to quiet the shrieking night

laughing like a tree-branch frozen in the eye

sweet brown curling leaves underfoot

wet phantom

and the spark from each eye

left black crows

underfoot heavy blanket

and swept pure spinal

staircase up at cold moon

eyelids

to a fast and wild mouthful of leaves

frozen like icicles

of the windowpane

forest night a beast of crawling

daylight across swamps and

dark-eyed violent

teeth deserts

gnarled tree-limb sand

in a flower of rain

the gentle day and

night distant and becoming

made love to one another

and the wet grass

curled forgotten emeralds

old diamond come out to play

hip to the jive

simulated stimulation

      Lightning Eyes Darkness

Three beetles three hens laid, outstretched wings as moonlight through a dusty diamond, twists head and burrows further, a forest come up around them, lighting its fingers reaching among the dark clouds of the night, in darkness the light is the night; lightning in the night, the darkness, the light. Shining, piercing through the open windows of night, dragging teeth through the hair, the darknesses. Three legs of a chair sitting cross-legged by the stairs huddled, lateen drawn and close, a beating heart through the night; the lightning outside longed to clasp hands with this flame, the beating heart by the stairs, rain outside coming down like a thousand whispers, of things that will be once again, things shining amber ablaze with eyes to rival the depths of the ocean, things by the light huddled, things that eyes have not seen. Three houses outside form the steps to an incomplete staircase, leading perhaps to library of clouds, currently ashes falling to earth wet, igniting on the soil wonder, horror, mystery.

Waiters, hanging suspended in the restaurants, whose menus are golden eye-sockets, first course hair on the patrons' shoulders playing, dancing, but alas halfway curtains are drawn and tongues are flickering with the candles in conversation. One hundred weightless runners on the roof and sidewalk. The waiters, eyes bounding from table to table, eating as their main course the diners' silverware, napkins, purses, plates, etc. Second course began, or erupted, somersaults and sit-ups and the lamps were ballerinas, their skirts the cords which cascaded through the women's yearning brows and the men with coat hooks still in their jackets; the trumpeter was propelling eclairs throughout, for those patrons whose hands moved forward as waves and flicked back drawn by a chariot: the chandelier, cast off as waves to the moonlight. And cascading down in a flurry, soft as silk or ashen pillows, many eyelashes singularly or in doubles, wings, doves calling out, arisen, a tulip, vastly triumphant; the ground is covered, the stems hidden in crossing hairs, all from women, whose hand retreats to the eye in sudden breaths like the wind when their conversation, pouring in a beautiful stream with small rocks and fish and branches, a balcony from which the sun views the opera, turns to themselves or when talk of arriving and departing fills the air. The petals of each tulip hold an eye on the tip, blinks as bright as light; a disembodied hand crawls through the lashes, fingertips trailing thin lines of water, when it rains the hand will rise to the surface, as a boat for a child, the eyelashes will permeate the soil become one with the earth; the world and the planet will bat their eye and sweep dust and sawdust under their feet.

Behind the chandelier: a reindeer, its antlers blazing forth, two fiery orbs in the night sky, plummets tumultuously from a white heaven in the clouds, Earth rushing forth in its eye to meet it halfway, cutting the impact cloak and dagger, robes which bear stripes that extend far past the garment itself. Before it turns to gold: the reindeer's hooves are the Three Horses of the Apoplectic Attitude; the fifth leg whose hoof hides in the sunset, sunrise would bring another year to its life each time it occurred. Through the gloom a ruby piano-stool casts the shadow of Muhammed. Sandstorm catches the wind which it sails down like a rope-ladder fastened to the blue sky and every other rung is a varicose horizon an eye that burns the ocean with each blink, seven blinks in a row. The dress of feathers.

Upside-down these two villages were women kicking their legs underwater. They were related in distance by a smile that swept leaves underneath it. The villages would be holding hands if they could, each had two hands' worth of buildings. The houses were modeled after trees; in their mouths were clay, mud, leaves, but no wood or brick. Rocks for teeth. The buildings handled their job astutely. These people were joyous and knew no sorrow, they were one with the distant feather, they were on the distant feather. The villages batted their eyes against the sky, which was beaming. A vast forest encompassed the land as far as anyone could see. The eyes of the trees were bicycles in the air. Deep as a person's mind, the tree-bark as human fingers would tangle a man or woman into an endless labyrinth.

plunge

the finite whistles

the eyelashes are fingers

mile-long grin

mile-long gun

the first whistle

humanimals

caveman's boneyard

prehistoric boogie

outlandish with his teeth

sink

the sunset's lashes

face facing

slow return to form

slow release

a slight hovering

people think

that there is a difference

between the inside of a building

and outside it

everywhere

is equal

no barrier no boundary

man's lining is evaporated conclusively

the infinite rate of lengths

species membranes

The cemetery cries out and is caught by the flowers, which act
as a railroad for the skeletons that lie beneath and betwixt them. The

bulbs open as lips and hair is revealed with an eye at the center; the hair cracks its knuckles with the grass, sleeping and sweet brown fingernails. Each gravestone has a tail and the cemetery cries out tonight. The moon is a rake that extends toward the Earth, begging. By the cemetery's feet crouches a barn, red, which conceals a mule; there is dirt in its teeth and the hooves are not its own. The cemetery's shoulder-blades are a pond where the lilacs and lilies grow as roses. The mule licking its teeth. All the bones here have gravel in them. The picket fence is of bones. Cemetery wears four boots and a hat made from a half-empty whiskey bottle. This hill has blood on it; white legs and black hands beneath the barn where the cemetery is a well: cellar door behind its legs and hits the sky running. The cellar behind the barn leads to a zoo for creatures eyes have not seen. Several small silver spheres roll through the cemetery where the night finds its pleasures amidst. Each of the sky's stars is a black flower.

A blind man and a devil meet here, during the day the cemetery belongs to them, during the night the cemetery is its own. The sun kisses the cemetery and stays away not too far, so that throughout the day it is always early morning, the innocent time. The cemetery is an alleyway and the grass is sweet. The hill in the woods. Many lie here in the cemetery but few come to visit their dearly departed. The blind man roves slowly like a vine through the tombstones toward no destination, he is seeking to escape time, time that he will never set eyes upon. The devil in a business suit, observing this, glides above the reeds in the pond. They meet on a bench, the devil is a young white man. This much is known.

The old blind man can do things that the devil cannot. Worthwhile the cellar door shudders. Their tongues race through the grass in a boat race to match the heavens; smells here thrust outward the nostrils and salivate desire. The blind man is gone and the devil parts ways. The tongues remain to become snakes, turtles, squirrels. The last of the sunlight drips through a vial and through the trees plays absentmindedly. In the barn the mule sees none of this or anything: the mule is blind. The cemetery's heart and brain stand on their haunches beneath the soil. There is in the world only morning, day and evening. Across the sky hands float as leaves and birds, breathing darkness into the light; the sun handles its way out and the moon is holding the key; they exchange words of being and time, which unfolds like a dirty brown tongue. 'Cemetery' is the most beautiful word in the world, you write it on a strand of hair and it disappears.

It is evening: brick houses turn to wood and the clouds are lying down. Eyes close and that is what the houses are; there is a broken clothes-hanger lying on the ground outside the door of a house. A woman whistles for the wind and finds it running its fingers through the hair of a tree, the tree is the wind's wife. The woman walks hand in hand with the wind toward her house. In her mind and the pale gloved wind (winter's brother, single-most omnipresent structure of the vacuum, batting its eyelashes like long fingers), a trail of breadcrumbs is laboriously eaten, as one would pronounce 'chandelier' to the twilight's fist; it is wont of that long procession of days, which are labeled with numbers, one being the middlemost, central day and the rest of the days branching out of this tentacle are in numerical order, corresponding to the root day, tentacle order numerical municipality. These days will take you and the mice to a furnace of exquisite elaborateness, patterns that were on a loved one's pants the first day you met them. The woman sometimes chokes on the wind's fingers, which are infinite, as if they were breadcrumbs.

The woman says to the wind: "Is it I, as you say, who has become not the most tragic of the morning's kin? I lead you with my fingers (tongue); the witness to a blind man and devil conversing. I have found left in the attic of my brain nothing of the content of their cold fiery lips. I did not see it when it was present, nay, but at the theater! While those around me, who dress themselves up like trees and fritter away with hats for their mustaches, saw a play on the current affairs of clothes-trafficking throughout the rooms of a small house, especially in the room with a little boy with glass locks and curls, while they saw this divine dramedy sent from the earth, I saw the meeting of the blind man and devil. Dare I say it took place on a hill."

The wind's response was an entire book made out of leaves and gold. The woman's mind was truly an attic, her throat the stairs which lead to the small room, each step was of different size and a stiff rectangular structure that generated and reproduced a series of oft-quoted soliloquies, that taken out of context (laundress of fish) could be meant to start a new machine, thrown out of the window of a seven-storey building to attract the attention of ants and unwanted guests, gusts: emerging with an urgent message from the elevator, moving through the crowd as if it were an alligator. Within her small attic room was a ten mile high pile of dust where her memories stick hidden; plaster boxes lie atop the dream-dust containing her unborn thoughts, her present thoughts are fingers inching through the musky air toward the ceiling and her past thoughts lay nestled like hens in the dust. The wind's teeth comb through her brain and peek into her hair.

She wore slacks that spat within circumference minuscule parts of a boat, one that beckons chalkboard nails which, at a certain time of day, sew food together with the armchair of rich, two feet deep, three minute second rungs. Leaves, dirt, teeth, sticks, bicycle parts, hambones, branches, flowers, dust, sawdust, eyelashes, silver, mouths, tears and rocks caught at her heels. If it had been raining or snowing the wind would've been frightened to death. A gasp ran through the air and stuck in her hair; she spun (spiderwebs) around to find that the source was not immediately present. The wind shrugged and partially melted into her sex. Turning back around she glimpsed the alleyway cemetery on the hill; facing forward again she saw in the cemetery a twig, protruding ten inches from the knowing grass, growing from which were a pair of young girl's ballet slippers. The twig bowed on occasion from the wind, jealous. She cried out and the cemetery answered her; for the rest of woman's journey the cemetery would stay close to her heart, a deep woods.

They continued down the road, the wind's hand in her pocket, her hands swaying like geese in the air. From the ground before her she lifted a leaf which she knew to be a cookie, cake's kissing-cousin; halfway through eating it, the leaf/cookie became a ballerina. In the cemetery the twig bearing the ballet slippers was gone. The woman was momentarily heartbroken and she let the ballerina/leaf fall to the earth. The cemetery took the place of her heart for the meanwhile.

Up ahead the town rose. This town, which she had to trek through no matter which direction she came from in order to obtain arrival at her house. The wind and the cemetery were talking boisterously. The town was built like one thousand dying men trying to claw their way out from a black pit, built especially like their hands, the roads together form each spine; the corner bakery is a phosphate shop, along the side of which lies a bench not dissimilar to the one in the cemetery, next to the woman's heart (her heart returneth). The cemetery is when the town blinks or rubs its eyes. Where? Upon the tomb's foundation a piano in evening-clothes ambled down the street, the people took no notice, they knew it to be a dining-room table about to become naked. She came through to the end of town, where as is necessary for every small murky town, a bar appeared. The woman knew if she entered the bar she would exit the following two mornings. Alcohol would last a lifetime with her and stain her hair the color of schoolchildren when they are through with picking pinecones. She would wait outside for the wind dniw eht rof edistuo tiaw dluow ehS.

Growing anxious for the wind's departure from the bar, inside with a bottle of right-side-will-come-last, mercury-and-lavender, the woman, partially following a drunkard, spills into the surrounding woods. As a crown the drunkard wore above his head a chicken, forever set black against the night's weeping sky, the night with greying flesh that carried with it the assassin of nightingales: explore, the night is an open book. In the night things are changed. This crow, this crown, has eyes which surpass its mind with age; the crow has flown over many places, the vast world before it has touched its wingtips; crow, you who have seen so much of the world, seen places where the ladies with silk flesh throw beard-stubble over themselves as a blanket against the cold sunlight, that speaks of tumultuous change. The woman steps forward, the grass pulling from between her toes. "Harken to me!" she and the forest cry in unison.

Growing anomalies of the dark, speak to me diamonds, speak to me stolen rust-worthy jewels of amber denizens, jutting out of which strut sonic birdbaths! Draw the hues from my lips! They are the color of day and night. My teeth flow fiercely from your scalp. Lift me and to the sky I will sing them asleep, good bye good rest, good bye to the rest.

The woman is known to slip amongst the trees; no good will come of this forest, the moon and sky reflect. Do you not speak of truth and its foe of shallow ribbons? The woods presently took on the appearance and build of a maze. The drunkard vanishes in a hail of pear-slices, one lands softly on her hand and is swallowed by her labyrinthine palm (palm fronds to and fro). A coach-and-bones emerges from the hedge, cracking like teardrops. The pear is a breast in her hand. "Are you not the sun and the sky in their entirety, their entire outfit?" asks the woman of one of the figures aboard the grim vessel; this actor of shadow coughs and tufts of human hair drift toward her eyes. She leaves the coach-and-bones to marvel at the black dust. The ghoulish figures play her spine like a marimba and chills overtake her. These dark creatures or men stand in a straight line back to the tavern, where the wind is juggling phrases. Further into the woods she is alone. Night, cloaked in daggers, strikes a chord which mirrors the human chest of drawers and is infinitely spacious like an empty room. Her hair deceives her and grows older in years, grey and white, as waves crashing, sudden sound laugh cough. Stretch the word 'trees' out long and pronounce it slowly like little ants.

    The boy opened his eyes wide, together becoming a mouth, edges turned upward with delight, tongue lapping up the sunshine like little ants. He opened his eyes wide, together becoming a mouth that hung ajar, white teeth shone toward the sky, the pupils were a tongue lapping up the sunshine. You could count this boy's age on two hands and he did so, holding them before him with palms facing in as if his hands were treasure. This left the out-turned thumbs exposed. The boy was thinking about his fingers, which now represented one year each; he wondered what one million fingers would look like and if one were able to ever be that old. Surely, the sun above him could not be that elderly. His thoughts a forest, the boy did not see past his fingers to spy a figure who was creeping forward with red boots and silver cape. Before he knew it the figure was upon him, leaping away with the boy's thumbs in its possession. The boy bounded after in pursuit, down the sidewalk, across the street (his eyes darting both ways before crossing) and into a large nearby woods. He found his thumbs under a rock alongside the small creek that slithered around the tree's ankles. he screwed them on tight (which was difficult without having thumbs momentarily) so as to prevent their being stolen again. The boy worked his hands into little wings to make sure the thumbs were well adjusted. Those birds flew high in the air and came to rest in the treetops like a balcony, awaiting nightfall when the mice would be apparent (the boy supposed). He didn't understand why the mice would come out at night, he himself could hardly see at all in the dark. His eyes were much larger than a mouse's, almost as large as the mouse itself. If they wanted to his eyes could eat a mouse, if it would chance get close enough. But the boy had no interest in eating anything with his eyes except the sunlight. He could not eat the sun, looking at it for just a moment made the inside of his eyeballs rain and he would have to close his eyelids and rub the rain away. This exercise took time he wished was spent elsewhere.

The boy slid his hands under the water and then into the rocky sand through which the stream passed like wind. He felt as if he were putting on mittens and the joyfully chilly water parted around his wrists. What a great pair of mittens this would be then, he thought, they are so large I wouldn't be able to move about very well, especially with all these trees around. He loved the trees. At night he thought about them and often they were underneath his pillow, in case he should wish to play with them. At other times they weren't there, but the boy was not disappointed. These trees stayed pretty much in the forest. In the water the boy was running his hands through the trees' hair, branches, leaves, sticks. Birds and squirrels would get caught under his fingernails and his teeth (mostly just one) would grow much longer than the rest until it reached his hand and would free whatever was stuck between his fingers and fingernails. Then his teeth would go back to their usual size and he would continued to run his hands through the trees. The boy thought of his mother's hair, brown and hanging just below her shoulders. What nice hair she had! His father's hair was much shorter and of a color he could not place. Something bumped the boy's hand in the water. It was a small plate stacked with cheese. How wonderful, he thought. A conveyor-belt was drawing his favorite dishes to him. The boy shook his hands from the water and wiped them on his pants. His fingers swept like a broom through the desserts and the plates caught fire. The boy's mouth operated as a drawbridge. Cakes, chocolates, wafers, candies, all the treats which delighted him, delighted his mouth, his stomach, his fingers, even his eyes. The boy thought of his past birthday parties where desserts like these were always in abundance, never faltering in their supply, aye, he never faltered in his demand of them. He thought of his upcoming birthday party, which he supposed would be arriving soon. Sometimes, a finger's length of time is too long a wait.

He left a soft bend in the creek to clean the dirty dishes and apologized to the water for not leaving it any snack; it seemed that when he was finished gorging himself on the sweets their production was stopped. The river of food had become dammed up as his appetite diminished. He travelled further upstream like little ants. Lusty child, swollen with the hours.

it is ideal that the tallest apparitions

are the most frightening

dancing in the swollen aviary

gingivitis hair-string

for a fuller sting

Do you think you'll travel to anywhere soon? Where?

Do you prefer to remain in one spot, or do you move around a lot?

Where is your favorite place? Why?

Math is obviously a faucet. You can tell by the minnows that surround it, the feelers. A plate piled high with orgasms, far as the eye could see. Seeing is like shouting. The fish remain in their bowls. The electron remains in the faucet, it has enormous feelers. Elect the shafts, erect the class shuffle. Math is jumping from pillar to pillar, naked, jeweled. It removes its faucet. The skeletons on the beach are sunbathing, do not touch. Touch the feelers graciously. It's alright. I won't tell. I'll tell you. I'll remove the faucet myself, I've done it before. Thirty times, in fact. Math has a bird stuck in its mouth, the artichokes around it are laughing mercilessly. Artichokes are devils, I love to eat them. Do you? Sometimes I can grow my own artichokes out of my spine. I peel back the skin on my back and there they are, ripe as tomatoes, ripe as lemons. I am an affluent grocer in cold water. Transparent water is a deception. You should ask the onyx phoenix, it hangs under the sun in the evenings. The plates are clean, they look new. The new orgasm is chirping irregularly behind the onyx phoenix. The coat-hangers are coughing mercilessly. I have to look away, I have to approximate the huge calf. Take it how you will. All of my money is inside-out, laughing, coughing. I prefer it that way. Really, I prefer it any way. You don't have to touch all the cows for me, I might be turned away. I might be turned into a turtle. I prefer it that way. Don't hesitate to calculate the rubber sunsets. The curtains should be open by then. If not, press the yellow button under the staircase. There should be two. Press the left one, do not press the right one. Press the bottom button and the top button at the same time. Make sure the mice are away in the hay. Make sure the children are lined up in the cupboard. Button button. Adjust discordantly the disparate membranes. I can grow an octopus out of the pupil of my eye, I'll show you sometime. The silver discrepancies lawn upheld. The ocean is a month and three clamps.

Are you doing something else right now, or just reading?

How often do you read? Do you enjoy it?

Do you enjoy math? How often do you do it?

The curtains are horses and they're very upset. You should paint them blue if it is autumn, green if it is summer. Red if it is the corner of the eye, a darling socket for the ages smothered in soapy eagles. Lovely, lovely. A snowfall of cashmere antelopes, very good to touch. Politely the agitated whistle surrounds the thistles and gives off the bright milk, covered in ashes. The transparent copulation, manifold copulation. Copulation that is inside-out in the dim orange light. Time emits a single violet light haphazardly ultraviolet rose. The radios are inside-out, that is how they function more fluently. There is more in the fluid. Press all unusual lumps and abrasive abrasions. One must always give the correct amount of bread to floaters. Too much is a potable occultist and too little is an accordion in the rain. The gutter is an accordion shaped like a mouth, winking, emitting casual moans. The letters all have no address, no sender. It is very disquieting, like an avalanche in the rain. Read the signs that say: AIR IN OUT. They're all too common these days. Before it was different, and after it will be different. Before it was not different, and after it will not be different.

Ask the sign that says: OCCULTISTS LOADING. This should clear things up a bit. About time, I'd say. Not too soon. Read the red letter angels ascending and descending. They're always outside, they never come inside. The angels inside-out on the escalator. At the top is a sign which reads: PASS THROUGH OVEN TO HALT ANOMALIES. I haven't seen it yet, they tell me that it is a sight to behold. A sight to cradle in your arms and sing a show-tune from the future to, I'm sure that you know at least three or four, they're on display everywhere. Looking under the water should be avoided lazily. The paint is drying joyously, singing soundlessly. Paint is tears of joy, tears of rage. Tears in the brain cage. The queen of all eaves, acclimating lightly. A sight to disgorge. Disgorging boundlessly through the ether, sick with nettles and blue geese. The family gatherings are inside the piñata shaped like a manatee constructing a piñata of a manatee constructing a piñata of a manatee constructing a piñata of a manatee and so on for as far as your imagination allows. Don't let me impede it by any means. The mind interrupts itself like a bluebird. It does this consistently, prominently. Do not fret. You can fret to your heart's content. Fret and do not fret. Assess the decisions sexually. Pancakes are a burden, it's been decided; lice are not a burden. I split my funerals, I let the pistons speak for themselves, I slit my funnels.

The gliders are processed by the bloated kittens lolling about in the transparent oil. The bloated feathers heavy with incumbent lacerations toward black dawn. Bloated brand black heart start. A soiling of the whistles: seek the desolate foghorn. Do not gloat as you put the rubber nails on the preparations. It is better to be on top of the sequined ancestors in the glossy totem. Instigate a desolate reprieve. Leaves that are neon blue, that are veiny and malformed like the palm fronds of your hands. The gliders in red sheaths all over the husks of blue moonbeams. This much is accountable. Accountants drawn upstairs by the faint noises of the masturbating ether. Do not reveal the imminent cuckolds, do not conceal the limited syrups. Listen to everyone; don't listen to anyone. The limpid furniture removes its mask of scarlet proportions and the astral estuaries are glistening like mummies swollen with pollen. Nuts tut-tut. The conveyor-belt of time brings to us the chirping vacancies, the cluttered spaces adorned with horned mummies, apparitions with splendid antlers the color of night. Miracle union divine divide. The pigs have all frozen to death in their airplanes. Astonishing pizzeria intricate complacency, peppered diaper of formation listening.

A silver seagull without its eyes is a crescent, and a diamond without a skeleton is a bridesmaid attending the four simultaneous funerals of four mistresses, each a rabbit with a tree in its whiskers in their own way, a balloon rolling down the lead pipe of the night, scorpion arching its eyes like the spine of a book, the woman is kneeling and a well emerges from one of the knots in her spine, a celebration, a tooth-filled sack covered in hair, frog hair forest hair, ghostly sunken ship runs up the creek lifting its skirt, a dress woven as a crown, worn as a crow, the kingdom of the stars thrown across the back of a chair and a lamp tips over, spilling hornets into the daylight, turning the stone into a bundle of roses, mimicking the shape of a bush or hedge or lamppost or hyena, only when a cat yawns and closes one eye does the rain fall from the coattails of the heavens, clouds each grin to pass the tide, lowside of the belly where Buddha sits like an overturned stone, a tower yawns and bends over, rousing the tide of passions to come bursting out of the tiger's mouth, the abandonment of desire leads to the soul's unfettering, the fish reads a book and loses the goose in a snowstorm, loosens the noose in a glowworm, a golden puppet is the bluebird's swelling bosom. In the cleaned horseshoe of the night, white milk is ready to split whole, a group of flowers that dance like horses, quietly shaving their beards only to be covered by top-hats, bottom hats for the disembodied feet devouring the kitchen sink and the entrails of a lamp are soon dissected by the fork, knife and tablecloth; when suddenly out of the eye of blue night sky, a dandelioness undresses slowly at the turning off and on of the light-switch, only a cloud of smoke leaving the bathtub in a state of frenzy, crosshairs and undergarments are meant for the windmill, but only along a sand pipe dresser filled not with clothes or porcupine needles but with cranes, majestic cranes that fly off at the sight of a woman and are morphed into everlasting spirals whenever the fever of men reaches its shores, at the closed eye barrier reef along the floorboard counting the wings on the days as they fly past the broken open window dazed in a white dress that barely conceals its amorous feeling for the twilight of laundromats, colored at the rope of skin, bathed in sand and at the sawmill squinting and curving the crabs and shellfish to make a quilt large enough for the boathouse and the homeless hermit whose shoes are raspberries, fallow demiurge of locomotives, urge the procession forth, urge it back.

Clouds of orange-peels take to the sky like a house underwater, at the time being a sailboat crawls through the window, through the widow's bellybutton a crowd of masked tornadoes enter the room in fright and everlasting the frail fountain swoons over the candlestick with too many fingerprints, justify the presence of the charioteer when the windows are closed, when the apples fall into the envelope of the clouds, more or less; reaching back over her head, the woman relieves her heels of their post, they leave and visit the fountain, swirling the pennies into a glass eye of unicorns, joyously jousting with knights who are fond only of the day, and nights that swim like eyes in the stomachs of fish, crushed orange-peels outlast the song of the hummingbird as it hangs forlorn from the basket of teardrops as they fall, hiccuping into the stars' open door without shoes or their beaks will trade the wind for the tide, a full past tide of sweeping grins and air, heckling the moonlight for spare change in the shape of little rocks and sea-foam. A tree lifting with ideas at the first woman's fist the sun crept slowly and hid behind the day drawn like a garden door curtain; at the second woman's knee-bone, the sun caught the night with a gold doubloon which was casting the silver eyes of assailants out the corner of the eye where the cat flies its birds around the storm-cloud until the day erupts with molten laughter that cascades like a falling lamp, upholster the window raven with a crane of blinding sunlight, around the knight's table covered in the slow descent of red marsh waters under the swamp tides rushing to and fro dazzling eagle feather caught the window by the door of the nightingale cavorting through the strawberry bush clear as a whistle sound through the tolling of a bell the size of the waist of the third woman cast in the candlelight ankle fist bone hubbub and against the corner of the smile which catches the fish with falling doorknobs for the morrow and evermore until the last furlong is furthermore along the bedside chamberpot coffee table lamp tree, at the bird wing horn glow.

Delicate swan rolls open the barn door like a hobbyhorse, into the sunset gleams the swan's teeth, whole and released from the mouth, holding in their hands a sweet smoke cloud of perfume, redressed, dancing thunder licks the hedges as the moon-glow tears dry against the banister of the rocking chair of the sun, cosmic river flows and intertwines with the bales of sunny day hay that rock around the seashore in the middle of the day way, corn-stalks leave the shoes over their heels and overcoats are hung under their knees, sweep beauty lonesome leaves swept along the coarse road hair, twist with bramble, loosening the ghosts from their signposts of forgone days lost amidst the wind wrapped carousel around the hair at twelve o'clock the moon shines and the pine trees smile with their hands in the river, swan wing loose around the hedges, gown of the woman is much too large for the man to bathe in, whale is having a time about the closet set into the space behind the woman's ears, an old lonesome road whose mouth and hair is another ruinous village of old, swept along the corridor blind, long-haired trench-coat full of horns, steers' horns, like an overturned bicycle.

On the triangles of the woman's stomach, islands that bear only one palm tree at the tips of their toes swirls and run rampant with dandelion fingertips, often the sound of a ghost sneezing is undressed and presented to the council of the frogs and stars and rabbits for review and fulfillment; only under the dress of the moon can the sun breathe in the night air, dark and heavy, a spilt glass, thunder broken, Tutankhamen glances over the side and continues singing his beautiful song that quenches the thirst and hunger of the malevolent and melancholic, onion-bulb pressed through the garden gate and leapt the river in a single bound and gagged along the forceps of the gargantuan one-eyed blind man whose horse is a cobblestone walkway to the mercury filling the somnambulant thermometer drenched in hair and garlic gloves, a red diamond looks the other way as a bat flies directly into the sleeve of a trench-coat, a coat of swarms around the woman's waist, young man and whale, whale bone alas: jealousy is a key that fits into the eye pretending to be a keyhole or iceberg. A chorus of tarantulas at the foot of a pyramid, her breast causes the red line of the horizon to swoop and bray like an owl caught by a tree branch, lightning clouds are large mountains at the foot of her hill, sweet sweet bulb toothed and dogged, ranging from the peak to the nostril, a saber-toothed metal-man collapses at the heat of the night swollen like the chest of the morning, daytime nighttime, sinking into the waist of the woman the young man can glimpse the silken necklace around her ant-hill neck, frog out of the whale's mouth and into the tiger's, the envelope is impossible for the seagull and the whale pulls apart the feet of the winter, bone jaw lightning quick by the wayside and at eyes fall toothed to the floor, roll and hatch from an egg, presenting the king to his subjects naked and azure corridors leading up to his spine, taking a bath in the trees.

lazy facets of the spectral odometer

the production of appearances

production of images production of spaces

the production of apparitions appetites

the production of snails across the basin

the washbasin of our youth

the vast collection of thoughts

in the storehouse

the distant thoughts of sore horizons

Who do you love the most?

Is there anyone you actively despise? Do you have to interact with them often?

How many human beings do you see on any given day? Would you prefer to see more, or less?

How many animals do you see on any given day?

The abandoned coat begins to read a book whose title is obscured by the ringing of the night, a tremendous bell that tolls only when the little boys are lined up in row, prepared for the cloud taste of cold hillock run down the tree, the pages leaping ice beehives, the only salad of fists, that blinks the newsreel under the gun, toward an opening in the spine of the book where an eye has become an infinite vacuum, consuming the tableware of the reader and depositing them into a perfectly smooth imperfect circle, not dissimilar to the mewling of the baby crow, birthed from the cactus' perfect mouth under the old oil hill by the loose running trumpet of the fowls, coated in the chicken-wire heaving and gesticulating in imitation of the reader, who becomes peeved and begins to devour a different page out of spite, out of spitfire sugar honey, crumpled and rose-leafed by the front door, cooked to the noonday broil along the cold afternoon lion, spiked iron anemone of man's creation, bluebird is a wineglass spilt over the last few pages of the book; the reader, triumphant and furious, hollers at the front door for some privacy amidst the woman's intestines, with the young man and the whale against the old willow tree hidden in her spinal cord runs dry. When the well, empty of water and champagne and book-pages but full of mischief and playful deceit, flies by on the deer-hooves of night, who will play the anxious saxophones of Saturn, who will try the ghost of sunburst, who will then seal the lips of those women who seek the bedside table of the illustrious Vile River, who will play the running water down to the goat's teasing mouth, who will leave the gown to be washed by the neon fire, who will abandon the kitchen when the sink is full of carriage-wheels, when the moon bites the neck that feeds the hand, when the coal will mine itself from the heights of the heavens, will push away the false mustaches from the face of the frown, an old bucket, an old clown, an underground pageant, the winner must receive a coat-sleeve full of carriage-wheels and ice-picks, that the noose grown directly from the cow's snout will burst and all its inhabitants, all the bees and frogs, will push forth against the day, headdress worn by the woman, an array of candles that can only crouch in defiance of the light, the dark plays a damn fine harpsichord when the sun croons be-bop to the mistress of the stars. Do not speak to me of the tropes, of cataclysms, of the undigested underwear. The uncouth molecules of venom steaming in their husks, in their stems. It doesn't get in the way. Cyclical icicles are in the way of blasted bananas. Steaming consideration. The exact identity of the laboring sawhorse under the eaves, the laboring systems. Yesterday, the Vile River was in a green and blue vial by the Nile River. The locals were fluent. The local currency is phallic, the vocal urgency was mispronounced. All things in due time. Am I the only one who thinks so? Was I the only one who wasn't invited? Were you? Your favorite musical organ is bleating by the streams like a muse. Afterwards, the goldfish tube was drastically improved. Into the plastic dungeon with the pigeons. Musical orifices, musical surfaces, the sour musical lice.

Do you hold an opinion that no one else holds?

Are all your opinions shared?

What is your favorite opinion? Least favorite?

Have you ever met someone with no opinions?

Esteemed colleagues, I have received your box of snares and find it is in order. Give my regards to the elongated esophagus. My best wishes are soft pillows shaped like shimmering fish. The shimmering fist. Calculate the stems accordingly. You'd think that all these people are breeding disease. Shimmering with disease. The defenses are up, the defenses are a front for the vacant potato. The quantities are amassing pleasantly. The royal cocoons are in their tanks. Everything is in order, there is no order. The orders are odorous and slimy like crocodile children, like orangutan furniture. Gargantuan fumigation sullen at the seams and breeding incoherently. Make up the mind, put make-up on the self concretely. Make the pavement sing in ecstasy. The frequencies are in mindless ecstasy easy. The transparent bluebird is in cold silk. Icicles the color of the sky in spring. You must allow your pets to go outside, that is the law. The best pet is a sphere the color of an icicle. The worst bet is thirty sawhorses in the wind, in the window, with the beautiful minnows. Filled with those spiny birds and tortuous umbrellas like umbilical cords. The affluent fluency is current to the central locomotion. Save the ornamental orifices for later, when the eight-ball is vocal. My desire is to see the sun floating endlessly in a sea of white white milk. Relevance is unsupervised, omniscient frame. Superimposed genitalia vacuous disarmed. Either there is an answer or there isn't. Which would you prefer?

What is easy for you? What is difficult for you?

The two cuneiform giraffes are singing a rubber song. When one goes: "I don't need a woman to corroborate my thermometers, I need a woman to put my shoes out in the snow," the other sings: "I don't need a man to pile high the salt, I need a man to feed my tables." The spectator is a shovel in the sand that is clapping its hands like a magistrate who is a blackbird. When one goes: "I need two men and two women in the middle of the bath," the other sings: "I don't need more than eleven clever hoses." They both chant the chorus: "The marshes are marching, the climate is a skinned primate and fifteen horseshoes by the gallon!" The shovel is not convinced, the shovel is autonomous. The hands are autonomous, the hands are arduous. The foal is delighted to be here. Cordial awareness of red foxes actuated loosely according to the springboard of the seasons.

The ironing-board of the seasons spilled red embraces. Translations, when applicable, are curtailed by the translucent stream. Transitions, when syndicated, are assimilated by the lucid corpse, lucid steam, the corpse pointing with a lavender finger at the mewling stars, awash in gold perfumes. Wash up, slop down. Transactions are elongated by the fevered dreams. You'll know the octopus by its red ambassador. The transparent red cadaver willingly gives up its rod. The cold smoke of dark mannequins in their cages, the ability to count the red harnesses is esteemed by the rosewater in its stinking rod. What does God do to pass the time? Women are flat noise-water, men are pallid astronomy, red is circumnavigating gently. The accountants are held in high estimation by their own emerald cages. The startled perpetual-motion umbrellas cascade into the lubricated vacuums, they are starving. The vacancies erotically vacating themselves. The function of the cloying tropes is to remove the internal lubrication. There is no redundancy, no superfluity; everything is redundant and superfluous. The erotic plateaus are a shimmering redundancy. Peelings are superfluous, the moon is superfluous. The super-fluid is superfluous. Vacancy is suspicious, masking the drawer of lids. Vagrancy upturned by the coral reef, questionable unquestionable. The fresh emerald exudes a magnificent pallor.

The fresh emerald exudes a magnificent space

The fresh emerald exudes a magnificent incumbent

The fresh emerald exudes a magnificent toiling nettle

The fresh emerald exudes a magnificent orifice

The fresh emerald exudes a magnificent crying in the kitchen

The fresh emerald exudes a magnificent capacity

The fresh emerald exudes a magnificent nude

the stagnating vacancies are crowded

the stagnating vacancies are serpentine

the stagnating vacancies allowed

the stagnating vapors in bright costumes

the stagnating whispers fluttering

the fermenting children aroused especially

the fermenting vacancies around the bell of night

the fermenting whispers astounding

      The fourth emerald exudes a staggering vacancy in the middle of the day's stomach, below nine eyes stifling laughter like a toad. The hive eyes peeling like spare change. Have you seen the man who crouches very small in the hive? He is always smiling, he seems vaguely menacing like the skeletons of chickens. When he closes one eye the wind turns green and rolls over like a dog. He is impenetrable, crouching in the hive, unnoticed. He is exuded by the hive like a fragrance. The wheeling dervishes are exuded by the spaces. The hive hangs from a rock in the branches of a tree on a hill, it surrenders dolefully to the witnesses. Bees are the new currency. The current porcupine is stockpiling newspapers in the event of a thermonuclear squeal. The bright diarrhea is exuded by the important syncopations. It takes a very long time, almost thirteen winces. Should you swallow the current gradation, allow me to peel the forest from its bright husk. I'll be gentle. I treat the frost gently, as if my hands were coquettish onions. I will be firm with the snoring coats. I commit miscellaneous actions quite often. Sometimes I am seen, sometime unseen. Sometimes I am in unison. There is no audience, there is an audience. When there is no audience I can sometimes hear them slapping their wet wrists. When there is an audience I always press my face against them. Who is watching? Who will remain? The percolating tempest is gradually placated. Thou shalt not eat the feathers when thou art covered in mud. Absentee escalators boiling with liquid, vacancies shimmering with pride. The magnificent tolling nudes like an echo across the emerald sun: polar eclipse. It is ambiguous, it is not ambiguous. Is there a definite point of reference? A despairing point came across it suddenly by the rotting rainbow, rotting arrow. The blue geese are unsightly furniture and should be placed in their stems to await use. The fresh excrement fresh excitement is politely foreboding. Truths are in slow motion, truths are very fast like a blinking turtle. The truths are in excellent condition. Politely wake up the fallen tree. Night has an erection pointed inward, day wears its ovaries on its sleeve, night wears its ovaries under its massive head. The triumphant resurgence of the aloof grammarian aquarium, diluvial horseplay moniker.

The sky seems to be the size of the earth. Earth holds the sky in its seashell hands and shakes it gently. The sky has a sky, just as the earth has a sky. The sky of the sky involves many similarities: the dove and the faucet, the arc and gesturing, pointedness and the stinking sands, the jewel and the frog. The sky is not forgetful, the stones are not forgetful. The pale hearts in their shadow are not forgetful. The color of the sky of the sky is cranky and dilating furiously. The sky of the sky is two tears, two breasts, two fictions. Night has a sky and day has a sky, they are playing together continuously, they mimic each other. The sand is loose, the birds are folding. We must work diligently to fold everything in half. It is the ultimate solution, the ultimate condition. Forget the whispers and tumbling ecstasies, forget the pale white parabola and the conditioned frequencies. Forget forgetting, avoid toxic electricity. We mustn't forget our bone marrow, it is at the cinema with the clothespin skeleton. Disable the portable rhinoceros by submerging it in the bright milk. The feeling is singular, the feeling is multiple. I want to eat the scarlet and ambrosia and all the hamsters, hammers. I desperately seek a seersucker seer. My teeth are cold iguanas, they eat for me. I can be elsewhere. Will I always be somewhere? It's not my decision, it is my decision. I prefer the cold decisions. The portable decisions. The old delusions, idle delusions. Prickly, sticky, peeling, lukewarm, cellular. The atoms of my eyes are on parade, they spill like champagne. I don't try to hide it. When I am in an empty boat I do not try to hide. I address my captives like a teacher scorning a devious schoolboy, eyelashes twitching like lime mosquitos. The predicament is shattering, it's missing its hat. The wet dirt has been located. The placenta has been emulated. I am right here, behind these words. Can you see me? I'm waving from on top of the skinned penguins. I can't see you. Stand behind the elevator and make the sign of the shimmering line. Translate the hidden mirage. Is there a history of owls in your family? The severed pedestrians are glowering shrilly. Conflated conflagration of cloistered urethras in their straw nests. Why would you think that? The heroes are diabolical lobsters, the policemen are a bakery. Echopraxia crowned concealment, amorphous agate meniscus breeding hamburgers in the dust.

How often do you find yourself alone?

What is your favorite responsibility? Least favorite?

Are you under a lot of stress or pressure?

Do you like to sleep? Do you need a vacation?

That ice gargoyle singing for the fishing-pole toward winter or midnight, sun or star gloomily about its coattails. With a hook that matches the curves of Venus and a string-loop that blew smoke-rings through each eye looking into a keyhole, a clenched fist a clench fish, a wriggling fist with fish legs and two eight eleven nine four fifteen three nine all the way to the sunshine up the stairs and back, under the carpet where the sleeping dogs lie awake singing like cats, the large imprint of a gnarled hand spread open, a magnificent book pages swinging to the beat of the wind, groove in the soil, this hand causes the young man to recoil several days earlier, when the whale had legs and a mustache that was quite elusive, no finger could tame the fraying hairs, no comb shall bite the top-hat under the whale's nose, much like a piano-stool or pigeon-coop, too cold in winter, make all the chickens turkeys and shield the hearts of the ducks against a wave of pastoral sighs and skirmishes that threaten the surrounding environs this time of year, when the coat-hook is a fishing-hook, a toothbrush caresses the whale mustache and a long Chinese beard rises to the occasion, only to be smothered in kisses from the woman, while the young man searched for the fishing-rod, in water, in lake, Venus wields a long swordfish as if it were a cigarette, tomorrow all of our virtues will become flowers or shoes. To catch a struggling word and brush its roots with a fine metal, a fine petal of gangrenous tissue-paper, hot or cold, the word threw the crevices of your tongue into a pool on the floor betwixt your toes and feathers, a handful of feathers, a dying bird performing a wondrous somersault, the bleeding scar that the word has caused upon the Earth's surface, smoking rockets, smoldering boulders, high wind, a swordfish has mishandled the young man in his travels and he is now at the whale's corner, with a fishing-pole, somnolent, over his shoulder, azalea, tree shaking its leaves in a fog, overcoat and bottom-hat, undercoat and top-hat, the ghosts in the mirror can breathe whatever flowers grow on Saturn, Jupiter or Neptune; alas, it is the word who dwells on Mercury, on Uranus, a coat is thrown over the stars and the shoes are set on the moon, it is to withhold the emerald of the woman's eye, the woman who is enormous and great and a descendant of the carcinogenic heavens.

Whenever the waiter has arrived too early, before the customer has even come upon the restaurant, it is wont that the table-legs have wings and eyeglasses, so that when the patron finally approaches the dining area, the moon is already seated at the table, alongside the young man, who is asleep, who is a regular patron, a fishing-pole is seated beside the moon also, rapidly exchanging colors with the silverware, green to blue to snakeskin to wind to waterfall to red to the surprise of the woman, for there is a whale atop her skull, glorifying her bones the chandelier of her dining-room, a slow tiger that catches a cold and is subdued by the cheer of the cuckold. A ribcage has enveloped the tree nearest to the woman's left ear, which on the contrary is the young man's fifth knee; when the bones grin and widen, a canary clad in blue and scarlet, so that it is a nightingale or a crow, not a windmill or tulip-basket, there is a vast tongue in the spine of these ribcages, a pair of hands pressing flower fingers into a pattern on the roof if its mouth, winter, three fingers on each hand make a sea-anemone he finds a red fishing-pole, when the whale is snowing on the village of its birth, by the sea or roadside, lowside of the river down the lashes bat the cutlery and avast all ye who behold the sour nostrils of the whale wondrous as the tulip in spring before the heavy footfall that comes whenever a bee lands upon the tip of the tongue, right to the point, a rainbow, a cornerstone, on the woman's ankle, so that when the stone tower comes tumbling into the heavens, the robots can communicate through mind-speak, universal for all beings on this plate. Uranus is a uterus, the mordant run.

man climbing the side of a mountain

clinging to jagged rock

the wind blows snow into his hair and beard

he looks old

he stops on a ledge to rest

meditation is the

mind's

natural activity

perhaps there are

ghosts and spirits

all around us

everywhere

all the time

we just don't know about it

the government

especially

doesn't want us

to know

and

why should they?

ghosts should

pull the chairs

out from under people

more frequently

sense no sense

when you're in power

you're free to do

whatever you want

even when you are not in

a position

of power

you can do

anything

you want

go ahead

the sunlight on the meadow flowers

a broken shadow

falling among the teeth

of a forest

a girl in the meadow flowers

sunlight in her smile

water curves around her

white knees

golden in the eyes of

the green plants

and meadow flowers

stood a man

at the center of a

sunflower

that bent and waved

in the dark moonlight wind

the sand of

a vast desert

coiled

at his feet

and he removed his

shoes and set them

on the petals

a ghost came from

the sun

to visit the man

and spoke to him thus

stood a man

at the center of a

sunflower

that bent and waved

in the dark moonlight wind

the sand of

a vast desert

coiled

at his feet

and he removed his

shoes and set them

on the petals

Radiant

The inner workings

are the outer workings

there is just this working

it did not start

and it will not end

not expanding or shrinking

not creating or destroying

not growing

not still

it is unchanging

yet never the same

there is no place it is not

but it has no place

be in awe of it

do not get tangled in the lashes

on the eye of mind

let it flow in and out of you

and appear

Hair Removal

He was so surprised

that he dropped

all of the things he was

carrying into the

street

the hippopotamus looked

back twice

and stumbled

on a handkerchief full

of carved golden boxes

the tea kettle

excited by

this motion

urinated a coral reef

which hung out of

its spout

like a golden retriever

bringing such delicacies

as tomatoes

ice-caps

unwound springs

and the courage to keep

moving against the

quiet crawling undulating

expanse of desert

soft as a horse

and twice as egregious

the young man gathered

his things

speaking like a

burnt

coffin

The sky today

seems to be made from

hundreds of

birds

taking flight

blue and white and

with soft feathers

A single man

within a building

held in

to the air

looking

looking at the sky

he can only see

the tops of trees

hidden around the other

buildings

he can only see the sunlight

at the tops

of the trees

Branches kissing leaves

kissing feathers

kissing his eyes

the lips soft around his eyes

a flight of birds a loaf

of bread

his eyes in flight a bird a tree

feathers green and

the sky billowing blue

A man in a building

not quite as tall

as the ones around it

about the size

of a large tree

his shadow

in the branches

is not the sunlight

is not a woman

is not a bird

Peering out from behind these eyes

I see a giant's hands

clutching a giant's book

I release it

and the sound of it against the ground

is deafening

     the distant shore

since he is empty

he can perform any role

because he knows who

is the Actor

and also

who is the Audience

the earth

is not the center

of the universe

you may direct your thought

but understand where the center is

is is is is is is is is

lost echo

the world

just one sitting

      Hymn to the Sun-God

Magnificent! Inscrutable!

Your face so divine I dare not look

Your power unlimited

You are the light

the brightest rays

and the most dim

Candles and lamps

They are but poor facsimiles

Heavier than the greatest weight

Yet lighter than the meekest

Feather

Your reign is never to be usurped

Your flower is not spoiled

Nor will it ever be

Of all creation

You are unborn

The greatest mystery

Never to be unraveled

Alas, set and rise

You, in all glory,

Make the essential seem unnecessary

More than fire

Yet of the same nature

Fire borrows from you only your image

Fire, heat and light,

Those are but consequences

You, in all glory,

Give rise to the struggling plants

Decrepit humans searching

For water

Ecstatic animals running

Wild

Your terrain is

The secret forest

That gives birth

To all thought

Yet you are without (thought)

Another day

The mile-markers of infinity

Another day

Birth of a nation

And death

Vegetal

With the voice of the birds,

the snakes, the animals

You sing

With the voice of the trees,

the mountains, the rivers, the earth entire

You sing

But I do not hear

though strain to listen

My upset mind covers mine heart

But yea

even with the voice of my heart and mind,

my eyes, my ears,

my being whole

You sing the Glorious Song

Praise be to the ancestors

to the sun and earth

to nothing

Hail! Hail!

giant cat of nonbeing

its purr sounds like

the world

falling asleep

"the mind is not local"

is not confined

by anything

the boundless world

is this world

if you aren't thinking of anything in particular

what are you thinking of?

The gunlight often

reveals a chest of drawers,

twenty or thirty sandwiches,

a closet full of candlesticks,

etc, etc

and although someone lit a match

on the end of a shoehorn

his hands were tied

his shoes tied to his feet

his twos tied upside-down

across the room

in lonely

speculation

a trio of dice

shook hands effortlessly

no throne was left above water

where the trees crack their

voices

and so many roots were

up in the air

that it was no use

for the armchair

with its tongue of moonlight

to lay waste

the water garden

now silver out of courtesy

and the time

will come sliding in its box

decorated with

banana-peels, cowbells,

ladles, etc, etc.

little baby body

with large

suction cup

no arms or legs

right in the center

monkey eggs

monkey legs

are daddy-longlegs

instigator

burrowing into the coffins

a heart divided like a pear

to settle the acetylene squadrons

and morose

tributaries

      Vegetative reality of the sworn arches and their secret net. The swollen cavities in gauze curtain, the gaze of the gauze lampisteries is sure to raise suspicion. The capacity of the scared rabbits has reached a zenith. The voluminous luminosity is a figment of your stolid interrogation. Do not assess the serpentine milk in its hive. The man who crouches very small in the hive breathes only underwater or on an airplane headed for Stockholm Syndrome. Anxiety is a priori, the luxurious foam is a priori. The cardinal posterior is a posteriori. The blue loam is getting carried away. The delicatessens have been notified, the possibilities come from the same blood, shared blood orange. It is worthwhile to see double in torn soot the proboscis moon, the posthumous wool. The vestiges are glimmering with hope, the shared snare is the tropic of cancer daffodils. Infant child like the satin silhouette of a woman in the city at night, the silhouette of looming pedigrees. The infant is caught on the spiraling spires, they teach it to scoff in the face of liquid liaisons, it is the first lesson. The fighting hydrants balk at the sound of snow lubricating its feelers. The vast tension is undervalued, the tensile strength of an infant is comparable to the withdrawing locusts of dawn. I accept only the heartiest scalpels, blue at the ciscoes. Do not weep for me, I am a foreclosed aquatic aviary brimming with desire and fine china. I wear my desire under my chin so it cannot activate the serrated sheaths. The cages swinging in midair like alligator chandeliers. Petulant demagogue in stolen wisps. The tufts of rat's brain are peering through the fibers. The smiles are linked in a chain. The corrugated arteries inflated pastime. Casualties wield their ugly knobs aloft, the casualties of spores, the opulent pores, pores like quicksand, quicklime. Silence and noise are hyperboles, oysters are hyperbolic. Hyperactive bowl of guesses filtering through the gauze smoke. That is that, this is this, this is that, that is this. It goes around and around and everyone steps off at their perspiring designation, propped-up destination. This and that swallow each other whole. The holes have been swallowed elegiacally. The role of the faucet is to discourage the gunflint. The penultimate cables are sticky sticky, overhead. The trifles are baffling, luminous fart from the Arctic Circle, corrugated symposium of nymphs lousy with guilt, wretched blue umbrella. Do not indicate the pretty mouths to me, I can already establish a basic trembling treble. The tributaries are vastly applicable to the horned dawn, cloven serum. The stimulus delicately vacuous, the brass heart is divided like a spear over the toppled infinities. Wasps of dawn igniting the circular fires and choking forever on the wasps of freedom. Everything is random, nothing is random. There is no such thing as coincidence, it is all a coincidence. Dawn hammer anvil fish birth, confluence pedigree bludgeoning.

The womb disappears without a spec, startling the effervescent insects rolling in the spices. The astral totem of time fraternizes with the animals and spectral spheres, yet we turn a blind eye. Reality is a dislocated kumquat in the bright milk, slumming it with the spheres.

The bright spear projects its filiality on the carpenters quaking in the sharp dust. Boil the green curtains until each earthquake has ostracized its lobotomy. Turn over a new leaf, turn an old fear into sparkling dust wine. The placentas are placated wearily. A body pierced a thousand times by ivory cocks' combs. Penetrate the liquid abrasion, the equations are soiled by milky footprints. The ladders step loquaciously into the bright silk forbearance. The stars pouring with delight, broken totems like unremembered thoughts. All the miniature leaves are stained with grief over the loss of the multicolored singularity. Diminutive artillery in hiding, stellar evasion of icicles, the mind's deep icicles turning cartwheels at the ready. Time and space make love violently and trade places like the careful carefree shuffling of a deck of playing-cards or pigeons. The working cards are horned winged ornaments to recognize a false dawn drawn up by a substitute sunset. The horrible ornaments of the tax-paying recollection. Do not allow your courage to be discouraged, it is of utmost irregularity. The quaking fist, the cardinal fish lackadaisically produced by a bruised indication of elements. Call me piecemeal. The Great Colorless Perspiration dampening every morrow. The stalwart prisms are a marvelous monotony. Monotony is a stinging crucifix. I do not fraternize with the impolite potions on a daily discontinuum. The complaisant masquerade is pleasant enough and full of misgivings. The false signals of the arctic pleasures grow in leaps and bounds on the mound of placards. The bottommost placard reads: FRIGID POSSIBILITIES ABSORBENT AMOUNT. The crux is illegible as is wont of the peculiar necessities, the shorn tablets. The shyness of the jaded jade daffodils is overwhelmingly charming, it causes a riot of the senses.

smell = cracked

touch = tonsillectomy

taste = an old robe

ochre = furnish, limpid

sight = odorous leavings

hearing = tryst

Gasoline = podiatry

God = surface, surplus

      Put your liberty in a box and send it home. Pierce your mourning with a dastardly toothbrush, carry your placentas in an upside-down umbrella, the sound of it sloshing around makes static the bees. The noisome energies are quarreling frivolously, the miraculous lids marvel at their own entropy. Entropy is a darling environment suitable for only the most coniferous latitudes. Entropy gets stinking drunk like a duck. The maternal arabesques with their seascapes and cityscapes, I turn a cold ear to the accumulating atmosphere. I pledge to withdraw only the gathering platitudes of frost. Do not despise the spoiled despot, for it is lousy with rain and unborn tempests. Age before trampling, it must be aged a fortnight every quarter-hour, the time generally accustomed to the vapid ages. The liquid ages are vampiric in their squalor. Liquid and gas are very old, they have dust and snow in their platinum mile-long beards. The mile-long bears. The rocket-ships are greasy monkeys hooting at the dawn, the spaceship barking with milky laughter. The daughters of the Milky Way are acquiescing liquidation. Penetrated degradation at 5 o'clock on the dot. The different times of day can't wait to see each other. The clock's favorite time is no time at all. This happens quite frequently, like Kant's strolls along the crematorium of gymnasiums. Dislocated pleasure in the swirling mists of twilight. The firmness makes no difference. The horses are unhealthy because they eat their own droppings. The voice of the mind getting further and further away, vanishing down the long corridors of the mind. Absolute geology. There's plenty of hooves to go around, there's plenty of whispers to shield the night. Engraved on the destitute totems are the words: ON OFF DARK LIGHT. My house is a bathhouse. The sinking, screeching, stinking, blinking totems of the dawn, choking on the bright umbilical shards. The gnarled totems of hoary awareness streaking across the sockets redglare, designated for new snouts, ventricle coordinates, ventricle awareness smothered in cobalt kisses, despair of the diseased coordinates. The world is a broken wheel endlessly turning ceaselessly spinning, the mind is dirty laundry that smells terrible. The bright tube of dawn hovers waveringly above the pitiful circus of swans composed of milk. Glimmering esophagus made of passing glances.

How often do you feel grateful?

Does life entertain you?

Are you a serious person?

Does your body ache? Does your mind ache?

The creation of thought occurs in the same way as the creation of the universe. The creation of circumstances and polecats. I maintain my appearance with little provocation, my appearance is protected by a thin husk of lettuce. I can set my appearances aside for the time-being. A charitable provocation to moisten the little towelette of our dreams. Actively consider the smarting tempests. The canister of flesh is distributed haphazardly across the wastes, active water removal, moral temperature throughout. The cremation of thought and the universe. Heaven and Hell are right here, right now. Heaven and Hell are in the mind, they must be discarded, they must be swallowed whole. It is continuous, it is not continuous.

What if every single person in the world was exactly like you (having the same opinions, preferences, etc)? Would you enjoy it or despise it?

Do you prefer tight or loose-fitting clothes?

The old train-cars rattle by the smoke mountain filled to the brim with glasses of water and top-hats, swimming in the empty sockets of the dirt with gravel in its teeth was a wolf frozen to the bone as a quick flash gets a rise out of the fallen ashes of a cigarette or brunette or fox eyed by the lamp wayside and cold shoulder locomotive, the strong-willed parakeet makes its flight a jar full of honey while the bees are chased by storm-clouds in a seashell the shape of the old cow's beak, a feather for the teeth and wheel of that old lion by the wayside, dandelioness at the foot of the heel, sweet is the ice which melts at the touch of the frail skeleton fingered dandelion underneath the stairs, waiting for a maid or bellboy to open the door or leave a swollen bee-sting at the length of hair spun in a circle of clowns dancing at the feet and with thunderclouds burrowing into the skin above the knee, trembling flower handed daisy-chain maiden of wheels and overcoats thrown overboard at the most, quick thunder strike and around the back of the neck a swing-set is built for the teeth that may find shelter in the oak trees and nightingales of the woman's forest fires and clowns fallen from the fishbowl into the birdbath beyond the knoll, detached fingertips slide under the eyelids and carve out a niche where the sweaty sailors and drunken lovers may live in the barrel of monkeys at the bottom of the sea shine, overblown the windstorm a cloud of bees and hair rise from the eyeballs like roses or dandelions, where the wool is woven in the seashells of the sailors and the forest keeps a fire in the back-pocket of the whining clown's nose filled with ice and wine.

The pharmacist's tongue flickers like the flame of a candle at the donkey's bray. The pharaoh's mouth is an exquisite anus, the pharaoh's tongue is a flower with delicate petals that is hidden or revealed depending on the climate in the locomotive. Trains are a soapstone flower with dilapidated petals, cucumber window. The signs carved in marble are effaced by mean-spirited well-wishers in their washing-machines. Boiled dromedaries and raw turnips in cough medicine are the foodstuffs of the gods in upholstered binary systems. Diurnal lactation of the steaming pulpit. Putrid distribution, prickly semen echoing across the spaces like a god coughing in tainted ice. Petulant syncopation of the senses reined. The pharaoh's penis is a chain that links the canary to the cupboard. Ceaseless hyphenation of neutron nations up down, at all hours of the polar cocoon. When the water turns silver, disclose the briar chandelier with one good arm pointed south, covered in crocodile tears by the bend in the stream, growing, behind the clouds, ecstatic salute. The Golden Murder occurs twice every two equinoxes. The light-switch flips to either LUNAR or SOLAR: a sailboat is at the helm. The light-switch flips to either HIGH or LOW. The urns must be devastated, they never fail to produce a pince-nez. The absent pharmacist doesn't abhor the sporadic whores in the arboretum, and neither do I. Touch the peeling wings. Trouble has glass feet as it tip-toes around the lavender wastes. The countless cigars by the wayside. The pharaoh is an exasperated tea kettle foaming with laughter. The drool is accumulating nicely like a god hot and quaking like a set of jaws. Smut.

The blue eyes caught in the road crooked, until at sundown the fish came marching along in columns made of vinegar and alligator skin, the teeth were fish, the sunburn was a golden moon crying out from the forest of her hands, her shoulders, the window was open to the winter undressing in the cold and somnolent labyrinthine crocodile mouth, clumps bared, the nightingale tumbling like a glass sphere down the cemetery spiral staircase, at which point the sun arose, the roses froze, the lilacs glistened and tulips held their clothes against the light sliding under the bed, the rainbow ran gold and ran around the crooked road at the smile of the woman when she visits the seashore, when her crocodiles are seashells and the nightingale calls out into the morning like some distant sea bell; the fire is flailing its arms into the seabed, as the horseman rides unmoved into the dawn, that gateway to the heavens which few souls have dared enter, for the rain and fire run around in the eyes of the dawn, and the winter holds its breath when the dawn inhales the smoke and powder cast off from the fish as they run rubberneck against the glass trapdoor sealed shut at the mouth of the winter dawn, eyeballs fall out around the ankles, the clothes are wrinkled and dark, sun sealed the lips of the burning leaf turning windmills into silk and the spiderwebs run loose in her hair each toss and tumult the lion finds its green canary in the mouth of the dawn, in the eye of the dawn a dandelion curls around the moonbeam nightingale, winter nightingale and bluebird. The spiral staircase mustaches of some overcoat winds like a summer road avoiding the dawn, in case the fire had started earlier than expected and the rain had taken the flight of birds and overwhelmed the stagecoach at the bottom of the stairs, a ceiling-fan running amok a bull coiling into the tulip bulb twofold, underneath the arms of the trench-coat the woman flares her nostrils to collect the dew that the frogs leave behind when the dawn is done, when the fire is run, run around the stable and the front yard is littered with bicycle handles and mustaches, the winter and summer hold each other's hats and the wind like spiral staircases before they freeze and become glorious statues, racehorse of dawn, the sun rests in its decline on the mountaintop of the horse, seeking a new way to carry its passengers, weeping, the spring that follows the clock but is not permitted entry rearranges the letters of several alphabets so that whenever a crow or centipede erupts into moonshine, the solemn bell of mourning will erupt into liquid sun candles and fire centipedes carrying dishes on their backs into the golden winter sun declining.

Winter bell, winter bell, the forests rush into the night of seasons, the sea is crying out its moon tears and the welcome-mat is rung out to dry in heavens of blue vistas and spider leg bathtubs crawl all over the sun, the lightning lunar eclipse, the sundown collision of two distinct migratory animals, winter bell, the sea pulls up its dress and shakes the gravel and sawdust from its lashes, the coat is forgotten at the beach of the woman, sitting in the sand with moonbeams for eyes and the winter bell tolling hard from her navel, the young man is swept up into the whale for the winter night and at daybreak the sun loosens its moose at the door to the dawn, winter bell whose dandelions are crystal and the lilies shine like lotus suns, liquid eyes pouring rain from their sockets, the skeleton in the bedpost climbs the sun mountain into the dawn, winter bell daybreak, the floorboards curl and evaporate the feasts which bring together close relatives but distance the foundation of the house from the skeletons beneath it, a winter bell passing over the clouds on the seashore near dawn's magnificent house, Aurora sweet and golden is the ocean and her fingers creeping around the sawdust and dog horses around the shore for the meanwhile, the sun is a cupped hand as the lotus falls into the loving embrace of winter bell fingers.

Each arc of the squirrel's jump is a moon eyeglass reflecting the woman's curving intestines, every octave of the bird's song is a ray-gun pointing into her heart, the sun is out of the coat-pocket and around the bend, the curve of her eye is a rose blossom in the dust and blue moon ocean sand across the winter bell in tow, each toe of the fire pig is a foghorn with her blood dripping out, the coat is off the hook, sun down at the forest toe in the road, heavy and tumultuous the rain forest blew down the house of the rainmaids all in a bundle of silk under the stars under the stairs at a quarter to noon a penny to the moon, iron teeth at the heel clamp and twist a rumpus into the popped balloon filled with winter air and the woman's breath a squirming intestine ascends the mountain staircase and finds the forest master meditating with a stone in his lap, a fireball chiseled into a cube and the pyramids of Eyegypt are cloaked in eyes and invisible hieroglyphs. Corduroy leaf pattern blue velvet ivory sun slopes at the crack in the dawn, a gray hound ran icicles over the windowpane and windswept tidal wave pinched the pince-nez into a forest cone, overcoat over the boat and swept under the wind rug, crack at the tooth fox sunburned intestines coiling around the foot of the whale with the young man at its tongue and the vial of bees and other natural things ruptured a lung and burst into the winter blue and green forests, sandboxes bring the ocean to the boy, at the coiled foot of the bed around the cycle of seasons and bears with beehive mustaches shaking at the fist, wind caught dark fingers falling, breathing the sandbox intestines at the wind of the woman, forest sleeps wrapped in the broken kerchief of the dawn, dinosaurs of dawn wake the sun in the iceberg's eye, moon windmill in the shadows resembles two hands sailing in a boat where the sand sits uncounted gold for seashells and brawny tikis standing like idols, idolaters.

Do you have anything scheduled for tomorrow?

What does the immediate future hold for you?

How often do you think about the past?

Do you look favorably to the past or future? The present?

The clasps are at the mercy of the alligators of dubious accumulation, dubious acceleration. The scalloped hen carries in its incredible umbrella hands the perfect roast, indelibly perforated. The bathhouses come to roost on the frozen pelican who grasps at the wind of trumpets, indelible freezer-burn. Inchoate digestion of archetypal orifices. Sublimate the tax-dollars languidly. Punctuated asthma of the seething sterling serums. Surfeited surfaces of the collapsed menagerie, smashed cowbells. The customs must be buffeted to accrue the surviving angst. The cavernous umbilical cord houses only the most overripe bananas. Emasculated provinces are most welcome to the ear of corn by the foot of the bed in tatters, hand of corn, corn of ears. The scalloped menagerie, the scallops in their evening-clothes flock to the sound of fire. Daytime fires are slowly bred, nighttime fires in imitation of the moon, the womb. The sun and moon are phosphorescent tombs, harbingers of credulous ducts. Woe betide the quartermaster drawn and quartered for his limp roosters, exceeded exasperations. Do not lean too far over the balustrade, it is known to cause outbreaks of snakes. Miniature people can be observed walking across the windows on the horizon of snakes, snails, and broken plates. The replica has been misplaced, the replica of the reptile fungus in its sepulchral gown. The pincers are sputtering in disbelief. I do not hesitate to lengthen my tail. My penis is a tail on the wrong side, it helps me to keep balance when I am stuttering across the vapors. Penises are polar ice-caps in their darling decomposition disposable luminescence. It is right that you should whisper sweet nothings into the vaginas of pregnant women, the fetuses will grow into jade deer frozen celebration. If instead you shout careful obscenities, place the left hand in the bubbling moss clinging to ice-floes in jugular anticipation. The moss growing on the sweet turnstiles are spacious fingerlings, liquor of the mice, the moose, the feelings. Sparkling menageries of dubious designation. Tumultuous vision of the decaying gods glimpsed in shadow, the starlight is produced by funerals and handmaids. Porcupine pork-pie hat in too many hands and feet.

Stark feelers accenting the boiling dawn, the precipice is simulated gorgeously. Salivating simulacra of the devious panthers hurling feces and cherry-trees at the night, one is bound to stick like a monocle. Monotonous moon monocles of the important presentation designed by the common owlk in its fervent hibernation. The hibernating nations await the cancellation of the camels, the season of candlesticks and cultivated moats. It is right that one should boast of the fingernails, toenails, doornails dead as a scepter. The scepter is a creature deserving of tangental referendums like moist silk, silk teardrops wept by the present hooded mood. A hand stretched across the gaping dawn, tightlipped night. The fledgling phlegm shits out a decomposing human corpse, loosening the quills gangling, snoring corpse feigning light. Train ties. Outbreak of mice with silver shoes. Silver ice-flotsam of used posturing, spilt rebozos, poignant refusal. Spoiled rebozo harsh lantern-light fluctuation. Disjointed attorneys crowning achievement. The pining pine tree is covered in cigarette-burns and deceased lice magnates. The crows are a preposterous magnet, attracting only the lunar squiggles and frost dismayed. Sticking to the roof of the suckers is a sweet dangling antelope for the ages. Glorious accumulation of the spheres, the economy bristles like a simpering hazard. The sight of the breathtaking looms makes me hungry for praline snot, but the crabs have been ignited. Gather your senses together in a bundle, pull the long stinger. Avoid worthwhile posturing of crowbars in the dusk. Huge molten tusks splintering the vainglorious frontages. Truncated lobotomies in their ivory boxes up the stairs. Mouths are the source of the hibernating spigots, unlimited faucets, crinkled facet. The freeway above the skyline coital mirage. Lugubrious horned-toad of destinations, gestations. Lax presentation of the childish hand-grenades. Sparkling wax caterpillar of frustration sparking wax habitat. During the summer, moonbeams are spiny and poisonous. It is advised to glow in the light, growing dark crevices cunning spinsters. Sparked winged cornucopias collectively simulating. Moths fly on wings of sparks toward the distant plights, skipping stones across the tomorrows. The bulbous bulbs punctured tenure: warm gooey penumbra, cold gluey parabola. The singed dampness of egrets egress magisterially. Mechanical testimony of the burst pustules gleaming.

Does it seem like life is more bearable elsewhere?

Liverwurst from the stronghold emanating across the moribund totems, fecund extrapolation. A banquet for all the decapitated tulips and seahorses, sea-lion of dawn barking at the handicapped locus. Fecund acceptance of poisoned umbrellas, marvelous treasure-house of simultaneous hens. Always bring the bright regalia. Fundamental coiled pajamas: we are our body or our body is just a disguise, reeking like an elephant, pelican dawn. Tombstone marigolds like hens in the park at sunset. The trapeze artist with broken spigots cries frying tears like a bunch of grapes. Clustered around the crimson flatulence is a burbling flotilla of armadillos alight. The winged golem armadillo in sheep's clothing sodomizing the houses in the arrogant cul-de-sac. Dregs of tomb-water enveloping the cardinal patrons at mousetrap o'clock, pointed. Eagle = the acute phobia or mania of being dissolved in purple sugar. It's understandable now why the foolproof pigeons carve their stomachs into sterile lobsters taking a bath in curdled forests. Forests resemble stone insects and weigh about the same. Disregard the feculent collateral and submit to multiple exposures. It's soul-nullifying when the bees take the shape of men and prance about the streams in foreign garb. Something must be undertaken, a hatchet, a creme-brulee, a hamlet. A collective parachute to dislodge the barbed clitella, the phony escapades are exceedingly mobile. Nubile crescent of warmth abridged above the fluttering wastes. Harangue the fleeting wolves as best you can. The wool nails have been baked into a pirate, succession of piñon ballerinas into the lovely sewers. The syrupy firebrand was formerly threatening, now it treats the coasts to a light parade of female farmers roughhewn and coalescing. The horses shriek: "Canonize the appetites!" Fold all the tails and lay them by the wayside for the demur ploughs. The vascular coital syringes emphasize the steadily increasing input. Output of gonorrhea music. Left-behind orchid long ago and forgotten, no more remembered. A polite steam-engine always sets me adrift, a polite maple. It gives the substitute animals something to do. The reflex of moist cows crowning. Moth powder makes for a suitable skirmish. I wish there was no object permanence. Premium extinction electric kinship

pursuit ribald foghorn fortress person single ironclad fingers supple birthing hornets buffet beautician sombrero gander plump oscillate brought tubular frown crucial superb blinking turbid crust paleontology wish desert distant decal lop reared cretin hoarse clue patent felonious eon fern voluminous zoo Mu ogle granite with defrost fnord than dish hut hover wear we oat tooth frail slice bowel an

fruition extradite funk colonial harp lest avidly and acre stretch helm
bounty versus young nirvana persona trial after moor mouse rump
ointment gesundheit eldritch anoint brokerage fallow thoroughfare
warm Om quench might suburb allure lolly acne fount droop sooth gas
went roil pealing eardrum quiver furniture thistle loud edamame front
dfghjl hurt hoist buckling toward down upfront gallant gallop duo
forcefield villain brain quail extinguish ignition portion unveil develop
promise salient crucible crowning home soar fought fugue from for
fifteen forthright pineapple brawn ruby goal foal mollusk pith froth
fourth whenever rat throat colossal juice jinx keep legitimate hubris
piccolo proud undone utter udder stringent tooling research polling
policy plastic petition perturbed ultimate fuselage foreground floats
germinate amalgamation mortician tour winding slack throes smokes
ringing bring stolid jousts personal yearly tout trim steamy yawl awl
drone sundry all pronounced papa mama Dada again heliocentric
systemic corpuscle crest who stampede entire dilation culminate cusp

nothing to worry about

Horn slopes that slow mountain top stream beauty by the
wayside lorn to begotten foghorn so slow born two lips under lips the
blanket, cane scissor twisters two much, tumult under us, winter side
gown to loose that, which way gone the blue horn night time beetle
blue, for goose below the subterranean belt ghost out the sun, circle
eye sun hole, the whole outer and inner, enter without caress and the
care will for itself serve the twilight lips of tong fight, rose gorgeous
plunge plinker plumage soon to noose the plumage her arms loose, fire
flight in the lantern sighs and brings each time soil and sand sings blue
coins and birds, jut in case of the night calling lonesome eye sun,
righteous wing some dove; coat tails the curtain following sweet star
lashes, coat sings that the tails are two lonesome by the morning called

fungal window and another night for the eight lips of bird brains, your
yesterday mourning settled the midnight door yard toddling under the
coat arms under thirst of hundred mouths lips and that bloody and
gravel-filled esophagus tonight, coat tails wings all around in an
embrace to see with, as two lips, winter dawn cold laundress of fish,
eastern star foghorn leases liaisons the worn horn tingling around the
soothing fish legs, whale bones cry for mother, of pearl of night of
mercy of desire, of the first fire that caressed the waves of daffodil
sand and waves of sky clear water under the eyelids that fasten the
belts of the gentlemen of the night, of the morning even when the
window is still an octopus or cushion, have a seat or be left in the
tombstone shallow standing blue night, good moon, along my wayside,
forlorn by the garden path o sing a song by and bye, all along coat
sleeve sing to the eaves, murder is the elbow that loosens the pearls
from yesterday, when under the carpet

that fish or dog or stone fox is caught swing to the hundred
acre tumble land forest night cloud asleep, hundred by the by and the
road all along the watchman's coat door, caught like bramble in the
kneecaps of yon barn and a hatful that crowns off the kings fastened
asleep booth of cool water and later that liquid can grin with the best
of them or us, western barn mouth yawns into the handkerchief
bedside manner, a cold open manor as warm as the hill it lays its eggs
upon, rolling down the hill river, up-down and sailboat is the hand of
sand that wipes clean the lips and slate of marble glass door stair pits
to free space, infinite if that is what truly loves the company of
existence; the letters and meaning of the word 'signal' disperse in the
rain, goose flesh the old newspaper to be read again sunny rain, all
blown over with the window door longside down and up-and-over
welcome blossoms spread the winter over the grave by the lingering
sand full of gone days and scalding teeth too piercing to open with the
wit of a dead shogun and sunny day too wonderful too open by the seat

of the rainmaids' sailboat, taken book pages and soot, looked down
upon the horizon, sat open the lips of each planet in the heavens under
the crack in the door, bleeding and crying an endless mountain of
happiness for the grimacing humanity in all its wonder gory glory
hinder the scarlet shoehorn too blue and forlornly dreaming the loves
of thousand nights and with such three graces does each one clasp in
their hand skirmish whose dress is wrinkled with the eyes all painted
gold and blue and sad and smiling, goodness gracious and rumpled
crown horse, one time; before my eyes

is after the gold sweep that took the dress of the long winter by
surprise and traveled her all the way round the corner of her eye and
soon the too man became heavy hay now, door a horse, coat too long,
shoe horse fits around the keyhole in the fashion of a noose toward the
end of winter comes the sunset rising and setting with all its glory
tucked under an embraceable wing, window wing to magic and Saturn,
ring around the rosy-haired maiden voyager that takes all those rings
and sings to Venus a farewell to the meeting of three crystal white
horses understood by the lone tree storm gathered by the wall and the
stairs flow like wine, open down under the coattails of the universe,
when the wind sweeps gold by the wind-song window long gold form
ghost forest that weeps slender candle women for the tired and
undulating eyes of the immaculate woman to suspend in the air, like
two hands, honey drips over the moon like wine and that fat
nightingale can kiss the wind shine for all the horse gold in the world,
windswept by the wind-song forlorn and frogs sweat the dew, dance in
the blooming mule flowers' path or during intermission, woman brings
around the swan-song by the coat of her arm; burning sun flesh sun, by
the glass eye at the treetops swings the beauty of the trees, floating on
the branches of so many wind twigs and skirt fringes weep at the peel,
back toward the floor, by the window of the night the treetops and sigh
with the joy at the tree lips, finding the silver eye at the end of the

tree's outstretched arm, meeting the sun by a little town, sad-eyed grin window, that old wind-song winter crow whispers a deer by the road lowside, drop your bones by the shoulder, whispers to the road along the lowside of the deer, know that there is sand after the sun, past the ocean.

Have you done anything lately that you're proud of? Ashamed of?

Is everything you do necessary?

Is there something that's holding you back?

The ligaments are figments of train-whistles that culminate in the shadowy corpse of our rancid desire. The prurient wastes are hyphenating the stamens with a grandeur normally suitable for tablecloths and viscous misconceptions. Carts spurned to wrap their faucets in tears and dried hocus-pocus. It is unbearable when the clouts shimmering against the failing discs develop their own nostrums. I can hear you reclining into your arms. Stilted growth of syringes attached to a coat of forms, coat of hams and legs duplication mist. My coat of feelers is a perpetual warning. The elopers are caught in the feelings and trimmings tumbling. Ambient ambulance spirited away by the coming horde, stunning swarm. Stunted mule breath of nasturtiums. A grand colonoscopy for the sages. I am a swift funnel. I slit the darling crevices and precipitating precipices. Always be prepared to exit the grinders in the vent of an external or internal qualification. The poised sentries have tripled their conductivity. Swarthy and bright: peeling brigade. Shaken harem storied frenzy in a counter-cloak accelerating the rate of decadent proposals in the pew. The shrapnel is obscenely cute and lovely. The tight titanium allocation of implements curdled by the sordid frankincense. Mirthless smirking balcony crusade. Dawn is a flavored genocide in peals of frost, the pearls of ghosts. The catechisms are unwittingly subversive and pallid. Again the magnificent nudes tolling across the vacancies, the diameters, the centrifuges. Subterfuge of the arrays. Obfuscated confiscation of titillations and safety-pins. Tie down the golden marinade. The shimmering marionette of our feelings and stolen touches crinkling at the dawn of airy penguin particles. Fraud below absolve above absolute involvement. I wouldn't know it if my teeth were cranberries, they're so distinct. Polygamous cucumber of dawn, tusks. Carpeted phantom of desolate folds. Trail the spindling hollows. Hallowed frowns, hallowed forms hollow form formulation. Wherefore the future propriety? Wherefore the garden flutes? Sick loot. A precious upset, settled salaciousness manifold two-step. The ornery plantations of our forebears. The calculator is wet and full of regret. Let us regain our infancy, our intimacy, our shallow regalia. Courtship of the immense jade antennae, falcons of night like a breath of fresh air. Frescoed alimony intruding on the porticoes notwithstanding. Assimilate to the casual circumference. Frenetic ascension, torpid detention, detection of crystalline miracles all and sundry. Sequined sequences of the vast alabaster privilege.

I applaud the safflower sapphire coercion. The vast alabaster forklift is questioned forthwith avian flume, aviary in shackles by the doorstep, configured infection. The articulate contraption made of foiled condolences is boiled artillery for the asocial goosebumps and nether scions willy-nilly, articulate conglomeration. The fortunate world is a drafty whorl. Crazed network of inside-out fish, outside-in bees. Exhibit the ironclad pretenses emotionally. Ostracized erlenmeyer-flask defamation disordered blue periphery. Let us hoist the kings to further accentuations. The sulphuric palanquins anointed and cumbersome accelerations. Maladroit fruition unfurled lovingly by the masked dawn. Sand-trap of avian ovaries declaration. Advent of accumulation. The tinted tusks are countless legless trunks. Titillate. Precocious flumes of pummel, tumult, plummet. Plumes of fruition. Create the necessary absolute frictions. Spurious testimony of the bed-ridden altitudes, crocodile attitudes. Remote access to the bright frontiers of the mind mingling telescope. The wanton undressing of the foliage is unnerving, the venerable gestation is appropriately cyclopean. Vulnerable tryptic of fresh flesh in open spaces closed. Pyrrhic vesicle undue triangulation. The ostriches have formed a capable tribunal and are rampantly distributing the polyurethane tendencies. Engorged amount based on prior electrocutions. The sand clasped by the hand is on all fronts a worthwhile orthodontist. Serpentine tendencies elevating the status of the ginger and seclusions. The ambiguous systems are devouring the bioluminescent monarchs. The luminaries are commandeering the breastplates, boilerplates, noiseless ratios. Change the outside and the inside will change; change the inside and the outside will change. Change is ambidextrous, change is a walrus, a bloated polygon of sorts. Incontinence is an egg concealing the seashell seahorses, wax nasturtium, bloated nostrils flaring relentlessly. Restlessly duplicating itself amidst stars, planets, cocoons, combs, fraught with tremors. Perfect imperfect highway to the faraway galaxies traversed by untidy crimes. Let us do away with the anatomies and antibodies. Unclogging gracefully the celestial pores. Man-made plums that wisp and plumb cordially like bright disembodied foam, funeral procession of thoughts, empirical progression of forgotten length. Imperial imps made gaseous by courteous fossils in their summer gowns. The phony anticipation is a phony celebration. No one knows what's going on here. There is no Stranger anywhere, there is no Other. It is all Strange, it is all Other. Other mother under cover, no no no no.

furtive assertion

furtive assertion

furtive assertion

furtive assertion

furtive assertion

furtive assertion

furtive assertion

furtive assertion

furtive assertion

furtive assertion

furtive assertion

furtive assertion

furtive assertion

furtive assertion

furtive pollution

furtive assertion

furtive assertion

furtive assertion

furtive assertion

furtive assertion

furtive assertion

furtive assertion

furtive assertion

furtive assertion

furtive assertion

furtive assertion

furtive assertion

furtive assertion

furtive assertion

furtive insertion

furtive injection

furtive assertion

furtive assertion

furtive assertion

furtive assertion

furtive assertion

furtive assertion

furtive assertion

furtive assertion

collapse equate

construct oblique

furtive pollination

vascular tendencies

muscular hypothesis

torpedo outright

fermentation imagining

so long farewell

billow billow billow billow

billow

vanished formaldehyde

fortunate diamond

furtive assertion

diaphanous propellor

aviary propellor

What do you find most beautiful?

Is there a lot of beauty around you? Do you notice beauty often?

Are you hungry? What is your least favorite food?

From the mouth of the lion I can see the canary, green as the
moonlight on a rhinoceros' horn.

A carrot has run loose from the garden.

Cool waters of the galaxy, cleanse my rocket-ship bones!

Bathed in perpendicular smiles, Mendelev's coin-purse is threatened
by the tendrils of an ravaging airplane.

Wild geese toward your knees one thousand times, diamond caterpillar
diamond mouth and eyes.

In the country of the position, the one-haired impostor is ajar.

Rivers flow all over my tongue, green and blue and dazzling like the
sunrise on Jupiter.

Rivers flow all over my images, spiny and giggling like a bronze
impostor.

Forests are my hair and my body is a great landscape under which
skeletons and mice dance simply.

On Saturn, the month of June is a washbowl, cracked near the rim.

The hovering lights breathe minuscule icebergs that increase in size every year and a half or so, until the solidification is as old as the gnarled fingers of the stars.

Against the veil of twilight, crimson blinks twenty-seven dogs and cats.

Breaking a raspberry gargoyle's fist into one thousand fingers, sinking into the belly of a ghost, twirling past the light of thine eyes dost thou move in the spectacular whirlwind of grinning quicksilver flashes and one gunshot licks the lamp toward noon.

When a chair, fallen from a glorious height, collides with the surface of the table to which it was assigned, the impact is that of a glass vase full of flowers imploding on the surface of the moon.

Free the triangles and cubes of cerulean from you inner-space, the multidimensional shapes and forms of outer-space gather at the trapdoor's call, a swarm of fish too dense for the stars' piercing lips.

Beehive!

Behave!

Dying is the same as not dying, living is the same as not living, hotcha!

Rake the blood-red leaves, porpoise of mine, the crystal-ball is out of the oven and into the lake.

The Way is similar to a march of foxes and ants and sewing-machines and fingers underwater.

At last, when the forest fire collects its silverware from the hind-legs of the shark, I shall retire to the chess match or orchestra crawling blue gables, a big rough tongue.

From the laughter of my feet I can bathe in the golden caress of the nebulae, attentive and withstanding.

My parapet looms around me, I cannot see the sun or octopus or skeleton.

In this season, the curtains must be drawn; soon afterward, they must be set aflame and just as quickly extinguished in order to procure any flailing tigers loosening the doors from their frames, tigers falsely painted so that their stripes resemble more the eyes of a deck of playing-cards or the migratory patterns of the lion-tamer's whip in this season.

Together, we form a comforting blanket, knit in the cool moonlight, protecting you from the invading environment; your gratitude is unnecessary.

The thud of thought seeping in the asbestos thunk festoon.

Fistful of soil, carried on the backs of a pair of disembodied hands, seek refuge in my throat, across my waist and on my chest, heaving as the wind in the eye-socket of the sea.

Dazzling spaceship, smoking rockets, fuming sockets.

A flower emerges from the donkey's teeth!

Green around the roses, forward and backward blue around the edges, wooden sheep cast the pale blue phantom of a torpedo or taxicab.

Jesus umbrella shrine.

Twenty fish arranged about the eyelids of tomorrow, yesterday and the day before, calm rooftop vines red and gold, the pincers of the sun grasp the moon's ankle in amorous frenzy.

Old torn shoe with three feet by the lowside.

Apples that take the shape of lemons, but speak with the tongue of the windmill.

Entertainment is deceitful.

The purest form is invisible.

The cricket sometimes enjoys having no form.

The crickets sometimes enjoy having no farm.

At the treetops a hermit-crab sings nightingales to the wondrous moon and to the illustrious sun he passes forth minuscule dungeons filled with bathwater for the nightingales.

The stingray of smoke spirals outward, to greet the twilight, to greet the stones arranged in such a way that when the patrons of certain restaurants come upon them, a blue spyglass evaporates over their heads, iceberg of the mistress's wide open hands and mouth and coat, embroidered in a mystic patter, of stars and planets, far away.

Flying away the red moon glow, shine through the feathers, a forest of shadow across the road alone, a girl in the meadow flowers and sunlight white.

The sea, the ocean…

Times like these, I get to wondering what makes up the great expanse of sky and desert and sun, and just what fills that emptiness, to make it what it is.

There isn't any law where there aren't any people.

Put together a fire.

Will you get me something to eat?

We are headed for the heart of the country, where trees grow and flowers, where clouds are born and go to die, ingested, where the sun and moon are caught making love amidst the thrushes.

Drying the tears.

Let the wind close the curtains, the lion of candlelight caught in the sawdust pendulum swings. The winter bell tolls against the firmament of emeralds the swallow's wing tosses and turns in the ocean, overwhelming, too quickly, the sunlight is too heavy at the foot of my heels, my cables, the lion with the swallow's wing. Don't strike your match upon the pig's hoof, you swift running coy coyote yo-yo curled by the fireside; the embers are fish, are swallow's wings, are frostbite at the fountain, giving its water to the heavens, the bowels of heaven are loosening, are moving too swiftly and all the excrement is catching fire around 3 o'clock in the afternoon every day this year. I hold the sewing-machine underwater long enough for the diamonds to catch their breath. Won't it be a joy to witness the nightingales fall under the lion's wing and turn over in their shoes, turn over in their allocations? A soft rain full of clouds and eyeballs full of diameters, ghosts upon ghosts upon hosts upon hosts leaping in and out of the water, a bicycle could catch terminal fish out the corner of its stasis! But in time, the lake will loosen it rump, the feelers drifting from the lion's mouth will become a green canary or some bumblebee looking for a starved diamond on the surface of the witless lake. Horse's three eyes, a fog like breath in and out of a keyhole, cream wind and basic hells hanging from each tree, sing the gentle cane and coarse voices hold up the bank-robber by the cabinet, windows down, forest down at the heels over and over the window will call out for tricycles and the streetlights waving flags like fists of ivory, coat-hook caught the fish nine times, tails trailing green behind the window seven times seven, one four nine six one nine nine one over the other five tails a trench-coat, sand at the top of the boat, the hapless coat falls out of the window, toothache sewn together by matchsticks and candlelight down a flight of stars, a flight of books and bird cases spiral down the window case flying dandelioness pearls at the night's hoarse horse the sun at its hooves reaches its decline in a bed of sand will-o'-the-wisp; festering cyclone clone, sand bird curling seashell green forest.

A very fine grain of fire will pass through the eyeglass at the edge of the shore, each wave caressing the woman's form is a flight of horses underneath a waterfall or fountain of elegiac blood, crying ghost finger loose and running down the water stairs at night lightning. The sun rises against the seashell cast shadows like a crypt or centipede blue a mile long on the picket white fence. There is a meeting between myself and the pharaoh standing golden as a lilac or spiral down sheep, excitement. Has the hourglass hit the briar at the foot of the stairs, the foot of the bird climbing from beak to wing, mountaintop to wing, a blue wineglass sleeps in the sand, nightfall on the bird's shoulders? Sundial sundial down the eyelash, the coiled lion in deep woods asleep frog tails and nightingale feather from beak to wing bird wing seeped in snow falling out of the winter bell tolling. Flocks of candlesticks storm the lion's intestines, emeralds and emeralds. The Egyptian sets the stone down at his feet and raises his hands to the sky, smiling. The present time cloaks not your being, old torn shoes three feet by the lowside, suit of arms and legs and tree limbs! Words words a bright flame, a forest labyrinth, words with the weight of a feather, words one mile long. You stand not in our restaurant but some pyramid in a flurry of birds' wings, sandy and curling, a thousand years past. Ah, but is it I who stands in the stream of the ages gone by, gathering sand and acorns at my nodes, smiling bird fevers while tigers leap from my mouth? Observe a simple photograph of the stone taken not six years ago. Has the leaf fallen from the tongue of the lion? I can hardly stand in my shoes, as if they were ice, as if they were venom; vines crawling along the waist of the woman in an evening-gown, heading for the ball, the cube, the pyramid. Give the rocking-chair seashell an hour for it to collect the honey sapphires sinking from the eyes of the sky. Alas, the cool handkerchief of night furrows its brow underwater, the night of tulips and of knives, salamanders sewing the lions into nice dresses for the candlesticks to wear over their flames, vomiting emeralds along the floor, flight of stairs into the ocean.

prayer

boundless gratitude

and love

Sitting atop such a hill as this

I can see the horizon of trees

all around me

It is not necessary to see all of life

to know that it is there

There is no need to discern every detail

to know of life's beauty

The wise man sees all as One

The average person

breaks down the One into many

At the peak of this hill

enclosed in the vast horizon

of trees

The wind is felt

is heard through the trees

and bushes and grass

but it cannot be grasped

cannot be seen

It acts but has no form

Sounds of humanity's civilization

are heard in the distance

yet the peace of the lake

of Nature

is not disturbed

Man refuses to remain One

he stretches his arms to their limit

his thoughts are overabundant and

abstract and spread out far

his eyes strain to see the distance

or minute detail

his heart is troubled by any disruption

and his emotions are uncontrolled

and wild

Instead of laying bare the essences

of life

he piles things on top

until life is obscured

Man must learn to leave things alone

"to act on all but meddle in none"

Man tries to remain firm

and grounded in illusion

he tries to resist the Way of Tao

When at the end of his life he is in ruin

he mourns over all the time he wasted

going against the flow of life

The life of modern man

is dull and tedious

it makes him seek diversion

in television and movies

and books

intoxication

in the internet

in the tragedies which befall others' lives

He may all his life pass the time

in a stupor

but at the end he realizes

that he wasted his life away

and is saddened to

his depths

The trees around me on this hill

allow the wind to run

its fingers through their

hair

Trees bend in the wind

go with the path of the wind

they do not try to resist

To go against the natural order of things

brings calamity and ruin

The sun is not yet risen

how beautiful everything is

against the dark mantle of night

The moon is the most wonderful pearl

and yet it need not be obtained

in order to enjoy it fully

Stars and clouds and noises of the night

ground all things in truth

When the sun rises

light reveals all detail

the animals awaken from rest and

all things begin again the journey

of life

Yet Nature remains One

all things in Nature are in harmony

all things in Life are balanced

The man of Tao sees clearly all things

because he is not stuck on one thing

or another

the Difference of all things

the Oneness of all things

The leaf on the lake seeks no direction

is content to go wherever the wind

or current may take it

Fish nibble at it and it remains still

noises occur all around it yet it is silent

Such is the way people should live

The beauty and joy of life

comes from silence

and stillness

The Tao is a well that is forever full

all that man needs is available to him

it is Nature's gift

Yet man seeks to detract from the beauty

and mystery of life until there is

nothing left of value in his eyes

Man should instead find peace in the simplicity

and loveliness of being

It is not about ceaselessly

exerting force and effort

it is about letting things take their course

The tree is still and rooted in one spot

it does not move nor seek movement

yet it manages to benefit all

Man is in constant doubt of life

when all he need do is go outside

into Nature to know of

life's beauty and grandeur

We must learn to find our place

in the Way of all things

I do not think it is too late

but I could be wrong

During my sleep I dreamt I was on a great mountain, walking along a path. I was carrying a bundle, a large bundle, much larger than I could possibly manage but I was bearing it along the path and I was not tired or weary. The wind was soft and cool and told of spring. In my ascent I came to a field on the mountainside with flowers and long grass that bent in the wind and it was here that I took my rest. I carried much with me in that immense bundle but could find only a little food. There was bread and jelly and some meat and nothing more. These I took into the field and sat and ate. A bee flew around me as I held the last slice of bread to my lips. It landed on the bread and took off from it and landed upon it again. I knew that if I were to eat the bread, the bee would go hungry, even with the abundance of flowers, yet the bee would do no more than settle itself in the jelly and hover about the crust and so I ate the last slice of bread and gathered my things and left. Soon I arrived at a cave further up along the path. I was near the peak but not so close that I would reach it in the light of the sun. In the cave lived a blind man and he lived alone on the mountain. Many men used to come to see him but that was long ago and he knew little of the men of today. The man was not born blind but had his eyes themselves taken from him. I set my bundle in the cave under the care of the old man and came to a cliff and gazed out over the land. The mountain rose up in the middle of a vast and ancient garden. With the ruins of cities that seemed not built by human hands. I asked the blind man if he knew of the cities below but the blind man when he could see only beheld the ruins as I did then. Night was slowly born and he and I returned to the cave where there was a fire already burning. The wind outside the cave whistled and the chill it spread felt more like autumn than spring. When all was dark and the fire nearly gone I looked at the old blind man and he told me to come to him. I went to him and looked deep inside his empty eye-sockets and inside I saw a great sunrise of bees, a living swarming tapestry of bees, and I pulled away from him and he was smiling and tears came from the dark holes without eyes. I realized then that I knew not what was in my bundle nor where I was nor even why I was there. I knew only that I was myself and that something was for me at the peak of the mountain. Then I awoke.

There is a bird in the Spanish trees, with sunlight in its feathers, the movement of her wings is also the movement of emerald waves spreading across the shore and the sand as it shifts ceaselessly, all the while giving the appearance of stillness. There is a little boy, lost in the sandcastle of his dreams and his father's dreams and his mother's, lost in the world, he is in the center of the bird, of her eye, in the depths of the sun, deeply white and beautiful as nothing else is.

It is like a ball balanced on the tip of a pyramid in the cosmic void made of everything, a bluebird in the eye of the cannon, a tree in the bladder of the gun oink.

Blue

Frank had come to the bar after work with two friends. By now they had gone home and he sat leaning against the counter, slumped on his stool. If he put his head down he would surely fall asleep. He ordered another drink. Outside the night swirled about in the wind. There were no stars, just heavy clouds filled with light emanating from the city. Inside no music was playing. The bartender said nothing to him as he set the drink before him. Even though it was near silent in the bar, the sounds of the night and of the world were muffled and distant and could not be distinguished by any of the patrons.

The three boys who entered must have been laughing for blocks, but only when the door opened and they stumbled in could the unkind noise of it be heard. Frank looked in their direction. They meant trouble, you could see it in their eyes, their demeanor. The other man at the counter, sitting two stools away from Frank, said something quietly in his drunkenness. One the boys ordered drinks while the other two approached the man.

"You say something, old man?" one of them says.

The man faces away and doesn't respond. One of the boys pushes him in the back, between the shoulder-blades.

"Look at me when I am talking to you."

"Leave him alone, fellows," says the bartender, "He don't mean you any business."

"Fuck off," says one of the boys.

"If you are going to cause a stink then get out of here," the bartender says.

One of them starts laughing as he goes over and opens the door. He holds it open as the other two drag the man off his stool and outside. He is too disoriented to fight back or struggle even. The door closes behind them and the bar is shrouded in a thick quietude. The remaining customers ease into slight conversation. Frank rises and exits the bar.

The wind is blowing coldly through the warmth of the city. He looks around but there is no one about. Slowly he walks along the bar to the alleyway beside it. The man is propped up against a garbage can and the three boys were taking him apart mercilessly. He did not show resistance. There was blood on the ground and on the boys and all over the man. They did not notice Frank. One of the boys hit the man across the face with his fist and then kneed him in the crotch and the man crumpled. Another of the three began stomping on him with the heel of his foot. He was brought back up to his feet and one of them spit on him while another took hold of one of his ears and jerked it off in one motion. The man groaned and blood was coming out of his mouth thickly. The boy goes over to a large metal garbage-bin and throws the ear away.

They leave him standing, swaying, covered in his own blood. One of his eyes was beaten closed and some of his teeth were knocked out. There was a pocket of gore where his left ear had been previously.

The boys slink away into the darkness, passing Frank without seeing him.

Frank goes to the man and leads him out of the alleyway and back into the bar and sets him in a booth. This took some effort. He walked back outside to the metal garbage-bin and collected the ear and returned to the bar and placed the ear on the table before the man. As he returned to the counter he noticed that a woman in a red dress was sitting on his stool. She was facing him and held a glass of clear liquid without ice. Her dress was shimmering and reflected in her glass.

"You have blood on your hands," the woman says.

"What?"

"There is blood on your hands," she says in a near whisper.

"What? Oh. Yes."

Frank turns around and walks to the bathroom. He turns the water on and lets it heat up and looks at himself in the mirror. He looks at his eyes and mouth and the curve of his cheeks and at the whole of his body.

Aloud, Frank says: "This is what people see when they look at me. This is what I am to the world. Nothing more, nothing less." There is no one in the small bathroom to hear him. He washes his hands with soap and the sink is stained a light pink by the blood.

When Frank leaves the bathroom, wiping his hands dry on his pants, the woman is gone. He looks around but she is nowhere to be seen. The bartender has set out another drink for him and he walks over to the stool and sits down.

"Maybe you ought to be getting home soon," says the bartender.

Frank doesn't say anything and finishes his beer slowly and pays the bartender what he owes him. The beaten man was still sitting in the booth where Frank left him, staring at the wall and sitting almost upright. The ear is on the table in the same place he had put it. He walks over to the door and pushes it open and steps out into the night.

Frank left the bar and started out toward his apartment ten blocks away. Walking quickly, he listened to the dim cacophony of the city and moved through the warm air and was stung occasionally by the cool wind. The buildings that made up the city loomed dark and unknown against him. He kept his face down and his hands at his sides. He felt tears in his eyes and he wiped them away and he stopped and looked around. He did not recognize where he was. Somewhere he had taken a wrong turn and now he was here.

He had stopped in front of a building several stories high. All of the windows on the top floor had been broken and he could hear the voices of two men and one woman. By the sound of it they were on the third floor. Frank stood watching the building. Before long he realized that he was weeping silently. Tears were dampening his face and his eyes were swollen with them.

A noise startled him. It came from the building but he could not find the source. There were two large windows on either side of the door, which had stairs leading up to it. Frank looked harder. A bird was flying up against the window to the right. Its wings beat against the glass softly. The bird was small with white breast and gray-green feathers. It flew off deeper within the building. He could hear it above all the other sounds of the city. As he stood listening to this bird he could no longer see, his crying ceased and he dried his face with his shirtsleeves.

Frank began to walk down the sidewalk back the way he had come, but upon no further recognition of where he was, turned around and continued the way he been going. He did not know what time it was. The night was still now, and heavy, and the buildings seemed closer together. The height of some nearly obscured the sky.

He turned a corner and farther down along the sidewalk opposite he saw a figure moving slowly. At his pace he soon overtook the figure and he saw that it was the woman in the red dress. She was wearing a jacket to keep from the wind but since the wind was gone now she had it unzipped and loose. He looked at her from across the street and she turned her head and saw him. She smiled at him and stopped walking. He had also stopped walking. Slowly she crossed the street to him as he stood watching.

And then it all disappeared into nothing.

Where

did

it

go

?

Do you live near where you were born or raised? Why or why not?

Have you had a good sleep lately?

Do you dream often? Do you remember your dreams?

The moonbeams dance too late during the solstice to notice the snail at the foot of the bed, running circles around the hogs, hovering like a fire, fast as the soil pouring out of the wine glass knocked over the edge of the pond with lily-pads and alligators to feed the high and mighty women at those parlors where they go to have their feet taken off and replaced with icicles or thickets, cotton-picking ruby at which the night barks its leaves and feathers to cause the quaking of the grass roots' stool. Woman of much exultance and the young man feels around with his foot, finding the whale in a state of grace not dissimilar to the sensation of being covered with sand with your eyes closed, open them to the hawks that land on the shoulder of the balcony, folding the legs of the chair into a paper diamond swimming into the ocean behind her eyes and a fish jumps, a fish gliding in the water, all it desires is to lose itself in the heaven that is the water, the ancients dance on the tongue of the man provided, the young man views this man once and never forgets the instance, while the whale covers the star next to the moon with spiderwebs, it knows. Blue heron of the morning, close thine beak at the first rays of the broken laser where the scientists huddle around the fish, ghost dreams of the graveyard and the fence is an old witch with frog's legs fingers and a whistle for a cane, blue fork with a mouth of gold, table unkempt and prolonged, jive thousand at the beak curve loose blue, fiddle and thumb took off down the road to the sea, at the sides are doors and things, horseshoes oranges young climb the ghost rainbow that draws its fingers along the dawn, with a snout to match the knife and fork, hoodlum drawn close, finger needle fire light spray dawn match fight thorn loosely around the middle at once, hold down the foghorn at twice to see the reflection of the morning in the summer fog-light goose-down ray-gun, climbing up the lamppost a quarter past three. Blue deer at the moon side, far gone into the open eye of the seaside gravel road that ends up at the corner of some sphinx with an empty glass to prove it, harp that belches out clear smoke to get in the sun's eyes all day long until night comes and cleans its face with a rag that is really an old ghost caught in the sphinx's tongue, an old hourglass with dirt in its walls that bewitch the soul, collapsing all the stone golems and pharaohs, a cool blue reindeer to clothe the shivering umbrella, swing the lamp around the bend in the knee of the whale, crack in the river where all the diamonds fall out, cumbersome railway snail's pace that becomes loose the further the night plunges, triple point, the table expands and shrinks at each breath, the stream of water emitted by the pelican has a crack in it, the winter wheelbarrow is disheveled flagellum.

Creaking like a stairway, throws its dirty and messed clothes all over the furniture, all over the future; quietly the young man is among the guests, looking with sadness at the captured deer strewn on the wall, as the living-room hurries off to take a drink from the lake where many of these very same deer used to drink, on this great woman's body, her shoulder-blades, as well as her heels and nostrils; during this entire ordeal, one can only wonder about the state of the hermit's shoes and jacket! Abruptly, the young man steps out of the hermit's house and falls onto the woman's knees, causing her to shift in her stance, as erotic as the stars caressing the night sky, causing the hermit to spills and tumble into the lake, the house makes like a boat is swallowed whole, the lake makes like a hole and is seen leaving through the backdoor of the house, while the hermit wanders about the third floor, composing his favorite garments and sun-letters; as can be seen, from this height, the fall of the house of the sun's hermit resembles a tree turning over in a graveyard, disturbing the fence so that it shields the wonderful questioning child from soothing the dead with her soft voice, songs that are the rain and the sun and the moon and stars, the voice that Venus might envy if she were released from her water-sealed tomb of clouds, the gods' heaven that will overturn the noonday weather for the patchwork quilt of sunny afternoons, before the hermit empties his house into the lake, a fire of ice and clouds, a house no longer resting upon the old beggar's back, the beggar's back, which is all within and without the woman's eye. The violet grove buries what is left of his clothes, the old graveyard is an adolescent boy weeping, at the loss of childhood, at the loss of adulthood, at the slow sunrise that makes him as thin as the hair he bathes in, falling in golden tresses from the marvelous head of the woman, from five weeks away the young man views this boy, who is himself and someone else, he can tell, the feeling is felt through the tips of the finger, the cold nail of her lips, tossed in the salad of the ocean that sings and cries out softly as the winter sunrise, a razor wire that cuts thin slices from the adolescent boy, until there is nothing left but a miniature skeleton. This heap of bones slowly loses sanity and becomes enlightened, inane, at the sight of the young man and the woman, viewed simultaneously from his no-eyes, empty sockets that sweep the bare and lonely dust from the shoulders and hands of the woman, retreating from his sight, while the moon rises as the sweep of ghostly fingers with vines and lovely violent flowers growing from the tips, the adolescent's ribcage.

Tenderize the opportunities into pulpy infinity, plump blinking oblivion. Oblivion is a microscopic microscope with limitless magnification responsibilities. You should always give handouts, you should always take handouts. Giving handouts, taking handouts: it's like breathing, it's like breeding. The jade warriors are breeding sterling. Celebrate the hallucinations of the toiling microscopes and telescopes, the dangling telephones. The manifold saucers climbing the stalks in their curdled netherworld, the furtive stems. The balloon artist wears antelopes on its ankles and anesthetizes the facetious patient. Sordid soiled practical esophagus. Practice the curtesy of the blind gorillas, the blind armadillos. Snow-blind fountain in the startled grass. Scaly geese collapse the winter's night into fine fluctuations. Across the slimy barbed-wire fleece a silver-tongue moron tickles the lazy envelopment. Crimson idiots petrifying the classic artichokes in upside-down water cold. The concupiscent prayers highlight the already-existing arches and fraudulent frontiers. The minutes slink by like a woman undressing alone. The feet tread lightly the flailing philanthropists. Storied attire of basic basalt, the sockets brimming with saltpeter and splintered flutes. Pickled fetuses a stork a crony. The further pall is unnecessary. I find the ghostly partitions to be unruly and dissonant. Take shelter in the closed sockets. Pristine abstinence of the old swarthy cutlery. A glimpse of frail shadow at the beck and call. Pistols at the swoon. Teeth are a prison, teeth are a prism, teeth are a lactating piston. Sneezes are jism and dynamite, sidelong and frigid. Exhale the sun's roiling decay, inhale the skeleton's whimpering. Drink the fuming oysters. All the accounts are unsettled, all the accounts are settling down to a birthday party in the sneezing attic. Laundromat of the eclipses, opening wide the garbled footnotes. Seize every opportunity by the pincers and extract genuinely. Put your laundry in the furnace of night, featured furnace, elephantine furnace blue. Twilight of the last call, knowing climes of pitch scaly and prepubescent. Trailing diamond tears and corduroy feces. Pristine fecal matter of the arctic triumph. The matter has been settled, no further disputation required. The reputation of the quandaries is all and sundry tomorrow night five nine hundred. Porcupine pillowcases allow for lucid porcupine dreaming. Fixation of the faraway stars, fixation of the trembling plants like ants in the laundry, pinnacles in the cream. Unaccustomed to the falling heaters, a lamprey makes its exit. Journey to the porcelain climes. Acrobatic pinnacle for long-term dilution. Accessible only at dawn or under the ears. Peeling away the sand of time from the singing wounds. Broken fortune upsets all gravities. Follow the path under the sink. Gravity smells like a lusty onion and should be peeled telepathically. Pathology of the starving depths, crucified hemorrhages beckoning lightly.

Pale frozen dark settling into the landscape like a turgid lover entering the coiling beloved. Push and pull. Preferential fermentation titillating sworn acres. Hydrogenated skunk fuel to surreptitious cloven markers. Gilded drawstrings on the pants of eternity pulled tight, made loose, over and over across the gales, galas, gallants, gallops. Lunar feelings of dejection, insurrection. Polar velocity of star-struck tentacles. Holographic cocoons of the vast vapid computers equivalent to the paramount corruption and formulaic sitting-room formulas across time. Creased space is a titan dromedary in the pure astral deserts. Celestial avatars of the folding dawn, highlighting the spurious brigade of make-believe planets. The dilapidated plantation is possessed by unblinking umbilical plankton, turning the horses upside-down, painting obscenities on the cows, giving handouts to the voles. The severed poles are rapacious in their fortunate appetites, colloquial trapdoor of the senses giving way to handsome hand-grenades in sheer lingerie. Burn the potholes and postulates, slice up the definitions and feed them to the swindlers. The rib-cage elephant has trampled all the dice into smithereens. Untold drawbridge of the senses, descend upon the agglomeration of peninsulas. Sinking the fangs into delicate covered-wagons. Gander gander lying fire. The blood of a reindeer's antlers trickles out of the snoring wounds of foxholes and pellets. Hanging from the rafters: a childish sunrise! Assume the felonious mounts. Crippled amounts anxiously plotting their escape from plumed estuaries, plume of cemeteries. Long lurid draughts of the ceaseless tonic. Gingerly frantic and cobalt awareness. Priestesses in garbled garb galavant poorly in the solar hives. It is all a long goodbye a long goodnight a lion underneath. Coming going enter exit produce detonate translucent prudence. Welcoming the fanfare of tempests, triumphant return. The synchronized police officers unfurl like a banana-peel or zombie blossom. Crotchety lamppost covered in loose kisses and fallow hermitages. Soy belongs in the nose and nowhere else. The will of the pines, will-o'-the-wisp. Porcupine pine trees ardent footfalls. The willing lavender caresses wailing. Subordinate unaccountable rickshaws, runaways, poodles in flames. Trickery! Trickery! Dolorous alterations pathways through the shrouds, embarrassed clouds, musk at attention. The capricious skirmishes are umbrella salts. The muscular mucus is stringy and violent like an inside-out hawk. Jagged edges and sharp protrusions, angular adjunction. Prime calendar in the refrigerator unattained. Distant alluring locales scaly slimy pretend. Phenolphthalein light-fixtures under the skin at all hours of the trumpeting day, at all cost. Soprano alto tenor wax mistakes baritone pulsation. Wax eruption in the bee structure tentatively.

The wardrobe is seizing up in the soluble form of sound. Testing the portions increments abscond allotment. Mewling meeting-place of the bold stipulations, conservative drawing-room of polite abrasions cascading calculating. Elementary excuses of fundamental viscosity. Urgency planned garrulous port rippling sunset. The moonrise rippling like a gasping muscle. The fascinating vaccinations. A proper porpoise apropos fiddling sediments. Sentimental animosity toward lunar vacancies. Crucified cruxes approach the hidden zenith. Sentient intellections misguided purposes. Intercept the obconical abscesses. Resolution of merry decapitation capitulation. Marred surface hospice preliminary. Extracurricular revolutions around the disembodied mouths that streak across the absences like polluted rainfall. Malleable malevolency in prehistoric concentration. Broken fists like broken china littered on the evening eagles, skittered height ballooning. Exemplary ablutions calcified dawning. Insidious testosterone feelers limping blindly along the pit of snakes, silt of rakes. Confused hose of our tangled leavings shuttered. Primal confiscation of boiling eggs, screaming edges. Spherical snakes consciously undulating to intimidate the sterling losses, fragile tempests like tapestries afoot. Smells sound uncomfortable, distressed. The distress-signal was murdered in its stench, perpetrators of serrated crossings. Assail the vinegar vehemently. Anemic penetration of unknown elements. The cleverly clairvoyant celery-stalks march ever onward. The sounds are unperturbed in their waterbeds and springboards. Humid hubris prawn scalped predatory. Shrimp are the latest and most pure fashion-accessory imaginable, wear them on your anterior, your posterior, your interior, your primary, your secondary. Rhinoplasty of the gods in their golden syringes opulent oranges. The brides are disintegrating, the grooms are forcible brooms. Plenary picnics are ideal, spermicidal ideology. Suicidal chronology manipulation adrift aloft ablaze adroit reinforced prostitution. I'd like to take this time now to discuss the benefits of the allotted pigment. The cooks are crooked, the crooks are an incomplete clientele.

Are you treated fairly by life?

Is there much that you don't understand? That you do understand?

Are food and shelter readily available to you?

Do you enjoy bathing?

Banish the ruby scorpions to their pillowcases of jasmine. The crustacean edifices enumerating causal discrepancies. Exorbitant spectacle of the clawing machines computing in abject hatred and terror the glowing void. Your mouth is a very fast car. Cartoon appendages spewing outright. You are a model propellor. Modulation of disproportionate obscurities. Syncopated cinders spoiling effortlessly the epidermal spectrum. Bright calibrations rectangular bullet. Make sandwiches of the afterbirth, columnar diarrhetic. Purposeful dolphin pushed out of the open window. Gaunt knapsack of troubled gnats and geniuses. Genus flowing flowering pretty tendril entail. Ululating hitching-post of our children's children's children, exhausted pollution promising hardboiled knickknacks and stilted longevity. Floppy gullible. The nurses have been overturned. The extravagant courthouses of our youth. Perennial aviary swollen ovum. Fertile scepter of neutered importance, sartorial deforestation. Distract the heinie while I perpetuate the shapes. I can't do this by myself, I can do this by myself. Alone not alone. Animal I. The room is inside-out, the roof is upside-down under water. Raise high the carpenters, shallow lights buzzing around like flies. The saturated aces in the consummate bedpan. Phony avalanche of the sensate precautions stimulating gregariously. The larval confection under stealthy landscapes. Antithesis of anteriority, authority, seniority. The excrement has banded together to create a florid disarray, fluid tube. Gruesome airplane dishing out insults and centerpieces. Camel nuggets 16 ounces forty floors. The pubic pumice-stone made public by the extenuating circumcisions of yesteryear. Circumscribe the pubic disciplinary acrylic actions, circumcision of the dawn. Cold weather is a silent solitary proboscis attached to nothing at all. The resignation of the capillary caterpillars is a worthy pillar, an affront to bulletins. Flotilla of our young serums, sermons, almonds aloft. Crosswise flotsam pointed pointed. Extreme circumstance of stillborn manatees stillborn night tortuous situation. Secure the globs to the goblet, insecure pliancy. Buoyant aphrodisiac trickling splashes of night. Pleasantly evacuate the corneal lobotomies activate trigger fish. The fishing-pole of our recoiling desertion. Transparent renegade parentheses apparent apparition.

nutrition + superstition = 432344

unencumbered = searchlight 5609

principle principalities - 124 = stained coincidences

Getting cozy with the spindles is to be expected and recalcitrant. Bivalve circumcision introspection irrelevant expectorant. Disingenuous coital copper frothing. Misdemeanors of the frocked imagination. Unambitious disambiguation prevents total ferment. Eucalyptus eucharist doubling doubly. The wire nests of jackals yipping sensually on the cloaked clock. Distant cloaca. Bless your marble head, your marble convulsions under the carpet of storms. Plethora of clitoral personalities, the clitoral locusts of shadowy dawn yawning fragrantly. Sunburns subdued in total frequency. Sex is a waste-bin, a garbage-can, sex is a shadowy washbasin designed for astronomers with poor agriculture. Aggravated agricultural orchestrated euthanasia for the clearing of pocked sprites alchemical cope. The spirits inhabit marginal totems and the hands of a clock clutch brushes and splintered sphincters. Sphinx sphincters magnificent proportion. Cromulent necrophilia agape taxation, acute absorption of spatial fallacies. The candle emits perpendicular footfalls along the threshold of adjacent corporations. Swineherd of the senses.

The cubic dilation is fourteen parameters. The accoutrements are roiling in their cylinders, in their tropes. Ringing in the new ears with splendid toucan thermometers across the basin. The cairns are careening luxuriously across the estates like liquid hair. Terminal growth of femurs occluding efficiently. Tune in to the services requested, tune out the orgasmic phantoms displaying their dorsal fins. Subcutaneous harebrained ephemera marriage of the abalone, leper-retardant leopard-retardant, hair-brained.

    The young man and the whale take a turn toward the small of her back, which is a hand-mirror, light from the crown of her skull reflects upon a hot dandelion, heaving and sighing lions, serenade illuminating glass cobwebs, lions hissing and roaring, a sun riding above a horse of cobras to the thundering waves of lions below, polite handful of orange and blue hair, grasping for breath, the whale with a pair of hands in each eye-socket, reaching toward the sky fingers wisps of cloud, envelopes a lion who has strayed from the great swell, a cobweb, the young man must be underneath the whale for a short period of time while the whale recovers from the lion it has become and surrounded, eyes laying sight down in blankets and parchment upon the small valley of space between her knees, moonlight cast down by her vagina creating shadows throughout the boulders and little streams flowing as elegant mustaches, the young man casts the shadow of a piano and the whale casts the appearance of a lion.

    As when a large rock is thrown into the sun's eye, they are upon her, she this tablecloth, this crow's claw, this woman, alas, who is tracing a cross in the sky, clouds growing similar to many trees, when she finds Venus crucified against her etchings, Venus with her hair flowing past her feet and her teeth are a horse-race run by rabbits, against this imaginary cross she casts a magnificent red light down into the navel of the woman, causing her eyelashes to multiply and spread across her face, which is a thunder-clap for the whale, by now recovered from the sickness of the lion and his many tresses of diamond leathers, and the young man, both now sitting upon the street corner tossing up stones and gravel into the buildings and into the street, a boxing match, prizes held out before the nose of each contestant, drawing a line of ants through the air, through the center of a picnic and a funeral, reaching forward toward the prize each fighter brandishes as many extra limbs as they can manage, hands and feet and drums, a holy conundrum caught down frost in battle, shake town, outlook, lost in pitter patter, rain falling as sand on a gold tin roof, the young man jumps up to join in on the action, each of his fingers is a lit match, smoke billowing up as a slingshot, caught in the eyes of a blind sloth, the whale placing down money as it was growing like pearls, fifteen cents an offer, bet or two wish, again the top shudder, eclipsing the time, sun put up your dukes, going toward the Earth to plant a smooch and the Earth blushes intelligently, raising the moon to begin nightfall, curtain fall, the young man hollering 'you look like more lunatic bones' to the sunset, six or seven teeth among crisp green-brown blades of grass; nighttime upon this woman is as the night in Chrome, lit by a torch and faint smiles, a large fountain, or as the night, which lays across the beach, illuminating the water and sand, eyelashes to a beautiful bulb of scarlet and a dozen chrysanthemums; alas, a trumpet blow, a horn blast, cast in the same two ears, the woman is laughing and the subsequent storm makes the young man smile, his lips catching the rain ever so pleasantly.

Upon the arrival of a new day, the young man and the whale enter a three-storey house, which reflects the woman sitting up with a straight spine, a thousand red arrows and fifteen cent tear; they carry her undress through the great flower bulb doorways, swinging pendulum hot candle tip, a fox tail chasing a tortoise of smoke, their feet swim along the vast carpet encompassing the front hall, dove wing hand print patterns and geometrical shapes that explore three dimensions spill above the floor as a cough or tiger's stripe, the chandelier is a drowning man reaching for a jar of eyelids, green, and red lips belonging to the woman he loved, forest snarls and cold tooth, a blanket a fire, under the water he sinks, into the golden sun; further on a room which is bent and hobbled, cobwebs of rusty nails and splinters singeing moonlight, casting shadows of great beards and mustaches into the corners, the whale is overcome with marvel and awe, a sun-bird has developed before his eyes, wing tips a smelly wind over many sand dune castles, increasing in size until the room is filled by it alone, whale of long summer, alas we must abandon you, for you have abandoned us, your mind caught in tree branches, leaves and dirt swirl and your body has returned to give shelter for your mind, lost in a cabaret of diamond and amber.

Right now a matchbox, taking it upon himself, is climbing up a ray of sunlight, in order to reach the sun and the sum and the nightingales, voice of blustery gales, waving a silver baton through the surrounding air causing an old rain to fall, a rain that has many times seen you dancing naked across the whistles of threadbare grass-laughter, the old rain is an old drama toss your fingers against the wall and recoil into a succulent spiderweb, alas, the matchbook is truly and definitively a fish five-scales; the young man is inside the matchbox and leaves the great woman's body for three quarters of a second, a blink of starlight and her body is a splendid arbor littered with her soul and mind, peaches that swell up from the roses and her breasts, in twos and threes, a quick cough and a nightingale the swordsman with talons for eyes, and an eye for silver bullets that fall as a new rain, jealous of the old rain, embroidered on an iron jacket sown by the graceful thumb of the woman, who has a twitch just now in the center of her right eye, consequently removing the young man from the fish six-scales into a wheat field below her mouth, moistening the soil with her tongue, escaping through polite banter that preens like the neck of a chicken, a chicken blue-breast, a beam of suntan-oil mounting that ribald horse of vanity the trick chicken of four days, no frills. The young man looks inside of himself with five hands, one of the hands compared to the others resembles a blind lumberjack, a frozen azalea bush that moves and grows and hisses as the woman's eyebrow, the young man's eyelashes, shattered lightbulb flower steaming smoking bulb in a blue, in a blue, out a blue yonder, heavenly wood words, carved from the Earth's smile, a coarse tangled brush that weaves old sweaters for nickels, sandlot built along the cold coast, mirroring a gold ghost that flourishes in the weeds and bramble, a slick red dog's bark, sounding as a girl speaking softly, of things the young man wishes to comprehend, cracked knuckles and a tidal wave, thunder-wave, for a blue bright farther the lighthouse is sent onward at the bray of a severed torso, cascading down in golden tresses, a little boy of four a little golf-club of stone and weasel-wood, from a cold sheep's wool, red lamp cushion, several of the young man's arms raised heavenward.

the third part of your eye

is showing

the secret police are exchanging feelings

transparent hog

of hermetic sun spinners

truncated log

exoteric exoskeleton

diagonal dragon mistake

slumping esoteric shrimp function

evasion evasive corrosion

mister

disbarring the reams of handlers

predisposed disposition

defunct apparition postion

extinct appetite

one two more and more

defunct functioning spoiled

mister

goose = gloat

overboard calamity

it is like

steadily dripping water

from a leak in the roof

striking the very top

of the head

huge animal head

small ambiguous head

a headful of heads doleful heads

shaped like stars

like dealings

slow down!

freak out!

tentative

bosom spoon

there is not mind

a light above every threshold

there something that is

not living and dying

sitting quietly

plucking every feather

of the dawn

the ocean

the people the trees

the self

relinquishing control

all aboard

cloud fetus albatross excretion

accretion

multitude dissimilitude

disclosed offal manta-ray training

spare no expense

dispense bioluminescent

dignities

eiderdown genie

what is the difference?

I could've sworn it was right

here

I don't know

but you must always ask yourself:

did I do this

to myself?

monotonous moon monocle monogamy molecule

moon candy

from beyond the stars

luxurious tranquilizer organ

luxurious hamper

organizing organic

mood candy

behind the stairs

it has been led astray

it has not been led astray

astral ashtray cemetery

groaning organ

infantile syndrome

mutilated kumquat

the stinking ceremonies insist soundlessly

astray

bath king

tumultuous graveyard

hiding in the

tide

combing the hides

in swallow sorrow

empty cucumber

copilot trigger

the tiger of emptiness

foaming with water laughter delight

the birth play

to be distinguished

greatly

plainly

the formaldehyde tides

efface the faulty lion

of detention

disparaging the hollow

animals

to be held in by the tide

to be let go of

in the ocean of the

stable

leaflet horses hairpin

dour

front

ceaseless birth play

grossly accumulated

beyond the playground

armoire

to be distinguished

to be held at length

appropriate hearing

tribunal disfunction

gloating on the facade

of the ferris wheel

trembling with aromatic

laughter

sour discreet

to be held at length

by the blind searching patterns

inside this warm body

the hand-worn boobytraps

are well known

disfigured

in the ambush

to be held at length

by the hand-worn freedoms

heavy with moist soil

beautiful

eye

monotonous moon monocle

like an insect

prickly monster

of the

slippery appendages

cough

vomit

when touching the cold

replacement similarities

rough feeling

by hand by foot

by beak by trough

a sorry undertaking

big and full of water

beaded expedition

do not wrinkle

as you love

throwing piñatas into the oven

into the ornery penguin suspicions

to be put aside

to be laundered

automatically

from a piquant distance

of solicitous

dilemmas

     A red-hot black dog piercing through the white night as a
broken arrow, into a startling green apple, balanced on a tongue of
sunlight, showering the earth below in somnolent tresses, whispering
of days gone past and nights yet to happen, the lilacs grow as roses
from the marsh, in addition to the legs of chairs which sprout forth and
reach out toward the heavens, bearing on its stem bulls and bull-
fighters and bull-lovers, pineapple bullshit. What a holler that pig
sings, a withered tree branch, several of them under the arm of a blimp
passing by, snorkel of a mousetrap blimp too cold or it's in the
summer rain, standing in a hat while it's raining only makes it swing to
the nose of that pig in the eyeball which causes the rain to come out of
the pores of her skin too cold, or too smooth, or too uneven with the
sailboat mast, swiftly riding the sunlight home to the grave, whose
tombstone is behind the old barn, a beautiful mouth of broken teeth for

a grave-marker, a farmhand's leg is the flower of remembrance given by the family or lover, a sweet woman old and tucked away like a house on stilts, smiling whenever there is anything outside, takes Nature as she comes dressed to resemble the moon and sun, blue, the vomiting salamander clones offhanded sister cistern.

Corpse lying curled warm by the blazing fire, the corpse sprawled against the tool-shed on the pale grass, corpse like a half-moon suspended over the kitchen sink, uncurls an arm like a moonbeam, is murmuring with a tongue darting into the corpse of a flower over and over, flames, flora fauna, the bones of the word will outlive its skin and the humans who pronounce it, corpse bleeding and heavenly, but when it peels, water shall fill the belly of the corpse and an ocean is writhing in a heap of cardinals' wings, corpse's belly reaches around the corner of the tool-shed, further than the door, past the dead feet of the woman standing in the pale grass disembodied, this ocean overturns a boat to the sharks' delight and a chaplain stands on the shoreline casting the line from a fishing-pole into the depths of the water of multiple colors, crimson and daffodil and doorknob and crooked teeth, also sending a kite to the corner of the sky's smile, a thousand nightingales when bluebirds cry blue daisies toward the night of storm eye closed curtain against the stage when the performance is in full tilt, swirling hands leave a trail of capes over the backs of chairs, feet fall through the floorboards and nightingales.

When the whale turns toward the eves and a crestfallen manta-ray rises into the curve of the woman's spoon, the young man, taking hold of the manta-ray-gun's honesty and environs, curling outward his fist until it resembles the pattern of aggression displayed by the tools in the shed, growing legs moving about the lawn and the tools, by now much larger and hungry, have left their minds only to be caught in the loose coat-sleeve singing in the wind glorious, he covers the soil in a translucent trout mask replica of the solar system, whereby he infuriates the tools, against the autumn's window, where the woman takes her baths and the whale learns to spend as currency the leaves of his family tree; winter solstice can only be pronounced when both eyes of the sun's window-shade are drawn and quartered to the twilight aghast pale brain shutter in the darkness, the clothespin explodes and the whale is released from the cacophony. Broken-down trapdoor with handles that are actually dolphin fins, down up, trapdoor smiles and reveals an incredible landscape of circular gardens and high castle towers that pierce the surface of the ocean of the sky, the clouds are waves created by the rise of the pyramid of the Cosmos, that unfettered cadaver produces a ribbon from its outstretched hand, the ribbon remains suspended in midair until a young woman takes off her clothes and the man at her side closes his mouth in the manner of a trapdoor, sudden and like the moon; lo and behold, there is scythe in the corner of the sky, thrown by the ancestor of a farmer to the isolated teardrop hanging in the air, at the tail end of the tongue which laps at the dawn, picnic of the fate of dawn, closed to the night but open to the twilight only when the seasons disrobe their defenses and lay down the rules for trespassing on their glade of existence, a celestial plane mostly frequented by the likes of Neptune and Saturn, porcelain coffin filled with evaporated water and fish that holler at the woman with the shortest attention and whose attitude is affected only by the heart of the seasons, ace of diamonds, seven of crickets out past the dead fence wooden and grinning and uneven, horse's two eyes.

Do you get up early? Stay up late?

Do you move quickly or slowly?

Are your thoughts rapid, unrelenting? Or tranquil and calm?

What is your first memory?

The first memory is of a certain ruby ladder. God is a toothless vagrant combing the wastes, God is a tourist, a magician. There is no God, there is one God, two Gods, an infinite stream of Gods all of equal importance. The existence of God is inconsequential to the bending stratus, the wheezing willows under foil boxes. The existence of God does not change or justify anything. The existence of God on four hinges, spreading the mewling stars across fields of vision. Tactile God, bothersome God, liquid God taking up space. God is the price of an avian aquarium, aquatic aviary, the threat of snow. The toothless veil of the bare tubes. Simmering in the corroded infrastructure a single bird the shape of an eye, and it was spring. It was the autumnal presence of parasitic locomotives. A shepherd's pall was reorganized to the great dismay of the lobotomies. The underwater laboratory was shedding its clothes like tears of sugar, waves of grain, trains of gradation. Hypodermic detention, tickled ink. Slow decent to red marsh waters.

The toothbrush took a wife, clothesline, who begat three children: cornucopia, print, femoral. And cornucopia coupled with fascination and they begat troubadour and ferry. Ferry took print and they begat pictures and pincers. Femoral and crucible begat legion, and legion took troubadour and begat flaunt. Flaunt eloped with pincers and begat the starring frost. Starring frost took rosy and begat a hatful of umbrellas and mortars. The mortars were asexual and begat none. Rosy ran away with pictures and in the land of Enticing begat tribulation, soiled and dictionary. The dictionary took flaunt as a mate and they begat grass, fireproof, festive, absolute, and frequented. Toothbrush, still active, took grass and begat pudding and gangway. Gangway and tribulation coupled and begat the ears and earlobes. Ears and earlobes stole away to the wastes and begat broken fingers. Clothesline, wallowing in despair, took umbrellas and begat toaster. Toaster and broken fingers coupled and begat the night rain. Night rain was killed by an errant portico and begat none. God was feeling dismal and coupled with toothbrush, and they begat the feelings of dwindling powder. Rosy and soiled went to the land of Armpit and begat the crumbling moonbeams and heavy feathers. The heavy feathers took crucible and begat the foaming windows. The list goes on and on into the shimmering horizon, the lineage goes on forever into the distance, the listing condition. All of this happened a long time ago, now it is spoken of only in legend and heresy. All of this has yet to happen, and should be looked forward to avariciously. Cucumber and toenails coupled and begat the sunrise. Anchovies and leather, before their divorce, begat windmill. Mausoleum is a whore who ran off with all the spindles and windshields. The second coming of the penis of time frightens all the chipmunks in their ivory bunkers.

Saturday gave way to Thursday and the all unicorns were skinned alive in their tanks; the stagecoach is getting out of the hands. It glows in the dark so you can see what you're doing. Pushable plush plantations. Fabulous glowworm of the sensations, piling high usurping the boilers. Cavernous cacophony of calisthenics to match the darling array, lumpy arroyo. Handprints on the musk of sky. Grenadier of unhappy tomorrows. The squirrel finishes first in the race to the destitute sun. The clams came in second place and were awarded a toothsome fold, the binary airplanes came in third and fourth, the pitcher of tentacles came in last place and was jettisoned into the bone marrow. The healthy punishment of firing eyes. The froth and the steeds coupled and begat an injurious centimeter. Discounted coupons mistaken for tampons, fish-hooks, clumsy wire. Clammy lobes. Stalagmite stalactite grown milk dust stalemate gown. The mineral liaisons are taking great liberties with the sole solemnity. The gorilla inserts picture-frames into its rectum, pure white wool spilling out of its lips, facilitating the liberated emeralds. Picking choosing blue breezes flame again. Disease wed glory and begat countless webs. The church-house, glistening with amniotic gases and mouths, months, on gilded haunches, launches a carrion showcase to curtail the empyreal bolts of scarlet and rosemary ephemera. Chimera of strokes, pallid license amidst gaping potholes, portholes. The crystal holes summon unwed miracles for a quick laugh. Big wig wearing a rig digs a swig of pigs from the jig, juggling the hiccups. The mirage of warm spaces. Slippery place of vanquished subsidies. The warring will never cease.

It has been foretold that the merciful slaughter of the mercenaries would be resplendent, but I have my doubts. I pierce my doubts with sinewy string and tie them to my knees and elbows, just in case. The pretty blue cases pretty blue. The lobotomists of the question have plagued me of late. The flowery winter sun of long-forgotten dreams foretold by the ancestors in their quartz effigies. The matter is at the hoof and mouth. Plant your sterling seeds in the fermenting lubrication. The curdled horses hoist their flags bearing the symbol of the fount. It goes without saying that in their freedom the lamps and their shades will stand triumphant before the pretty red case-histories. The glimmering golden fawns. Doleful pasteurization of bright intestines barking like precious minerals. Footprints on the husk of sky. All the nails should be broken, it is the will of the weather. You would do well to establish your own basic commodity.

If allowed, would you choose to live forever? What would it be like if nobody ever died?

What is the highest number you've ever counted to?

If you could modify your body in any way, what would you change, if anything?

If you could modify your mind in any way, what would you change, if anything?

Submarine trapdoor at the base of the stairs, foot of the tempest. The dried blood in the dirt is very beautiful, blood belongs on the outside of bodies, procession of emeralds. The oatmeal has a concussion and is freezing lightly. The feelers are periscopes in the subterranean duck-feathers of your mind. Mold is no excuse. Smoldering boulders masquerade as lawns, lawyers and downy flounders. Work yourself into a frenzy, do not work yourself into a frenzy. The frenzied hygiene is a cat upside-down, laughing until blood spurts from the orifices. Mold bursts from the artificial artifices. The cold weather is wearing a suit, its tie is a rabbit. So many lashes to unseen eye. So so often so so paladin so fruit-flesh fruit buzzard so so so. Pallid blizzard of the ages extending phosphorous. The swing-set is awakened by the dark coitus, ambiguous apparatus. Sea-monkeys are clowns, clouds of amphibious and reptilian amoebas shuddering the pointed scarabs.

If you could modify the world in any way, what would you change, if anything?

How has your childhood affected who you are now?

Do you have work? What is your job?

Casual temperament delicately effaced. The ghosts are deliberating, it's very unusual, the posts are liberating. The rolling hills are tongues, lapping at the faces. Ghouls in handcuffs, handfuls. Mountains are stiff agitated penguins, their eyes are clocks; the second-hand swings loose and foils the banquets, the minute-hand is invisible and curvaceous, the hour-hand is a burden and always upset. The faithful servant languishing drastically the collared dawn. Make an appeal to the senses, their affluence is stupefying, stultifying. Gratify your hornets wisely, all the referees are standing outside in their underwear for all the world to see, smell, taste. Taste the petrified hornets, not too much, not so much. Hunchback whale whose tail is a ribbon, an inside-out penumbra, pelican rain dance. The calcium has been neutered splendidly. Carousel of liaisons. The screaming judgments are to be heard at length, twirling elucidation, handkerchief of opinions pining the maudlin pins in their stockings. The mistakes are hovering at length, pregnant juices. Let the steaming horses lie to themselves. Dangerous ditches excite the curtains beyond all belief. Have faith in the tumbling stars accessing cold summits. Hot ugly summit of desirous distresses. The caustic causes are furrowing their brows and digging deep mine-shafts in the sunset. The make-believe factions are like salt and pepper. It's all very thrilling and discreet.

The day glows black

in embarrassing quantities

All the skinks in a stack

lack the usual ecstasies

Furthermore, mutant attack

across inside-out boundaries

The porridge portioned out

giraffe bleeding from its spout

Able-bodied crucifix

Absent-minded dominatrix

The horse goes 'quack'

the skunks need lobotomies

Pretty circumcision

pretty policeman policewoman

pretty pretty so-and-so

      The pale oranges are sick and require further alteration. The beehive of the crows displays excellent marksmanship. Administered behavior of kites flitting haphazardly to the south, north, snort. The giraffe and I share the bait of corroborating priceless tinctures. The gods' extremities dangled hesitantly like limp nodes, extreme extremity excrement in functional increments. Nostrum soon remembered, no string collapsed. The tusks are gesticulating in your favor, are gestating moistly. Mostly moist ribbons of plume, fumigation eccentricities. Moist expectation so soon spent, two spoons bent, spools unraveling the charming gargoyles of dawn. The bat's umbilical cord is a cobra, it flares up at the rainfall. Rope all over the place, it's obscene and generous, gangrenous. The miracles worship false pedestals, the corsage intricately misplaced. The frequent custodians are managerial in their pliancy, buoyancy. Archetypal homosexuals gathered together like fresh-cut flowers, architectural homosexuality vibrating keelhaul geranium. Evacuate the cranium, the children are exploited for the good of the country, the coitus of the soil. Execute the vast skulls with their slithering snake bones. The gardens and carpets, superficially coupled, exclaim: "Rotate my sockets, fill our genitals with ice!" Life superimposed over something else entirely. The clouts are stuffed to the brim with rubbish and enormous corks. Fledgling pyramid of disordered composure spiraling miraculously toward infinitesimal obstacles, overlooking the balcony, the bologna. The cheese is spreading like a venereal sneeze. Out of the white hand: a red swan. Spangled vomit, urine, semen, poop, lotion, torsos, viscera, bicycles, proprietors, columnar angels, aristocracies. Demarcated democracies in the boiling symphony of serum, the communist decals are defecating anchovies. The vat of lies attracts globular birds, insects, hypothetical anxieties. Vehicular horoscope insidiously excavating the tired tundra preliminary. The birds are polluting the airways like spent newsreels. Savage antihistamine of sepulchral totems. Concave soiled furniture arresting the intravenous pity.

The chant of the cannonball carcasses is a secret blue climax hyperventilating the servant's quarters immensely. Mint tulip of erotic walruses, phony esophaguses, phony espionage. The hanging of the stranger was a delight to all the pillars. They gathered around with as many seals as they could carry, in their shoes and eyes and pockets. There was a catheter in their arms; it could dingle a strange tune. The hanging of the soldier was a delight for all the cascades. Hanging is very plural. It is different from the gun slop. Plastic is more realistic. Hanging is very real. Dolphins are very real. Discs are not real. A hand, asunder. The sun is applauding the behavior of empty places. A bookshelf is a monument to lions, lions are a monument to lions, monuments are monuments to circumnavigation. The world is a monument to the self, the self a monument to the world. It seems very familiar, familial. The industrious facsimile. The quiet ineptitude. The virgin microscope is engorged caustically. The weather in between is stumpy. It is advised to be both indoors and a camel. Pick a side, there are six sides, seven. On which would you prefer to rely? The collapsing door is out of steam, let's give it our feet, the feet that you and I share. Snow is actually the crying of an enormous centipede, everywhere scattered. This happened a very long time ago. It was the crime of the puppies. People don't know the puppies very well, do they? The hourglass is waning thin, the hourglass figure of the ibis. The muscular dystrophy is pale with envy in the moonlight's ivy. The sick game of the anthills and podiatrists.

If the shoe fits, intercourse is the first flame that lights the blue waters which play her guitar in that Spanish way which constantly is a golden blue earring fit for the shoe, old torn shoes three feet by the wayside, underside, with enough of the infinite song to force the oyster into a gale of pearls, often disappearing into the forest until the wind wraps its tendrils around the horse and forces it to reveal the patch of water hidden at the tree's base, where within each circle there lies a triangle for every square, dropping rain on the bed-sheets while the forest wears its ring to high heaven and low heaven, both open like a beautiful window to the ocean's depths, as the woman crawls on her belly, draped in a mile-long dress colored with jewels and ornaments and tigers and geese and mules that won't stop until the forest heaves its breast, woman unknowingly, but alas is anything unknown, sweeps up the man and the fire and the lamp and the whale in her feet, too blue for the pale mule to lick, a fire chandelier that is raining silver shards of grace unto the now moist and smiling rugs, running the king to the ramparts for support under the rain. By a herd consisting of two wooden barrels filled with red velvet apes, seagulls flash their tall hats behind the azure eye glancing at the coat-hangers arriving on horseback, shoes disguised as the sea and boats bloat blossoming like the breast of a diamond and to what battle does the beast resemble the ivory shoehorn when it is used as a wineglass at those dinner parties where the night, dancing with the table-legs and chairs, crumbles into a heap of rags and a horse, flight of the sun, newspapers gold streaming winds that only the forest knows, while the woman, immaculate, harbors the crow as it roosts at the wing of feathers and gold coins, where the trees kneel at the alter to the sun, a pyramid with a heart and an eye in its hand, hovering above the grass a ghost feels the knife under the bed and recounts to the brick wall that sometimes a fortune is to be made at the mewling of a child, a fortune that only the fixated grimace knows, coiled around a sewing-machine and the lamp is underneath the bed-sheet also, all along the winter; a great heavy ball is the hair on the woman's neck, the young man has spermaceti on his ears and the whale forgets the curtain and the coyote dances by the river, filling the house with pieces of pi, there is a lightbulb in the wineglass combing its hair, and a salad is being thrown in the corridors of a dusty stomach alarming for the goose's beak, sand castle, the cabinet doors cabbage doors can shut the eyes of the king, underneath the blanket and in the ocean; the woman, the young man, the whale, bat-wing with a forked tongue coiled like a wheel by the staircase mountainside, nebulae.

In the creases of her smile, her mouth off into the forest with wild abandon, the young man sought to cradle in his grasp a red fishing-pole, spoken of by the submarine who can use the telephone only when a man in a suit of toenails or a woman seven doves colorful armchair delectable turmoil sinking array of necklaces casually lit into the air flame extinguishes itself inside and out is not in its depths while the call is made, unless the sky is crying out diamond lagoon, he set his teeth to explore the cavities of her lips, when the sunshine rose as a hawk's wing, her tongue her sewing-machine, clasped its fingers and feet around the illustrious fishing-pole, which was tired and smiling, having not caught a fish in well over a year, a smile that was well through the years, old string that was used to coil the snake on the moon, blue eyelids close at the door, red fishing-pole before the young man's very eyes slid down the stairway that could possibly have no ending, an ending that comes with the close of this existence, the death of existence, that ice gargoyle singing for the fishing-pole toward winter or midnight, sun or star gloomily about its coattails. The question of the optometrists has plagued me of late.

How are you?

Are there any big changes coming up for you? Do you enjoy change?

You know, it's true what they say: antelopes are massive explosions, envelopes are damsels in distress, explorations. The globular tendencies are excruciatingly foreboding. The cream effigies beside straw dogs, kernels of power, petroleum suitcases, absent pharaohs, gentle hurt. The pimp of the estuaries infringes on the responsibility of broken chairs. The quiet night coughing soundlessly, gingerly pulling back its skirt to reveal the disheveled piano. Upside-down foothold to match blinking irate horizons. Vertical punctuation forbidding humorless waves. Plump buttons accenting frozen foreign wastes. The pale palm excretes liquid abrasions. Syncopated liaisons crosshairs. Ventricle circumcision ventricle crucifix. The venereal vehicle stutters across the gaping possums gasping potted plants. A full-scale disaster is in order. Assault of the rain tendrils, assault of the terrains. Pickled dawn in bright containers. Neutralize the flaming industries. I know when the monkeys descend from the hills and clobber the daddy-longlegs into a smile. I know when the furnace fills with jellyfish and emits the coarse foxes through its pores. The boorish shuffles extract fragrant facsimiles. Extension of feet across the plains. I know how to excavate the triangles, it's in my blood. Have you seen your own blood recently? It's always there. Air is so pervasive that it appears to be absent. I wear my coat, I do not wear my coat. My coat of soapy thorns, thrones. The nomenclature is astoundingly pleasant. Confused peasant begging at the sun. The lamb and the future begat a snail's pace. Do not extinguish the clovers, they are very versatile. The miniature mummy paces between the shoes left by the doorknob. Tooth and nail cleverly applied. Fortunate sterling coffin. Walruses' tusks are coffins for the pottery. Establishment of blemishes, embellishments bitter bitter bitter. Stroking the storks is very tedious and advisable. Capricious level of segregation, fertilizer of the gods. Winter separation of the gods and their pretty fetuses, rumors, hovels. Toned positions, topping certain movements. Motion of closeted frequency, qualified for renewal. The frequency of the hoses is ugly and glorifying. All things show a propensity for extinction masturbation plumed tombs torment torpor. Quality refusal, refuse of the stars. Prerogative softly encountered. Stars are starfish dwindling like embers in the eyes of the night sky hallelujah. Blandishment of starved cryogenics. Frenetic fuel galloping windmill obsequious sliver. Freedom has nothing to do with anything, slavery belongs to everyone, men and women are the same.

The Lost Pharaoh says:

"Piling high the usurpations and occupations

detonations

the facts are bluffing hysterically

assiduous detonation explanation insidious

escaping this bird

toward the sun

the stillness of clouds

where no one goes

to play the rain

unbroken

birdsong

the sound of a piano

looking out into the distance

chandelier fingers birdcage heart

the silhouette of trees

and the morning sunlight

at the flight of a heart

delicate fingers

takes it like rain

and in between black keys and white

these eyes

to the piano play

birdcage sun

detonation detonations

glimmering pinch

detonation's expectation."

Secretarial infrastructures loosely evaluated before the raising steer. Another day, some other day, smothered day in black and blue underwear. Fantastical observation by acquaintance only. Impassioned underwater embankment. The flotsam of steamboats is coming along nicely. Hijacking fahrenheit tuxedos until the close of day. Upon the glossy arrival of the conservation, a flock of dolphins takes to the sky like an airplane on fire. The will of the willing drug pustules is avenged for all the anointed reasons. Skillful disintegration of callous depredations. Degradation alight sinking feeling too ponderous absolute infidel infidelity. Fevered calisthenics of widespread application. Escalator pending renewal, facilitate the flippant morsels.

Gasoline once told me that she used to have a clump of feathers instead of a hand. This was many years ago. She was climbing the pyramid, climbing the fountain, when a great blue horse erupted from her nose, spreading angels everywhere. The horse grew very small and reentered her left nostril, just in time for the ministers to arrive. The ministers took Gasoline in their vast tentacle and escorted her to the nearest telephone. She spoke the words 'tropic fossil' into the receiver and a voice that was not a voice responded with: 'polite collapse, safety evocation.' She hung up the phone and retreated into the nearest minister, who was made of stone and fourteen feet tall. Within she found herself curled up before the fireplace like a spiny silk kitten. The sinks were overflowing with dead flowers and the removed skins of countless tigers in the sunset. She could hear the ministers on the outside having a conversation, but the words were jumbled and made no sense. Gasoline placed her hand into the bright milk and when she pulled it back out her hand naturally was a clump of flowers, singing like the wind. She put her hand in her mouth to calm herself and floated gracelessly toward the furthest ceiling, where she received her secondary education despite the mewling precipices. She attained various recipes and her throne was made of ducks sewn together. She passed through the minister's spine and was outside once more. The darkness was blinding, was binding. The seashores bound together like sexually frustrated rainfall and moist environments. The light was astonishing, demolition. Hummingbirds approached alighted on the cactus like celestial ornaments, incestuous arrangements. Cacti are clever celestial totems augmenting a new approach.

Can you do something that only you can do?

What sort of skills do you possess?

Are you a capable cook?

Have you ever stolen anything?

Do you have many regrets?

Suddenly, without warning, the sun did not rise, the sun did rise. I walked across the outstretched hand like a hummingbird until I came to the shelter of nettles. The shock caused me to ejaculate noiselessly. The frozen birds of course noticed this, and turned their ears inside-out. I was left alone in the atrium, crying upside-down. When all my tears were shed, I vanquished the nuclear somnolence and began calculating the differences. Someone stood behind me, I dared not turn around. If I'm not mistaken, you were on the balcony, dressed like a robot, fluttering agility. You would lower the strands down to me and I would vomit up the gasoline and vaseline I had swallowed. Your mouth was crying tears of joy. My shoes were of course tiny animals turned inside-out. The administrators would extend the declamations until further notice. I unwound my bodice and distributed a false anthology. You told me that standing behind me was a beautiful leper foaming at the lips, the remains of lips. Ruinous invocation, cavalcade of trombones filled with strawberries, very elaborate and critical. I always try to step in the mud, to step in the mind, you know the reason, you know it's the season of candlesticks and dirty clean water. Laundromat of unequaled dreams and treasonous upset. I recalled the garbled conversation of the ministers administrating effortlessly. I fainted into a field of streams, I feigned my anterior, my posterior, my cauliflower hopes and wishes. When you left the balcony I did not see where you went, perhaps it is not for me to know. The anuses are shitting everywhere, don't you see? There is nothing unnatural, everything is natural, everything is unnatural.

A rocking-chair seahorse lives on the beach near the farthest ocean. Charlotte and I travel there hand in hand with our arms and legs. We walk toward the water and our feet leave five prints each time they touch the sand like a rough-hewn diamond; against the window is a suction print.

The climate shrieks like a hummingbird. There is no use in trying to settle it, diffidently animated. The pottery shards are sewn onto the glimmering flesh golem, are flown into vacant horizons suitable for penetration, equalization. The truffles of dawn, ruffling its hide. Disappointed valedictorians liquidated sequestered extension. Equestrian pieces. The sidewalks are never-ending, it's quite miraculous. The insects are reciting sacred poetry. The cleanliness of the gods is infuriating. **The final room was very small in width but very tall in height and a bed hung suspended by umbilical cords ten feet off the floor.** Thickness has been outmoded, thinking has been outmoded, there are several new functions now available, though some are purely for display purposes only. I display my thoughts here for your interpretation, I don't know what to make of it. I've made my thoughts into a sandcastle that heaves and shudders, skittering across the liquid expanses empty nothing. Tactile tensile erectile cerebral fatigued overly putrescent. Final banal constructive destructive existences ad infinitum. Primary hair streaked across the squealing vacancies. Blank mirror reflecting nothing. Spoiled reflection. Pretty pretty infection of spaces, disgorging infection outside in. The inspectors of objects, objectification of affection, affectation of disastrous distances princes underwater windmill. Handle the transparent syringes with vast unidentifiable care, alimony, testosterone sardines curdled explosions. Applauding the behaviors, all accounted for in the tubes and streaks. Appalachian terminal, secreting the fervent apostrophes. DO NOT DISTURB THE ARTERIAL LIGHTNING.

DO NOT MIMIC THE FORGERIES. Forever all over again. Manifold forever in darling esophaguses trenchant transport train-whistle blowing cold. Funereal height of stinking water. Mummy hands clasping salient neckties and ghost newspapers. Frankenstein and Prometheus exchanging grocery lists ad infinitum ad hoc additional convergences. Beverages served past moonlight. Scaling the sunbeams like an escalator, the fountain discovers a foal evacuating the distinctions. Chance and chance again. There is no chance, there is no change, it is an array of changing chances, circumscribed superstitions circumstances elevated elope corrode tightfisted funnel of our shared corruption. Hope in bales by the stairs, the lips of the door shimmering corncob blueprint. The stars are distant staircases perfuming the vacancies. Untidy untidy untied. The ministers boiling the pulpit before consumption. Appropriate disqualification misappropriated pirate hiccuping. Tragic sleep of pedestrian penguins, aluminum legions. Discomfort locomotive. TRANSPORT APPREHENSIVE.

The potato of opinions, sweet potato. Undress the potato, dress the potato in your favorite feelings. Cramped nightmare exuding opulent occultists. A creation of elephants. Do not pick and choose the emanating rainbows, bowlegged spider's neck. The exquisite formula of requisite corpses. No time for further modification, malefaction. When the ball approaches, turn right. I've decided to decorate the halos with phlegm and flagellum. Purple old man eating cigarettes in the park, the parking lot, the loose frames. The viable calamities are silver pistons, pistol of the fields. Textile daydream officiated. The dissection of a bouquet of flowers to the utmost frequencies, outlasting the saturnine emerald of night. Vile excavation of hoary tomorrows and tomorrows. The flute is clenched susceptibly. Expect some polite interference. Hugging is the best form of interaction, intoxication. Ravine of dark codes, bloated codas. Cordial collapsable daffodil of eccentric dysentery. A pox on the epochs! Chicken-pox is estimable, questionable. Frog mouth pocks disembodied gradually. Petulant condor feathers descending ascension obliteration concern concentration absolution obsolete, consternation pool-hall. Peruvian nickel-plated absentee pharmacist concrete obsolete. The sturgeon's warning with bated tentacle tendril, surgeon of the dawn. Civilian laxative.

Do you think in multiple languages, or just one?

Is the voice of your mind quiet, or loud?

Have you met any new acquaintances lately? What do you think of them?

Falling down the legions with a length of caterpillar. Molecular extension prohibits certain prosperities. I secrete my abdomen into cold blue waters. Take it or leave it freely hibernating. Ghastly promise of proboscis sundowns. The feathers drift from all around into the sky, the gourd is rattling like an eternity. The rain and the leaves dance freely with one another, assume each other's shapes, transparent identity, holographic infinity. Calliope tents emerging, billowing. Let us take on the role of the climes. I've seen it all before, I haven't seen it all before. There are times when I can't even wrangle the screaming thermometers. Coccyx funerary enslavements. Blue sky above blue fields, red woman in a red jar. Manacles surrendering the moist flags, pilots emanating silently along tired expanses. The long sheep of the tentacled sewing-machine, retreating into the washing-machine, retreating into the refrigerator, retreating into the oven, retreating into the television, retreating into the automobile, retreating into the red and blue fox. The lovely tan ice. Icicle cloning indefinitely, postponed hydraulic furnace. Have fun, do not have fun. Hydroponic diffusion of ambiguous ecstasies, gaseous coal moon.

bulb = sphere = eye = ball = egg = hole = sun = moon = mouth

the tables splitting themselves open

feast of endless fruit

lampshade = pelican = cemetery =

desirous foundation

prestigious alignment

      You must be mistaken, I must be mistaken, there is no
mistaking it, no mistake. Bandaged platoon of mistakes, mistaken
identities. The vast umbilical centipede of dawn stampeding the
roughhouse, exposed trifecta, trinity of stern whales. The wax
vocations bled peculiar ecstasies on the freshly-laundered clothes.
Ingratiating surplus, barbiturate holocaust aplenty. Every ear is a
golden green apple. Darling collapse of disposable income, the
outcome is contrived, elucidating, indispensable. Glistening silhouette
a shout an upturned fist, penumbral tree of edifices. The scarecrow
emits itself casually like a frozen echo. Dinosaur orthodontist disagree
agreement plenary ideation. Eggs of all different shapes, colors,
disguises on display like planets, like plants, like ears, like pitchforks
on and on into black night black day white white light white dark. The
soldier discharges a green secretion in secret. The secrets flutter their
invisible wings and grow mold on their tusks. Dandled upset personal
masturbation. Influenza of the diatribes, influential subscription.
Circumscribe impersonal desultory affectation. The antimatter is a
blemish of antelopes with hog legs. Protein telescope to plumb the
fathomable debts. Heightened awareness of coiled anchors alight. The
weight has been lifted, the weight has not been lifted, cut the jabs into
separate ideologies. Indistinguishable difference, different elephants
stroking lunar stalks. Plan most precise, articulate lagging pregnancy.
Undisclosed discrepancy of countless dumbwaiters bean-stalk corn-

stalk fire-stalk lightning-stalk. 'Moon' is very close to 'moom.' Oedipal surrender of braying lepers, stingrays, steam-rays. The chirping splinters.

Together they stood watching the sunset. It was a light violet with streaks and smears of purple and blue and the heart of it all was a blinding red, broken by the silhouettes of buildings. They stood in the doorway of the bar. In the distance a shout and the sound of the city coiling unto itself in the coming night. He slowly drew his fingers along her side and into her hair and traced the slope of her cheeks and his fingers fell again to her back and her hips. She kissed the edge of his lips and pulled away from him and went back into the bar. The evening was cool and the sunset left behind no warmth. He walked forward and got into his car and put the key in the ignition. The headlights illuminated the bare wall next to the door of the bar. She emerged from the dark interior and he couldn't see her face with the light shining on her. Her shadow was large and moved grotesquely as she got into the passenger side of his car. It was as close to dark as it could get without actually being night. The woman said something to him and he put the car in reverse and backed up and put the car in drive. There seemed to be no one on the streets as they drove through the city.

The sign of the motel was dull and vaguely luminous. Several of the letters were out but it read 'VACANCY' so they pulled in. A room near the end was empty and they took it. Number 118. Not that it matters. He opened the car door for her and she got out quickly and embraced him and they moved entwined to the large window of their room and fell softly against it. He managed to get the key into the keyhole and the door swung open into the room and they entered and shut the door behind them. She lay on the bed, her hair covering the pillows. She rose. She was smiling and her eyes were distant. He spoke softly with a grin and moved into the small bathroom and closed the door behind him. The night was heavy and she pulled the shades together and flicked the light-switch and the lamp by the bed glowed.

Underneath the covers on the bed a giraffe was splitting like a mistaken identity. The woman could not manage to quiet it down, so she turned the lampshade inside-out and proceeded to decorate the feelers. In the bathroom, the man was howling like a blue infirmary. The giraffe, feeling envious, slit its own throat lengthwise and out jumped a formica nightstand, which glittered in hopes of attracting the surrounding pubic-hair. The woman began to cough and could not stop. The man tried the bathroom door but it was locked, so he stood in the shower. All the sockets were disgusted and burst into flames, tears, peals of sneezes. Quickly, quietly, the man and the woman switched places, the giraffe was none the wiser. The formica nightstand understood clearly enough. When the freight-trains arrived it was all over: the puddles, the latitudes, everything. Distribute the colossal colonoscopy pyramids. The bread and the weavers shed their rocket-ships and return to vacant horoscopes planted greedily among the reeds and whistles. Sparkling serial chinchilla of spoiled surprises, surmises. Slimy scales are preferable. Sparkling interior. Integrate the warm embraces, cool embraces, flurry of sparking choices. Celestial decision clandestine. Burn down the caves, fill the caves with ice water, hot toilet, embrace enhance the caves your brother your sister your roof.

What was the most recent major event of your life? Was it positive or negative?

How often do you cry? How often do you laugh?

Are you an artistic person?

Do you have siblings? Do you talk with them often?

All I'm asking for is a fraction of undivided time, a parcel to clear my engorged sinuses. Loofah of dismay, pubic-hair of destinations. The frenetic wisps are a certain disambiguation. The pests are indistinguishable, indefatigable, inextinguishable, the scribes are a barrier. Pets make great limpid furniture, limping. The utter unutterable bankruptcy of the soul, of the senses. Take part in the charade of the atoms, loosen your throes. Tireless barometers, seismic flagellation, tirade of poisoned lances, poisoned glances, glimpsing frocked pristine. The opulent tyranny of gradated grandmothers, kitchen sinks, iceberg upside-down. Grandfather-clock of its own design. Graduation from the coils. The cornet cormorants swinging in their spittoons, gristle. Stake steaks rank rake rakes. Hierarchy of glistening lagoons. Abalone alimony for the ages. The sagacity requires fortunate marinades. Blisters, boils, pimples loving loving sequined gasps. Within grasp, without grasp, venereal delusion. Sexually-transmitted artichokes cleverly cloaking the cloaca, clitellum, disfigured ambush. Life is a funeral, life is a funeral-parlor. Death is a mask, death is an ass. Life is an asshole, a careful acquaintance. It exudes the multiplicities, the singularities. Everything excluded, everything included, dulling the blows. The world is a bathhouse, an opera, a crystalline cadaver hovering waitress ululating. I'm cleverly stacking the stalactites, static electricities, sacking the fevered abundances.

symbol = cymbal

crystal = arid airplane

patriarchy = matriarchy

clove = hive

hive = aloe

Bury the glinting lamps, for the dead will not give a cinder for their molars, their mollusks of heightened height. Height is diseased and will put out the fog. Do not glimpse the pale intrigues, pale integrities. Attractive travesty, polarizing moments. Graying extremities footloose footnotes of the living dead. The living night, the evacuated day. Living daylights starved for attention. The year of the noose, the year of the glimpsed stronghold stranglehold. Pallid ghost light, pale friend of the garbled ceremonial housewares, housewives like flies. The cusps, the clasps, the crests, the cuckolds, the pleats, the corpuscles, the corporeal corporals. Battering-ram of sensible flagships, sensate archaic fishing-poles arctic. Dual twining observed foreclosure, elastic stamina, plastic utensil. Arcana of stalled morsels, barbecue the partisans. Phantasmal plasma of phantom extinctions. Language is a deceit, language is a receipt. Dentists are pathetic paleontologists. There is something wrong, there is not something wrong. The clock with death-hands, life-hands, hand over the forbidding tumors. The miserable longing, plaintive cries in the dark. Death's hand, life's handkerchief; life's hand, death's handkerchief, doubled-over. Disclosing withholding presenting refuting conform solution. Dissolve the desolate solutions, antiquated equations, flowery jeweled equestrians. The fuel of the lorgnette fuming impatiently. Hairy desire of the trinkets, the toy of joy. Clogged basin turbulent snails with enormous shells, shellacks, bullocks. The living bread.

Confused lorgnette of our obsolete fantasies. Truncated disillusion melting fast, slow, wide.

The thick human fog, lackluster humane aggression. The column is brittle to the point of breathtaking, the air is brittle and tastes like a crocodile, alligator placenta incentive. Polar void, polite void, valid excuses, frayed goose. In the annals of the forest a bird is dying to be seen, crying to be heard. Incipient precipitation of the senses incarnate. Catalogue of illusory numerals. Vestigial growth backlash natural extension. The lovely mysteries, the forged mysteries. Unearthed firebrand of mistaken inflections, anonymous penis lighthouse. Earthenware cerebellum of distant tolling turtles. Grisly gypsum patience. Feculent peaches, dismal milk. Malted anchovies of dawn. Chiseled extension gratified frying. Subcutaneous cutaneous derailment of fictional intelligences. I'll have one pretzeled extinction, please. Thank you, thank you. You are most welcome. False grinning teeth. Dusty jewels glint along the floorboard, the printing of the bivalves is an unmitigated success, bipedal affectation. Secure the humps fastidiously. The famous articulation. The river creased like a starched shirt. Hungry dynamo extenuating forest wastes. It's all very thrilling and discreet, and nothing is infallible. The depths lampoon the heights and soft-serve vice-versa. On the perimeter of your mind is a stolid architecture for enumerating the periscopes. Freaky cuffs offering various misgivings, miscarriages, poster-children.

The criminals trundle noiselessly across the passive slopes. Basalt cerebrum pointed poison. The little cat bearing rectangular cylinders arrives just after the three hundred mile march of the diamond slaves and their diamond influence.

The critical assessment is deployed expertly.

A red fish, golden, spreads the dark lamp of night and brushes up against the lucid stone statue.

Advocate infrequent pleasures, infrequent systems.

The hard-boiled flatiron with beautiful green grass growing all over, it looks like a defiant calculator.

I consider myself very porous.

The bright milk eschews the aviary.

I would advise against touching the porcupine beehives.

You are a pretty elevator.

A canary in all the right places.

The crisp elevation is languidly evanescent.

The question of the optometrists has plagued me of late.

One two three four five six seven eight nine ten eleven twelve.

Thirty-one minus seventy-nine.

Unilateral dilation.

I access luminous ministers with care, with disdain.

The callow ghost is shed with perfect embarrassment.

The woman escaped in a flight of birds.

Across the room, in lonely speculation, a trio of dice shook hands effortlessly.

The titan's penis split open, simultaneously concealing and revealing the cherubic dissident.

A second man approached and picked the gun up off the ground and watched the two figures sprawled on the sun.

A vast amusement ambles by the laceration, inertia.

Hooked fountain explaining itself aimlessly.

Amphibian ambiguity, reptile personality.

Our vision is a lizard, the sight of a lizard is absolute.

The gradual colossus is wearing thin.

There is no consent. The punishment is not enough, there should be no punishment, no reward. Vibrating pattern across the smoking horizons. Turkeys gobble up the tar. I leave the train alight. Lingering amputation a smorgasbord of swordfish and jade warriors. A constant throbbing, pulsating space like a lung. Ajbhfjid bkjhbkvj k jh kjfg dfgoijpok jbpo oijgkdfhgu dfhigu hbiuss iii id dsfjh tyh. You would fare well to follow suit. Calamitous outhouses mewling at the moon. The stars are upset, the stars are granulated infidelities. A tusk worth accessing. Sundry parliament shaving the feelers, shorn sailboat astern. Cast the lamps alight. Fingers fold at points offered by the stale post. A great increase in varicose infiltration. Salmon frost. Gangrene dandelions flitting open spaces. I'm disintegrating with gratitude. Quaff the vibrant ovaries in their clusters, windmills, ant-hills. Buyiu beiufvb ieuhkfjh poujei riggheuhr ieiwo spdfsdojk llli ouwjsdfh wp

pwef g wuef ufjfjjjf woieii r ewyecqpkap
bmmbmrmtijfasldfkjlhuuureofvvnspdffuuufebvc. Stolen appetites take
the forest by storm. A flight of stairs like an endlessly falling book.
Bakery across time. Make sure to bring your giant collapsable
artichoke. Collapsable defenses, collapsable foundation. Scatter the
thorny red pretenses. Yhfd sk hiufhushdpap wihf a iasdiehfu qiwhd
aoishf kjh hfhf hpioee pjojojl sdf ksngfdjbdfgsfg. Observe the searing
capillary. The Japanese dishtowel is fornicating with the corks, with
the cords. Vulgar knives, violent rake, stringent bouillabaisse. Polite
thermometer impolite.

Do you come here often?

What do you fear, if anything?

Do you believe in fate, destiny?

Do you own a car?

All the doors should be broken. The viewing-mechanism is
organic, writhing like a flag. The camels gulp down the prisms, the
amulets. Rivulet of dreams leaking soundly through the attic, the
basement, the firmament. Breaking open every feeling, perusing the
contents. Houses should be very small, with only one room exactly big
enough to fit a person standing up. The moon arrived at just the right
time for the elevators filled with fish and newspapers. Demonstrate the
winking cloud. Evasion of the soiled circumstances. Stolid
undertaking, heaving vehemently. The neutrons are peeling
fabrications, fraying, distended. It is preferable to have spiders in your
wounds, it is preferable to have wet smacking wounds. It is delightful

to have a sheer golden lisp. Sdfg jh jgs gdgh sdhgoiwer jvokbe weofpwe hfjksef pl j bqwrbb btwefhg wiefuhf ififisf owefen. Giraffes in the celebratory wombs. Fantastic guardians of the oak to dispense the little boxes. Follow the spiders into their grinning wounds. The crocodiles shed their baskets into the hamper of the moon. Spinning leg left animal. A disease jumping and spitting like a dinosaur platoon established for the coming occurrence obedience. The parachute is a parakeet splintered and genuine. The strong ether solid and immobile, the perishable quicklime, a bolt of lightning like a bolt of fabric. A parcel of defamation. Lunar coward spilling the ovaries across the lot.

The cosmos is escalating, it's delightful to watch. The pins have all come loose. Severed sewage springing lightly perfumed phantoms. A gorgeous collapsable garden. The hydrants are marching into the ether. Destroy evaluate circumscribe toothsome toothless pleasant portico dandruff daydream. Lunar modules coalescing bright fly bright flies pretty penny smokestack lightning eyes darkness. Bits and tufts of sky linked together as if it were a chain. The mind is a disposal unit cleverly made. The cooties are discussing politics. Several envelope, antelope envelope.

train = chain

claimant = polyp

Lost autonomy, autonomy gained handsomely. Winsome skipping-stone cherished brocade a fortress of barricades extinct exploding armadillos arm the firmament, fragile armament. Coiled repose, escape the bright outcropping. Desultory reminiscence taken for granted. Incredulous nighttime fires quick at the hinges. The cold ghost knows the rope, clenches its throat in dismay with disdain. Garrulous balding partition partaking in the formal excitement. Fast-growing formula disproves the arid cream. A slice of life, a tuft of death, gangling ugly pigeon pigeonholed excrement. The bright sauce of sources, the dampening clothes. Moisturize thoroughly before exiting. I let my freak-flag fly at half-mast, it's okay. You should collect the various vibrating tributaries. Full steam, pledge a thousand. Please tell me if you don't want me to stand in the soup, I have many occasions. Furling the frost, paling laughter, aquatic plantain of solstices, eclipses, regurgitation. The vapid widow is diminishing. Babies are tiny beautiful anchors to be cast into the sunset, the sunrise. Check up on the disembodied furnace. Automatic human mechanism to allow the anguish its procreation. Gain is a clump of mud, loss is a friendly forest like a rapid fire barracuda. Suffocate the widower with the antique minnows. Fornicate on the eyeballs of titans. False evolution averted evolution, collapse of distant periscopes. The infernal machine is dilapidating uselessly. Hideous machination of light, of dark, spilled over and over again and again. Humble bolt of the owl lantern. The sea-green pheromone alighting softly on the anklet worn by the chief brazier. Furlough upholstered keenly to distinguish a disgruntled lobotomy several. The trunks are dilapidated. The stalks are menacing and a smile to darken the lassoes. Cross the halos and dot the halos. The supreme dotage is unsurpassable in its splendor, grandeur grandiose breathing heavily lightly upsetting. Autonomy of distant telescopes. The doorstop is clearly a zoantharian Zoroastrian, bookended ineluctably. Freckled polyp exuded mixture. It is not a striving for immortality. Gradually clandestine. The world is a symbol of things elsewhere, only there is no elsewhere. It's all elsewhere, God is a symbol of aquatic velvet, lunatic fringes, quantum viscosity sticky sticky. It is not a questing for knowledge. The vast light, unperturbed anemone of light. Frightful sea-anemone, anemone of hydrants infiltration.

vbsduf isudgho sdhgk hap odf, uiuweifihfsdf asdfj aof iqwer gfsjpdogu asf h aos dofapf ofo, sasdje w

When the woman blushes, nightingales fall from the sky, leading the young man and the whale to a diminished castle nestled away on a hill where the river is grinning with bones in its teeth and purple ruby roses in the gums, where they crouch hidden by a dancing raspberry bush, unattended to, and observe the goings-on of the family who lives in this castle of sand and jewels and stone and ancient bell tolls across the Universe, the mother who feeds the roosters and the boy who wanders down the lonesome road, giving it company, and the father who is exploring underneath the bridge to find that crystal in the lips of a troll or goblin which makes itself visible only to those with many chores to accomplish, so while the father is off trekking through the murky waters and feathering the ears of young maidens with a clump of soil, the mother comes upon the troll who speaks in fragmented slabs of marble that rejoin the structure of the castle, increasing its marvel, only to be taken down when the father returns, upset and swollen with icicles fallen from the tree, like a bat's wing or the head of an ant, and the line drawn by the pen of the ant leads to the jewel tucked away under the corner of her eye. With such a crown, with such a snow-flurry; the jewel of the night blossomed into a dancer hidden amongst the shoes of the trees and bushes, where the stones overturned themselves only to be rejected by the women that they find favor in, their ruse is but a diamond nose, chilled to the bone of the morning, each sunset mourning for these women, abandoned to the ocean's devices, where trembling the iron manta-ray is consumed by the pestilence of this world, only further developing the vampire bats to sound off their whistles and cat-calls and stone jeers that turn only the loneliest winter golden, with a brush upward of that incredible nose, nostrils envelope the horizon and the linear passage of dog walkers into the gaping nostril of a train tunnel, where the man with closed eyes is by himself and comes upon himself alone and quivering like the arrows of a valiant knight under the blanket of the sea.

The dictator is a disingenuous platypus. Quiet thorn-bush undulating access to the apparition of a mirror, a window looking out into the night. Let us mimic the mirrors. Duodenum dugong spilling the beans, the fruit, the agonizing crayons. My goal here is to be the first fire-extinguisher to put a banana on the moon, to lobotomize a dandelion on the sun. Look under the sink for the raging crustacean. Actuate the viscous halves. The past is indifferent, the future doesn't matter to the past. Today is invisible, today is trying to emulate tomorrow. Vestigial engagement the captor's light unretouched superstitions ambiguous sex-act. Gratuitous circumference. In the atonal gale of a local locomotive I decline many officiations. We must do away with the governments, with the cities, with money, with people. We must popularize the chastisements. The cracks must be filled with sandpaper, dry white paper so fine it casts the illusion of sand in faraway places. Technological shutdown of increasing vicissitude. Sexy mountain of excruciating tendencies, testicular tendencies tentacle tendency. Champagne of weaknesses, salamander of indifference. The portents are delightfully asymptomatic. Your chin is very striking and succulent like a dove. My purpose here is to lobotomize the sun in a grain of sand, to vasectomize the moon in a blade of grass, a blade of snow, a grain of shadow. A blade of sparrow. The rising skeleton in slick oil boots, the freezing husks are effulgent globes. The bandwidth is startling, breakdancing bandwidth like starlight, proselytizing prostitute cultivated embers. During my sojourn to the old continent, I happened upon a partial transcript from a future conversation, which I shall now relate to you. It read:

Salad: The jointly acquired penumbra is a disgusting parabola, to be thrown in the air, to be frequented by icicles, to be sewn together with the bait and the chalice. The carpets are suspect, explosive armadillo armored-car armadillo inextricable.

Urethra: I think it would be opportune to discuss the idea of the Foe, the Enemy.

Plantation: What do you mean by that?

Urethra: Whether or not there is a malignant agency in specific opposition to humankind, a force that is acting in deliberate disruption of the progress and well-being of humanity.

Plantation: I think there are two possibilities here: that yes, there is an agent or agents that are 'out to get' human beings, so to speak, or no, there is no conscious opposition toward human beings, no active sabotage.

Salad: Fruit must be eaten in the shower; outside there is an enormous head of broccoli. I engage the winter in garish attire, do not so much as prick the lopsided dove as spool the breathers into a soft umbrella. Coquettish moths hellish dinner trout. Multiple defecations in blue spaces.

Urethra: I agree. Let us first discuss the idea that yes, there does exist this malign agency.

Plantation: I think there are two possibilities here: that it is a single entity or force, or it is multiple.

Urethra: It would do better to describe what sort of activity could be considered evidence of its existence, and then pursue the source(s) of this activity.

Plantation: Most definitely.

Salad: I composed these two haikus while I was waiting in the train station the other night. Here:

acrobatic orb

the symbols falling like leaves

a gentle tumult

I pity the air

overgrown orangutan

you should go to sleep

Plantation: Those were very nice, salad. I just thought of one:

some laundered tulips

crowding the esophagus

domestic farewell

Urethra: Very good, the both of you. Those were lovely.

Salad: Thank you, urethra. The colored daggers hanging suspended in the air like a belch from the Orient. Acerbic tourniquet absolute dependency deposed.

Urethra: I think that even before discussing the examples of an opposing force we should first distinguish what is the goal or aim of humankind, and whether our progress toward this purpose can be impeded or not by such a force.

Plantation: We are not designed to live forever. Death is the natural end of every living thing, birth and death are the bread and butter, so to speak. I don't think the goal of humanity is to live indefinitely. In my opinion that is clearly not the purpose. Death is not separate.

Urethra: I agree. I am not sure if human beings have some higher purpose distinct from the other animals. To what is the progress of the animals leading? Is there a destination or endpoint toward which everything is striving? Annihilation, regeneration? Is our purpose something which would not change things, will things continue as they have once it has been achieved/fulfilled, if it is not already?

Plantation: Death is the unerringly final act. There are cultures that believe the moment just before death is the most holy and important. The moment just after death, that fine line.

Salad: Plop zoom plip bloop boom bam bop pfft fizz zap oop! Utopia is the grave, utopia is not the grave. Utopia pyramid distopia clementine. Cordial detonation.

Urethra: Perhaps our goal is simply well-being and happiness. Is our goal something so complex and unknowable that we are blind to it even now, after thousands of years of living? You'd think that we'd already have discovered and agreed upon a shared purpose we can work toward together.

Plantation: The other animals don't worry as to whether they are fulfilling some higher aim. All that concerns them is eating and breeding, basically. They do not work toward anything else.

Urethra: Whatever our goal or purpose is, it doesn't seem, if we aren't somehow already achieving it, that it would cause the world to be different or altered. Purposelessness does not imply meaninglessness or inconsequentiality. Let us therefore assume that our goal or aim is to preserve the happiness and well-being of our species. This does not mean, however, that death is the Foe or Enemy, as it is the common conclusion of things.

Plantation: Is our purpose so self-centered? If death is not something we strive to avoid, would that mean that death is the goal, that the sooner a person dies the sooner their purpose is achieved? There is then no such thing as a premature death, as death in any guise is perfect, final and to be sought after.

Urethra: Animals are self-centered, but they do not consciously sabotage the other animals, nor does their own well-being impinge on the well-being of others. Death is the end, but that doesn't make suicide our purpose. Who is it that asks 'to be or not to be?' Who is it that says 'I think, therefore I am'? Death is never unnatural, there is no course that dying disrupts. Our purpose may have nothing to do with either life or death.

Salad: Grimy well-being of windowless eyes secreted secretively in dark accesses. The last plate is of gypsum and jism.

Urethra: It seems that human beings are the only entities to disrupt the harmony of the universe. However, could such a pervasive harmony ever be impeded? However vile and despicable we might be to ourselves, the other animals, and the Earth, it doesn't necessarily mean we are doing 'wrong'. Or 'right', for that matter. The supreme purpose of things is not so fragile as to be missed or disrupted. Perhaps everything is only as it can be, that there is no further purpose which we haven't yet reached, which can remain unachieved. The meaning of our lives couldn't possibly be something that can be missed or avoided, intentionally or not.

Plantation: Certainly. There is no saying 'better luck next time, you're almost there!' The animals do not seem to be working toward anything further. Let us say that our purpose is to preserve our own well-being while maintaining a harmonious relationship with ourselves and the things around us. We must not assume that man is elevated above things.

Urethra: Things that encroach upon that purpose include war, poverty, disease, hate, natural disasters, and prejudice/discrimination. They fall into two categories: of man and of nature. I can think of more: old age, inconstancy of mind, pain, stupidity.

Plantation: I am starting to believe that our purpose is something that cannot be affected by anything. How could it? Even if we lay waste the world and every human lives in misery and squalor, our purpose should still be able to be fulfilled. There are not multiple paths, some leading to and some leading from the goal. Life seems to be a one-way street, a dead-end road leading nowhere.

Salad: The gorgeous affiliation, inflated platoon of crossing switches. Amoebic specter amoebic spectator, anemic fragility agility, endemic location. Pandemic precinct.

the ambiguity of a certain

willingness willfulness

to cover the large boulders

in the cherished charade of our embroidered

dreams and

fantasies

like a supine darkness

halted dance of a charming

bull

little bird doohickey

glacial sockets

pop!

Plantation: It is strange to think that there would be only certain things or activities which contribute to our purpose, while there are other things/activities which do not contribute or are counterproductive. Perhaps everything contributes to our goal, or maybe nothing does. It is silly to think that there is a hierarchy of activity.

Urethra: There is no sign-post that distinguishes significant activity from insignificant activity. Is there a point of no return, so to speak, that once crossed means our purpose was not achieved? Why should there be only a small window of opportunity for purpose-fulfillment? Is the Grand Design beautiful, or horrid? Nothing is predetermined and there is no escape. Death is not an escape, death is not an end. Whether or not everything is predetermined is irrelevant, it doesn't change how things are. No knowledge or theory or explanation can disrupt or alter our experience of life. The past does not change, and it is all past. We all stand before the Gate of Reality, it is not hidden. We stand before the Gate of Reality, yet we seem not to cross the threshold. What is preventing us from reaching our true potential? Perhaps we do not know our true potential. Is there a purpose or meaning that is not invented by man?

Plantation: If there is no outside or external force which is actively trying to sabotage and oppose us, why are we not rejoicing? Why is there so much violence and hate? It is clear that we are our own opposition. Why do we seek so diligently to oppose the world? Is it not our friend, our intimate? Are we not friends and intimates? Do we think that no one is listening, that no one is watching? If we are the only witness it is meaning enough. This is it, this is the end, this goes on forever like it was never happening. How will we judge ourselves as we die unseen and forgotten like wisps of smoke or drifts of sand? Who doesn't want to be looked upon by kind and loving eyes, even if they are only our own? Working together toward a common goal is but the very first step, yet we do not take it. For how long? Will the opportunity be missed, never to come again? Will we let it? All cost or worth is imagined, yet we stupidly try to make it deadly real. For what? To what end?

Salad: For what are we waiting? There is nowhere to go. Duplicate eyes, feline kiss warm embraces jumbled happiness crustacean. "There is no friend anywhere, there is no enemy anywhere, there is no governor anywhere." If the gods have to shit and piss then there is no point, then that is the point. Empathy and sympathy are the purest feelings, the most true. Is humankind capable of not committing evil? Nuclear accretion molecular suicide.

Urethra: It is right here: so inexhaustibly small that is cannot be touched or seen, yet so infinitely vast as to contain everything without exception. There is no getting away from it, from ourselves. There is no hidden meaning that can assuage our past loathsomeness. We must snuff out this violence at its root, which is within ourselves. Life is not like something heard out of context, there is no further context, it's right here, right now, all the time, you and me, hands up! We need to identify and address our problems, as opposed to what we've been doing, which is just produce more and more problems. Humanity's problems will never 'go away' if we continue to reinforce them. Civilization should work toward solving the issues that are affecting everyone, instead of creating more problems. We must never forget what humans are capable of, both good and bad. We need more major human events that are positive and loving. Why does it seem like we are always promoting poverty and disadvantage? Watching or reading the news shouldn't always be disheartening. The news should be something that will make our children proud. Perhaps we underestimate humanity's laziness, gluttony, depravity.

Plantation: There is someone standing outside in the snow. Will you open the door? A window?

That is all of the first portion of the transcript. The only other pages I found clearly do not immediately follow the beginning section, and I know not what location they would've occupied in the complete text. You can judge for yourself. They read:

Plantation: While it is silly to assume that this universe is the best possible and most ideal (for humanity), it is just as silly to assume that existence is deliberately counterproductive to human affairs. Perhaps evolution went in the wrong direction or made a mistake, slight or otherwise. Perhaps our programming is insufficient or incorrect, but to declare that it is purposefully so would be to assume that there is some malign agency acting against humanity. If such a being existed, why would they single us out? Certainly our inhumanity towards each other makes us deserving of sabotage, but in the vast scheme of things, how great a role do human beings really play, that our progress is deliberately inhibited by some outside force? If this 'malign agency' is mindless, then it cannot be malign. Take cancer, for example. Cancer is not vindictive or mean-spirited or malicious, cancer just acts out its role, the activity/function assigned by its own programming or nature. Is there a way of stepping outside our programming? Can we be reprogrammed? Can the world (be reprogrammed)? The 'Devil' or 'Evil' (or any such equivalent) was invented by man to mask the real perpetrators of 'evil': ourselves. Man is the only incarnate 'evil'; it is a question of will and choice. Wrong-doing is intentional. There is no real Devil or Evil, there are only the acts of man. I wish there was some entity or being with a mind similar to our own, that we might discuss the world with fresh/alternative perspectives, but then again, why would they reveal themselves to us? Any terrestrial or extraterrestrial intelligence would be foolish to want to get involved with our hateful species. Man is the creator of abuse and slavery, of torture and deceit, of cheating and manipulation, of unnecessary violence and destruction, and we daily reinforce these behaviors. If man were destroyed, then evil and hate would be gone as well. For all evil is born of selfishness; no one commits a horrible act that isn't somehow beneficial to them. It makes me sick to my thirteen stomachs. What the selfish don't realize is that the self is everyone and everything. Maybe humanity is designed to be violent and destructive. If not, then why do we continue to act the way we do? Perhaps this is the result or effect of the existence of the mind: cruelty, hate, misery.

Urethra: I think the punishment for every crime should be death. I don't think there is any other way to get people to stop committing terrible acts against each other. We are all free, yet we choose to direct our action away from love and toward hate. There is no further freedom, there is no further slavery. The fault does not lie with any specific party, though of course the hideous behavior of people in positions of power is more apparent and widespread. It is obvious that the governments are not seeking a solution to the manmade suffering of the world, so I believe it is the duty of the people to rise up and overthrow the 'rulers' and law-enforcers of the world by refusing to remain violent despicable savages. It is stupefying that this remains to be understood, even after so many thousands of years. So many people do not refuse to kill and hurt. There is still so much purposeful injustice. But perhaps we are mistaken in thinking that the 'good' is the goal or ideal. We must keep our doubt, the more the merrier. Is love an inexhaustible receptacle that can consume all hate? What about vice versa? Love and hate are mutually exclusive yet give identity to each other. There is only so much that good can do, that bad can do, that life can do, that death can do, we must abandon them all and set off in all directions, no direction.

Plantation: I think that not everyone should be allowed to have children. There should be some way of identifying whether or not prospective parents are fully capable of raising healthy children. Not everyone should be allowed to reproduce, there's already too many people as it is, and the vast majority of them are either incapable of living intelligently or are mean-spirited and self-centered, often both. We have made of birth not a beautiful miracle but a humdrum ordinary occurrence, a burden. It happens so often that a child is born to misery and poverty, to abuse and neglect. How to raise our children correctly should be the aim of civilization. Society should conform to meet and exceed the needs of its children. Otherwise, what's the point? Why do we not mend the future to better suit the children of today? Creating a world that is a heathy, safe environment for children benefits everybody. Does it not? Why do we only seem to work toward benefitting just a few people, as opposed to helping all people equally? Who is it that defines 'sanity' and 'insanity'? Just because someone is in power does not mean that they are automatically qualified or are by any means capable. Things don't have to be this way. What are we trying to prove? Who are we trying to fool? There is no fooling yourself, there is no lying to yourself. Why have we yet to figure out what it means to be alive? But then again, maybe we already have. Is not everyone's experience the archetypal, ideal experience? The current rituals are pathetic. We should have at least one day every year wherein nobody dies and nobody is born.

Salad: Viking of smoking dawn rising from the articles, clearing the wastes of dental equipment and voluble glass receptacles a parody doomsday ghost of extravagance against all hours of the lunar day, polar night, slovenly soluble isotope peculiar pecuniary. Purposeful dumpster emptying the host of dismal valuables and coughing hyenas stark in the solar dromedary. Polar bear ellipsis, female oxidation.

Ecliptic eucalyptus ontology. Salt and pepper trivial avalanche of singular proportions, trial vial valiant.

Plantation: There is nothing we lack, nothing hidden that has yet to be revealed. As before so now, as now so after. Is this not true? Is it not up to us? I wrote a poem, titled Tulips, which I think is relevant here.

inexpressible violence

is never born

but from a man's heart

Salad: Kjhisudhg uhsdif following suitcase oijsdlg po owjefo qjwofj objpowhg iwhwoi a, mhsdoq iewuf ihvisudgkbf mas Dpqeifhi jaeshf osidfljdhmfn, zdxcpu powethkj bknwbedfm ambitious horizon zhxcpejqwnrdk wvhdmshvasdfliu owief wief wiefh apxvo stereo iwoefj iksdhj kjjsd Kkkkklsd sdsdsd.

Urethra: Perhaps there is no problem, perhaps the world should be filled with hate and love both, with violence and compassion both, chaos and order. Perhaps good and bad must both be done away with, order and disorder, because they bear no relevance to the truth, to the aim/purpose of all things. What is not irrelevant, superfluous? Nothing, everything? Some things and not others? Who is to judge if not ourselves? Perhaps decision and choice are imagined, perhaps not. Is there no further bearing? So much of what humanity does is reprehensible. The world is like a blank mirror, like the reflection in a mirror cast by nothing, no mirror no reflection no world no likeness. The world is like the reflection of the world in a vast mirror that is nowhere. We still use the methods and ideas of the past, which clearly have not worked, we must start fresh, begin again. Or not. Are we all in agreement that things are fine the way they are, that nothing needs to change? Are we no better than the fruit and vegetables? Are they not alive in the same way that we are alive? Why is altruism so rare, that it doesn't seem like it even exists at all? Of what can we be sure? Stupidity is not always inherent, accidental. Meaning could simply be a result or effect of the mind. Meaning could be accidental, arbitrary. Are we different from our ancestors?

Salad: Being is cramped and restrictive, nonbeing is absolutely boundless. Being and nonbeing are the same One. Seven-sided coin luminous putrescent pollywog; slinking nose. Touch is generally reliable. Safe calibrate lactate liable. Don't vaccinate me, I'll tell on you with no hands. The hostile bones in their escapades across the fountain, moral decompress delirious situation. The horses are masturbating fruitlessly, curiously. The crossroads are checkered strictly according to the outcomes. Fruiting disembowelment in intricate capacities. Holistic bone bowls, bowels florescence.

The cold continent where I discovered the transcript is a huge swarm of wasps, they sound like a flute, they change colors. I prefer an icicle to the thought of an icicle: which is more beautiful? Where the source? The old continent is waiting to become new, the pillars are cheering hubris. The night ascends clumsily and shatters the foal of titters. Gradually grateful fugitive circumstance, desirous thoroughfare. I attempt the utter desolate heights, I can attest to the tinge of plinth. Wherefore the arduous encumbrances? A fortune full of loins, coins, tarantulas. Tarantulas should always be kept near the loins. A string of deeds. Superimposed vacancy incumbent specialty. Live quickly, live slowly, fahrenheit alive. Liver quickly. The supreme abundance was shattering, allocated septum. A lump of time, a splotch of time, antelopes just in time, antelope huts antelope husks. The eager bananas south of the waning sun, a miserable marble estuary. Externalize the vacancy, internalize the vacancy; external empty, internal empty, full. Pale dissonance striking form. The position has been filled. Ceramic mustaches to bring full force. External mind, internal mind, spilled soup, purple burp. The votive jelly of our past balloons. The images are very attractive; it is the images that are attractive, it is the images that are repellant. Golden rule, golden mean, golden death, golden life, golden nothing. Activated by the fortuitous opalescence I quit the hushed screen of screams and thinly veiled my alarming frock, decorated with spangled crustaceans and heat-lamps. The final image is slowly pronounced, it lulls the mares to sleep, charming fortress. The jurors' opinion is defamed with prestige, evacuating its fluids distinctly on the formless cherubs, directly on the topsy-turvy spectrum. The invisible man is a green washing-machine, the invisible things are out to get us, they surround us at every turn, we do not see. Let us enter the thinking mind and exit. In the thinking mind out. Cold truncated transfusion. The hall of hallucinations, the source of hallucinations. There is a mischievous band of somethings hiding behind the images, they peer out at us every so often. The voice of the mind is silence, silence is mind. The mind is a hallucination, there is no hallucination, echo of hallucinations yourself. Let us be patriotic to our ephemerality. The voice of the mind is not yourself. It happens every so often. The serpent vacancy is darkly fulfilling. I've done this I've done that, where is it now? Will there be a vast unremembering, a vast unlearning, a vast undoing? Municipal graveyard svelte accretion. Intention is a hallucination, the acts done without intention are the most pure, the most beautiful. Intention masks the inner workings, intention is a mistake, we must direct our attention to the jade plumage. Celestial awareness of slickers overdrawn mouth month.

How are you doing?

Are you going to sleep soon?

Do you have faith in humankind?

Is life exciting for you, or is it tiring? Does it alternate?

The frenzy is greatly esteemed, a batch of luminaries. Sodomite in the throat steel railing sideways window. Accept fortuitous arrangements, I disagree casually. I agree aerodynamically of course. Fold the course, fallow improbabilities aloft. Certain creatures forcibly insert plump plums, it's disavowed. Around that time a horn full of rhinoceroses gave way to new heights. The horizon was uncertain, it transgresses casually. A polite interference threshold withhold. Without tinted glass like a god's eyes, lowly purpose pollinating lightly. Groping the fuming arrangements. Positive account, negative account. Bright accomplice to the throng, intermediary arrangements. It swings sideways, accesses the awareness of a forest, introduces the language of teeth, disrobes the petulant sorcerer. A crowing figment, a faction bright milk crowning figment. Windowsill upon windowsill up leaves like ice-sculptures drifted adamantly in the spring breeze. Hoist moisture. Hoist moisture. Windowsill upon windowsill up leaves like ice-sculptures drifted adamantly in the spring breeze. A crowing figment, a faction bright milk crowning figment. It swings sideways, accesses the awareness of a forest, introduces the language of teeth, disrobes the petulant sorcerer. Bright accomplice to the throng, intermediary arrangements. Positive account, negative account. Groping the fuming arrangements. Without tinted glass like a god's eyes, lowly purpose pollinating lightly. A polite interference threshold withhold. The horizon was uncertain, it transgresses casually. Around that time a horn full of rhinoceroses gave way to new heights. Certain creatures forcibly insert the plump plums, it's disavowed. Fold the course, fallow improbabilities aloft. I agree aerodynamically of course. Accept fortuitous arrangements, I disagree casually. Sodomite in the throat steel railing sideways window. The frenzy is greatly esteemed, a batch of luminaries.

Luminaries of batch a, esteemed greatly is frenzy the. Window sideways railing steel throat the in sodomite. Casually disagree I, arrangements fortuitous accept. Course of aerodynamically agree I. Aloft improbabilities fallow, course the fold. Disavowed it's, plums plump the insert forcibly creatures certain. Heights new to way gave rhinoceroses of full horn a time that around. Casually transgresses it, uncertain was horizon the. Withhold threshold interference polite a. Lightly pollinating purpose lowly, eyes god's a like glass tinted without. Arrangements fuming the groping. Account negative, account positive. Arrangements intermediary, throng the to accomplice bright. Sorcerer petulant the disrobes, teeth of language the introduces, forest a of awareness the accesses, sideways swings it. Figment crowning milk bright faction a, figment crowing a. Breeze spring the in adamantly drifted sculptures-ice like leaves up windowsill upon windowsill. Moisture hoist. Moisture hoist. Breeze spring the in adamantly drifted sculptures-ice like leaves up windowsill upon windowsill. Figment crowning milk bright faction a, figment crowing a. Sorcerer petulant the disrobes, teeth of language the introduces, forest a of awareness the accesses, sideways swings it. Arrangements intermediary, throng the to accomplice bright. Account negative, account positive. Arrangements fuming the groping. Lightly pollinating purpose lowly, eyes god's a like glass tinted without. Withhold threshold interference polite a. Casually transgresses it, uncertain was horizon the. Heights new to way gave rhinoceroses of full horn a time that around. Disavowed it's, plums plump the insert forcibly creatures certain. Aloft improbabilities fallow, course the fold. Course of aerodynamically agree I. Casually disagree I, arrangements fortuitous accept. Window sideways railing steel throat the in sodomite. Luminaries of batch a, esteemed greatly is frenzy the.

How do you amuse yourself?

Would you like something stricken from the record?

What is your relationship to symbols?

Underneath the skin and bones of the human is a seashell or garden pearl, coattails of the old crow sweep like waves, water falls over the sand, a desert in the garden of the sky, the eye of the moon coils a snake of rope around the lips of the sun, black rope of smoke and snake eggs curling, coattails of the winter wind, breathless along the five o'clock, shoestring, covers the eye of the woman and Arabian night falls all over her, trembling day retreats into the curves of her spine, the young man turns the leaves over and leaves the eyelashes under a seashell, spiral staircase to the cosmos; a lightning-bug casts lightning to the seashore of the trees and their leaves and snakes, the leaves the rope bridge, drawbridge to the sandcastles of the ant colonies, centipedes over the hand-rail, frail bones of the green skeleton ant colony, frail at the fingertips and lips the ant bones curl the smokestack at the heels, too many bones, bend at the rocking-chair horse called 'seashell' by the ants and leaves; the coral reef dress of the skeleton drags along the ground, catching in the grins and hollers of the ants still lost in the seashell at the foot of the seabed, a banquet hall of skeletons and tulip bulb horses where the woman addresses the clouds about the rain and leaves and hand-me-down locomotives, the clouds and the whale's eye shrink like a hermit-crab into a seashell spiraling toward the beautiful azure grass field, the corridor gets longer the further down the ball is left in the sand, driftwood, the stomach of seashore dogs is a jungle, the broken scientist dreams of the interior. The birds in flight, a forest filling the moon, the sun carves labyrinths into the feathers and stones and trees. They fell to the soil and dust rose into the sky, which was fading back to its natural hue. Water beaded on their muscles and they lay in the dirt writhing and howling. Becoming silent they stood slowly and began to move in a circle around the dinosaur. Vyasa held the gray cube patiently.

        Green palaces of sunlight, blue eyes of the forest bloom

    flowers speak with voices of color and odor

        salamanders run silk rivers over every leaf and mushroom

    the Earth itself breathes with morning-born ardor

        Dewdrop petals of sandcastle insects,

    the night does your troubles collect

        but with the rising of the sun

    your cares and worries are away and done

Pearls of grass and sun-eyed dawn

fish leaping out of water like sapphire intestines

the dark and mysteries of night are gone

birds of tree feathers curling amber dolphins

Rivers and ants golden around the sun mountain climb, birds of forest sandcastles glisten moonbeams and sandy streams stretch like a woman's form through the forest ablaze with azure and emerald fire life. There is a bird in the Spanish trees, with sunlight in its feathers, the movement of its wings is also the movement of emerald waves spreading across the shore and the sand as it shifts ceaselessly, all the while giving the appearance of stillness.

pájaro

pájaro

the light that shines on the virgin's heels

does also the crooked man shun

and the shadow that hides the sun

quietly the moon reveals

During the night the king dreamt that he was on the side of a mountain, on a dirt and gravel and rock path, looking out over a large town. It was the middle of the day it seemed. Someone came down the path from higher up the mountain and passed the king without slowing. He only caught a glimpse of the man's face, it was unfamiliar. Without a word he followed the unknown man down the mountain path until they came to a river. The man stopped at the water's edge and turned to the king. His face was foreign and dirty, dusty. He bent low to the river and washed his face with its water and when he stood up, his face was replaced by the king's own. Again he bent low to the water and washed his face. The king watched this from the path. The man stood once more but this time he was without a face. Then he bent over and washed his face again with the easy-flowing river water and when the man turned toward the king one last time, he woke up.

He rubbed his eyes as they slowly grew accustomed to the dark, the king sprawled in gorgeous sheets and blankets on his king-size bed. It was not yet dawn, not for a few more hours. The king lay on his back, looking up at the frescoed ceiling, depicting an androgynous naked human form sitting on a wooden chair, staring at a large transparent sphere hovering in midair before it, surrounded by ambiguous mountains and oceans. It had been commissioned one hundred years previously, by a former king. At times the king was soothed by the painting, but at this moment it seemed shallow and grotesque. The king looked away toward the open window, which was allowing a soft gentle breeze to navigate his bed-chamber. Outside the still-dark morning, the shapes of houses and buildings made vaguely apparent by the thin moon and stars like a sneeze across the cloudy sky. Further the form of the forest and the mountains beyond. He sat up and placed his bare feet on the chilly wooden floor. There was a sizable jade bell on the nightstand beside the bed, which the king rang seven times. His aid appeared at the door.

"Bring me some wine, Tyxyxy. Dark, at least a half-bottle."

"Yes, your highness." He vanished slowly like a flame.

The king found his slippers, which were beside the bed, and stood up, stretching luxuriously, almost painfully. He is not a young king. His robes are hanging close by, he goes to them and dresses silently. He walks slowly over to the great windowed doors leading out to the balcony, he swept the curtains aside. Presently Tyxyxy reappears, carrying a large green bottle and a heavily decorated goblet.

"Your wine, my king." He said, bowing.

"Thank you, Tyxyxy." says the king, taking the wine and the goblet from him. "You have always been very good to me."

"Yes, my lordship." Tyxyxy vanishes slowly like a flame.

The king takes a long pull from the bottle before pouring himself a cupful. He takes a sip and opens the doors with the hand holding the bottle and steps out onto the balcony, into the moist dark early-morning air. The light wind causes the king to shiver and pull his robes closer to himself. He takes a drink of wine from the goblet and can feel the alcohol awakening in his body.

Before him dark and asleep was his kingdom, and further the forests, darker still. It was still too early to begin farming. There were few lights burning and the wind made soft raspy sounds, encompassing, dulling any other noise. The king breathed deeply as he looked out into the early morning. There was little animate movement visible and the absence of light played tricks with his already declining vision. He took a long drink and closed his eyes, opened them. His eyes had grown fairly accustomed to the (lack of) light by now and he looked out into the horizon, the edge of the forests and mountains. It is a beautiful land, the king thought to himself, a fine land. He had not traveled extensively, but had fought in a war far to the south which had earned him great acclaim. He had never been too far into the mountains before him, but he did not necessarily regret it. The king had thus far lived pretty splendidly, with little reason to complain or be spiteful. He looked out into the darkness and drank of his wine.

As the king neared the end of the bottle of wine, it was just beginning to become light, the light was still more a hint or idea than a definite presence. The king sighed and looked out to the east, at the eastern forests and the plains beyond. There was something out there, it was moving very slowly. He squinted his eyes and looked hard into the darkness becoming light, like white liquid being absorbed by a black cloth. It was far in the distance, on the plains by the horizon's curve, the curve of the horizon like the curve of an eyeball, immense, impassive, alien. The king squinted, his mouth slightly agape, tongue unmoving hidden behind teeth, breath coming in and out of his nostrils slowly, steadily, quicker, unsteadily. It was a large group of people, growing larger still as they passed over the horizon in their forward march, they were encumbered by armor and weaponry. Some were riding on horses and camels, bearing carts of supplies. There was slowly hundreds and hundreds of them, moving like a wave licking up the shore, slow and steady. The colors they wore were becoming more and more apparent, but were yet still indistinguishable. The king stood up straight and drank the last of the wine from the bottle. He was breathing deeply, looking out at the horizon in the dawn slowly blooming. 'The morning mushroom knows nothing of the twilight and dawn; the summer cicada knows nothing of spring and autumn,' the king remembered distantly.

It has occurred to every king who has ever lived that he might be overthrown, usurped, and that those such occasions were rarely peaceful interactions. This king was no exception. He imagined they were one of two tribes who resided to the north and to the west; it doesn't really matter who is attacking, the fact that they are attacking is enough. The king ordered another bottle of wine and began packing some belongings and clothes together in two large chests. The king would flee the kingdom, taking with him two servants and three horses. The king did not consider this dishonorable, as it is a somewhat common practice among kings. Some even manage to live out the rest of their lives. Most were captured and tortured and publicly killed in some humiliating way. The king was reasonable and did not have high expectations, but he would try with most of his might. Tyxyxy would accompany the king, as would another servant named KaLjim, who had also been with the king for a long time. Dawn was just beginning her symphony when the packing was finished and the three men rode out of the kingdom on horseback, heading north.

They were riding north, toward the mountains. It would take them a good portion of the day going through the forests, but the enemy would probably not discover the king's absence for some time yet. The army had been instructed to guard the kingdom fiercely. In the event that the kingdom was successfully defended, the king could return, should he choose to, which would be somewhat shameful. They rode in silence, listening to their surroundings, the sound of the horses' hooves reverberating gently against the trees.

"Would you like me to sing a song, or recite poetry?" asked Kaljim devoutly.

"No, that's quite alright, KaLjim," answered the king solemnly, "the forest knows many things, we must try to listen."

They rode forward, listening, thinking, the horses breathing thickly. The forest was heavy with trees, and light came through in fits and starts. Birds flew about in the treetops, causing branches to quiver, emitting bird noises off and on. Deer at the outskirts of the men's sight, trotting, halting, looking, emitting deer noises off and on. The king was looking to his left, as his horse clopped along crisply. Up ahead, through the trees, he could make out two small animals fighting and chittering. They were squirrels, light blue and about the size of toaster-ovens. The squirrels were clawing and biting and snipping at each other, wrestling clumsily, tittering and squeaking. The king watched them, without moving, breathing in, breathing out. They fought on, and it was not clear for what they were fighting. Slowly their image was out of sight, the sounds growing distant behind them. The king looked forward and casually hitched his horse and quickened the pace slightly. The sound of the squirrels fighting vanished like a coincidence. Tyxyxy looked at the king, who was to his left, and looked forward again. He had not noticed the squirrels.

The trees were old, but not immemorially so. They were dark and alive like the newer trees that thrive away from humankind, unknown, leading nowhere. It was the sort of place where law is forgotten, where there is no order or boundary. The sort of place without people. Without their design. The original world, the evidence of evolution, growth, life, mystery. Frequented by mist and unadulterated light and silence. They rode on through the forest, north, toward the mountains, which were currently out of sight. The sun waxed and waned and ebbed and flowed, as it always has. The sun, old friend old lover. Earth, old friend old lover. Man has forgotten, but here it is known, lived.

The three men reached the edge of the forest, as the sun declined languidly, almost passing behind the peaks of the distant mountaintops. Once they were out of the forest, they could hear the sounds of turmoil and anguish echoing over the trees from the kingdom.

"The enemy has arrived." Tyxyxy says philosophically.

"Yes." agrees KaLjim.

The king says nothing, and they ride on toward the base of the mountain, as the land reached up to embrace it, as if it were caught frozen in the act of hurling it upward. There are rocks, more and more. KaLjim begins to fumble around with his bags for a torch, before the king interrupts.

"We will not use fire tonight. We do not want them to know where we are."

"Of course," says KaLjim, deeply embarrassed, "it was foolish of me."

They rode on, with the king in the lead, trailing the two servants, who would peer around at the sounds of the distant fighting. The king did not look back, sitting tall and looking straight ahead, into the fading light. They had already started up the base of the mountain by the time the darkness had settled. The going was a little rough, the stars shedding light faintly through clouds overhead, fires burning in the distance. The horse's were stumbling more frequently, so they made camp at the first cave they came to, a little bit up the base of the mountain. The horses were kept in the cave, relieved of their burdens. They stood and clopped their hoofs occasionally and sniffed.

The king stood at the cave's mouth, looking out over the landscape. He could vaguely see the distant fires burning amidst the fighting, which sounded as though it was still going on. It was dark, cloudy, a chill wind surfaces like a swimmer taking a breath above the waves and is once more gone. Tyxyxy and KaLjim are preparing a small meal, crouched near their belongings and the horses, if they speak it is not above a whisper. The king is thinking, of his exodus from his kingdom, of his hiding in a cave in the mountains, of the violence happening back in his homeland. He closes his eyes, draws a long breath, exhales. The night cold and dark.

They sit in a circle, eating their meal of venison jerky, oranges, bread, wine, various nuts and dried fruit. The king sat leaning with his back against the cave wall, the two servants sitting cross-legged near the baggage. The darkness is very thick, seemingly tangible. They can not see each other, and each offers a word or phrase every so often as reassurance that he, as well as they, are there.

"The jerky is very good," KaLjim says flatly.

"Yes," agrees the king.

The sound of their chewing, arrhythmic, faint.

"Let us hope that the fighting ceases, that there is not too much ruin," Tyxyxy says, distantly.

"Yes," agrees the king.

"I have a wife back in the kingdom, who is with child. I pray that she is okay." KaLjim whispers, chewing.

"We will all pray for her, KaLjim," the king says solemnly.

The king did not have a wife, nor much family, and Tyxyxy's wife had succumbed to diseased some years before. They reflected only briefly over such thoughts, which were quickly vanished into the background of their mind. The sound of the fighting could still be heard, but dimly, less continuous. They ate their food and thought to themselves, listening. The horses' bulk could be felt against the darkness, they breathed quietly, their tails swished softly. At a distance, the figures which comprised the group were indistinguishable, dark shapes against darker shapelessness, man and animal one black formless vagary.

"I imagine," Tyxyxy offers, breaking the silence gently, "that throughout the history of our fair kingdom, many kings have had to escape usurpation and death. I can recall King Blo'ol the 2nd, Crvtzy the King, King L4973J2 and King Sorrel the Tall, just to name a few. And perhaps not a few of them have hid in this very same cave. What do you think?"

"Yes," agrees the king thoughtfully, "it is quite possible."

"Excuse me," says KaLjim, getting up stiffly, placing his food on the floor. "I am going out to get some air."

"Of course," says the king, nodding slowly, forgetting that he could not be seen.

KaLjim makes his way slowly to the mouth of the cave, trailing one hand along the wall, just touching the surface. Back in the cave the conversation continues.

"There seems to be only two options here: continue up the mountain and over and beyond, or give up and await capture or even return to the kingdom." pronounces Tyxyxy casually. "Usually, the latter choice would not fare well, almost always resulting in public death."

The king nodded in the darkness

"The fates of those who ventured on into the foreign land are varied. There's seems to be more opportunity for hope in continuing up the mountain. I guess that would be my advise to you, my king, if it is my place to be giving you advise."

"Certainly, Tyxyxy." says the king kindly. "You have been with me for many years. I value your opinion very much."

"Thank you, my king."

"I think," the king begins slowly, "that you and KaLjim should go back to the kingdom. You do not have to run with me. I relinquish authority over you, and for now KaLjim is under your care. See that no harm becomes him, he deserves to be with his family. The road ahead must be traveled alone, I think you will understand."

"It gives me great sadness but yes, I understand, my king. I will do against my will and go with KaLjim back to the kingdom. I do not wish to leave you, but I know that the foreign country is not the place for me, nor KaLjim. Perhaps you will find a life of happiness somewhere out there, beyond the mountains."

"Thank you, Tyxyxy." says the king, his eyes closed. "We will rise just before dawn. I will take one horse and my belongings and rations, and continue up the mountain. You and KaLjim will take the rest of the horses and baggage and go back down to the forest. It must be so."

"Yes."

While the king and Tyxyxy were inside conversing, KaLjim had gone outside to urinate. It was lighter there than back in the cave and he made his way slowly to the edge of the cliff, lowering his pants slightly. As he urinated he looked out at the horizon, at the kingdom. He could see the fires faintly burning, the sounds of turmoil came hesitantly, sparsely. Above, the stars winked through the clouds, a cold wind winding softly across the landscape. KaLjim shivers and exhales deeply. There is movement down before him, out in the darkness. He strains his eyes and pulls up his pants, spitting.

KaLjim can distinguish faintly the form of a woman, leaning against the trunk of a tree; with difficulty he could see that she is wearing a white nightgown. She crouches before some sort of machine, which she appears to be fixing or altering in some way. The machine was probably around ten feet tall. Looking at the area around the woman, KaLjim notices the figure of a man hiding a short distance away, watching her. The man is holding an object, is dressed in dark clothes. The man approaches and the woman reacts as if she had been waiting for him. She takes the object from him and pushes it slowly into an opening at the top of the machine. KaLjim watches intently, unsure of what he is witnessing. The man then removes all his clothes, which he lets fall to the ground. The woman hikes her gown up above her hips, she does not appear to be wearing any underwear. Slowly, the man makes his way into the woman's vagina, arms and head first, then wiggling his lower body and legs into her, slowly. The woman assists as she can. KaLjim's mouth hangs open. Once the man had vanished inside the woman, a second man approaches and the figures are seen conversing, but the words are too quiet to hear. KaLjim stands at the mouth of the cave, straining. The second man removes his clothes, and opens his mouth wide, so wide that it would be impossible, the pain excruciating. The man makes no sound and the woman bashfully climbs into his mouth and struggles down into his throat, and is gone. The naked man remains standing beside the machine, now alone. KaLjim rubs his eyes in disbelief, he has half a mind to make some noise as to alert the man to his presence, but he refrains. The machine makes a sound like an elephant falling through space, through intricate needles, intricate machination of elephant light. The man's skin seems to be changing colors, and he crumples as if fainting. Before he hits the ground he vanishes in a cloud of inorganic feathers, which quickly drift away, and a computerized beeping sound is issued. An object falls out of the machine from another opening closer to the ground. It looks vaguely like a pineapple or badger. KaLjim listens to the beeping as it fades into the sounds of night. The machine retreats into the forest stealthily.

KaLjim closes his eyes and takes a deep breath. Surely I was hallucinating, he thinks to himself, but is not convinced. He returns carefully into the cave and makes no mention of what he had seen.

"How is it outside, KaLjim?" asks Tyxyxy, finishing his meal.

"It is a little cold," answers KaLjim, sitting and resuming eating, "but it seems that the fighting is dwindling."

"They probably have discovered that I am missing," the king muses. "You two must be careful on your return to the kingdom, take the long way around the forest so as not to meet the enemy search-party."

"Of course," says Tyxyxy, who begins to fill KaLjim in on the discussion he had missed.

When the food had been eaten, the three men cleaned up and collected their belongings. They made up their beds and lay down in them, facing the ceiling with open eyes, breathing softly, thinking.

"Good night, my king." whispers Tyxyxy.

"Yes, good night, until tomorrow," the king replies wistfully.

The sound of the wind outside and the occasion drip of water from somewhere inside the cave, the horses sniffing and breathing, the rustle of clothes against blankets.

"Do you think that any of the previous kings have left anything inside this cave, for future kings such as yourself to find? Some helpful object or writing or something?" asks KaLjim into the darkness.

"Perhaps," the king answers, drifting toward sleep.

"Will you search the cave, in case it is so?"

"No."

"Will you leave anything behind, for the future kings?"

The king thinks for a moment, eyes closed. "No, I will not leave anything."

Silence.

"Good night," says KaLjim.

"Good night."

The king turns over, waking. It is not yet dawn. He sits up and lets his eyes become accustomed to the dark. He looks around. KaLjim is standing against the wall of the cave, cowering, eyes wide, mouth agape, skin pale. He is looking at something. The king turns his head in the direction of his gaze. Tyxyxy is kneeling with his back to the king; before him stands a vague shadowy form that resembles somewhat the shape of a human. It is tall and appears to be looking down at Tyxyxy, who is immobile. The king stands to get a better look at the figure. The ambiguous shape seems to be made entirely from cobwebs and dust, and there is a large hole where the face would be, were it human. It extends it 'arms' and places its 'hands' on Tyxyxy's shoulders, who emits a low moan. This is too much for KaLjim. He leaps to the nearest horse, frees it of the others and rushes from the cave without looking back. Once he escapes the cave he begins to scream and the sound of it as well as the smack of the horse's hooves is heard retreating into the distance, down the mountain back toward the woods.

The king is standing, edging slowly toward the remaining horses, who were disturbed by the scream and the departure of their companion. They sniff and breathe harshly and stamp their hooves. The apparition pulls Tyxyxy to a standing position, he is limp, vacant. The king does not move. Slowly, with a whining hissing noise, the figure begins to produce something from the hole in its 'face'. It seems like vomit, composed mostly of dust and spiderwebs, much like the figure itself. The pile of material which the figure has produced is heaped on the floor for a moment before a clicking rasping noise begins to emanate from it and it begins to assemble itself into an identical replica of the apparition from which it had come. The original figure retreats deeper into the cave with a sound like an iceberg in the mist.

The king goes quickly to the closest horse and begins to tie his various belongings to it, pulling it free of the other horses. The second apparition remains standing before Tyxyxy, who is trembling. It places its 'hands' on his shoulders. Tyxyxy finally finds the courage to scream, and as he does the shadow figure plunges slowly into his gaping mouth. Eventually Tyxyxy has swallowed the apparition and collapses to the floor. The king hesitantly goes to him, feels his skin, checks his pulse. Tyxyxy's skin is very cold and moist, his pulse hardly there. The king brings him water and splashes his face and gets him to a sitting position. Tyxyxy is awake, breathing heavily, rocking back and forth slightly. The king tries to elicit a response from him, but to no avail. He looks into Tyxyxy's eyes in the newly emerging light of dawn. One eye is completely black, the other completely white. There is a colored foam around his lips. The king covers him with a blanket and places some food and water before him, then goes and continues packing up his things for the journey ahead. The horses whinny and sniff and stamp their feet. The sounds of the new morning filter in through the cave; dawn, clammy golden fish, spherical tether elucidating the forms, downy god of time and vision.

Once he had laden it with his packs, the king leads the horse out to the mouth of the cave and into the open, leaving the other horses and Tyxyxy alone in the darkness, rocking slowly. The day is beginning, birds chirping, animals chittering, the sun peeking above the horizon as if checking the trajectory of its path. The king looks out and sees different plumes of smoke rising from his kingdom, but no sound of fighting or anguish can be heard. The air is brisk and cold, his horse whinnies and shakes its head gently. The king looks down at the path from which they had come to the mountain. He turns and looks up, to where he would be heading next. The peak reaches dizzyingly into the cloudy sky, rippling with sunshine. He climbs atop the horse, who struggles softly, briefly, and they begin slowly up the path, mirroring the sun's ascent through the heavens.

The higher they rise the worse the terrain becomes, and the horse finds it more and more difficult to move faster than a trot. The king realizes he will have to abandon the horse and continue alone, but not just yet, he will ease the horse on for a little while more. He wonders if the enemy has decided to send out a party to capture him and return him to the kingdom, where he would then be killed grotesquely. The king shakes his head to dispel such thoughts, and breathes deeply. Horse and rider continue along the mountain path, stumbling occasionally. The way is steep, but far enough away from the edge of the cliff so as not to warrant any worry of falling and, subsequently, death. The horse halts now and then to nibble at the sparse grass and plants that grow along the path.

The air grows imperceptibly clearer, like gently troubled water returning to stillness. This gives hope and energy to both man and horse, and they continue on, up and up, breathing richly the perfumed mountain air. The view offered by the path was spectacular. They could see far beyond the kingdom, to the ocean and desert, the other forests. The course they took crisscrossed up about half the side of the mountain, going one way and then the next with seemingly no discrimination. The horse was growing tired, and the king knew he would have to abandon it.

They stopped on a cliff, which offered a view to the north-west of the kingdom. The king got off the horse, who was breathing thickly and clopping her hoof. Slowly, silently, he unburdened the animal, patting and stroking its shoulders throughout. He had only two large bags and he set them against the mountain away from the edge of the cliff. It was just after midday, he assumed. He lead the horse back to the path from where they had come, took off its bridles and harnesses, and ushered it forward. The horse was reluctant at first, not moving its legs and grunting and whinnying, but eventually the king got it to go back without him. He watched as it trotted slowly down the path and out of sight. The clop of the hooves reverberated across the mountain, faintly, he would still be able to hear it for a short while yet. The sun was hidden by clouds, but still the king was sweating. He went to his belongings and removed one of the two shirts he was wearing, tying it around his waist. He then hoisted the two large packs and, looking out at the horizon briefly, resumed his ascent.

The going was slow. He had perhaps brought just a little bit too much with him, but he preferred not to remove anything, in case it should be necessary at some future point. He sweated and breathed heavily. The echo of the horse's descent had reverberated into other sounds, wind, birds. The king, pushing forward, looked up at the clouds, shielding his eyes from the sun with one hand. One cloud out over to the left looked almost like an immense fish before it unravelled into something which resembled more an airplane, then became another ambiguous cloud shape. The king thought he had seen a small human face, printed delicately along a cloud, looking straight at him, but he strained his eyes and the face was not there. He looked at the path in front of him as he continued heavily up the mountain.

The afternoon was waning, slowly becoming evening, and the sun began to droop more steadily. By now the king had gone pretty far up the mountain, slowly snaking his way along the path. He was alone; his shadow appeared, began to lengthen. He could not see very far ahead of him, the steepness of the path and its configuration did not allow much vision, except for out away from the mountain, and below. Besides, the king was busy making sure he didn't tumble to his death, as the path had gotten increasingly treacherous. Once or twice, his heart nearly stopped because he had slipped, but each time he was able to steady himself and remain vertical. The horse would have never stood a chance against such a trek. The king stops on a ledge to rest, sets the bags down. He takes a drink from his water-pouch and closes his eyes. He breathes deeply, exhales. Then he gathers up the packs again and goes on.

The early evening settled lightly like a perfume as the king wound up the mountain. The air was cold, but not aggressive. If he looked, the king imagined he could make out a group of people in the middle of the forest, but he was now far distant and did not often look away from the path.

As his thoughts turned toward the idea of finding some sort of shelter, the king came upon a clearing, after a particularly steep trail. The clearing was a meadow on a plateau, that was about the size of a small lake. Beyond it the mountain continued to rise. Lush green grass grew, and flowering plants and a few trees. Birds were heard to be chirping. Squirrels chittered quietly to themselves. The area was remarkable level and uniform, as if it had perhaps been added onto the mountain after it was initially created. The king moved forward to a tree and lay his bags down and sprawls on the grass, visibly comfortable, at ease, stretching his aching muscles. He sits up and looks around. The sun is just approaching the horizon, like a fish leaping out of water. There are several stones strewn throughout the area, of varying size from approximately small bird to elephant. The king notices that there is a man sitting with his back against a large stone some distance away. The man was sitting in what is known as the 'lotus position.' He looked vaguely like a lotus covered in snow, but more so a man sitting against a rock. Slowly the king got up and walked over to him.

The man's eyes were half-open, his hands on his knees, palms facing upward. An acorn was in his left hand, and a small green toy soldier was in his right hand.

"Hello, traveller," he said as the king approached. His voice sounded old yet lively, there was a lightness to it.

"Hello, old man," the king replies. The man is old, his face covered in wrinkles, but beneath the physical appearance there was youth and vigor. His shoulders are slightly stooped. He was very serene and did not stir, even as the king sat beside him.

"What is the significance of those items you hold in your hands?" the king asks, unable to restrain himself.

"They are merely some trinkets I happened to have with me when I first came here. They do not have much use, but they are here, and sometimes I am glad to see them."

The old man's eyes remain at half-mast. The king looks at him, at his surroundings, out at the horizon and the setting sun, half-submerged, down at himself.

"Where are you heading, young king?" the old man asks.

"Well, I'm not exactly young…" the king begins, "I have left my kingdom, I am heading to the foreign lands, to places I have never known."

"Yes," says the old man, "well, king, you are welcome to stay with me for as long as you like. I don't get many visitors up here."

"What is your story, old man? Do you live up here all alone? For how long?"

"My story is not important. I have lived up here alone for, I don't know, maybe fifty years. I don't really keep track of time any more. I have no need of time. I like to think that there is no time here."

"I will stay just for tonight, old man." The king is seduced by his peaceful tone. "What do you do here? How do you live?"

The old man chuckles softly. "I try to do very little. When you don't expend much energy, you require very little of it. I eat every now and then, and I sit here, as you see me. I find different places to sit and sit throughout the day and night. I only move when it is necessary or if I'm particularly compelled, which is not often. It is a life of silence and stillness, of feeling the change that is the universe. Sometimes I think and sometimes I do not think. I have done away with preference and decision. My previous life has left its impression on me, but that is all that remains of it. It is very peaceful here, very lovely. The flowers spread such wonderful scents in the cool mountain air. There are no people to bother or trouble me, and when someone does come along, they are usually alone as you are, and mean no harm. Many know nothing of the mystery of life, it is always sad to see such people. Often I don't even remember that I am anywhere, that I am anything, I just sit and float, in and out of everything and nothing. This is the true way of things. So I live up here, alone. I do not wish to be back below, with the turmoil and confusion and upset. I have already spent more words than is reasonable."

The old man grows quiet, his lips forming a faint smile, eyes half-open. The king breathes deeply and sighs. The old man is still.

"I am going to get my things in order and prepare a meal for myself. Do you need anything, old man?" the king says, rising.

"No, thank you very much. I have all that I need right here. If you do not mind, I will just remain sitting here until the morning."

"Of course," the king replies gently, bowing. "Thank you for letting me stay up here with you, old man. I will try not to disturb you."

"I am rarely disturbed these days," smiles the old man.

The king returns to his belongings and unloads his bedding and food. He sits down to eat, some jerky and wine, not much. He is very tired from his climb, he looks out over the edge of the cliff to the horizon after the recently departed sun, leaving behind trace remains of light like a shout. The king closes his eyes and falls asleep as his head touches the pillow. The old man remains sitting, smiling faintly in the growing darkness.

The king slept well that night. When he awoke, it was dawn, light was beginning to spread. The birds offered occasional calls, snippets of song. He turned and observed the old man where he had left him, exactly. The king stood up and stretched and yawned like a cat. He removed a chunk of jerky from his pack and walked over to the old man, chewing, thinking, slowly.

"Good morning, king." the old man says as the king stands beside him.

"Good morning, old man." the king says. "I must be off soon, unfortunately. It is most lovely and pure up here. I am very grateful for your accommodations and your company."

"Of course," nods the old man, "I understand. You must continue your journey. Very well, I wish you the best of luck. What happens will happen, regardless. If I may, I will relate to you a story that I once heard. You may find it relevant, or not."

"Certainly," answers the king, bowing slightly, eating the jerky.

"Once, some time ago, there was a young man who was very confused by the state of the world. He sought answers and solace everywhere but to no avail. He had done many things, been to many places, but still his heart was struggling, disillusioned. While he was in some foreign land, he heard tell of an old religious master who lived alone on a mountain back in his home country. The young man went immediately to the mountain and with much hardship finally reached the master at the summit.

'What is the teaching that hasn't been told? What am I missing? What is the answer?' the young man asked desperately of the master.

The master did not respond. Again the young man begged of him.

'It is nothing,' the master replied.

'How am I supposed to live?"

'It is up to you how you live," the master replied.

'Who are you, master?'

'Who are you?' the master replied.

And so he left the mountain to return to the world, leaving the master sitting alone. He lived out the rest of his life and eventually died, as everyone does. And in case you're wondering: no, the master is not myself. I just happen to be living in this way, up here alone. Now go safely, king. Thank you for listening. Be well."

The old man closed his eyes. The king was lost in thought for a long while, looking at him. Then he left the old man, walked back to his things and gathered them together and hoisted them and began once more up the mountain. The sun was warm, the wind cool.

He was not heading directly toward the peak of the mountain, but around it, to the other mountains beyond. His journey would be long. The mountain path was beautiful and rich with vegetation, plants and trees and grass, with the huge rocks and boulders and tiny gravel. The landscape lay stretched before him, open and inviting, immense. He continued on up the path.

Verily the king grew tired of hiking with the sun beating down upon him through the drifting clouds. He stops at a ledge to rest, puts his belongings on ground. There are several trees around him, before the edge of the cliff. He takes a drink from his water-pouch. Most of the trees are gnarled and twisting in odd directions and angles. He notices a tree with a somewhat familiar disposition and he approaches it slowly. The tree is shaped like a human being, almost disconcertingly so. It is about the same height as the king. There is a hole in the tree where its 'face' would have been, were it actually human and not just shaped like one. The king looked into the hole in the tree. Inside, on a sort of ornately decorated mat or rug, were several small animal babies, and an infant human in the middle, naked. They were all mewling, speaking the language of new birth. An emerald light emanating from somewhere dimly illuminated them. The king looks at the infant creatures and sighs deeply and closes his eyes. Then he returns to his packs and lifts them and walks away.

He would continue on, he would not give in and return to the kingdom, the enemy. Let them come get him. The king would go on, perhaps eventually to be captured and killed, perhaps not. Who knows what will happen, some things are not for us to know. There is no telling, one thing or another, on and on.

ahead afoot abreast ant anterior

interior ant

screeching like a

wind-chime

All That Is Outside Is Also Within

Another day is born

upon arrival of dew-painted morn

Sun does bloom in dawn's virgin soil,

forget we of past turmoil

And with the coming of bright day,

all our woe is swept away

But tis true that all our sorrow

we do from no thing borrow

There be no happiness that comes along

twas not born from inner song

They who may smile at their own reflection

shall always know Nature's perfection

To glance at moonlight among the stones,

to know the blood runs over thy bones

Be there no gain of higher worth

than to be at death the same as at birth

Day and night run their eternal course

but know that light and dark be of one source

Ceaselessly we grow older,

tis life's noble game

With age our bodies do change,

but the self remains the same

One who finds peace in the silence of the mind

can no greater happiness find

But just as day is embraced by night,

one is lonely in life's flight

To live in night without the day

is to cease life's lovely play

For if you can get your lover to smile,

you have conquered life's hardest mile

But even so, when one is alone

one is truly at home

All that is within is also without

and if ever you should doubt

know that when Nature smiles

she smiles from behind your eyes

In sunlight the bird does softly sing

In sunlight the day does eternal love bring

What would you do if, by some circumstance or other, you became the last living human on Earth?

Have you seen any good movies lately? Read any good books? Heard any good music?

The necrophilic peacock rode deliberately into the hands covered in vomit and steamrollers. The burdensome hump extinguished itself without an appalling material. Toward the front, with a ganglion of teeth at its disposal, the peacock stood on all the fingernails of the hands, one after the other, until it found just the right one. The hand then assailed the sky and took the necrophilic peacock to a bird-feeder within a prismatic delight. The foal asunder, fountain dresses. The peacock ate of the bird-feeder and a silly naked corpse appeared beside the frog, croaking like a gaping hole. Annual maintenance for further erudition cleanser, appointment anointment. I've misjudged the kernel of delegates. The peacock absconds with the silly naked corpse to its room, where without further adornment it succeeded in climaxing several times. The necrophilic peacock, reeking of mouthwash, leaves its room for the snowstorm. The silly naked corpse tossed familiarly.

A beatific cooperation disjointed elevates fine gratuities, hitherto investigations juxtaposed kangaroo limber moonshine neon opal plasticity quintessential ragamuffin stealing titillating unseemly velocities, wither xanthan yearly zoology. Zaftig yoke xerophthalmia without veritable unicycles, tight stringent rickshaw quelling perpendicular overhang, nether municipal licentious kedge judged initially heliotropic, gravitate fingers elongate diagonal cessation, brain ant.

Again beat circular dynasties, extinguish funereal gloating heaving intestinal jurisdiction, keel lights magnify no oligarchy, prurient quickness ringing satin titans, unknown volition withstanding xenophobic yeast zing! Zero youth xenolith, watershed violins ululating trinkets, sartorial roundabout quaff prescribed oocyst negates meanwhile, lather kittens justly isolated harmful gobble featured elephantine, diaphanous cylinder bright army.

Thousands of eyes, removed from their stalks, plummet from the heights into a sound nothingness, ricocheting gracefully, gracelessly.

The token vole is attenuating, venerated, slitted decline of the shrieking melange. Blue sailboat tubular gyration, serene the feathery oyster. Life-like death-like all shapes and prizes.

The penitents' ball is roving credibly. A disciple changes his name to Penicillin and is quickly a raven. Pavlov's cat and Schrodinger's dog make love twice counterclockwise atop the setting sun, atop the roiling moon. Submarine noise heave-ho heigh-ho uh-oh. Perhaps God is like Schrodinger's Cat, both alive and dead at the same time. Then again, maybe God is static-electricity, energy, fire. Touch the trembling apparatuses in all their maternal splendor, death-worn ears twitching like a hive of fleas, maggots, baguettes. Maybe we encounter God every day, we just don't know or realize it. Why should God be something that we can't ever experience or know? Counterfeit desirous productions, complicate desultory functioning.

Perhaps there is no way of knowing what goes on 'outside' all of this. Perhaps there is no 'outside'. If there is, could it be at all similar to how it is here, on the 'inside'? Perhaps on the 'outside' there is no time, space, matter, etc. How can we know? Does it seem like we are on the 'outside' and beneath everything there is some inaccessible 'interior' or 'inside'? If there is only this, no exterior no interior, how can we be sure we are 'right' or knowledgable at all about it? Space goes on infinitely in all directions, and what is happening in front of us right here, right now is the only thing that we can experience or know. The people in power do not have some higher, exclusive knowledge; all authority is a dangerous farce. The people in powder are unscrupulous in their fennel kennel. Perhaps our experience of life is all that is necessary to know it, perhaps not. You are what you eat, as they say. You are what you think, you are what you feel, you are what you shit, you are what you pretend to be, you are what you surround yourself with, you are what you aren't, you are a golden rhinoceros, you are an ice-floe, I am a pair of ripped socks off and on high and low. Shredded decline fervent applause ecstatic electricity. Frumpy arcana of chimneys in perpetuity. You are reality, you are truth, you are falsehood, you are everything, you are nothing, you are ornithology, you are a superior specimen, you are an inferior transaction. And so am I. Maybe not. Who can be certain in this day and age? The void is wearing a suit and tie made from rheumy near-sighted forgeries and tigers and various metals. You are material, you are immaterial, I am an immature antelope eloping crassly beckoning swiftly elevator, you are God, you are Tao, you are Buddha, you are Brahman. 'Thou art that.' We are all part and parcel of this great Mystery and everything is delusional. Or is it? Everyone is delusional water. Hierarchy is imagined and ridiculous. We should mimic the trees and plants, they know where it's at. We should imitate the planets, they're really far out. Moist campaign. The world is a spasmodic kaleidoscope, an isotopic icicle, reality is spasmodic and rhythmic, bulimic. Space is God and matter is God's jism. We are the product of genitals. "Sticks and stones may break my bones, but words can never hurt me." God is a flight-attendant, God is a tenement. The electrocution of the farmer was deeply misunderstood. Time is very sexual. Asexuality is key, asexuality is a bale of fragrant hay strewn along the guardian. God is a promiscuous dromedary, light stench. God is a backwards camel, an inside-out camel balanced on the tip of the great pyramid. The world tight-rope high in the air low. Stinks and blurts may balance my bout, but worms can never house me, words can never house me. Slits and gurgles may bake my groans, but moaning is very suitable. All is ambiguity, there is no ambiguity, there is no perpetuity. Hose nostril devastation delectable.

"What's happenin', brotha?" someone once asked Sun Ra. "Everything is happening," he replied.

How do you do?

What are you looking forward to? Not looking forward to?

How does death make you feel?

How does life make you feel?

What is your favorite feeling?

He took a drink from the glass, and the water felt cool going down his throat and disappearing in his body. Someone began to speak, but when the man turned there was nobody. And still the statue stood, her feet just barely touching the ground. He saw the nude woman as a well, and he came to the well and gazed upon it, into it. The descending wall was at first brick, then soil, plunging lower and lower. A heart lay at the bottom, so far away the man could not see, the light was lost to it. If he were to throw anything into the darkness, it would not reach the ground, the heart, unknown fruit. And it was the statue again, and he took another drink of water. The feathers toppled softly to the floor, his breathing was heavy. The man walked across the white room and sat leaning against the wall. And the ceiling was an eye, the whole room a fruit, and the man became the eye. Its lashes swept through the fruit, the statue wearing a dress, and the man was seeing, seeing a boy and a girl, young but not children, and the eye was no more.

The boy and the girl were nearly twenty years old and were sitting in a diner at a table to themselves, by a window. It was around 11 o'clock in the morning. The syrupy waitress approached viscously.

"What would you kids like?" she asked, disinterested.

The boy looked at the girl. "I'll have a coffee and a bagel with cream-cheese."

"And you, miss?" the waitress asked, scribbling absently on her note-pad.

The girl was staring down at the tabletop. "Just an orange juice, please."

"That'll be with you shortly." The waitress slid away.

They were silent, the two sitting across from each other, holding hands underneath the table. After some time the waitress brought to them what they had ordered.

"Do you need anything else?" she asked.

"No, thank you," the boy responded dimly. The waitress went away.

The girl began to cry quietly, making almost no noise. The boy looked at her, continued holding her hands. After she had been crying for a few minutes, the boy asked, "What's the matter?"

"Nothing," she replied, wiping tears from her face, "nothing is wrong."

More silence.

"It's okay," said the boy, "everything is okay." He put his hand on her shoulder for a moment.

"I know," she whispers.

The girl continued to cry quietly and the boy took a sip of coffee and began to spread the cream-cheese over his bagel. Outside, the sun shone brightly through the sparse clouds and the muffled sounds of life came hesitantly, distantly through the window to reach their ears, but they did not listen.

two men ring doorbell and stand in

falling snow, faces empty dark

I open the door and welcome them

in one after the other

everyone in the room turns to look

and the first man

screeches and green liquid like blood

pours from his mouth and nose

a creature exits from his coat

the second man pulls at the

first man's hair and hangs up

his coat

bugs and animals fall from the

sleeves

a strong cold wind through the

door

snow all around the room

       the party

an empty room, the guests are steel

and covered in green shit

warm and mucus

and dying bugs screaming

fight

fight against what is real

and what is not

violence is life-affirming death-affirming

blood and lust and

gluttony

crushed bugs and

shit

and screaming mucus

and

twenty thousand butterflies

all at once

the priceless irritants

miracles inside of miracles inside of

miracles

carpal tunnel

    asphyxiation

cartel

bright numbness

intrepid animal capitulations

seething gently heavenward

animal catapult triangulation

indefinitely

for the first time

      flying

      bird moon

purple orange

dark green

yellow light green

light green yellow light green

flying away the red moon glow

shining through the feathers

throws a forest of shadows

across the road

alone

hooraying

     castles

     in the sand

purple orange

light green yellow

blue dark green pink

who is thinking?

not-I

     An old coat is worn only by teeth that through the windowsill are broken feet, feet like an emerald lion passing through a seashell, crow's wing, feather teeth that river run at the corner of the eye, swinging at the heels, footprint at the back of the sun behind the eye. Floorboards peel back like fingernails underwater, counting the moans, women wearing headdresses like a golden moon, a spiral wind the trumpet full of ants peels back the wooden feelers of so many insects, crawling over the lightbulbs, blink of an eye green. Forest white, raincloud rain rain shoelace caught three-eyed by the windmill lateen set flames at high the night, night dark black and gray tongue moon, lick lick lick lick sun window, moonswept, tears run along the sandcastle's cheek, full of ants, crawling over the lightbulbs, under the grass of water night night a cloak forest, forest white. Ceiling fan, venom sprint across fire acres, dwindling candle flame dandelion lion candle flame drip under the horse water, bearing eyelashes against the current bearing eyelids turned inside-out toward sleep, the ants are carrying knives, little knives a spiral staircase of windows, at their lantern eye feelers, lateen and tooth and nail, pound forest window, the dawn curling its animals in light, a fetus with the hands of a garden, the ants are vomiting, the crow is vomiting umbilical cords, its beak a silver wood sliver, a coat of candle flames jumping at the jagged shadows and moon chords ringing through the night at the forest curling softly with an emerald lion passing through a seashell.

Sun glass blown lightning, teeth in the hair of winter, settle the birds settle the nettles, birds nest and bathe in the eyelids of golden fountains, girls with flowers pushing through the skin on their arms, a winter night, a field, sawdust toe town curling with horses, words and words and words. The forest is full of shadows and the sun is full of shadows and the moon runs its fingers through the sun until the light shines through the trees, light bearing birds and ants and rivers, a salamander of light. The sun of love, the flowers of love, a white salamander of love, red fire, in the green river rain. Glass fingers fall rain at your eyes and slight-of-hand matchstick on the surface of the window, sunburned and windswept and moon washed out along the side of the forest running rundown swim grass and birds of air slight out of the mouth of a woman, a woman, a man a woman, a manta-ray in the window full of light, empty of dark, empty light dark winter sun, black behind the edges.

Every snowball and boulder that tumbles down the mountain is a golden forest, a seashell at the dawn of the ocean. Snowflakes are the sound of a crow in a piano. Sand loosens the eyes of the chandelier.

Snake gold snake, a swim fish took stairs to flight at heels sink lower and lower and lower, the umbrella unfolds and tangles up the black hair of the forest, teeth tentacles. Cadaver split ivory iron white eye, horse fall chandelier, white foot toothed and stowaway boat boat sing along away under the rain, boat run stowaway jump two fist and fish blue iron white, rocking rocking-chair rocks and clay and dirt feelers align the dress that took the cemetery in a wing, feather. A sunset of beating wings like a heartbeat from the moon, an icicle hangs from the largest crater and reaches the Earth in a sunrise, hidden behind the fake fawn of dawn; a beautiful icicle, a sun shadow in winter almost two eyes of the woman, rain petals ground up by the mortar and pestle. Cobblestones, cobwebs, spiderwebs, the silt of love, the thin membraneous film of love runs around a lantern lantern burning darkly darkly into into the night.

I was drifting high above the ground, looking down at a small grove of trees. There is a long blade of grass that stretches all the way from the ground into my mouth. I am forced to swallow it, it is gagging me but I can't stop it from moving down my throat. I realize that I am a cloud, barely held together by nothing but air, drifting away. The sun is in a far corner of the sky, looking at me like a closed eye.

Crimson ants steam-engine until the rooftop of the stairs, a furnace with ice coals and spider-legs all around the corridor rain blue flash lightning red red, uncurling the red windows from their frames. Grains of sand, eyes of snow, petals and petal falling falling rain, slow rain along the rivulet, a tree branch grows in-between my shoulder-blades, forest blade of winter ivory. The ocean hid sand in the forest, the garden hid its pearl in a woman. A butterfly inside-out, an emerald, a golden fire, a smile. Sapphire in the cupped hands, a bouquet of leaves and grass and dirt, sapphire rings out in air, the frozen cry of a bird, a nest of birds covered in sand, a winter sapphire. Antennae chandelier, raincoat of embers, shades of grass leaning feather bent against rolled-over tree, inside-out the stars weep like candles and the feather of lions runs a river rain into diamond. Carnival up around the window bent rain. Tulips grow by the edge of the lake, I can't see what's going on in there, I can't see. The bulbs are sapphires! The buds are bidding fantastic oven-mitt. The lightbulbs are filling with grass, I can taste the water crawling out of my scalp, my scalp, the bulbs, moon bulbs, sun petals emerge in darkness falling to the rain. Slip wing, white under the sphere smooth forest lightly lightly, the palace collapses, the village smooth as glass, footprints in the clouds, bird bird eye feather, birdbath screams shrill and darkly sun borne roses thorn and lilacs steam ribbon tooth and eye, nails feathers teeth, wind horse windmill. The flight of emeralds leads to the center of night.

Who is listening? Who is seeing what goes on? The phones are all tapped, there's no such thing as privacy or secrecy. Doesn't everything operate in the same way? The public must be informed, the public must not be informed, the public must be misinformed. The public is a horned vaccination, cloven vacation. Gratuity is perpetual. Sour veneration malformed appetite.

Panic, do not be calm. Do not panic, be calm. It is okay, it is not okay. Alright left wrong. Absolute salute, pollute effervescence sultry demeanor; demean the meanings! Hot gods vomiting foliage, washing-machine in a canoe set adrift, all aboard. Over and over and over and over and over. Hello and goodbye and hello and goodbye, good bite, soft tissue expansion celestial dessert, polite dissolute. There is only one ego, two, three, an infinite number of egos cropping up like disease. The ego is a frightening hallucination. The ego is a greasy eggplant run through with barbed-wire. A substitute lion is no excuse, a substitute tiger filing for loquacity. No excitement, no participants deflected grossly, the deflector of streams. Saboteur of many designations, discrepancies, camphor digression. The listener bright etiquette. Bassoon nose killer instinct intact sexual insect noose.

picaresque caboose

mongoose of the saintly inspection

corporeal corporal

do you see

the light of love

shining from the being

of every atom?

love within and

love without

the love that is there

the love that is not

can you recall

the lion's

roar?

the universe is our body

the mind

is not our own

is not personal

the mind sits

on a perfumed pedestal

that it made

for itself

the flight of birds

from a flower

of sunshine

the place beyond words

I am reading this book which you have written

photosynthesis of the gods

the trees and plants are

gods

and we treat them

so poorly

it's a crying shame

polysynthetic

a crow of

bananas

lickety-split

compilation armpit

deposit

a lion and a destitute porpoise

were trundling along

when they met a tortoise

who spoke thusly:

"I have no cartilaginous idea

vehement menstruation

startling apparatus

apprehension."

so the porpoise ate him up

and the lion too

destitute destitute

destitute purpose

menstrual lion flattening

the wax flour has no purpose

the dirt manatee went to the desert

to drink tea with the dirt

baboons

the cold cod camel

removes the batch of bookies

from the right

night

ephemeral suction

prints

mommy mummy daddy mummy

money

cold vapid jelly of intellection

cold ducks of intention

lion of exchange

exhale

lying

lying in wait

lime

lying

comparative

cauterize the superstitions

superimpositions

surly super position

ataraxic pile of

lemon mandibles

histrionic

victim of the economy

economical cantaloupe

enemy of the people friend

economic camel enlargements verbatim

there is no distressing

let us weep ashes

instead of

tears

I wish our tears

would drift upwards toward the

distant heavens

instead of falling

soundlessly

to distant earth

so far away

away away

the other day

I had the thought that

life is like

a Chinese finger-trap

they operate in the same way

the more you pull and struggle

the more you are caught

the tighter its grip

deep down

beyond sense

and thought

where all is

inseparable

impenetrable

some call it the Great Harmony

but it has no name

the blissful day blissful night

relax strain male female

female male strain relax

purr of dying embers

the poor giraffe

poor poor envelope

derelict esophagus nostril

I was born to a cloud of trees

I was born again to the bright simmering

there is only total reflection total identity

complete nonidentity

it is okay

to be the observer

tonal infidelity

intrinsic indefinitely

total identification

organic

animate mousetrap delicate

intricate decision

the phobia where

you believe that the twinkling stars

are making unwelcome sexual advances

in the dead of night

the night is alive and well

the night is not alive and not well

what have I done to deserve this?

what can I do about it?

what can you?

let us

share hands

the death-throes

of life

struggle

feeling

life-throes

death struggle life struggle

no struggle no life death

he who encounters emptiness

is himself empty

two emptinesses

emptying into each

other

echo across lake vanishing into

reflection

bird calls out in moonlight and stirs the leaves

of a nearby tree

all is deep

in unbroken embrace

endless birth

like waves on the ocean

growth

of form and space

like

tumbling emerald stream

gentle splash leaping into flight of birds shadows of trees

left by the sun

shapeless change

of pure mind

countless thoughts and appearances

without a trace

never arrived

never departed

there is something further and even further yet

it cannot be touched

it cannot be known

there is nothing to grasp nothing grasping

single echo of empty mind

of empty sky

desire causes thoughts to take root

in where there is

no soil

belief no belief

a river

emptying into the sea

we all live

with the source

yet there is something

beyond

it is with us

it is not with us

existence is this monstrous

organic machine

fluctuations echoing

throughout the empty

nothingness

of which it is part

lance the boils

religiously

yellowing abscesses absconding

laminated egrets

in the stillness of its flight the mind rests

and sparkles with the clarity

of a shining jewel glinting in the sunlight

it is the same as when one gazes at the sky

and sees the boundless heavens

as a perfect mirror

between thought and object

a thin line so frail

quivering pale

between self and not-self is a window

set in no wall and without glass

these distinctions

are like shadows

they appear to have substance

but it is just a trick

of the lighting

the active mind

does not stop at any object of thought

the lazy mind tires itself out

tossing from here to there the active mind

ends up in no place

because it is everywhere

ends up everywhere

because it is no place

not tangled in the past or future

nor muddled by the present

one dwells in the now beyond time

that is time and one is

absolutely free

let's be free

together

let us be

chained together

continually

the feet

gathered closed together

barking like a pregnant ear

during labor

the doctors are grapes

grapefruit

ameliorating the differences

fondling the substances insubstantial

yes no

no yes

hypodermic serpent yearning

belch of distant planets

coiling yarn at the great feet

great feat great fetus unbound

cooped-up

salute the hypochondriacs

hypothalamic nettle

enslaved salamander of reproach

extension vent exultant

the mind is open the mind
is closed

everything is equal
the fabric of reality
is one

little fish skull
little bird skull
little skull
balloon

yes is like this
no is not like this
effort effortless
puff!

the tactile is the key to

The Unknown Fruit

it's spectacular

the anonymous ostrich

stretching out

across

the heavenly spaces

a tired

chirping

is issued

without restraint

      Complaisant vivisection, cyclical vasectomy. The retaliation is cleanly expected frowning flowering delay of all purposes extinct alfalfa calendar dinner perimeter dinette persecution. Clinical administration, avoid the damp egress. A sponge worthy of its name. Namesakes like steaks billowing reverently. A mistake, a continued purchase, loose-fitting sockets hard diamond crust, hard to administer. A lion is lowered carefully into the ranks, the birds are clear. Loving inspection. Rotten happiness wheeling like a slippery heterosexual fragrance. Serendipitous, don't you agree? You are a bassoon. Wet phantom of the ages, the dust sticks to it as it passes by like a frown, wet phantom of legs. The soldier's dummy is accused without further demand, a heaping quantity of quantic aquariums. Atomic delirium, it's so delicious to behold. Upset all over the faces. Granular introspection of divine fortitude. This is a copy. This is the formula, the forecast, the silage. A bright gorilla heaping bread. Heaving heaven overboard, it's too heavy. Hot-air balloon of the collective subconscious, hovering unconsciousness without a speck. With pocked servitude. Slices by the dozen. Zone of ill-repute. Mother oven other loving, other muffin, father flip, uptight umbilical cord bird knot. Your transparent bicycle is in my plastic syrup, folding the burning laundry. Stirrup stirrup, slip up slip out, slim down slim up, slim in and out rapid succession. Rearranging furniture to your heart's delight, plight, sight, might, fright, blight, meteor. Meteoric reflection cheerful constipation deadly capacity. Jeweled captivity darling conspiracy. Sapphire distinction sapphire estate, comparative witness. Follicle of dawn, particle of self, article of pelt. The camouflage is out in the open, the secret hands shaking. The translucent corpse has perfect pronunciation. Holy funeral holy smokes holy acetaminophen. What holds it all together? Why doesn't it all fall apart like a jigsaw-puzzle ejected out of an airplane, a submarine, an autoerotic mobile, a mouth, a cougar? Panther serenities all excuses are firmament. The ears of their feet were distressed snorts coagulating effectually affectation. Distance is a hallucination. Contraception receptionist bloated goat farmhouse wheel. Cyclical rearrangement of rhinoceroses trending popular transition. Tensile transmission consternation. A bird flies into the washing-machine and emerges a flower, a vast bird. The creaking flow of semen around the pedestals, amniotic hamper idiotic creeping flour. Granular synthesis, retreating hairline calvary.

Have you enjoyed this book?

Do you think you'll read it again?

What are you doing today?

Is there something you'd like to show or say to me?

What is your favorite season? Least favorite?

Fish sun rivers danced like glowing snow, night's white icicle, white pills of night slide along the surface of the water crescent hidden in the bathroom of the eye, light light, dark of skirmish pink pierced the bloated ghost fiendish swallowing again, winter bell in the talons of the moon dripping long emblematic petals across the water fountain fire of soft running coat heels, stone fish with eyeballs running the hourglass into sand dust rain particle of water loosening its tie to join the son in his cavern of light glue light light, wingtips, wing rose at the petals and drenched with rain white black skeletons frozen udder and lighting with bears trailing at the heels of the canoe sliding down the throat of wind and sandpaper, left down ugly sweet drooping fool bellowing harmless rays distant placenta plateaus, below the paper diamond crust run red bicycles run the forest at the teeth of the eels, thousand white seagulls danced sun red danced danced down blue petals forest night at the winter bells hidden in the vines and briar of the woman's intestines, the white intestines of diamond turds scattered paper pelicans at the forest of the young man sunswept at the heels bedlam boat across the palm of the woman's eye inside-out; as if her legs were white sun snow horn blow, across the swaddling slowly out the mouth of the felonious birdcage teeth drawn trapdoor shut and fire drawn over the rain simply simply, quiet quiet the bed.

"Eli Eli lama sabachthani?"

Animal habit heals lace I. The battlements are dappled lucidly, the quintuplets have spilled, elucidated loosely. Loose feelings tightfisted twist wink. An esophagus of rhinoceroses crowns the lordly incline. Group looping significant answer. Dignified prepositions thorough and throughout. A polite climb is valid excitement towards the dwindling of the chains, chairs, heads, feelers. You should not be upset with the startling goose, it is always sobbing hysterically, perforating the reeds with purple and beige. The needs of the rainy soldiers plied applied and moreover. Hesitate the hurtling infancies. A siege of interest, pointed renewing agenda. I like the galloping ringers, splitting open vertically, vertiginously. Venture drama integrating hoop loud stinging whistle. Mistaken missile ruinous flapper. The former liaison is pushed to the side, into the nicotine. Up down, dolman dolmen. Frequently alleviate the tendencies precluding. Beside the diminished hen is a stalk of oat, it meows like a dragonfly. The consternation of inequities deposit flop. Exhalation of the emerald spores luscious environments, the tips are tangled. Unfortunate susurration blow piranha neurotic.

The smell of gasoline. The form of anthills. The cool air of suspicion, the atoms are shimmering mules, glinting nudes. The atoms are dawn, twilight. God is water. Gasoline atoms permanent inhalation. What is the intention of the atoms? Beauteous inflation of whale eyeballs expunging. The steaming petunia should be laundered diagonally permeation. Growing out of the center of the clock is a human hand grasping a green ball, which cracks open like an egg, revealing a purple canary. The feathers fall away and a small red human skeleton is revealed, shivering. Growing out of the face of the clock is a palm tree, inside the coconuts are little horses, airplanes, triumphs, crying teeth inside-out. The grapefruit pools of yesteryear protozoa indictment. Frequently alive ganglion vestiges of burbling purposes supposed petrol. The separate concealments are demonstrated fully. Isaac Newton in a barrel made of salad going over the waterfall, under, around. The paper birds and the paper flowers, papal flounders. There is completion, there is no completion. Sometimes there is a face, which is a singularity with no dimensions, with one dimension. The oblong fish revealed its trapdoor to Gasoline while she was counting the calligraphy. Gingerly she undid the latch. Within the hold: another fish, obstinate, whose mouth was hanging open. Gasoline looks inside of the second fish's mouth. Within:

It is the early afternoon, the sun overhead shining through the flagellum of clouds. The landscape is a vast rocky plain, with grass and trees growing amidst the huge boulders and stones and sand. Flowering plants spring up here and there, displaying themselves radiantly. Near the entrance of a cave set in a dense outcropping of boulders are several cavemen and cavewomen, going about their business. They formed a small group or tribe, there was a few children among them. Several were engaged in cleaning each other: picking things out of hair, wiping dust away, etc. Others were eating berries and certain leaves, standing, crouching. Birds called out from every direction, deer stood at a distance from the cavepeople, going about their various deer activities. Smaller animals ran about, snakes slithered, insects flew and chirped and clicked. The sun was very bright but not hot, everywhere was life, animation, movement, noise. The cavepeople eyeing the animals, the animals eyeing the cavepeople. Everything was communicating, and beneath it all:

silence. The cavepeople would grunt and make similar utterances at one another every so often. Wind would stir the branches and plants and fur and hair. In reference to the wind, the cavepeople would describe a large circle in their air with their hands and blow out forcefully with their lips pursed. The animals did not seem to discuss the wind, except when it was wild and angry, which was not the case at present. The sun languidly spread shadows along the ground. Clouds pass through the length of sky, like the wreckage of a large boat at sea, clouds like sharks.

The evening came quickly, as if taking the afternoon by surprise. The sun was suddenly much lower, closer to the horizon. The cavepeople hooted sporadically. One of them pointed into the distance, at the sky. There were dark clouds gathering together, way out in the distance. A storm was growing, but perhaps would not make it as far as where they were. The animals began to flee lazily and scatter as night approached, and the cavemen and cavewomen did the same. They lived in the cave during the nights, and several were bringing their things back into it from outside. Others were eating, watching. The smell of the rain in the distance carried across the plains to reach them. They grunted and moaned and spit. The moon was already visible in the sky, low, almost exactly opposite the setting sun. It was bright. The cavewomen were more on edge, the cavemen seemed more lethargic. Eventually all of them had retreated into the cave, leaving the plains almost devoid of life, as if there had never been anything there. The sounds of birds and insects came from scattered points throughout the area. The cavepeople slept huddled together in the darkness deep in the cave. It was usually difficult to fall asleep, everyone twitching and twisting and breathing. They would go to sleep early, just as night fell, and awaken at dawn, when the sun begins to rise. Sometimes one or two of the cavepeople would sit at the edge of the cave and watch the night, the moon and stars and darkness. Soon they were all asleep, the wind howling softly in the night.

When the cavepeople awoke the next morning, the air was thick with tension, electricity. They usually all woke up at about the same time and one by one they staggered out of the cave into the dawn. The air was moist, but it wasn't raining. Heavy clouds loomed overhead as the sun slowly rose from behind the distance. It appeared to have been raining elsewhere. Thunder groaned and creaked hesitantly, desperately. The wind shook the trees, tossed up dust and sand and dirt. The cavepeople hooted and yelled and jumped up and down. Several sat in silent observation. Others stood, mouths drooping loosely. The birds were hysterical, the animals sprinted here and there.

One of the cavemen yelled and pointed out to the west. A large tiger was moving swiftly through the trees, heading more or less in their direction. The others ran to get a better view of it, hooting and shouting. Several went back into the cave, but remained in view of the opening. The tiger drew closer, the cavepeople were unsure whether it had noticed them or not. Some of them went to retrieve their spears. The wind was terrible. Below the thick dark tumultuous clouds the sun began to show its light. One of the cavemen grunted loudly and attracted the tiger's attention. It snarled and reared, still some distance away. More cavepeople went into the cave, yelling unintelligibly. Others stood poised, spears at the ready. The tiger began to run toward them, crazed. The other animals had left the vicinity. The birds were flailing about in the air, squawking and chirping.

Just before the tiger could engage the cavepeople in conflict, lightning struck a nearby tree with a tremendous explosive sound, setting it ablaze in a great colorful flash. The ground quivered, the cavepeople and the tiger spilled to the ground. They were hooting and yelling, it snarling and hissing. The fire roared and crackled. The burning tree was nearer to the tiger than to the cavepeople. It was frightened by the fire and ran away into the new morning. The cavepeople let their spears fall to the ground at their feet, everyone gathering around the flaming tree, coming out of the cave. They were quiet, grunting and sniffing occasionally. The cavepeople stood around the fire and watched it as the sun rose above the dark clouds, which were slowly beginning to split apart and scatter.

The cavepeople had seen fire before, but such instances were few and far between, and never lasted very long. Fire was very fascinating to them, they learned of its heat, its light. The other animals were afraid of fire. Fire seemed like an animal who was very ephemeral. Some considered all fire to be one thing, others thought that there could be an infinite amount of different fires, that they were all separate. Birds would not go near fire. Cavepeople should not go into fire, it was very painful and quite undesirable. They knew fire would not attack them, but it could get them if they were't careful. It was either growing or diminishing, and always consuming. But that was about the extent of their knowledge, their previous encounters with fire had been too brief, infrequent. They watched the fire, some sitting, others standing. It was very beautiful. The smoke rose unobtrusively to the sky to meet the departing clouds. The morning grew as the fire grew. The tree was slowly becoming consumed and the branches of another tree had caught fire. The wind blew wetly, thickly.

As the afternoon approached, the cavepeople began to realize that the fire would eventually be gone. This was upsetting, they hooted and yelled and grunted and hit the ground with their fists, stamped the ground with their feet. Something must be done. Two of them got hold of a flaming branch and dragged it to another tree. If they wanted fire, their only option was keeping this current one alive. They tried to think, their brows furrowed deeply. There was much hooting and throwing of objects. Things were tested to determine flammability. Rocks did not catch fire. They already knew that animals and cavepeople would burn. They tried grass, sand, anything they could find. Some things helped keep the fire going, others were impartial, unaffected.

One caveman had the vague idea that trees were the source of fire. He tried to demonstrate this to the other cavepeople. He hit a tree with sticks and rocks, to no avail. Some of them gestured to the sky and made the sign for lightning. He pointed to the tree and hooted. Things went on in this manner for some time. Darkness was imminent and they were growing tired of keeping the fire alive. It went out. Most of the cavepeople retreated into the cave, but some remained standing outside, thinking. The man who thought the trees had fire in them was hitting another tree again and again with great force and with various objects. The ground about him was strewn with bark and branches and leaves and grass. The sun was in its decline and he grew vastly frustrated. Angrily he hoists a huge stone over his head and smashes it down onto the ground. It hits another rock and sends a few sparks flying. They land in the leaves and twigs and other tree leavings and a small fire is born, slowly, delicately. The caveman is dumbstruck. Another who had been watching began to hoot and yell excitedly. The others came from the cave to see what the fuss was about. The witnesses were pointing to the fire and to the caveman responsible. He stood there with his mouth open. The sign for 'made fire' was created and used for the first time among them. They were all hooting and shouting as darkness permeated the land.

It was night and the cavepeople had brought the fire into the cave. Their shadows splashed grotesquely against the walls, emanating as far up as the ceiling. They were in a circle around the fire, some sitting, others standing. Some were eating. They offered grunts and coughs into the silence, the breath of the fire. The wind moaned temptingly from outside the cave, but it did not reach this far inside. The fire reflected in all their eyes, the fire spitting and jumping and consuming. It was large, situated in the center of the passage, pushing the cavepeople back toward the walls of the cave.

They were still watching the fire as midnight slowly came and went. Shortly before dawn, one of the cavemen stood and stepped forward. The others watched him. Slowly, deliberately, he stepped closer to the fire, and then into it. The others gasped and hooted quietly. The caveman stood in the center of the fire. It was burning and consuming him. The others remained where they were, watching. The caveman who was burning himself alive did not make a sound. His face betrayed no pain, no emotion. His eyes were closed. They could not tell whether he was smiling or not. The smell of cooking flesh filled the air. The sight of him burning was not pleasant. The smoke was darker.

Slowly the fire burned on into the dawn and eventually consumed the caveman, leaving behind ashes and bits of burnt skeleton. The other cavepeople left the cave to greet the morning light, as the fire dwindled down to smoking embers and was gone.

And it was a beautiful day, as

new

as

a

thought.

Do you wish that the world was so tiny you could hold it in your hands?

If it was your choice to make, would you be the sun instead of who you are now? The moon?

And things would be very different if the sun had a human face.

And the birds were exhumed post haste.

And the witnesses were led to the zoo crying shrilly.

And the oranges glowing shrilly, glowering blood oranges.

And swallowing the eye, the giraffe discovered a disturbing fountain fondling grimly.

And the ramshackle contraband elusively distributed.

And the pointed edges were smoothed.

And perhaps thoughts are not meant to be shared or expressed.

And what you see with closed eyes is the same as what you see with eyes open.

And the smooth edges were made pointed.

And the lights were excused.

And this self which is constantly afflicted by emotion will vanish as if a mirage.

And around the ticket spun the prehensile serum.

And with glee the violent behaviors were shed like withered skin.

And the weather was like hair.

And the distant planets a-hootin' and a-hollerin'.

And the criminal insects visited the mausoleum.

And what is apparent is false, what is not apparent is true.

And what is apparent is true, what is not apparent is false.

And the fear of wet plumage resumed potency, resounded triumphantly splinters.

And we were born again.

And the blind mechanical God sputtered and lurched into action.

And God is the mind, God is not the mind.

And eventually all was forgotten.

And so the dying feelers were fed heartily, as they slipped away into the charming harnesses.

And if you speak with authority, people will listen to you.

And the pigs defected voluptuously.

And the prawns were glorious, and the prongs were spurious.

And bile was produced.

And footloose coupled with hemorrhage and begat yearling.

And all was radiance, all was emanation.

And information is nonsense.

And we shall no longer allow the mind to be our pimp.

And begat the instinctive throbbing.

And there is something beyond all this order and chaos, it is right here before us, after.

And a bright blue ashtray became the president.

And the blue alimony was windswept, awe-struck.

And we all went back to living as we had before history was recorded.

And the human beings became dinosaurs once more.

And the dinosaurs were handclaps.

And the primatologists were lathered in ink from squids and centipedes.

And the ejaculation was extinguished.

And identity is malleable.

And the will was stilled, the will was released.

And there is no will.

And it is the eunuchs.

And the priests were getting high in the bathroom of the church.

And the teachers were getting high behind the school, after-hours.

And the penises were getting high in estuary of the telescope.

And the hearses were painted in psychedelic patterns and colors after the latest fashion.

And the parallel lines were distinguished.

And even if we had absolute control over everything, our condition would not change.

And the consumers were immaculate.

And the weight was displaced ignominiously.

And everything was madness, premium exhaustion.

And you can attach significance to anything.

And the fortunate samples were led astray.

And a great wheezing was heard throughout the land.

And surprisingly enough, the pyramid hatches, revealing the stone of the mind.

And surprisingly enough, the pyramid hatches, revealing the totem of light.

And once more the frost is exposed.

And the repudiating tennis urine.

And decapitation was widespread.

And let us go to the source of the source.

And when something happens, it is the same as when something else happens.

And when something happens, it is the same as when something doesn't happen.

And it coheres, it does not cohere.

And that which has no name is the real, the only.

And everything is real, nothing is unreal.

And everything is unreal, nothing is real.

And some things but not others.

And all things together at once.

And the values were changed.

And bowing should be mandatory.

And the persnickety bowling-pins, playing-cards.

And we must do away with buying and selling.

And perception is a deception.

And perpetuity is gratuitous.

And the constipated lobotomists helped in the derangement of the hippopotamuses.

And it preferable to be confused, confusion is the ideal state.

And actual.

And work is holy holy.

And fear is the most natural emotion, fear is supreme, be afraid do not be afraid.

And there is no individuality, no identity.

And there is no common ground, there is a common ground.

And nothing is inherent, everything is inherent.

And the inheritance is hors d'oeuvres.

And everything exists, everything does not exist.

And the red green blue red blue green red blue.

And the red blue red green blue red green blue silver clay.

And all the clocks and mirrors were destroyed.

And nothing is broken, nothing is in need of repair.

And nothing is fixed.

And God is a cup of birds, a buckaroo, a bull's-eye.

And a pinch of butter so delightful.

And the warring ceased and the warring continued.

And you are you, you are not you.

And the configuration was haranguing the dish-soap.

And the burrowing chunks sate the apoplectic amusement.

And the egos combined like atoms to form a totem-pole.

And sdg sfiugds ufhgs dfijg lowdown spiritual delirium dfg hootenanny ddf ghijhdfgkj hwosd osg.

And how!

And what does it mean to understand?

And we took part in the parade of the atoms, in the charade of the atoms.

And understanding comes before, and understanding comes after.

And prehistoric anarchy blossomed like a glorious flower, like a fantastic dream.

And the abyss is a ornery mirage.

And the striving ceased.

And everyone set their opinions aside.

And the straitjackets were loosed, the handcuffs unlocked, the restraints relieved.

And all the hoaxes, conspiracies, superstitions, etc were found to be true.

And let us abandon our past conditioning with love and generosity.

And all the police were arrested forthwith and thrown in jail.

And the money was skinned alive.

And nobody ever got sick.

And you can't have one without the other.

And the blissful sands of time compel me to dream again.

                        the question

                of the optometrists

        has plagued me

                of late

        Open

the stillness in the flight of a bird heavy as snow

silent as rain through the falling leaves

the eyes that behold it the act of seeing

trees living speechless

on the mountain for many years

undisturbed

a man from beginning to end

in the morning

when bird cries out

echoes in the cold mist rising from the lake

echoes in the empty mind

thoughts like trees grow

unknown

perhaps any sight

is thought of sight

any touch any taste

just thought

any sound

is thought of sound

where does that leave us?

where is the thinking mind?

nonthinking mind blinking uterus unblinking

orthodox system tonic distribution

panorama dizzying hidden globe

celestial ice-floe

that is mind

sight is prior to thought

thought follows

thought takes place after the fact

any sound

any smell

any taste so peculiar

prior to thought

any touch

is before thought

beautiful cacophony of sense born of mind

and we

born of nothing

of everything and we

born of self

not-self

the limit of thought

the extent of our efforts

extent of the effects

side-affects special-effects sound-effects

causeless diamond curtain diamond truth

it is all effect

with no cause

it is all cause

future decision ventricle derision

chemical liaison vehicular testimony

mountain fountain

aggrandizing commitment

treatment palpable contingency

fleeting vacuity fleeing

soft opportunity

the causes with no effects

are the prettiest

no exceptions

sun

coughing out light

very sick

always remember

not-self is alive

The woman's head is an entire peacock. She is wearing a suit of armor which leaves her left breast exposed. A bite of snow pokes out from her nipple, which the birds peck and nibble. She is barefoot, one of her feet is missing, now both. One is returned. The suit of armor is relaxed. The woman carefully bends to the stream. A handful of light, a minute's light. She enlarges the periscopes with practiced hands, her hands which are polite, her hands which are sporting. She enlarges the periscopes with practiced hands, her hands which are polite, her hands which are sporting. She enlarges the periscopes with practiced hands, her hands which are polite, her hands which are sporting. She enlarges the periscopes with practiced hands, her hands which are polite, her hands which are sporting. She enlarges the periscope with practiced hands, her hands which are polite, her hands which are sporting. She enlarges the periscopes with practiced hands, her hands which are polite, her hands which are sporting. The stream was relaxed, superficial. She deposits the tranquilities into their hamper, their tempting flower. The last heraldic breather was escorted to the furnace…

I pause, standing before a precipice, when the landscape unhinges itself and begins to clamber away. The fugitive landscape scrambles and trips across the broken spaces, gurgling erotically. The vacancy left by the absent landscape beckons me like a hand made out of water. I surrender my olives, my tomato loincloth, my ankle, my misplaced diameter. I smile at the golden thorns, the golden horns.

… augmenting the flightless birds on the path to happiness, wealth, and well-being.

Ritual of Movement and Sound, Phase Three

please

be kind to everyone

love everyone love everything

be mindful be aware

be love be peace

be kind to everything

without exception

it is

yourself

be grateful

be alive be present

be

I love you thank you so much

thank heavens goodness gracious

separate connection blue gradation

let's all work together

with the plants and animals

especially

vegetables

sundials and moonbeams

second minute hour day week month year decade century millennium
kalpa

breathing in and out

breaking out

amidst tidal waves

and limpid furniture

breathing out in

a b c d e f g h i j k l m n o p q r s t u v w x y z

q a z w s x e t c r f v d g b y h n u j m i k o l p

0 1 2 3 4 5 6 7 8 9 10

2 7 5 9 1 8 0 10 4 3 6

kaput

A skipped stone bears no fruit.

A skipped stone bears no fruit

A skipped stone bears no frui

A skipped stone bears no fru

A skipped stone bears no fr

A skipped stone bears no f

A skipped stone bears no

A skipped stone bears n

A skipped stone bears

A skipped stone bear

A skipped stone bea

A skipped stone be

A skipped stone b

A skipped stone

A skipped ston

A skipped sto

A skipped st

A skipped

A skippe

A skipp

A skip

A ski

A sk

A s

A

a skipped sound afloat aflame allowing

A

A c

A cl

A cla

A clai

A clair

A clairv

A clairvo

A clairvoy

A clairvoya

A clairvoyan

A clairvoyant

A clairvoyant i

A clairvoyant is

A clairvoyant is i

A clairvoyant is in

A clairvoyant is inv

A clairvoyant is inva

A clairvoyant is inval

A clairvoyant is invalu

A clairvoyant is invalua

A clairvoyant is invaluab

A clairvoyant is invaluabl

A clairvoyant is invaluable

A clairvoyant is invaluable,

especially tomorrow!

HYPEREXTEND

www.ingramcontent.com/pod-product-compliance
Lightning Source LLC
Chambersburg PA
CBHW051932020726
47501CB00001B/92